As Though You Were Mine

J. MARIE RUNDQUIST

Red Adept Publishing
Unlocking New Worlds

For Andy, who continues to stick with me through everything.

Chapter One

When I got the call telling me my brother and sister-in-law had died in a car accident, a tiny hope buried deep inside of me fractured and fell away. I didn't realize I'd harbored the dim expectation of one day forging a new bond with him until I discovered it could never happen.

It hurt. It wasn't a keen, engulfing hurt but a quick jolt of disappointment that then disappeared. I reacted with logic. Brian and I hadn't been close for ten years, so it made sense that my heart couldn't summon profound grief.

And yet, with Brian, it felt like there should have been a chance. Once upon a time, we and our sister, Layla, were the LBJ Society—Layla-Brian-Julie. Only I never liked how the sibling nickname got the order wrong. Apparently, the presidential reference held greater sway than our birth order, LJB.

My heart seized in relief when I heard that the kids remained unhurt; they weren't in the car with their parents. Brian and Elaine had two kids—four-year-old twins, Lucy and Mikey—and their safety overrode my conflicting feelings about my brother. Though my boss told me to go home, my immediate need for answers compelled me to make phone calls from the break room. *The twins. Where are they, and what will happen to them?*

Three phone calls later, I had my answers, stunning as they were. The kids were in emergency foster care with a friend of Elaine's who ran a daycare the twins attended on Tuesdays and Thursdays. In a little more than a week, they were coming home with me.

Me. Brian and Elaine had named *me* guardian of their kids. Not my happily married sister, living in some house she was waiting to fill up with children, and not some couple who were probably their best friends from church and had kids of their own. Instead, the kids were to live with the aunt who'd never wanted children and who'd willfully chosen the single life.

I didn't go straight home. My apartment suddenly seemed empty and lacking. It reminded me that I'd remained decidedly alone. I headed to the Grey Shade, a men's gay bar in downtown Minneapolis that was co-owned by my best friends, Gemmi and Sean. The bar wasn't open yet, but Gemmi would be in the office.

I found a parking spot on the street, and when I walked to the back door, I almost smiled at the music floating through—"Soul Power" by James Brown, one of the few '70s artists Gemmi and Sean could agree on for the bar's playlists.

Gemmi and I used to rock out to '70s music when we were roommates, and we had so much fun trying to convince Sean to have a '70s night at the bar. Our interests spanned the entire decade.

"Girl," Sean had said, "if I thought you meant the right kind of seventies songs and not the drivel from that era you enjoy, we'd be talking. Have some self-respect, will you?"

"Zeppelin, Stones," Gemmi started.

"Clapton, Boston," I chimed in.

"Nope. Not happening in our club, my charming but woefully-out-of-touch-with-the-queer-scene friends."

"And you're calling it a 'club' instead of a bar, you walking stereotype," Gemmi scoffed. "There's another problem right there."

He put a fist to his heart. "Damn, girl, where's your head at? We are not just 'a bar.' We are the *it* place in the Warehouse District."

Despite our protestations, we were fully aware he knew what he was talking about. Gemmi was the money and the brains, and Sean was the heart. Gemmi always ceded to him in matters of style.

Music spilled out from inside the bar, in spite of the early hour. I pounded on the door, hoping Gemmi would hear me. When no answer came, I second-guessed my decision to go there. I had to call my mom. Oh God, it was going to be awful. It had been hard enough making the calls to find out information about everything. I hardly ever spoke to my dad and sister, yet the burden would probably fall on me to tell them the news. I pulled out my phone and steadied my fingers to text Gemmi. I needed moral support.

The music stopped, and the door opened.

"Mai!" Gemmi used her Puerto Rican–influenced term of endearment for me. "What fun! What are you doing here?"

When I didn't answer, her cheerful expression changed as she pulled me inside. Instead of leading me to her office, she directed me to the bar, had me sit on a stool, then rounded to the other side to pour me a drink. "What'll it be?"

"A Coke."

She filled a glass with ice, and before picking up the soda gun, she reached for a bottle of Jim Beam. "And with a shot?"

I shrugged and let her decide.

She mixed the bourbon with the Coke, slid the glass over, and leaned forward on the bar, the beads at the end of her electric-green-highlighted box braids clattering on the surface like thrown dice. "What happened?"

I told her about my brother, and she asked all the right questions. She asked how I felt, of course, but knowing me as well as she did, she also wondered if I had guilt over not feeling more upset than I did.

"How can I help?" she asked.

"You can help by telling me how in the world I'm going to raise Brian's kids."

"His kids? Oh, wow. Sure you don't want me to make this drink a double?"

I managed a brief smile and shook my head.

"When do you get them?"

"Next Tuesday unless plans change with the memorial. They're staying with a woman named Lynette and her husband, Dan, up in Duluth. We agreed—well, she suggested, and I agreed—they should stay with them until we get things squared away down here with the funeral and everything. Is it up to me to figure out all these arrangements? I haven't called anyone yet, Gem. How am I supposed to talk to the kids? How am I supposed to do any of it? I don't know how to raise kids. I've never wanted to learn how. Why would Brian and Elaine leave them with me?"

Gemmi held my hand. "You've always told me how much you like filling in with the childcare room at the community center. And my nephews love when they get to see you."

My head dropped, and I dug my hands into my hair before they fell again to the bar. I reached for the stack of coasters nearby. In fact, when I filled in at the childcare room from time to time, I enjoyed myself. I considered the times I spent in the childcare room as I mindlessly built a structure with the bar coasters. I liked to play Legos, blocks, and cars with the kids. Or read stories to them. Little Grace had sat in my lap as we read *Fox in Socks*. She giggled each time I took a deep breath to rattle out the tongue-twisting verses.

I didn't dislike kids. They said funny things and loved it when people played *anything* with them. However, liking children and wanting to have them myself meant different things. Unfortunately, most people didn't understand the concept. Friends, family, and strangers often found my womanhood lacking because I didn't want children, which also surely meant I didn't like them. That often led to opinion number two: I must be terrible with them. On the other hand, if a kid did like me, we would close the conversation circle with a discussion of how I was defective for not wanting one of my own.

I pushed down my makeshift house, scattering the coasters into a haphazard mess, my brain and emotions mimicking the chaos. Gemmi pulled my phone out of my purse and slid it toward me through the disarray.

"Call your mom, babe. We'll figure out the rest later, right?"

I nodded, and she slipped away to her office to give me some privacy.

66 Julie? I can't talk right now. I'm in the middle of a showing."

I wasn't sure why Mom answered the phone if that was the case, but I was glad she did because I couldn't bear to wait for a call back. The queasiness almost overpowered me. "It's about Brian."

"Oh, honey, whatever he's done now to offend you can certainly wait to be shared with me later."

"No, it's not—"

"I can't talk. I'll call you—"

"*Mom.*"

Something in my tone pierced through. When she spoke again, her voice dropped. "What is it?"

"He's dead."

I wasn't sure what to do with her silence, and my gaze cast about for something to ground me. Stray scuff marks along the baseboards on the floor earned my filmy focus. I started to tell my mom what happened, then background conversations on her end interrupted. In a brisk voice, she told me she would call back and then hung up.

I thought my nausea would ease after breaking the news. Instead, the sudden disconnect jarred me as conflicting emotions flickered around me. The shock of losing my brother faded, but the bits and pieces of the news about my future with the kids still stunned me.

My mother's call back sent those pieces scattering.

"Was it fast? Did he suffer?" Her words came out in pinched, shallow tones.

"They didn't say. It sounds like it was pretty quick."

"The kids?" Her pitch rose. "Were the kids in the car too?"

Her fear stabbed me. I rapidly assured her they were fine, then I told her the rest.

"Really? He left the twins with you?" My mother's voice remained thick with suppressed tears, so I couldn't tell if her comment expressed doubt or hope. Given her lack of involvement in raising my siblings and me, maybe she was grateful Brian and Elaine didn't leave their four-year-old kids with her.

I closed my eyes and dug a knuckle into my forehead.

"All things considered, doesn't it make sense?" I asked, ignoring my doubts.

"Oh, Julie, yes. Yes, of course it makes sense. Despite everything, you were definitely the obvious choice for Brian to make. He isn't... wasn't very good at showing it..." She couldn't hold the tears back. "He loved you very much."

Her grief overwhelmed me. I hated being the one to give her the news. I hated Brian not only for dying but for dying without warning, without any chance to figure out exactly where I stood with him. Without any chance of eventually becoming a real aunt for Lucy and Mikey. Without any chance of pulling him away from the damn church that preyed upon him while he was still young and vulnerable.

"Where are you, Mom?"

"I'm in my car, outside the house I was showing."

"Go home. I'll meet you there, okay?"

She murmured an assent, and as I left the bar and started driving, I considered my mother's words. *He left the twins with you?* I could question Brian's decision all I wanted, but when it came down to it, technically, the kids were already mine.

Chapter Two

I beat my mother to her place and let myself in, remembering the days I'd come home to an empty house, and I cringed about the awkward times when it *wasn't* empty. I called out after stepping inside, ensuring old mistakes didn't turn into new ones. I had a knack for finding unfortunate surprises where none should be. My father feeling up his secretary in his office. My mother giving blow jobs to the landscaper.

I closed my eyes and tried to let those memories go. I mangled the technique Gemmi suggested and blasted away the thoughts rather than gently blowing them as though to say, "Poof! Gone!" I wasn't yet self-actualized enough to believe it could be so easy. My huffing and puffing at them like the Big Bad Wolf razing houses worked for me.

I waited for my mother in her kitchen, since she would enter there through the door to the attached garage. I stared at nothing in particular until I caught sight of the photo resting on the windowsill next to the coffeemaker. I picked up the plain silver-edged frame to see a trio of faces from a worn-away memory. Flanked by my brother and sister, I wore my red graduation robe with a carefree smile. It was the last time all three of us were together. By that point, we were already a family coming apart rather than reuniting.

As a kid, Brian gave us all smiles—and maybe an occasional frown of apprehension—with his adventures. He climbed trees, flew over jumps on his bike, and sailed through the air from his swing to a spot a little past the ones he'd landed on before, trying to outdistance himself every time. My sister and I could make him laugh with imaginative play one moment and quickly have him pouting the next when we told Mom and Dad the broken dishes or carpet stains were his fault.

As he grew older and developed a mind of his own, Brian changed. I supposed our parents splitting up didn't help. Then my sister left, and eventually, I did too.

Instead of finishing the job of raising Brian, I moved out right after graduating high school, much like Layla did four years before me. I had this idea I would still check in on him, and I did, but he also turned into an overly independent and argumentative adolescent.

His exact words were "You're not even smart enough to go to college. Why should I listen to anything you say?"

By the time I matured enough to realize his words and attitudes reflected common teenage rebellion, it was too late.

I would know better with his kids.

I startled at the sound of the garage door opening and fumbled the photo back to the windowsill. When a couple of minutes passed and my mom didn't come through the door, I opened it and caught my breath. She sat still, her hands and head leaning on the steering wheel. I should have offered to pick her up.

I hurried to the driver's-side door. "C'mon, Mom. Let's get you inside."

She nodded, and I helped her out. When she stood, I took her into my arms. Her grief seeped into me, and while I hadn't yet internalized that same pain for the brother I had no connection to as an adult, an image of a smaller Brian, giggling as he flew high on a swing, hit me and wrapped tightly around my chest.

We made it into the kitchen. When I offered a glass of water, she waved me off.

"I definitely need something stronger, honey. Cabinet by the fridge."

I nodded and pulled out a bottle of vodka.

She shook her head. "Scotch. Straight up."

I changed bottles, poured, and put the drink in front of her as I joined her at the table.

"It wasn't supposed to be like this."

I knit my eyebrows together, frowning. "What do you mean?"

She worried at the beads on her bracelet. "You weren't all supposed to be trying to get as far away from each other as possible as you grew up. Or trying to get so far away from me. Or your father."

"I'm here with you, Mom."

"Yes."

She offered nothing more and took another sip of her drink. She was right. I barely talked to my dad, and my sister and I only exchanged birthday cards. The last time I'd called Layla was a few years earlier, when I'd left a message on her answering machine, congratulating her on her marriage to Sheila. They married in California. They didn't invite any of us.

I tried to have a relationship with my mother. We lunched together every couple of months, and sometimes, she texted me funny things people said about the houses she showed them. I called with news about my latest job. She told me all my earrings, rings, and tattoos were scaring the good men away. I told her marriage clearly wasn't all it was cracked up to be, given she kept having relationships with no purpose or direction and Dad had remarried and divorced several times since splitting up with my mom.

She and I shared a fairly typical mother-daughter relationship, even if the shallow tone of most of our conversations was the norm. I never learned how to have a tight-knit bond with her. She hadn't, either, which was part of the problem.

I reached for one of her hands and squeezed it. "I mean it, Mom. I'm here, okay?"

She turned and placed her other hand on top of mine. She nodded, giving me a watery smile. "You're right. You are. I appreciate that, honey."

"What do you need me to do?"

I didn't expect my mother to put the planning of Brian's memorial entirely on my shoulders. Or nearly all of it. My mom wouldn't physically go to the funeral home, so we filled out a funeral-planning guide online, and I went there later to finalize the details, including writing the obituary and setting up the arrangements for Elaine, my sister-in-law.

To make up for her avoidance, my mother agreed to call the rest of my family and to contact them again when we determined a date and time for the service. I still had to contact Elaine's parents. It was a toss-up as to who had the more difficult job.

I was to send Elaine's body back to Washington State immediately. When I asked about planning a joint memorial, Mrs. Masinsky swiftly refused.

The conversation was awkward and terse. She thanked me for seeing to the details on my end and gave a brief, sympathetic comment regarding the loss of my brother. She made no reference at all to the kids. When I mentioned them, she cut in and said, "Yes, yes. I imagine it is all very sad for them. Arrangements have already been made?"

She made no reference at all to the kids. When I mentioned them, she cut in and said, "Yes, yes. I imagine it is all very sad for them. Arrangements have already been made?"

She "imagined" it was very sad for them. And I "imagined" asking her about her perceived sadness and whether she foresaw coming out to visit her grandchildren.

"Yes. In their will, Brian and Elaine stipulated me as their guardian."

"Good. Well, thank you again. Very sorry for your loss."

The end. She hung up on me before I could say anything more.

Given my mother's reaction and despite my own, I found Mrs. Masinsky's words and tone disconcertingly brusque. A few years ago, Brian had mentioned Elaine had no close ties with her family. However, he didn't share any details. I figured she was at least still in contact with her brother, since he shared the same connection to the kids I did. I decided to add as many details about Elaine as I could to Brian's service. She shouldn't be cast aside.

I hoped Mrs. Masinsky would be different—softer—with Elaine's brother when breaking the news to him. Thinking of Elaine's brother made me wonder why he hadn't been the suitable choice for their guardian. Maybe he was married. If not, maybe the old-fashioned attitudes about women being caretakers had nosed their way in. I wondered if Elaine's brother would feel relief or resentment about not being chosen. Or maybe he was aware of the potential arrangement because he and his sister talked to each other sometimes. I couldn't guess.

With the arrangements for the memorial completed and communicated to my mother, I found myself with extra space for my stomach to churn as I stressed over my future. My whole life was about to flip completely upside down in three days when I headed north to pack up the kids and bring them back down with me.

I'd met Lucy and Mikey only once in the past four years. *Once.* Pretty pathetic considering the supposed bond we should have had.

I'd finally traveled north last spring on a recruitment gig for the department store I worked at for about a year. They wanted me to set up a kiosk for the career fair at the Duluth campus of the University of Minnesota. Brian invited me to dinner and to spend the night after the event.

I saw Brian's family's old-fashioned style during dinner. He was clearly the breadwinner and head of the household, while Elaine was the caretaker. Lucy and Mikey were in daycare only a couple of days per week during Elaine's volunteer work for the church.

Brian presided over the meal. He asked questions, listened attentively, and reacted in all the right ways to his kids' stories. He nodded when we all used "please" or "thank you" and eyed us with disapproval when we didn't. While the kids overflowed with stories, their parents tempered their enthusiasm, saying boisterous behavior was inappropriate at the dinner table.

When Brian excused Lucy and Mikey from the table, he and Elaine continued their exceedingly polite discussions as though they were putting on an act for my benefit. Conversation remained superficial. We asked and answered basic questions about our jobs then talked a whole lot about weather. Minnesotans were experts with weather talk to fill the empty spaces. *Do you still have a lot of snow in the Twin Cities? It sure has been cold, hasn't it? I hope this long winter means a long summer.*

If I'd thought we would find some inroads, our inability to move past the surface chit-chat taught me differently. As the older sister, I probably should have known how to ask the right questions to get us talking. Our distance only highlighted my social deficiencies.

After dinner, they shooed me away from helping with dishes, so I went to find the kids, who were sitting patiently if not a little dejectedly in front of a computer with an error message on the screen.

"Hey, guys, what's going on?"

"It's broken," Lucy groused.

"It breaks lots," Mikey added.

"Let's see if I can help fix it."

They made room for me, and I explored what made their computer "break lots." In the meantime, voices rose from the kitchen. Mikey slipped off his chair and shut the door to the office, obviously a familiar practice. As I worked on the computer, the disagreement continued, though it never escalated beyond the tense tones. It sounded like the unraveling of a tightly wound family, and when I glanced away from the monitor, Lucy and Mikey were sharing a chair, holding each other's hands and stuffed toys, a doll for Lucy and a rabbit for Mikey. I hurried through my clean-up of the mess of files and potential viruses plaguing their computer.

"There! How about you two teach me one of these games, huh?" I raised the volume to let the bouncy arcade-type music distract us from the unhappiness in the other room. Within moments, we giggled and cheered as animated vegetables went on adventures in order to find hope and grace for their friends. A few minutes later, the arguing stopped, and Brian stuck his head in to tell the kids it was time for bed.

The kids successfully roped me into reading them their bedtime stories and tucking them in. When I came out of their room, I found a note from Elaine regarding a prior engagement with some sewing club, and Brian had gotten a sudden call to help with something at the church. So much for reconnecting.

At least I'd had some time with the kids. Nothing magical had happened, but I'd discovered their origins didn't matter. They were my niece and nephew, the way they were supposed to be.

I currently had far less idea of my new role or of how I should feel about it. As I prepared for them to be truly mine, I hoped a maternal switch would flip on.

By the end of the next day, after I'd worked out final details for the memorial, planned— with my mother's help—for the kids' arrival, and listened to my sister suggest I should transfer guardianship to her and Sheila instead, exhaustion had signed a lease with me.

I came home to find Zach, my ex-boyfriend, sitting next to my door, reading a textbook. His legs were outstretched, crossed at the ankles, his messenger bag propping up the book on his lap. His fingers tapped a rhythm like they always did while he read, because while he pursued one passion in pharmacy school, his other love was music. He played drums with a jazz group almost every weekend and a day or two during the week when he wasn't interning at CVS Pharmacy.

Seeing him in his usual pose involuntarily endeared him to me. Our relationship had lasted a couple of months, and while he wasn't the most attractive man—he had a crooked nose, and one ear was higher than the other—his kindness won me over.

The past couple of days, however, had taken their toll on me. My reaction to seeing him in front of my door both heartened and irritated me. Zach was a complication. I didn't like having to deal with him and whatever it was he hoped for by showing up unexpectedly.

"Hey!" He smiled as I approached. "You're home kind of late from work, aren't you?" He scrambled up from the ground.

I didn't understand his clueless enthusiasm. It was like he expected me to fall into step and give him a kiss like we hadn't broken up a week ago.

"What are you doing here?"

He shrugged. "I missed you."

"Now is not a good time for all of this." I slipped by him and unlocked my door. Yet he'd already eased past my defenses with the casual and seemingly sincere "I missed you" comment. I let him follow me inside.

"What's wrong?"

"*What's wrong* is we broke up, which usually means we don't see each other anymore."

"You haven't missed me?"

"My brother and sister-in-law died, they left their kids with me, and no one thinks I'm fit to be their mother."

"Wow, Jules. God, I'm so sorry." He closed the distance between us and wrapped his arms around me. I didn't have the energy to second-guess it; I sank into his embrace. There were a lot of reasons why I broke up with Zach. His gentleness was certainly not one of them. I *had* missed him.

It felt so good to have someone who wasn't buried in the mess surrounding my family. Someone who simply held me without arguing or questioning everything. He led me to the futon in my living room and kept me close, one arm around me.

"What happened?"

I filled him in on the past couple of days, and each day proved harder to share than the next. Case in point? Earlier in the day, my sister, Layla, had driven up from Rochester—about ninety minutes south of the Twin Cities—to my mom's place, where she lost no time in pointing out how unprepared I was to raise our niece and nephew.

"Do you have anything ready for them?" Layla had asked. "Do you have any idea what you're going to say to them? Or what you'll do when they're here?"

"No, I don't. Maybe it's because I was busy taking care of getting Elaine back to Washington and planning a memorial no one else wanted to do."

"That's funny. I must have missed the call asking me to help."

"*Mom* was the one—"

"My fault," my mom interrupted. "Okay? It was my fault. I did the extra phone calling and told Layla it was all under control. And Julie, honey, we understand it's been stressful, but you have to admit—well, you and the kids..."

"What? What about me and the kids? Do you mean it would have made more sense for them to go to Layla and Sheila? Or you? Do you think I don't know this? Do you think I haven't been telling myself this over and over for the past day and a half?" I dug my fingers into my hair and wanted to yank it all out, anything to distract me from the emotional overload.

"You could transfer guardianship over to me and Sheila," Layla said.

"What?"

"It seems like you agree. Sheila and I would be better suited for taking in Brian's kids. We've got two stable incomes and live in a great neighborhood for raising children. We would love them and be excellent parents for them."

My mom had spoken before I could. "Julie's got a steady job too."

"A community-center front-desk clerk with no college education is not what I'd call someone who has a job with a future," Layla countered.

As she and my mother argued, I'd imagined myself free of the burden, the weight of responsibility suddenly thrust upon me. How easy, really, to simply sign some paperwork and let the kids be Layla's responsibility. My life could go on as it was before... everything. It was, after all, what I'd agreed to when I originally donated my eggs. No obligation. It seemed the perfect solution.

Yet my heart recognized the truth. When I'd agreed to help Brian and Elaine have children, Brian might have treated it like a business transaction, but I didn't care about the money. It didn't matter about me not wanting children. Offering my eggs to help someone else have them gave me purpose, and when "someone else" meant family, it wasn't a tough decision.

Elaine had some condition that contributed to an extremely low egg count. They used my eggs and Elaine's brother's sperm. Sometimes, I thought of the *Friends* episode in which Phoebe told people she was having her brother's babies when she really meant she was *carrying* her brother's babies. When Brian initially told me about the fertilization plan, I had to work out the genetics piece in my head. It was all good—Elaine's brother and I weren't related. Got it.

"Why not use an anonymous donor from the clinic?" I'd asked.

"We can't let our baby come from just anyone," he'd said. "Who knows what kind of person is donating eggs?"

"Me, Brian. I'm the kind of person who is donating eggs."

"Exactly. This keeps it to known factors. Family."

"Why me and not Layla?"

"C'mon, Julie. You know why."

Oh, right. Because Brian was a homophobe. Maybe that factor should have kept me from helping him. I didn't know. Possibly the guilt from not finishing the job of raising him compelled me instead. I did all the blood tests and took all the shots. Gemmi patiently suffered through my hormonal craziness throughout the process. Then she and Sean had taken me out to the bars to drink until I could almost forget it when the only thing I got from Brian in return ten months later was a birth announcement. Not a thank-you. Not an invitation to visit. Not even a phone call.

Hence, the continued mixed feelings I had about Brian's death.

In the end, it was irrelevant whether some biological imperative had led Brian and Elaine to name me guardian. I held no misgivings about giving them my eggs, nor did I truly have to think twice about taking in their children.

To Layla's credit, she hadn't pressed when I declined her "offer."

I didn't tell Zach everything, especially the part about the kids being biologically mine. I couldn't explain why, exactly. I didn't believe he needed all the details because we were no longer a couple, and besides, Zach often had strict opinions about random stuff. I wasn't sure how he'd respond.

It was surely a mistake, but I let Zach take care of me. He cooked dinner.

"I'm looking through your cabinets and fridge, and wow, you reverted to your Twinkie ways fast," he called from the kitchen.

"Do you think because we slept together, your cooking genes transferred over to me?" I yelled back. "Didn't you have to take a genetics course?"

"Ah! Genetics must be coming later in the program." He stuck his head around the doorway and grinned. "It's really because you've never been willing to learn. I'll teach Lucy and Mikey how to cook so they won't grow up as helpless as you in the kitchen. Hopefully, Elaine has some gene to pass down to make up for this Mercer family deficiency."

And there it was. Assumption. Slipping in the idea he would still be around when I brought the kids home.

I made some mistakes that night. *Letting Zach cook for me?* Mistake. *Letting him hang around after dinner and watch TV with me?* Another mistake.

Feeling the warmth of his body next to mine on the couch and then later in my bed?

Just the mistake I needed.

Chapter Three

The day arrived for me to head up north to Duluth to pick up the kids from Lynette Caswell, their emergency-foster-care and daycare provider. And as much as my sister and I had argued regarding the best home for the kids, Layla and Sheila showed up at my door first that day. Gemmi and Sean followed soon after then Zach and my mother. All save my mother were headed to Brian and Elaine's house to pack up the kids' furniture, clothes, and toys. My mom planned to ready the spare bedroom in my apartment and stock my kitchen with easy-to-prepare, kid-friendly food.

I hadn't expected help. I was used to going it alone. Yet the sudden surge of support gave me a much-needed shot of courage.

Lynette's neighborhood reminded me of any small town with rows of neatly organized, slightly weathered single-family homes, each one showing off its distinct style. Small front lawns were still mostly snow-covered—a dirty, wet, slushy snow common for a Minnesota spring. Our location two hours south had proved enough of a temperature distance for us to enjoy a lucky, snow-free April in the Twin Cities, at least for the time being. Last year in late April, a storm had dumped a foot of snow on us.

After leaving everyone at Brian's house, I debated where to go next, already losing some courage. I considered checking into the hotel then recognized my stalling tactic and forced myself to go straight to Lynette's. The next day, I would meet with lawyers and a social worker and take the kids officially into my custody. Despite the will's clear language naming me official legal guardian, nothing would be final for one hundred eighty days, per state law. For forty-eight hours, I'd been bargaining with the universe for us all to survive six months in one piece. For probably the two hundredth time, I wondered what Brian had been thinking with his decision.

I slowed the car to look at house numbers and found the right one. Lynette's house had a slightly tired appearance, but the driveway was clear of snow, and the curtains and blinds were all open. The openness reassured me. Lynette had nothing to hide. I sat in her driveway, regretting for a moment my refusal to accept anyone's offer to come along with me. I told them I didn't want to overwhelm the kids, yet I wasn't sure they would remember me from my visit the year before.

Thinking of everyone taking care of things at Brian's house bolstered me, giving me the wherewithal to take a deep breath, get out of the car, and go introduce myself as the most unqualified person to care for two four-year-old children.

The woman who answered the door was close to forty, with long blond hair pulled back into a ponytail loosened, presumably, by a busy morning's work with young kids.

"Julie?"

"Yes."

"Come on in. I'm Lynette."

I stepped through the door, and my eyes traveled across the neat row of character backpacks, diaper bags, and winter clothing hanging on their respective hooks. I tried to guess which ones belonged to Lucy and Mikey. Lynette already sounded stronger than when we spoke on the phone. She asked about my drive and paused.

"Brian and Elaine were good people. I can't tell you how glad I am they've got family to take their kids. To be honest, they didn't talk about their family very much, but I remember Brian talking about what you did for them."

I wasn't certain how to process her information except to analyze the unfairness of Lynette—who had played no role in the twins' conception—having heard more about Brian's appreciation than I had. I shoved the thoughts away to make room for more immediate concerns.

"Everyone's eating lunch, which is why it isn't as noisy as it is usually," Lynette continued. "You hungry?"

"No, thank you. I'm okay." Well, obviously not okay. My nerves were shot to hell, but at least I could lie well enough.

She led me to the kitchen, and thankfully, I spotted Lucy and Mikey right away. I stood in awe, overcome with emotion. Those were my kids. Mine. I would be responsible for their lunches moving forward. And their breakfasts and dinners. I swallowed my anxiety.

Lucy had thick brown hair pulled back into a ponytail with a mind of its own. She seemed small, and Mikey seemed smaller. He had darker hair, almost black, cut neatly around his ears. Five other kids circled the table, and some of them greeted me with a cheerful "Hi!" or "Are you going to eat lunch with us?" Peanut-butter-and-jelly sandwiches were the main course, with baby carrots and goldfish crackers. Lucy's plate was nearly empty, while Mikey's appeared only picked at.

"Lucy, Mikey, your aunt Julie is here. Can you wave hello?"

I gave my most reassuring smile as Lucy offered a small wave and Mikey stared at me. *Oh, Mikey. I think I understand exactly how you feel.*

"Mikey hasn't been much for talking since..." Lynette drifted off. "In fact, if he's done any talking in the past few days, I haven't heard it. He and Lucy are pretty close, so it's possible he says stuff to her when no one's around. Lucy's been a little off, of course, throwing fits more often than usual."

I wondered what "a little off" meant, and I decided I didn't want to know what a "fit" consisted of. Fear crept up my throat. I asked for a glass of water.

"Oh, sure. You know, they'll all finish eating in a few minutes. Then they normally have some quiet time with books or napping, and we'll have some more time to talk and figure things out."

I stood holding my water, certain I appeared utterly useless and also like the worst aunt as Lynette helped clean up the kids. I started clearing the table, something concrete and secure to do. When I got to Lucy and Mikey's place, I paused.

"Should we pick out a book together to read for quiet time while Lynette gets some of your friends down for naps?"

Mikey still only stared, but Lucy agreed and returned my smile. They led me downstairs to the play area, and as Lucy picked out a story, I noticed Mikey holding his stuffed bunny.

"Hey." I knelt by him. "I remember meeting this bunny before. He must be pretty special, huh?"

Mikey pulled it closer.

"Don't worry, sweetie. I get it. He's important! I bet he's helped you through a lot of stuff. I used to have a dolly I kept close to me all the time too. She was one of my best friends." Huh. I wondered whatever happened to Dolly. Dropped off at the Goodwill or Salvation Army, no doubt.

"Mommy and Daddy don't like him to have it," Lucy said, returning with a Dr. Seuss book. "Lynette says it's okay, but he might not be able to bring it everywhere if you don't like it. She says we have to go live with you. Are we going right after this story?"

"No. Not until tomorrow." At least, I hoped it wasn't until tomorrow. "As for Bunny, you can bring him everywhere you want to, okay, Mikey?" Wait. Kids were pretty literal. I quickly added, "Except in the bathtub and swimming. Where should we sit for the story?"

We found a place next to the couch, and a couple of other kids joined us while I read aloud from *Green Eggs and Ham.*

"Have any of you tried green eggs and ham?" I asked them.

"I did!" one dark-haired boy said, leaping off the couch. "One day we had green eggs, and then another day, my daddy made red ones. It was like they were bloody!"

"Ewww," a curly-haired girl added.

"It was cool."

Lynette popped in. "Okay, kids. Lucy and Mikey's aunt and I have to talk. Time to find your own quiet activity, okay?" All except Mikey scrambled away. Mikey had sucked his thumb during the story. He simply sat next to me, holding onto his bunny, and I was reluctant to leave him. Somehow, his proximity felt momentous. He could have scrambled away at the first opportunity, yet he didn't. It was a ridiculous thought. I'd read one story out loud and thought I'd found the magic spell.

"I'll be back in a little bit, okay? I'm going to talk to Lynette," I told him softly.

I needn't have worried because Lucy was already coming back with a coloring book and crayons for them to share. As I stood and walked away, I thought I felt a light touch on my leg, but I wasn't sure. Lynette led me to the other end of the room, where she still had eyes on the kids while we talked in low voices.

I asked straightaway, "How have they been doing?"

Her eyes drooped with her mouth following suit as she sighed. "The first night, they did fine. I don't think they fully comprehended what happened. I'm sure they still don't. I think to some extent they now understand their parents aren't coming back to pick them up. The second night was kind of okay, too, until Lucy figured out something was up, and Mikey picked up on it and shut down. He's never been one to talk much anyway, but I'm not exaggerating when I say I haven't heard a word from him since probably the day after the accident. A couple nights ago, he woke up screaming. Scared the bejesus out of me. Especially since he hadn't been making any noise. Took a while to calm him down. I offered to have him come sleep with me and Joe—" She sighed again and shook her head. "He wouldn't do it.

"Sometimes, they'll interact and play with the other kids like they always used to. Then yesterday, Lucy started having tantrums when things didn't go her way. Throwing things. Screaming. Insisting she wanted to go home."

I thought I might throw up. I was so nervous and wished I'd at least brought Zach with me.

"Honey, are you okay?"

No, my dear Lynette, I am not at all okay. "Yes, I'm... Well, I'm a little nervous." Understatement of the decade. However, if I were Lynette, I wouldn't want to learn I was sending children home with someone who had no experience whatsoever. Or that the kids would probably be better with her than me. So I shifted. "Can you tell me about things I should for sure pick up from their house for them? Some of my family is there now, so if there's anything in particular, it would be helpful to know." I was glad I'd made a list of questions. My mother helped. Zach had come up with this question, talking about how his nieces and nephews always seemed to have toys or stuffed animals or something else they had a specific attachment to.

"We have most of the important stuff here. I ran over to their house the night of the accident to grab some clothes and the rabbit and so forth. I imagine you don't have many toys, and with spring coming along, you might want their bikes if you can fit them."

Bikes? I didn't know where those would go. I hoped my apartment building had some rentable storage-closet option. Gemmi and I had never needed it, so I couldn't remember if our complex offered that. I nodded. I refocused on my last few questions, which dealt with allergies, strong likes and dislikes with food, and any special medical conditions.

My final question worried me. *Should I take them with me to the hotel today?* I hoped my relief wasn't too evident when Lynette suggested it would be easier for everyone if I didn't encumber myself with the kids while gathering items from their house and working through official business.

"Join us for dinner, won't you? It'll do the kids good to see you again before tomorrow."

I agreed and talked to Lucy and Mikey.

"Are you going to our house? Can we go too?" Lucy asked.

"Sweetie, I'm sorry, no. I'll pack up as much as I can, and whatever I forget or don't have room for, we'll go back another day to get it, okay?"

I received a reluctant nod, told them I would be back, and drove to the hotel to regroup.

Dinner at Lynette's house was far warmer than the one at Brian's the year before. Laughter abounded—at least from Lynette's kids—and interruptions garnered no rebukes. Lucy and Mikey remained reticent, causing me to seesaw between believing it was a good thing for me to take the kids from an environment so different from what they were used to and horribly wrong to remove them from a specifically happy one.

Afterward, we played a game of Memory, which Lucy was remarkably good at, while Mikey colored. The first page he worked on showed meticulous control—no stray lines. Colors met expectations with green grass, blue sky, and brown hair. The next page turned out more Hyde-ish. Clouds were red, frogs were black, trees were purple, and crayon marks scrawled across the page. It wouldn't have surprised me had I not seen the perfectly colored page earlier. Mikey might have been silent in voice but clearly not in emotion.

The next morning cemented the new reality and gave me my next family surprise. Sitting in the waiting room at the law firm where the probate process would begin—and the custodial transfer process as well—was my father. The lines around his eyes were more pronounced, and his entire expression gravitated downward in fatigue and sadness. Despite the waves of grief emanating from him, a small funnel of hope opened inside of me. My confidence rose a tiny bit with his presence.

"Dad? What are you doing here?"

"Making sure you understand everything discussed in this meeting."

"How did you know when and where to come?"

He set aside his newspaper and looked at me with an expression that was a cross between exasperation and something like paternal kindness. "Your mother called me. My morning appointments were nothing I couldn't shift around, so I agreed to come." He leaned forward and rested his forearms on his legs. "*You* should have called me about this."

Years of independence paved the way for my response.

"I would have been all right on my own."

He nodded, a ghost of a smile tugging at the corners of his eyes. "Yes, I imagine you would. Maybe you'll let me do something for your brother by allowing me to help his sister be sure of all the details."

I agreed. My father had his own firm, and while probate law wasn't his specialty, he still understood far more of what I was about to hear than I did. Besides, I liked that he'd traveled all the way up to Duluth for me.

We heard a mix of good and bad news. The kids had trust funds, accessible when they turned eighteen, to cover some of their presumed college expenses. Any remaining cash on hand came to me, but it sounded like it wouldn't be much after probate fees and other outstanding debts. I could, of course, apply for Social Security benefits on the kids' behalf. However, not much else remained. All other assets, such as investments and the future sale of the house, were going to Brian and Elaine's church. My father balked at the news, making me appreciate his presence even more.

He argued the financial scenarios of an established family, a church, and a single woman who had no plans for a sudden family. I listened as he mapped out a plan to contest the will. *Is this what I want?* On one hand, Brian was my brother, and maybe his wishes meant something to me. On the other hand, I'd looked at my budget, and I had no faith in its long-term sustainability.

"Everything we have has come to us by the support of our prayerful community at the One True Path Christ Community Church and therefore by the grace of God," the arbiter quoted to us. "It is your prerogative, of course, to contest, but understand those words came from Brian and Elaine. Go against the provisions of their will, and you go against their direct wishes."

"They're dead, so their wishes no longer carry the same weight as the needs of their children. My office will be in touch with you next week regarding the undue influence of their church. Now, let's move on and take care of the paperwork for custodial care."

They're dead, he'd said so casually about his son and daughter-in-law. He was present for me, yet he also said he was present for Brian. I didn't have a close relationship with my father, so it surprised me he hadn't sided with Brian. Then again, maybe he'd experienced some of Brian's more recent unpleasantness, but Brian was his son. My head swam with contradictions, and I didn't like my new perspective about my dad, whatever that perspective was. Complicated, I supposed.

Paperwork and the process for transfer of custodial care went smoothly and without incident. The social worker said there could be a home visit at the six-month review date. However, with legal guardianship falling to another family member, they sometimes skipped the review unless they had reason to investigate the children's environment. After a few more signatures, we were done. The kids were officially mine.

My dad and I walked out together and paused outside the door of the building. Dad was tall and broad-shouldered, something I saw favoring him when settling cases. Plenty of gray had entered his hair, and it showed signs of thinning, although not so much as to make him work to hide it. In fact, it led me to believe maybe he intended for Nora to be his final wife. I had no idea, really, but Trevor Mercer was a good-looking man and had always worked hard at maintaining his appearance. Fine clothing, spotless higher-end car, fit body. Probably because he was always chasing women other than his wife. At his current age, he looked more... settled.

"I don't know about this whole contesting thing," I said.

"That's why I came. I'd hoped your brother changed the conditions of his will, but clearly, this church distorted his common sense. Miracles don't feed and clothe children. Money does. Plain and simple."

"You saw his will before now?"

"Of course. He asked me to look it over back when he revised it after the kids were born."

"You knew I was to be the kids' guardian? Why didn't I know?"

He frowned. "I assumed you did, especially since Brian argued with me about the choice. He was quite adamant it should be you and not Layla."

It occurred to me my dad meant he had argued in favor of Layla over me. "And now you're telling me you don't think I should be in charge of his kids?"

The spinning got worse. I searched for some place to sit down and spotted a bench a couple of yards away. My dad followed and sat next to me.

"Julie, that's not what I'm saying. I figured if he wouldn't leave any decent financial means, then he could at least choose Layla, who you can't deny has a better-paying job with excellent benefits plus a partner who also works. Financially, it makes sense."

What the hell is he saying? It's all about the money?

"Look. I appreciate you coming up and helping. I'm not sure about the will. I mean, he must have had his reasons, right? Let me think about it. For now, I'm going to go get the kids and figure out this whole parenting part first."

He stood and patted my shoulder before reaching into his jacket pocket for his card. "Think about it but not for too long. Don't be a martyr, okay? An unnecessary sacrifice won't help you or the kids."

I glanced at the card, grateful to see an email address since I didn't know if I would manage another proper conversation with him. I nodded and thanked him.

"Julie? Please drive safely."

He turned and walked away. It was a couple of minutes before the tone and sentiment of those words settled in.

Chapter Four

As we drove to the Cities, Mikey mostly stared out the window. Lucy, however, joined me in jamming to the radio. I primed Lucy with chorus lyrics a few beats before the band sang them. It worked for a couple of songs before she abruptly stopped without any explanation or response to me trying to revive it. There were limits to how long someone could pretend to be happy. She wasn't singing in the car with her parents, only the questionable stand-in.

We ate dinner at McDonald's, a new and exotic experience for the kids. God, already I'd messed them up by feeding them junk food. Lucy cried upon discovering onions and mustard on her hamburger. To my surprise, scraping away the offensive ingredients mollified her. Perhaps the tantrums wouldn't be an issue after all.

We arrived home, and the prep work my family and friends had put into my apartment made me more grateful than ever. A couple of toy bins edged the living room wall, which the kids delved into with proprietary fervor after dinner, allowing me to check out the bedroom and make a game plan for settling them in for the night.

Their room looked as close to being two separate rooms as possible while sharing the same space. *Who thought of that?* Layla or Zach, I guessed. *Smart.* Their beds lined opposite walls, and their dressers stood back-to-back, sides pressed against the wall across from the door. What little had been on their walls at home appeared there, including the blue and pink crosses—probably Zach's influence—and the stained-glass ornaments—likely my mom's idea. I attributed the new glow-in-the-dark stars to Gemmi and the string lights to Layla or Sean. Homier than what I remembered from Brian's house, the room was still crisp and pristine, a far cry from the free-spirited blend of chaos and trendy décor Gemmi had given the space when we were roommates. It wasn't an unwelcome change. Between their room and the other odds and ends added throughout the apartment, there was a sense of completeness, the illusion of a real home.

Gemmi and I had been roomies until a few months earlier, when she moved out to live with the love of her life, Demitry. She had good taste, but it involved so much *stuff*.

"Mai, it's like I robbed you," she said after moving the last of her things out. "Did we sign a prenuptial agreement or something? Where is all *your* stuff?"

"I'm a minimalist. I can't be bothered with material items."

"Oh, right. I guess you won't mind if I grab some of your extra rings and earrings?"

She had me there. I did like my accessories, and I missed some of the designs formerly sprucing up the walls. I wasn't big into art, and framing photos seemed like a lot of work. Gemmi was right. I wasn't a minimalist; I was lazy. I imagined the homey atmosphere of Lynette's place then the more austere one of Brian and Elaine and contrasted both with my apartment. Having more stuff in my place made it more complete, anyway. I didn't know about more comfortable.

Despite the naps the kids took in the car on the way home, they welcomed bedtime without any fuss—a small blessing for us all. I was equally exhausted. Instead of going to bed, I flopped onto the couch and flipped on the TV, hoping to blank out my mind and push away the gaining momentum of a headache.

At first, I was confused that I couldn't find any late-night talk shows. Then I realized it wasn't even nine o'clock yet. I laughed at the absurdity. I'd had the kids for less than a full day, and keeping my eyes open for thirty more minutes proved impossible.

Around two in the morning, shrieking cries woke me. I bolted upright, cringing at the crick in my neck from the unfortunate position I had fallen into on the couch. I wasn't sure which kid the cries belonged to and, bounding into their room, saw it was Mikey. I scooped him up and into my arms. I rocked him with all four of his limbs clenched around my waist and neck, his tiny sobs shaking his body.

"Shh. It's okay. You're safe. I've got you." I rubbed his back until his cries subsided, and when his grip loosened, I pulled him away to ask if he wanted to talk about his nightmare, only to find him already asleep again. I marveled at the phenomenon, especially since my heart still raced. His cries had been wrenching—full of fear and sadness. Remnants of his grip lingered as I nestled him back in. Lucy slept soundly in her bed. I arranged her kicked-off blankets around her once more and risked dusting my hand over her head in place of lifting her into my arms as I had with Mikey.

I walked to my bed and tucked myself in, hoping it would work as a relaxation technique. It must have had some effect, because I drifted off to sleep and into my own bizarre dreams.

The next morning, I opened my eyes and stared at where the carpet met the wall, my cheek resting on the edge of the bed. The warm body pressed against my back explained the view. I slowly rolled and gently fell to the floor. I turned to find Lucy snuggled in my bed with her doll. Based upon stories I'd heard or read, I thought twins were supposed to be inseparable. I'd expected Lucy and Mikey to be curled up together in one of their beds.

I sat on my knees on the floor and stared at the soft rise and fall of Lucy's little body as she breathed. Her back was to me, and her wild hair inhabited most of the space around her head. I was tempted to crawl back into bed with her but decided I needed to get up and figure out what in the world I was going to do with two four-year-old children all day to distract them from the reality of their new and awful situation.

I'd told family and friends I didn't want visitors for the first few days. The changes were overwhelming enough in having the kids and me get used to each other. Besides, I'd already envisioned everyone watching me like a hawk to see everything I did wrong. Layla would have no problem verbalizing all her criticisms. I couldn't deny that the hours stretching ahead seemed daunting.

One step at a time across the rickety bridge spanning the abyss below.

Mikey came out of his room at the same time I came out of mine.

"Hey, buddy. How're you doing?"

A thumb in his mouth and Bunny gripped tightly next to his cheek, he contemplated my question before shuffling toward me. I squatted to offer him a hug, and to my surprise, he walked into my arms. I gathered some courage through embracing his small, warm body.

"Do you want to help me figure out breakfast?" I felt more than saw the nod. We continued into the kitchen. Mikey crawled into a chair while I opened the refrigerator.

"Eggs?"

He shook his head.

"Yogurt?"

Another shake.

"Cereal?" Hmm, no movement. Not a no but not a yes either. Time to show him the options. I pulled out the first choice from the cabinet. "Cap'n Crunch?" I was positive it wasn't the best thing to give a kid, but I figured, *Fuck it, his parents are dead. Let the kids have whatever kind of cereal they want for a few days.*

He didn't want it, though. I reached for the ones my mom had bought. "Cornflakes? Cheerios?" A nod! I almost laughed at how excited I was for the ridiculously small victory. *Julie's such an amazing mom. She figured out her kid likes Cheerios! Throw the woman a parade!* I finished getting him all set up with his cereal then heard Lucy call out.

"Mama? Daddy?" A frightened voice. "Mama!"

I hurried into the room and sat next to her on the edge of the bed.

"Where's Mama?"

The pit of my stomach filled with marbles, heavy and knocking into one another in my panic. Some of them threatened to rise up and choke me. "She's not here, honey. Neither is Daddy. It's just me. And Mikey."

Her eyes cleared as she more fully awoke. I wrapped my hand around one of hers.

She looked at my hand and slowly pulled hers free. "Where's Mikey?"

"He's eating breakfast. Would you like some?"

She slid from the bed and raced into the kitchen, probably to double-check that I was telling the truth about Mikey. *It's what I would do.* When I followed her out, she pulled a chair right up to Mikey's at the table, as close as she could. Safety in numbers, I guessed. A little jealous of them for having each other, I felt stupid for being jealous of their situation at all.

"Do you want some Cheerios too?"

"May I have toast, please?"

She had an über politeness I remembered from my visit a year ago. I opened a drawer to find two kinds of bread—white and wheat. My mother to the rescue. I would never have thought of having both choices.

I pulled them out for Lucy to see. "White or wheat?"

She pointed at the wheat.

I popped two slices into the toaster. "Do you want jelly?"

"Yes, please."

I wondered what the chances were there would be choices of jelly in the fridge. Pretty high, apparently. Those tiny things improved my mother's reputation. As a rule, I didn't normally have extraordinary expectations of anyone, but even I marveled at how my expectations had lowered in recent days.

I buttered and jellied her toast, and my first smile of the day came from watching Lucy put the two pieces of bread together like a sandwich.

"When your dad was your age, he used to eat his toast as a sandwich too." I'd forgotten about the little quirk. As caught up as I was with his unpleasant adult tendencies, it would probably be good to remember how I had really liked him as a kid.

"He says everything is better as a sandwich." She stared at her toast sandwich without taking a bite.

"And with a pickle, right?" I added, hoping the idiosyncrasy would help dispel the melancholy.

She nodded, and her eyes twinkled. The small bit of happiness had already transformed her face. A connection. I crossed my fingers and hoped the day wouldn't be so hard after all.

We made it until lunch.

Lucy didn't like any of the food choices. When Mikey assented to macaroni and cheese, Lucy merely scowled.

"Mama cooks ours on the stove. You're doing it wrong!"

I made the microwaveable singles. I considered it a safer choice than the stovetop version. Macaroni and cheese wasn't some gourmet meal, but I didn't want to take any chances.

"It's the same thing, just in different packaging. This way, you'll get exactly the right serving," I said.

Even I caught the lame reasoning she likely saw straight through. I had no idea what else to say to convince her. My nerves were fraying. Between Mikey's silence and Lucy's strong personality, I spent my morning continually seeking approval from one and placating the other. I couldn't remember the last time I'd been so intimidated by a child.

I allowed the macaroni to cool and gave the kids some baby carrots and milk. Lucy stared at her macaroni and ate a carrot before risking a bite of the offending pasta.

"You're wrong. It doesn't taste the same."

"I bet you could try eating it anyway, huh? It can't be that much different."

"I don't like it!" The sheer volume of her yell froze me in place as she threw her bowl to the floor then followed up with the carrots and almost-full cup of milk. "It's all wrong! You did it all wrong!"

Before I could process the explosion, she raced to her room.

I stood in the middle of the kitchen, stunned, staring at the artificial orange clinging to the gray carpet fibers, the carrots rolling to different corners of the kitchen floor, and the milk spatter everywhere, including on me. As the shroud covering my brain slowly slipped away, I heard Lucy crying and saw Mikey in his chair, legs up to his chin, arms wrapped around them, and his head buried in Bunny.

I reached out to steady myself on the counter, closed my eyes, and breathed deeply. *Okay, Jules, get your act together.* I took another deep breath then scooped Mikey into my arms and carried him into his bedroom to find Lucy curled around her doll on her bed. I sat with Mikey on one side and gently put my hand on Lucy and discovered my own trembling calmed considerably. With the calm came a degree of understanding.

Of course it was all wrong. Everything was completely and horribly unfair. My disillusionment with my parents might have come when I was older, but when I was four years old, they were still my world. My dad's lap was cozy, and my mother's hugs chased away my tears. Lucy, Mikey, and I might have had a good morning, yet it wasn't home. It was an unwelcome, never-ending visit with the unknown stranger.

Lucy sat up and nestled into me. "I'm sorry, Julie," said the little muffled voice.

I held her tightly, and every emotion I had rolled into pride and sympathy for the child who'd shown me that whatever I thought about her parents, my opinions had nothing to do with how the two had loved and raised their children. "It's okay. I know it's all going to be hard to get used to."

We sat, the three of us, for a few more minutes, and I suggested a new attempt at lunch. "I bet you're pretty hungry, huh?"

She nodded.

"How about a sandwich?"

Back in the kitchen, Lucy picked up her food and dishes without me asking. I invited her to help make her sandwich, mostly for self-protection. She chose her jelly while I spread the peanut butter. I asked if she wanted to do the jelly, and she readily agreed.

As she ate, I cajoled the less-traumatized Mikey into picking out a story. The selections appeared narrow. There was no sign of a book like the *Green Eggs and Ham* I'd read to them at Lynette's place. Almost all were adapted Bible stories or about God. That wasn't a bad thing, but I didn't know if any *silly* religious books existed. Kids needed silliness.

I was in serious trouble with the whole religion angle. They were moving from a home with parents who were devout Christians to a place with an aunt who was a lackadaisical believer in anything. I wasn't sure what my role was—whether I should continue down their parents' path or mine. I didn't have a path, religious or otherwise, which worried me.

Mikey handed me a book, and by the time we were halfway through, Lucy joined us on the couch, and we settled in for a period of calm. After a couple of stories, I suggested the TV. *Clifford the Big Red Dog* was on, and as we watched, I considered Clifford's enormous mass of compassion. I figured we could all use a big red dog to help us out.

I took the grace of the moment and tried to pack it away for the coming days when I would surely need it. As hard as I worked to stay in the moment, thoughts of the challenges ahead and whether or not I was up for them flooded my brain. I needed to look upon it like a new job. I'd had my fair share of new jobs, and each one had its own tests, whether they were mental tasks, physical ones, or simply dealing with people.

Kids? Another test. I hoped I could pass it.

Chapter Five

I clearly had no idea what a tantrum meant if I'd thought Lucy's outburst on the first day home defined one.

On day two, she didn't stop at throwing a dish to the floor. Anything she could get her hands on went flying. Mikey fled, and I stood in complete shock as she swept away all the dishes then knocked down chairs. After she tossed three different toys from the bins in the living room, I finally unglued my feet, crossed over to her, and bound her within my arms.

She kicked for a few seconds before her screams subsided into a more familiar cry. Waves of relief worked through me, as I had no idea what I would have done if she'd fought me.

"Okay. It's okay. That's right. Calm down. Shh..."

Little by little, her body loosened, and her breathing slowed while the cries receded. I sank to the floor with her in my arms, and we sat, still and silent.

We journeyed through the rest of the morning slowly and carefully. Once again, Lucy tended to her tornadic destruction and helped me scrub the carpet. Part of me felt unsympathetic. Another part recognized how Lucy joined me without complaint, and it wasn't like I made her do it all by herself. It seemed a good sign.

The sun filled the sky, and we took a walk, touring the neighborhood in a fresh way, an aimless exploration reminding me of a path leading to Lake Nokomis, one of the popular urban hangouts in the nonwinter months. We also found the playground I passed all the time on my route to work but obviously had never given much thought to before wandering by it with kids. Though areas of the park were still muddy and wet, we finagled two dry swings and traversed the bouncy bridge enough times to bring smiles to Lucy and keep Mikey engaged. A stop at an eclectic coffee shop completed the rounds with caffeine for me and slushies for the kids.

We made it through lunch without incident. Confidence tiptoed back into me. I suggested stories, since they bound us together.

Mikey handed me one about David and Goliath.

As I read, Lucy moved in closer and said, "Daddy reads with different voices for everyone."

Her use of the present tense jerked my heart, yet I also appreciated hearing the tone showing that maybe Brian wasn't strict and rigid *all* the time. "Should I do voices too? Mine probably won't be like your daddy's, but I can try it out anyway."

"Okay," Lucy agreed.

I looked at Mikey, who also gave his permission.

As I began, Lucy leaned forward, and I spied her disbelieving glance at Mikey, who I couldn't see quite as well in my periphery, though I thought I caught a twinkle in his eye as he brought Bunny up closer to his face. Later, as I finished the story, I discovered a hidden smile. Joy filled me upon seeing it and wiped away every terrible moment we'd had since leaving Duluth. Lucy remained in a fit of giggles.

"Oh, was the story funny?" I asked innocently.

"Daddy does voices, but they aren't like yours at all! Yours are funny!"

A trick I'd learned at the community-center childcare, using unexpected voices, thankfully had gone over perfectly. I read Goliath's voice like a mouse, David's with a Southern twang, and God's in a pathetic mix of my attempt at Australian and a truly misguided Irish.

I deemed my solution to the lack of silly books to be successful. I added a trip to the library to my list of activities for the coming days. My new plan was to read to them all day, every day.

Lucy made it clear that plan would never happen as she jumped up from the couch and pulled out the cars and a racetrack.

I looked at her brother. "What about you, Mikey? Cars? Blocks? Colors?"

He slid down from the couch and grabbed a car then the blocks and put them both on the floor in his own spot before taking my hand and leading me there. He quickly set up a couple of blocks in a line then did the same in a parallel setup before taking his car and driving it between the two rows. He wanted to make his own track. I dug in and divided my time between playing with the little town he and I created and watching Lucy's races every time she told me to "Watch this, Julie!"

The knock on the door threw me, as I had forgotten a world existed outside of the tightly woven three-person one comprising our past forty-eight hours. Glancing through the peephole, I saw Zach. Irritation crept in as he again showed up when he wasn't supposed to. I breathed in and out, focusing instead on my tiny relief upon seeing another adult face as I brushed away my aggravation and opened the door.

"Hey."

His smile defused some of my annoyance; the kiss took care of the rest. Zach's arms around me restored some of the strength I hadn't fully realized had been leaking away. We stood in the doorway, and I rested my head in my special place between his shoulder and neck.

"What are you doing here?" I asked.

"I had a little time between class and my shift tonight. I missed you. I figured maybe I could meet the kids. I also kind of thought it might help you remember I still exist."

That wasn't an unfair reaction. I had ignored his texts and phone calls. I replied to his and everyone else's initial "did you get back okay?" messages then left the rest alone. I hadn't had time to talk to everyone and didn't know how to prioritize my time. I resolved the problem by not giving any of it away. I didn't have a handle on how Zach should fit into my new life. Considering how supportive he'd been, I tried to remember why I broke up with him in the first place. Despite my request about no visitors yet, I told myself that him wanting to see me and meet the kids was a good thing.

I flipped my head at Zach, motioning for him to come inside. Moments before, race-car-track noises had filled the living room. It suddenly yielded silence. The kids had disappeared.

"Hide and seek?" Zach suggested.

"They must have gotten nervous. Hang tight." I walked down the short hall to their room and found them holding Bunny, Dolly, and each other's hands on Lucy's bed. If they hadn't looked so shy and nervous, I might have taken a picture. Their sweet faces mirrored each other in expression and manner. I knelt on the floor and leaned into the bed, putting my hands gently on their feet.

"Hey, kids. My friend Zach is out there, hoping to meet you. He's got a few nieces and nephews of his own, and he's extra excited to meet mine. I'd love it if you came out and said hi."

They stayed silent, which was only odd for Lucy, of course.

"What if I brought him in here? Only to the door, and all you have to do is wave if you want to."

Mikey looked at Lucy as though to seek her approval, which she gave with a nod. I smiled and told them I would be right back. After giving Zach the conditions, I led him to the bedroom door.

"Hey, guys." Zach waved.

Lucy returned his wave, and Mikey tilted his head.

"Zach plays in a band, and do you know what instrument he plays? The *drums*."

The corners of Lucy's mouth gave a little upturn as her eyes brightened.

"Ba-dum-ba-dum-ba-dum, boom-boom," Zach sang out, miming with his air drumsticks. "You'll have to come by my place sometime and try them out."

"We've got a recorder." Lucy bounded off the bed and darted past Zach.

"We can have our own band!" Zach responded enthusiastically as he followed her.

Mikey stayed on the bed, still uncertain. I held out my hand. No go. I held out both arms, which proved the winning combination. His arms wrapped around me and brought to mind his two a.m. activities, the ones I wasn't sure he remembered. At least in our current situation, he wasn't sobbing.

"Where is it?" Lucy's shout had me rethinking the sobbing.

The grip around me tightened. My stomach clenched, and my heart pounded. I didn't know if I had the energy for another tantrum that day, and my nervousness increased at the idea of Zach witnessing it. I wanted to stay with Mikey in his bedroom, to hide out and let Zach face it on his own. In fact, I thought, as an unreasonable flush of frustration came over me, it would be only fair because the tantrum probably wouldn't have occurred had he not shown up. I'd made it clear no one should visit. Yet there he was, showing up unexpectedly when I'd told him not to. The fragile peace the kids and I had reached was destroyed. Anger replaced anxiety, giving me courage to charge out to the living room and face them both.

Already, toys were everywhere as Lucy unsuccessfully searched for the recorder. "I want my recorder! Why didn't you pack it? It's *mine*, and it should be here! Let me go!"

Zach had grabbed her, and though it was presumably to stop her from tossing more toys around, my anger bubbled over.

"*Zach*. Let. Her. Go." Never mind that I had restrained her in the same way earlier in the day. I couldn't handle watching a stranger doing the same thing to her, however well-intentioned he was.

"Jules, she's—"

"I know. Please let her go."

He released her, and she shot past Mikey and me and into her room.

"I think you should go."

Zach looked at the mess then looked at me, with Mikey still trembling in my arms. "I'm sorry."

"This is why I said no visitors at first." I didn't trust myself to speak in multiple sentences for fear I would go off on him like Lucy did or because I might fall apart. I couldn't fall apart.

"Okay, I have an idea first. And then I'll go. Please?"

He didn't wait for my response, which was probably wise because I would have shot him down. He was already heading to the kitchen while pulling from his pockets small prescription bottles with no labels that held his spare change and keys. I followed him.

He dumped the items out of the bottles and started digging through one of my drawers. Finally, he pulled out a package of microwave popcorn. He yanked off the cellophane then tore open the bag of unpopped kernels. He dumped some into each bottle and replaced the caps. He turned to me with a bottle in each hand and shook them.

"Maracas." He shook them, the rattle of the kernels giving off an easy, rhythmic pattern in his capable hands.

Some of my anger slipped away, and between Zach's calm and the quiet from Lucy, Mikey's stress decreased too. He pulled away from me and looked at Zach, who gave him a smile and handed over one of the makeshift maracas. Mikey joined in with the rhythms.

Zach passed the other bottle to him. "Wanna take this one to your sister?"

Mikey slid down from my arms and disappeared into his bedroom. Without Mikey's presence to give me purpose, I sank into a dining room chair, hoping the table and chair together would prop me up. Zach started cleaning up the toys, but I still wanted him to go. I wasn't sure how much longer I could keep it together.

"Look," he said, "I know you're mad at me for coming by, and I really am sorry. I'm going to help clean up my mess, and then I'll get out of here, I promise."

I didn't answer, because Lucy appeared and started picking up toys, too, which made me want to cry, although I wasn't sure why. Maybe it was pride in her knowing how to take responsibility for her actions. There was something else, too—sadness. Sadness for the little girl who had to go through too much and who was handling it the best she could. She *should* be mad that her recorder wasn't where she wanted it, and she *should* be at her own house with her parents, who knew exactly how she liked her macaroni and cheese. Yet she was overcoming it all with grace. I wanted to crumple that grace and throw it out the window. *Let it all out, kid. Fuck the world for doing this to you.*

"I'm sorry for throwing my toys, Julie. And yelling."

The small and sincere voice crawled into my heart, where it would stay forever. "It's okay, honey." As I wrapped my arms around her, her head went to the same spot where it belonged, just as mine had with Zach. And with a different sort of grace, I discovered I'd already fallen in love with these children.

"Can Zach stay a little longer? He made us these fun shakers!" Swiftly, she jumped away and skipped with happiness.

"Maybe. Let's ask him." It was my peace offering. Zach's presence might have tipped the delicate balance the kids and I had for a while, but had he not shown up, it would have been something else.

"Not today, buddy," Zach said, and I heard the regret in his voice. "I gotta get to work. Later this weekend?"

"Okay," Lucy agreed and, without giving him another thought, began singing a song to go with their shakers.

Mikey showed the most minute sign of a bounce on the couch while shaking his own prescription-bottle maraca.

Zach leaned in and gave me a kiss.

"Thanks for the maracas," I told him. "It was good thinking."

"Can you guys come on by soon?" he asked.

"Maybe. Can you please wait until I call?"

He agreed, and after he left, I searched for an instrument to join in with the living room band. I dug out a beer bottle from the recycle bin and blew into it to create a deep and hollow whistle.

"Yay!" Lucy cheered, and I almost wished Zach had stayed. He would have joined in with some percussion, and the kids would have gotten a kick out of his antics. He really loved playing the drums. I enjoyed watching his enthusiasm when he performed with his band. He moved a lot like Lucy did.

However, we had our own fun. We sang and danced to our music then plugged my iPod into the dock and played our shakers and bottle to pre-fab tunes. Mikey rocked a little, and we eked another smile out of him. His face was a whole different kind of beautiful when it happened.

Before bedtime, the smile disappeared, and red and black colors streaked across a page in deep, hardened tones, crayon chips sticking to the paper from the pressure during the coloring session. Later on, I woke before he did, ready for the piercing, heartbroken cries to punctuate his sleep and tear my heart into pieces.

The cries came. I calmed him, then back in bed, I calmed myself with thoughts of popcorn maracas shaking a gentle, promising rhythm.

Chapter Six

"When's the last time you've seen Grandma?"

We were headed to visit Mom for our first true break from our little bubble. I always thought it strange she had kept the house we grew up in since she hated doing all the yard work and general upkeep. However, she'd taken up gardening and hired out all the other stuff. I imagined it increased the property value. She did have pretty flower beds, causing me to assess my lack of plants. A vision of Lucy dumping them to the floor or all over the furniture convinced me not to get any yet. The current bonuses to my mom keeping the house were a garage and driveway. She agreed to let the kids keep their bikes at her house and ride them in her driveway. It made more sense than us lugging them up and down the stairs in my apartment building. When I told the kids, I glimpsed a flicker of enthusiasm from Mikey. Lynette's recommendation to pack the bikes had been spot-on.

"She brought us Christmas presents," Lucy said after some thought.

"Cool. What did she give you?"

"I got Dolly, and Mikey got a tow truck. It has a hook that pulls out and attaches to other cars and trucks. You turn the crank to lift the car up!"

I smiled at Lucy's excitement over Mikey's truck, guessing she played with it a lot more than he did. More often than not, Mikey preferred coloring and drawing over her louder activities. Lucy was visibly busy in her play. She liked a lot of different things, and rarely did any of them involve her sitting still. Reading stories successfully captivated her for longer periods of time.

"We don't have that tow truck, do we? Should we add it to the list of things we need to get from your house?" As soon as I said "your house," I regretted it. I wasn't sure how to work around the topics of home and parents. Hearing about their parents affected them on a hit-or-miss basis. There wasn't much sense tiptoeing around them because if there was anything I'd learned in the past two days, it was that the kids weren't stupid. "Your house" felt deceptive. My place wasn't home yet either. They understood on some level their parents weren't coming back, but I couldn't guess whether they applied that understanding to their old house too. Lucy's silence following my question made me wonder about the direction of her thoughts.

We passed my old elementary and middle school, the two structures still attached as they were when I attended. Kids not much older than Lucy and Mikey flew down the slides, rode high on the swings, and chased one another. I'd been a swing person myself. It didn't require the tricky navigation of friendships I never fully mastered. I was happy to leave the school years behind.

I parked on the street at my mother's house, keeping space available for driveway bike riding. As the kids got out of the car and glued themselves to my side, I admired the pretty picture. The lawn showed signs of emerging from its long winter dormancy, red and yellow tulips bloomed vividly along the front walk, and bright-green hosta shoots flanked the edges of the flower beds bordering the front of the house, leaving wildflower remnants too early yet for bloom. It felt like a grandparent's place, regardless of my mother not falling into the role easily. Of course, Lisa Mercer was a Realtor, and experience told her the value of a homey exterior.

Mom opened the door with an excited smile. "Mikey! Lucy! I'm so glad you came to visit me today."

Lucy suddenly looked up at me with panic in her eyes.

"No, no, no, no. Don't worry, honey. It's like I said. We're all visiting. I'm staying. I promise." Promise or no, Lucy gripped my hand tighter, and Mikey did the same. We shuffled over the threshold, and my mom offered chocolate chip cookies and snickerdoodles.

"Both Julie and your dad always loved snickerdoodles," Mom told the kids with a wink of conspiracy.

It was true, and I hadn't had a snickerdoodle in years. Cinnamon beckoned us into the kitchen, warmer due to the heat from an oven about to offer us scrumptiously fresh cookies. My tongue could taste them already as memories came back to me of sitting around that same table with the same cookies and hot chocolate after playing hard in the snow. Baking and cooking. I often forgot about the little piece of domesticity in my mom until it came to holidays. I remembered she used to do a lot more baking and cooking when we were growing up. I almost suggested that Grandma might bake cookies with them sometime when I recalled why the cooking side of my mom had slipped my mind. She wasn't a fan of us helping her.

"The mess," I said aloud. "You never liked the mess."

She looked puzzled.

"When we tried to help make cookies or cake or whatever. You'd cringe every time we spilled flour or sugar all over the counter or floor."

"When you're stuck at home and forced to be the only housekeeper, you can imagine me not wanting extra work. I let you help sometimes, and when I didn't want the help, I baked after you were already in bed or while you were at school."

She understood my implication. I wanted to have enjoyed those times helping her make cookies. However, she didn't give them to me. Moving on, she told the kids about several things she had from their house because we hadn't been able to find space for them at my apartment. They knew about their bikes, but she showed them the sandbox in the backyard, rejuvenated with their toys and new sand.

It was enough to propel us out the door and away from accusations.

As the kids dug in, Mom and I sat on the patio. "Hopefully, Lucy and Mikey are like you kids always were with playing outside. It was a saving grace, I tell you."

"Even when Brian was jumping out of trees?"

She laughed. "Don't you mean when you were pushing him out of them?"

"Hey. We weren't *that* mean... most of the time."

Mom's voice broke a little. "True. You and Layla were good sisters to him. I'm very grateful we managed to raise you two that way."

I swallowed the lump in my throat. Her grief seeped into the space between us. I reached over to take her hand, and we sat quietly until Lucy yelled out happily.

"Here's the tow truck!" Her head disappeared as she plunged into the bin, reemerging moments later with the Christmas present and letting whatever toys were above it fall to the wayside with a loud racket.

"She was looking for the tow truck?" Mom sounded hopeful.

"Yes. She said it was a Christmas present from you."

She smiled. "Well, I'd bought it for Mikey, but as long as one of them enjoyed it, I'm glad. I couldn't always be sure they were getting my packages."

Her statement depressed me, and it wasn't about trusting my brother to do the decent thing—it was how it highlighted the relationship none of us had with her. It felt weird to simply be in her backyard, hanging out with her. Our times together usually had a purpose, such as a holiday or helping her with some home project. I wondered what it would mean for us with grandkids in the mix.

Growing up had often felt like being in a water park. Much like standing out for long stretches in lines for the best slides, exposed to the elements as we waited for the bracingly cool water, we would wait either for my mother to spend time with us and show interest in our stories or for our dad to be around enough to play with us. Then we'd have those short, euphoric times when we got their attention while we shot down the slide or worked on a fort or project together. Those short rides down the slide were never long enough. Given the choice, I would choose the lazy river. Fewer thrills, but at least we could all float along together.

When my parents started cheating on each other, it was like they were cheating on us instead. We clearly weren't enough for them. I lacked the skills to be bright and shiny. Layla had the loud personality, and Brian had bike stunts and adventure. I didn't know what I had.

As an adult, I still stood at the edge of the chasm separating us, uncertain how to cross it and get my mom to be more interested in me.

"You didn't by chance run into a recorder with all the other toys you brought back to your house, did you?"

She shook her head, and I spilled out a tired sigh.

"How are things going, honey?"

"As well as expected, I suppose. Let me tell you, where Mikey falls in silence, Lucy has more than made up for it with her tantrums."

She chuckled. "I guess you've discovered the first thing she's gotten from you."

"Tantrums? Me?"

"Oh yes. You had quite the lungs to show off when you were unhappy with something. Layla would cover her ears and beg me to 'make it stop.' You stopped freaking out not long after Brian was born. Kind of the opposite of what usually happens, really. I guess Brian brought out your caretaking streak."

"*Layla* thought I was too loud?"

That prompted full laughter from my mother. "Go figure, huh? Your sister was never shy, and she liked things a certain way, but she was much more reserved and didn't fuss as much if she couldn't have something. You, on the other hand, were very passionate about what you did or didn't want."

Passionate. The word brought to mind Mrs. Lasky, a member of the community center where I worked. Mrs. Lasky always had tidbits of "wisdom" to pass along—as well as a plethora of unsolicited advice—shared with a little squeeze over my hand and wrist and prefaced with a heavy-toned "honey." "Honey, you really need to put on some weight. You're wasting away." "Honey, don't let your man get away. You're not getting any younger." "Honey, that cupcake is going to go straight to your hips."

Recently, she had accused me of not having enough passion, and too many coworkers were hanging around, jumping on her bandwagon. "Yeah, Julie, we never see you get really excited about stuff. What do you really care about, anyway?"

The question cut me with its tone and implication. "Just because I don't jump up and down and shriek about things doesn't mean I don't care about stuff," I said.

"Name one thing you really love, something that gets your heart racing."

"TV," I said. "If you interrupt me while I'm streaming an episode of *Bones*, I'm likely to go off on you."

"You know what?" Mrs. Lasky said. "I'd really like to see you go off on someone sometime."

"I'm pretty sure part of why they hired me for this position is precisely because I do *not* go off on people."

"True," one of my coworkers conceded. "Not even Livestrong Freak can throw her. If lack of passion can make her calm for Freak, let's call it a win."

"Livestrong Freak," named that for wearing not just one yellow bracelet but three, accompanied by every other item from the Livestrong web store, was our resident visitor hyper-addicted to exercise. He criticized our personal trainers for doing everything wrong, our staff for not enforcing rules strictly enough about equipment and space use, and every other little thing not meeting his expectations for the day. Sometimes, he yelled. I usually picked up the walkie-talkie as a silent reminder that I would call security, which often worked. The first time I ever had to follow up on the threat, our one security guard for the entire facility was nearby and responded quickly to escort Livestrong Freak out of the building. Most of my colleagues usually argued back or placated him. Unfortunately, their response often strengthened the guy's arguments.

I didn't see any point in getting worked up over him. If not getting worked up defined lack of passion, then I didn't see how it was such a bad thing. So as much as my coworker had defended me, she also agreed with the others.

They weren't wrong. I had little going on in my life, which I guessed made me a little boring in my coworkers' eyes. I liked my life as it was, though, and didn't see why everyone always had to have a burning desire for something. Floating along peacefully had been working for me.

"Can we ride bikes now?" Lucy ran up to us, bobbing up and down on her toes as she clapped her hands.

"Of course, sweetie," Mom agreed, and as we moved to the front yard and the garage, I asked my mom about photos. I'd thought it might be nice to print a couple of pictures of their parents for the kids to have in their room. I couldn't find an Instagram account for either Brian or Elaine, and while Elaine had a Facebook account, she had never accepted my friend request. Her profile image hadn't been changed in a long time, so it might not have made much difference anyway.

"I dug all around but couldn't find any. None of you do pictures like we used to. It's all digital now. Layla didn't see anything on their desktop computer in their house, though, either, and if they had any on phones or something, they're probably lost or destroyed from the car wreck."

"You don't have any?"

The question clearly pained her, and I wanted to kick myself for once again spotlighting the sorry mess of a relationship she had with her kids.

"The last time I saw them... I didn't think... I took pictures of the kids but not of Brian or Elaine. I have a pretty picture from their wedding at the office. I'll scan it and send you a copy."

"Look, I know you and I haven't really been close or whatever, but I won't keep you from seeing the kids or anything."

God, that sounded bad. *I still don't want much to do with you, Mom, but I won't be filing any restraining orders because I'm so magnanimous.* "I didn't mean that quite like it sounded."

"No, honey. It's okay. I understood what you meant, and I appreciate the effort you're putting into this whole thing. I know it's not at all easy." She took my hand and smiled at me. "One thing at a time. You tackle the new-mom thing, then you can figure out the other mom thing if you still want to."

I had a brief flash of being young again, craving the affection my mother suddenly offered me.

I wondered what it would mean to figure out the "other" mom thing.

Chapter Seven

When Layla and Sheila arrived the next day for a new round of acclimation, Lucy and Mikey opted for sequestration in their room. Layla could be loud, so I thought it was a good idea. She came on strong, which was an admirable trait, though I was sure it had gotten her into trouble. I kind of loved how she didn't care, except when it annoyed me.

Sheila, however, might have had some influence on her, as Layla seemed much more subdued, especially upon discovering that the kids had hidden rather than face another new thing.

"What's in the bags?" I asked as they set the brown grocery sacks on the kitchen counter.

"Zach told Sheila you're good for nothing in the kitchen, so we brought everything we need to bake cookies and later to have a proper meal instead of some questionable thing from the microwave."

The tension must have crossed my face like a marquee, because she immediately followed up with, "Oh God, Julie, lighten up. It's a joke."

"I know. I don't care about the joke. It's… Well, Lucy's been a bit temperamental with meals. We might want to clue her in to what dinner will be before making it."

"Temperamental as in not eating?"

"No. As in throwing it across the room."

"Ah. Things not going well?"

Not wanting to give Layla the satisfaction of my failures, I answered, "We've had moments. It's going as well as expected."

"Of course it is," Sheila cut in. "I'm sure you're doing great."

She and Layla exchanged a look, and I decided it was a good time for me to check on the kids. "You might want to work on your game faces a little more before I come back out."

I tried to shrug off my irritation as I entered the kids' room and had some success when I saw they were playing quietly on the floor with their farm set instead of huddled together on the bed. Lucy commanded the animals while Mikey lay on his stomach, leaning over slightly on his arm while he scooted a tractor along the floor. Their calm floated over me. They were so beautiful. My mother said she thought Lucy looked like me. I didn't see it—except for maybe the hair. Her hair had already proven a challenge, as it was thick and easily tangled. It quickly earned the use of all my expensive hair products to manage it with minimal tears. We'd been only partly successful.

Mikey's dark hair was shorn close and easy to manage. His eyes were just as dark with lashes most women would die for. Because of those lashes, I wanted to see what he looked like with slightly longer hair. I thought it might help him appear less serious. He was a kid; he should look like one. I saw traces of Brian in him, but it was more of an overall impression than any specific feature. The resemblance made sense, though. Possibly, Mikey looked more like Elaine's brother.

"Hey, kids." I joined them on the floor. "Your aunts would love to meet you. They've been wanting to meet you for a long time."

Mikey paused and sat up, looking as though he might be ready. As he often did, he looked to Lucy, who had no response.

"They brought stuff to bake cookies with you and a dinner sure to be better than what I can cook."

"What kind of cookies?" Lucy asked.

A smile tugged at the corners of my mouth, and I tried to hold it back. "I'm not sure. Should we find out?"

"Can I crack the eggs?"

"Probably."

Lucy stood then reached down and tugged at my hand. With their small hands in mine, we headed to the living room, where Layla and Sheila still stood as though uncertain we would welcome their presence.

"You have lots of rings like Julie has," Lucy observed of Layla's fingers once I introduced the two of them.

"Would you like to try one on?"

Lucy nodded. Layla sat down and splayed out her fingers. "Which one?"

Lucy left my side to examine her choices. "This one." She pointed at a braided wood band around Layla's right pinky.

Layla praised the choice, and as she slid it off her finger and onto Lucy's pointer finger, she looked at Mikey. "What about you, little man? Wanna try one on too?"

He studied her for a moment then looked to me.

"Go ahead," I encouraged. Instead of going to my sister, he held up my hand and pointed at the silver band I wore on my left thumb. "Mine? Sure." I had never thought about their interest in my jewelry, which helped me imagine plenty to do in the future. They couldn't exactly try my earring collection, but I had plenty of rings and necklaces to play with. After twisting off the silver band for Mikey, I dashed to my room and rifled through my boxes to pull out anything I didn't want to get wrecked or lost and brought out the rest. *Jewelry as the icebreaker with my sister and sister-in-law. Unexpected.*

And though I should have anticipated it, the icebreaker turned to potential frost with Lucy's next question after she continued to study her aunts' wedding rings.

"Where are the uncles?"

"Which uncles?" I asked, although I was sure we all understood her question, especially given what we knew about Brian's ignorance.

"The ones who go with Auntie Layla and Auntie Sheila."

Layla squatted next to Lucy. "There aren't any. We are auntie and auntie. Sheila's my wife."

Lucy's brows furrowed slightly. "I thought only daddies and uncles could have a wife."

"Aunties and mommies can have wives too. And daddies and uncles can have husbands. It depends on who you love."

Layla reached up for Sheila's hand then looked into Lucy's eyes and smiled.

Lucy smiled back. "Your rings are pretty."

The questions might come back, but Lucy seemed satisfied with the conversation. I smiled at Layla and Sheila, pretty sure they were as relieved as I was that Lucy didn't already harbor Brian's prejudices.

They all moved on to games, and I stepped back and watched with satisfaction as Lucy smoked my sister in Memory and Mikey showed off his steady hand in Jenga. They moved seamlessly into the kitchen for cookie baking, and I took the time to clean, something I hadn't done for several days.

I found something cathartic about scrubbing the bathroom clean, a predictable task yielding a predictable and satisfying result. The sink didn't yell at me. It didn't freak out about the scrubbing bubbles, nor did it care what kind of cleaner I used. It didn't interrupt my sleep or make me guess what it needed. Cleaning didn't normally relax me, but I decided not to question the solace it provided. And the solitude. It had been only a few days, and already the lack of quality alone time disheartened me. I was used to regenerating in front of the TV for the better part of each evening. Just me, Michael Weatherly or maybe Ice T, and Hostess.

I believed my mother when she told me it would get easier, I really did, and it had been only a few days. I wallowed in self-pity anyway. I sat on the edge of the tub and took in some deep breaths. It was time to stop feeling sorry for myself. My life had changed, and it was time to deal with it. I tornadoed my way through cleaning the bathroom, and by the time I finished vacuuming the kids' room, Mikey appeared as though he had a happy secret. When I took in the great aroma worthy of my mother's cooking, I let Mikey lead me to the table and discovered the reason behind his happy expression. He'd decorated place mats, and mine showed a drawing of someone I thought was me with him and Lucy and random pictures of rings around us. He had a knack for drawing, and I had only minimal guesswork about who and what everything was on the place mat. Based upon other pictures of his, I had an inkling there might be more to his drawings than those by other kids, including Lucy.

Layla's place mat had her next to a sun, Sheila's had her holding a heart, Lucy's showed a windy racetrack, and his depicted a bunny lying on its side at the base of a tree trunk. I studied it briefly before giving him a hug for the wonderful surprise.

As we ate dinner, Lucy dominated the conversation. She had doubled her listening audience and therefore took advantage. She opened up about life in Duluth, although upon a close listen, she avoided stories about home and dwelled on places they visited, church, and the kids at Lynette's daycare.

As Lucy chattered away with Layla and Sheila, I communed with Mikey. I pointed at my plate then at him and put a hand up in the air in a gesture that asked, "Well?" I wondered what he thought of dinner. He smiled and rubbed his tummy. I pointed at myself, then at the kitchen, and followed up with both hands mimicking an explosion.

He giggled. Out loud.

I couldn't help my expression of pure shock and joy. His return expression worried me, making me think I'd scared him away with my response. To hear the beautiful sound felt like I had been tucked away in isolation and discovered music for the first time. I quickly put my hand to my mouth and mimicked surprise. It worked. Even though he didn't laugh out loud again, he put his hands to his mouth and hid his obvious grin.

"What are you guys laughing about over there?" Layla asked, suddenly privy to our quiet corner of the table.

"We're cracking up over the weird miracle of how much better the dinner you made is over all of my meals combined. I'm soaking up the laughter because come tomorrow, we're all going to be crying again."

"Auntie Layla showed me how to make everything, Julie," Lucy said. "Now I can help you!"

"You sure can. What a great idea!"

In the meantime, Lucy volunteered to help with the dishes. I washed, she rinsed, and Sheila dried while Layla and Mikey disappeared and did their own thing. I couldn't have asked for a better introduction between the kids and their aunts. Their bond formed willingly and quickly.

Later, after Layla put the kids to bed, Sheila ducked out to take advantage of being near an IKEA, leaving Layla and me to our own devices. I popped open a couple of beers for us while she put some cookies on a plate, and we sat in my living room in a strange silence while our buffers shopped or slept.

"So, the Mayo. Do you like working there?" I opted for the lamest conversation starter ever.

"Ah." She shook her head and gave a rueful smile. "So, that's where we are right now, is it? Look, I was a bitch about your job before. I'm sorry."

"What? No. I wasn't trying to bring all that up by asking about your job. I mean, you were right. It's not like I'm climbing some great career ladder. The benefits aren't anything great either."

I had calculated what my new paycheck would be with the kids added to my insurance plan. Add daycare and a bigger grocery bill, and my budget got tighter and tighter. Plus, my boss had balked at how much time I was taking off, reminding me of all the unpaid days since I hadn't been there long enough to earn vacation time. "I like the people there, including most of the regular guests and members. And I'm not just a clerk. I supervise the fitness programming." God, my defense sounded pathetic. I opted against mentioning I was hourly and not salaried.

"I know, and it's cool you like it there. I was being a snob and taking my anger at Brian out on you. I mean, turns out they're your kids, right? They go to you. I get it. I do."

I thought about how it had been for me when Layla graduated and went off to college. The house became quieter, and I no longer had her around to share responsibility for Brian. Maybe Brian came up against loneliness, too, when I left. Instead of letting me go, he got angry. Maybe it was my fault he'd submerged himself in religious circles responsible for shutting down his compassion for his sister who dared to love another woman or me, his other sister, who dared to hold marriage and children at arm's length. I would do better at taking care of his kids than I did in taking care of him.

"Remember when we used Mom's makeup on him?" Layla asked, slipping into my secret, self-recriminating silence.

I smiled. "And painted his nails?"

"And draped him in the curtain sheer we took down from the living room window?"

We giggled over the memory and how we made up ourselves and had a fashion show with towels laid out end to end as our runway. Mom had come home, and we thought we would be grounded for the next three weeks. Instead, she joined us, snapping imaginary pictures and calling out commands to stop, turn this way, blow us a kiss. I always loved it when she surprised us and joined in our play. It made me feel like she'd wanted us after all.

"How about when we made him take his bike off that jump?" I asked.

"The little shit totally nailed it."

"It was probably good Dad came home when he did. I'm not sure Brian would have safely navigated the next level we would have made."

"He looked beautiful flying off that ramp, didn't he? Landed and did that fancy skid brake," Layla said.

"Grinning ear to ear."

"We created a monster that day."

We clinked our bottles in a toast to our conversion of Brian into a daredevil. It wasn't our fault entirely, but we sure opened the door for him to try more and more crazy things.

"See how far I can jump from this swing," he would say. Or "watch me flip off these monkey bars" or "look how high I can climb on this tree."

I hoped it hadn't been a cry for attention. He broke his arm only once, and given how often he pushed the limits, he got off pretty lucky.

"Too bad he turned into a real monster later," Layla added with an edge to her tone.

The depiction took me by surprise. I'd not been shy about being first to criticize our brother. However, classifying him as a monster seemed extreme.

Brian had started in with his disapproval of Layla's "lifestyle choice," as he put it, by the time I finished high school. Layla took us all out to dinner for my graduation. I didn't remember much other than the end, when Brian asked her if getting out of college and having a real job had finally cured her of her lesbianism.

When it came time for his graduation, Layla refused to come.

"He's only eighteen," I emailed her.

"Which is old enough to act like an adult. You had a full-time job and were supporting yourself within a couple of months of graduating. He's still accepting handouts and spouting off as though what he says doesn't actually affect people. I sent him a card. I don't owe him anything more."

She made me reflect on my role with him. I should have pressed him more when I was still living at home—when he was younger and more malleable. By the time he was eighteen, he'd already traveled far down an unfamiliar road and sent the rest of us on detours away from him.

"Really? That bad?" I asked.

"He used to send me brochures for all of those fucking 'sexual orientation rehabilitation' clinics. He'd email me quotes from the Bible about my 'sinful' way of living and offer paths of atonement. Then came the links from all the shit anti-gay propagandists drummed up whenever a gay-rights issue arose somewhere in the US."

As if she didn't run into enough harassment from strangers, her brother had to intensify it. I gulped down more of my beer, which only worsened my upset stomach. "I'm so sorry, Lay."

"Oh, I haven't gotten to the good stuff yet. He found out from Mom I was serious with Sheila, and he stepped up his game. Texts, email, snail mail, I got it all on a weekly basis. He resorted to quoting other religious dogma against homosexuality—Orthodox Judaism and Islam. He likened our future children to being psychotic and murderous because our immoral home structure would seep into their brains and pervert them."

Good God.

"That," Layla growled, "was the final straw. By then, Sheila and I were solid, and I got my job at Mayo. I moved in with her, changed my phone number, and deleted my old email account."

"That's horrible. Why didn't you press charges for harassment?"

"Because he's my brother. And because of Mom. She convinced me not to. I promised I wouldn't if she promised to never ever, even under threat of death, give him any personal information about me again."

I stood, suddenly unable to absorb everything she'd revealed. I wanted to shake off her words, her truth about our brother pressing upon me without permission. I hardly talked to him but never guessed him to be so creepy. Or *that* awful. I didn't see how that could have happened to him.

I faced Layla, realization dawning on me. "Are Brian's twisted views why you wanted the kids? So you could be sure to reform them?" As soon as the words left my mouth, I regretted them. Daggers flew from Layla's eyes, and I took them in. "Oh God, I'm sorry. That was a shitty thing to say." I put down my beer and paced. "No wonder no one in this family wants to have anything to do with each other."

"Oh, fuck, Jules." She stood and put her hands on my arms to stop my pacing. "It *was* a shitty thing to say, but it wasn't all wrong. It's complicated."

"What if all of Brian's awfulness rubbed off on the kids? How do I undo any of it?"

"You already are undoing it. You have a good heart. Plus, they're young," Layla said.

"I don't know what that means."

"It means they're resilient and moldable. And you'll show them, because your heart guides you. They're only four. It's not like they're aware of any of the shitty stuff Brian did. For all we know, it wasn't his normal thing. He probably figured he was called to some special duty to save his sister or something."

I took a deep breath, allowing it to fill me with a temporary confidence. I grabbed Layla's hand. "I'm sorry."

"Since when are you no longer a hugger?" She smiled and pulled me in.

"I'm glad you're here," I told her. "I've missed you."

"I've missed you too."

After Sheila came back and picked up Layla to go to their hotel, I opened my computer and began looking for photos of Brian and Elaine. Someone out there must have an unprotected Facebook account or public photos. Or the church site, maybe, since they were active members. It took some work, but I found a few and downloaded them. One was of Brian and Elaine with another couple. Looking at the tags, I figured out the other two were Shannon and Chad. Shannon and Elaine took up the center of the photograph, arms linked and their heads leaned toward each other. They looked happy. I almost considered friending Shannon until I realized the awkwardness behind such a decision. And honestly, I had no reason to think their friends would be any easier to tolerate than my brother.

I had a friend request from Lynette, and I hesitated before accepting. Then I wondered what, exactly, I was worried about and added her. She seemed fairly active on the site, although it wasn't her business page, and she probably limited what she posted to kid photos. I found one, though, of Elaine and the kids. It was one of those Mother's Day photos—each kid pressed up on either side of Elaine, looking joyful. I wondered if there had ever been a similar photo with my mother. I wanted there to be one.

A few family photos were on the church website. I figured once everything with the estate settled, more photos and effects would materialize. A sense of urgency came over me. We couldn't wait. The kids needed the pictures as soon as possible. I sent them all off to the in-house photo lab at the local drugstore for pickup the next day. If the kids needed more, I might contact Shannon after all.

I considered the images of Brian and Elaine's friends and the hole created by their deaths. A wave of sadness washed over me as I thought of how often in the past few days their friends had picked up their phones to see what Brian and Elaine were up to only to have reality hit them. Guilt seeped in about how those who should have felt Brian's death most keenly barely registered his absence. *Would Brian have come down for the funeral if it had been Layla? Or me?* My heart pounded faster, my breathing shallowed, and I realized the whole situation angered me. *Damn you, Brian, for judging me in life and in death. I'm doing my part*, I wanted to scream at him. *Again.* Whereas I couldn't determine what Brian had ever done for me.

Nothing. That was what. Suddenly, I knew my dad was right. Fuck the church for taking everything I could use toward helping me with the kids. They said the kids came to them by the "grace of God." I didn't think so—unless God was living in my ovaries, I was pretty sure I had a hand in that grace. I got up to dig out my dad's business card from my bag and shot off an email to him from my phone, telling him I wanted to contest the will. I didn't know what it would mean or if I would be successful, but when I considered my budget, especially after looking at daycare costs, I felt more confident it was the right thing to do. I could afford everything—barely—but if we had an emergency, there was no way I could swing hospital fees without them taking everything I had.

As quickly as my blood pressure had risen, it whooshed out of me, wearing me out. As I returned my computer to the dining room table, I noticed Mikey's place mat sticking out from under mine in the stack. I pulled it out, and my heart about fell apart when I discovered what I couldn't see earlier. Bunny lay next to the tree. Behind the tree, though, colored in brown crayon to look like bark, was a picture of a child—Mikey. Hidden. Unseen. I held it up to the light, and the eyes and mouth on the face were simple, straight lines. Not happy or sad but emotionless.

I choked on my own heart as I considered whether that was how he felt or how he wanted to feel. I wondered if that drawing reconciled his nightly screams with his all-day silence.

I remembered his laugh at dinner, and I placed his picture on top of the stack, determined he shouldn't be hidden away. I would get his sweet laugh again, somehow. I thought of Lucy and her offer to help me cook. It seemed foolish, but our dinner and the kids' reactions were important. I desperately hoped to get a sliver of laughter again, if I could replicate the situation.

I texted my mother. *Will you teach me how to cook?*

In thirty minutes, I had willingly contacted both of my parents in the name of Brian's children. I guess he'd done something for me after all.

Chapter Eight

We went into the next week slightly calmer and ready to see the world beyond my apartment and neighborhood. I took the kids to the community center to meet my coworkers and to discover a surprising and overwhelming care package. My colleagues and some of our regulars had donated books, toys, and gift cards to Target, Walgreens, and Cub Foods.

"It was the next best thing to a baby shower," one colleague said.

"The place is falling apart without you, Julie," another colleague told me. "And Livestrong Freak claims we're double billing him for his membership dues and is threatening to sue."

"He said the same thing last month too," I replied. "I already proved to him it wasn't happening. Go ahead and tell him to sue."

My boss, Carl, wasn't anywhere around, bringing me a sigh of relief. My position at the community center was health-and-fitness program liaison. I managed the class schedule and supervised the guest services desk. One of my coworkers told me the position used to be called the health-and-fitness program supervisor. Carl changed the name because it sounded too close to his own position as community program director. It was ridiculous to think a salaried manager who oversaw all the center's programs and personnel would be threatened by an hourly employee simply because of a title but whatever.

The secondary reason for the visit was to let the kids swim, and they showed off how well they did it. Aside from the showers and hair session afterward, the activity put us all at ease for a good two hours. I pocketed the idea for the rest of the week.

The week also started the race to visit and decide upon a daycare. Earlier that morning, I charged through phone calls, and after the first thirty minutes, I'd crossed out fifteen places. As large as the list was, there weren't many daycares within my price range or in a workable location that still had openings. I simply crossed my fingers and hoped for the best.

The first place we visited was loud and dirty. Lunch dishes still covered the table, and the kitchen looked like it hadn't been cleaned in days. We couldn't step anywhere without tripping over a toy. The second place wasn't much better, and I scuttled the kids out of both homes before I asked the first few questions on my list. It was only the first day, I told myself, and I tried to remain optimistic.

Unfortunately, the fear I might actually leave the kids at such a place entered Lucy's heart. She determined I was doing everything in my power to make her unhappy.

"No, that's not how you play the game. You're not supposed to sound like a lion."

"If you want me to play with you, then maybe you could help me with how to do it," I said.

"I don't want to play with you. I don't want to be here. I want to go home. Why can't we go home?"

When she finally let me pull her into my arms after the subsequent thrashing of toys, we cried together at the injustice of throwing us both into places we'd never wanted to be.

"I have an idea," I told the kids as I pulled my phone out of my purse. "While we go up and down the aisles, I want you to take a picture of everything you like to help us find out what to buy in the future and give Grandma ideas for what she can teach us."

We were on our first grocery shopping trip, an activity I'd always heard horror stories about from other parents, so I didn't hesitate to give them the task in hopes it would take us through the store quickly and painlessly.

Lucy readily agreed, and both kids watched closely as I showed them how to work the camera on the phone and reminded them to hold it carefully with two hands. With Lucy's unpredictable behavior, it was dumb to trust her with it, except she hadn't had any major meltdowns in public places. I decided to risk it.

It turned out to be a good decision. The kids got a kick out of taking pictures and did great with turn-taking. I loved seeing what they found for their photos as they recognized items from when Elaine had cooked, even if they didn't exactly know how the ingredients figured into the meals they liked. I was betting on my mom to help fill in the blanks.

Zach, oddly, showed disappointment when I told him about my mom offering to teach me to cook. "You've never taken me up on my offer to teach you."

"I didn't really care about cooking before."

"Obviously." He laughed. "But I always thought it would be fun to cook together."

To appease him, I agreed to take the kids over in the evening to try it out. I wished I looked forward to it. I sensed a very different atmosphere between having my mom teach me and cooking "with" Zach.

My premonition proved accurate after we arrived, and he told me his plans. He was making some kind of vegetable casserole, rolls, and chicken cooked in a fancy sauce. All I thought of was restaurant food. I could normally handle boxed food, and suddenly, "cooking together" for the first time didn't include a single box of easy steps. I tried to tamp down my anxiety. Maybe it was less complicated than it sounded.

"I wanted something more challenging than I normally make," he said with enthusiasm.

"Except 'more challenging' for you is several levels beyond my expertise."

He gave me a little side hug. "It'll be fine. C'mon. Let's head to the garage first so the kids can bang on the drums for a while."

Zach's apartment building had an external structure with garages, except Zach used his as a practice studio. He hung insulating blankets on the walls not only to allow for noise dampening for his neighbors but also because he used it in the winter. When Zach wasn't studying or working at the pharmacy, he was in his garage. He and his jazz band frequently played at small venues throughout the year.

Lucy's eyes lit up in the makeshift studio, and to my surprise, when Zach let her loose on his drums, she didn't go wild. If she had, Zach would have taken it in stride. It was an appealing feature of his, that placidity. With Lucy, however, I saw a new side of him—teacher. He showed her how to hold the drumsticks and the different ways to play on each part of the drum set. Lucy ate it up. As they moved on to trying out a rhythm, I looked over at Mikey, who stared at the electronic keyboard.

I switched it on, handed him a pair of headphones, and pressed down on a couple of keys to encourage him to do the same. He put a shy finger on one key then another. I wondered at his hesitancy. I doubted it was the first piano he'd seen. I'd seen Brian's hold on structure; possibly, he hadn't allowed the kids to touch one. I reassured Mikey of his permission to try it and showed him the different buttons for changing the sound. The demonstration got him going with more confidence.

I stepped back to enjoy a moment of harmony. Watching Zach leave Lucy to her creative exploits and joining Mikey in his jam let me imagine that things between us could actually work. I hadn't seen a future with him before. Lately, though, I was trying to see an alternative.

Zach's dinner plans started out well. I invited the kids to use butter knives to chop vegetables for the casserole. They formed adorably misshapen crescent rolls from one of those Pillsbury cans. They lost interest after roll making, and there was still much left to do. The casserole, which needed at least thirty minutes to bake, hadn't made it into the oven yet, and we had the fancy sauce and chicken to somehow time along with everything else. The cook time for the casserole alone had my nervousness building since it meant we would be eating well past the kids' normal dinnertime. I'd brought extra toys for them to play with, but I didn't know how long the kids would last before we encountered a Lucy meltdown.

"Do you want to finish the casserole or start on the chicken?" Zach asked me.

"I have to finish mixing everything in this pan for the casserole, right? I'll finish up the casserole. We need to get it in the oven and get things moving," I told him.

"We're doing fine. Why are you stressed out?"

"Because the kids are going to be hungry, and I'd really like to avoid another tantrum from Lucy today. Why didn't we have regular vegetables?"

"Because this sounded like more fun." He put his hands on my shoulders and gave them a gentle massage. "Look, let's let the kids have some extra crackers for a snack."

I sighed. I had no doubt crackers worked for his nieces and nephews and other kids—it worked with Mikey but not Lucy. She needed substance. "Lulu will need more than a few crackers. I'll make her a peanut-butter-and-jelly sandwich."

"A whole sandwich? She won't be hungry for dinner."

"Then I guess she won't eat much of this elaborate meal. You're going to have to trust me on this for once."

"For once? What does that mean?"

I bit back a curse as I tore through his cupboards and pulled out a knife, bread, peanut butter, and jelly. I bit back another curse as I saw he of course had natural peanut butter, which tasted completely different from Jif. Extra jelly had a chance of disguising the difference. "It doesn't mean anything. Forget it. Keep going with dinner. I'll catch up after I get Lucy squared away." *If* I got her squared away. The peanut-butter thing might undo our whole evening.

I hated feeling anxious all the time.

"C'mon." Zach's hand rubbed my back after Lucy ended up downing the sandwich with barely any comment. "She's fine. See? We're almost done with getting everything cooking, and then we'll be able to sit and relax for a bit until it's all ready."

I tried to relax, jealous of his tranquility plus a little irked at how he brushed everything away. I should have left the kids with him for the rest of the night and found out tomorrow how it was all "no big deal."

With my luck, he would have zero problems. At least I would get some sleep. It really wasn't a mystery why I was on edge, given I hadn't had a full night's rest in over a week. Mikey's nightmares continued to trouble me. I'd searched the web for ideas about sleep, grief, and child development. What I read was it might simply be his coping device—his subconscious dealing with what his conscious self couldn't yet handle. Then there was the whole idea of his speechlessness too. The entire thing seemed a thorny mess.

I called out to Mikey to see if he would help set the table. He nodded, leaned into me briefly, then accepted the first set of plates. Zach finished preparations for the meal before leaving everything to simmer, brown, and heat. He pulled out a bottle of wine and presented it to me as a server in a high-class restaurant would.

"A glass of zinfandel, my lady?"

"Yes, absolutely." Wine to go with my whine seemed highly appropriate. I took a sip and let it rest in my mouth a moment longer than usual before swallowing and willing it to work its magic and relax me.

I sank into a chair at the table, and Mikey, who'd finished putting all the silverware in place, crawled onto my lap and snuggled into me. That action alone produced a calm more effective than the wine. I wrapped my arms around him and kissed the top of his head.

"He looks good on you," Zach said, his voice caressing and his eyes taking in all of me at once. I felt warm and nervous at the same time. For a moment, I saw his intentions for our future. His future.

Despite getting a late start on his new career, Zach was pretty put together. I admired his confidence in knowing what he wanted and how to get it. Of course, he was sure of what I should want, too, which was pretty much what stagnated our relationship the first time.

Dinner, when finally ready, went over pretty well, as Zach had predicted. The kids might have eaten more rolls than fancy chicken, but they also enjoyed the complicated vegetable casserole and acted polite and gracious for the entire meal. As we cleaned up, Zach pulled me into a deep kiss and suggested we stay the night.

I knew what he was asking, while he didn't really understand what he would get. I wasn't prepared for Zach to see the pain threatening to drown both the kids me and in our weakest moments, such as the tantrum sure to come later in the evening, Mikey's middle-of-the-night screams, and my breakdown that often occurred amid everything. I built a protective wall, causing my irritation to resurface. The irritation increased as his hands wandered over my body.

I pushed away from him. "No. Things have been turning out okay today, but it's inviting trouble to press for more. They're barely getting used to being at my place, let alone trying to throw in something new."

"It was just a suggestion, Jules. I wasn't trying to demand anything. You don't have to get so bent out of shape."

"I'm not sure if you've noticed, but my whole life is a little bent out of shape right now."

He leaned back against the counter, crossing his arms and dropping his head. "Yeah, I know."

I wasn't sure whether his tone indicated compassion or accusation.

"I kind of figured you'd say no. Then again, I also thought you'd turn it around and invite me to stay the night at your place. Wishful thinking."

Some of my aggravation slipped away. When I'd opened the door to him again, I knew what I was doing. Or at least I thought I did. I always saw Zach as a good guy. He was still a good guy, and I might not have understood his situation, either, if our roles had been reversed.

"I need some more time. The kids need more time. People keep saying kids are resilient, and maybe everyone's right, but it's not instantaneous, you know?"

"No, it's not. I also don't think you have to let everything about what's happened take over your life. You've still got a say in how things go."

I stepped closer again and gave him a weak smile. "It doesn't really feel like it right now." My hands found his. "I'm just running along, trying to keep up."

"Maybe if you took advantage of the equipment at the community center, you'd be in better shape." His eyes twinkled as he released one of my hands to put his own through my hair.

"Hey," I protested, feigning indignance. "I've at least cut down on Swiss Cake Rolls."

"Does that mean you won't be sharing our dessert tonight?" He kissed me then let me go and grabbed a box of Little Debbie Devil

Squares from the cabinet followed by a Fanta Orange pop from the fridge.

I laughed. "You probably should have led your 'stay the night' argument with this."

"I thought about it. Or better yet, I should have held them for ransom."

"Well, all I can say is if the kids didn't already like you, this would have gotten you the win. I mean, it's always worked with me."

"Bribery gets you everywhere."

The playful Zach was exactly the one I needed for the rest of our night. Casual, funny, and accepting. I stroked the ridges of his ears with my fingertips, and I pulled him into a kiss.

"I had fun today," he said. "I can be your running buddy."

"Aren't you already?"

"Am I? I feel like you're keeping me at arm's length."

He wasn't wrong, but I also didn't want to launch into a "state of our relationship" conversation. So I gave him an answer that also wasn't wrong. "It's all pretty new still. I just need a little time."

"Okay."

Considering we had broken up recently and slid back into the situation with each other, there wasn't much else for either of us to say. Although I could officially say yes to him and make it clear we were solid.

"You've been great. You really have. I'm glad you're in this with me," I said.

"Is that the Little Debbies talking?"

I grinned. "It really is."

Chapter Nine

The third daycare we visited showed promise. In fact, everything about it felt right. Unfortunately, the provider told me she'd met with another family earlier in the morning, and it looked like one of the two openings would go to them. She promised to call if things changed.

The remaining visits all paled by comparison, and I was running out of options. I had to console myself with "good" equating to "good enough," even if it wasn't great. Everything since losing their parents was barely even "good." In some ways, I figured it was ridiculous to think the options weren't better by leaps and bounds than what I offered the kids and knew how to do. Then I would see how Mikey reacted in each situation, and I was positive I couldn't bear to leave him with just anyone. While Sheila had helped prepare me with questions when she and Layla visited over the weekend, it was up to me to make sense of the answers and trust my instincts. I didn't have a grasp on what my instincts should be. If Mikey didn't have a death grip on me and Lucy didn't scowl, then I chalked that up to progress.

The next daycare we visited, run by a woman named Sophie, was clean with busy children. They had a lot of options for play—arts and crafts for Mikey, building supplies for Lucy. Sophie had a couple of kids of her own. She was young and energetic and said that most days, she implemented a preschool curriculum for the older kids, which would be good for Lucy, who seemed to need more stimulation. The schedule posted on the wall showed detailed organization, and I'd recently read about the importance of structure for kids. It made them feel more secure. Until learning about that, I hadn't been keeping any schedule with Lucy and Mikey except for mealtimes. It was no wonder Lucy fell into tantrums and Mikey still didn't want to speak.

At first, Sophie expressed some misgivings about Mikey's silence. However, the more she and I talked, the more at ease she became. It probably helped that he was such an agreeable kid. In the end, we left with a copy of her contract, and I was fairly certain I'd found the kids' new daycare.

With one burden lifted, I moved on to the next.

Unlike their parents, the kids accepted pretty much everyone I introduced them to. Sure, they were shy and didn't always jump right into interacting with someone new, but once they crossed the threshold of unknown to simply new, they fell into step. When I mentioned we were going to go meet their grandpa, they didn't resist. In fact, Lucy startled me with her observations as we sat on the couch together after reading a story about different kinds of families.

"Mommy and Daddy said we didn't have grandpas, grandmas, aunts, and uncles like everyone else. But now we do."

"Do you mean you didn't think you had any?"

I watched her for a moment before she settled on a shrug.

"Grandma—that's your daddy's mom and my mom too. And Grandpa is both your daddy's dad and my dad."

"Really?"

I nodded. "And you met Layla, our sister. Did you know your daddy had another sister besides me?"

She shook her head. "You came to our house once."

"I'm glad you remembered! We read stories together."

"Do we have other aunts and uncles?"

"Your mom has... had a brother. At least one. I don't know if she has other brothers and sisters." I remembered my Facebook photo investigation the other night. "I don't think so, though."

"What about grandmas and grandpas? My friend Emma has two grandmas and three grandpas."

After my conversation with Elaine's mother, I better understood Brian's vague explanation—or lack of one—about his family. Complications cropped up all over the place. I hadn't yet contemplated the idea of revealing to the kids the true nature of our own relationship. It was something to consider in the future, the timing of when they would need to know. Or want to know.

"I guess you have another grandma with Nora, Grandpa's wife. Plus, you have another grandma and grandpa in Washington. They're your mom's parents."

"Is Washington another country?"

"Nope, a state." I pulled my laptop over and opened it up. "Let me show you on a map."

Mikey had been listening to our conversation, and he and Lucy crowded close to the screen as I taught them about cities, states, and countries. I pointed out Minneapolis and St. Paul and Duluth. Then I showed them Washington. Lucy decided it was far away and wondered if they would get to meet their other grandparents.

"I don't think so, honey." It pained me to say it, but I also didn't see what good a lie would do.

"Because they live too far away?"

"Maybe." It was as honest of an answer as anything. They lived too far away in more ways than geography.

We met my dad at his office for lunch. He and his partners worked out of a street-level office park at a cross section of residential and commercial zoning. Trees, a pond, and walking paths surrounded the building, creating an environment very different from the high-powered, sterile one fitting the stereotype associated with lawyers.

The receptionist recognized me right away and greeted us with a warm smile. "You must be Julie! I'm so happy to finally meet you and the kids." She stood and walked around her desk before shaking my hand. "Trevor's been looking forward to this all morning. He came back a few minutes ago with your lunch. I'll take you to his office."

My father's office was a couple of doors down and, naturally, on the window side, which he and another woman were standing next to when the receptionist ushered us in.

"Here they are," my dad said, his expression bright and inviting, so much different than our past couple of encounters. When he smiled, it made me think "daddy" and not "father." My heart tugged for my childhood Daddy days.

The woman was Tamara Resnick, the attorney handling my case. He introduced us briefly, but Tamara couldn't stay, as she had a conference call to attend to before meeting with me. My dad crouched and took in his grandchildren, who had predictably gripped each of my hands and attached themselves to my side as soon as we entered the building.

"I bet it's sort of strange to see your gramps for the first time. I've been nervous myself to meet you two. I can tell already you've figured out your aunt won't lead you wrong." He stood again. "C'mon. She's not going anywhere. We'll all eat lunch together right here at the conference table."

He pulled food out of the paper grocery bag, which included sandwiches and at least one pickle. I smiled, remembering for certain where Brian had gotten his pickle habit.

"What?" he said with a sudden expression of mischievous surprise. "Would you look at this? There are *doughnuts* in this bag. How did they get in there?" Out of the bag came a white bakery sack. "Let's see. There are two chocolate doughnuts. I think those go to you two." He looked at Mikey and Lucy, who grinned. "There's a bear claw for me, and this jelly-filled one must go to my Jujubee."

"What's your Jujubee?" Lucy spoke for the first time, unable to stay silent when she needed answers. Too bad that was the one she suddenly needed. The only thing keeping me from feeling ridiculous about my dad's pet name for me—one I hadn't heard in years—was my silly joy that he'd also remembered my favorite doughnut.

"Not a what but a who. It's your aunt Julie, that's who. Jujubee is what I used to call her when she was your size."

"Kind of like how I call her JuJu and she calls me Lulu?"

"I'd say exactly like that."

We ate the doughnuts first, much to the kids' delight, then tackled our sandwiches while skating around a history of nonconversations between father and daughter. I asked about Nora. She worked as a financial planner and had one daughter who lived in New York. Nora and my dad had been married for three years. He asked if I was seeing anyone seriously and if I liked my job.

"Yeah, I like my job pretty well," I said.

"Any room for advancement?"

"Not really."

He sighed. "I wish you'd go back to school and get a degree."

"I'm not cut out for school."

"That's fear talking."

"How do you know? Maybe I like my life the way it is."

"Then it's laziness. You're too smart to keep going nowhere like this."

I sat back and crossed my arms in front of me, and as soon as I did, I felt like an immature high schooler, but it was appropriate, as I remembered a similar conversation back then. I had done a good job of letting him down. At age eighteen, I had figured it was payback for him letting *me* down. "I don't even know what I want to do," I admitted, surprising myself as those words—those thoughts—escaped.

"So, you start out with the basic intro courses and see what sticks."

He took my silence as his cue to move on about why I was there. Crumpling up his sandwich wrapper, he spun in his chair and dropped the paper into the garbage.

He stood and looked at the twins. "Okay, you two, do you want to play a quick game while I get JuJu started with some boring paperwork we have to do?"

They agreed without hesitation, and after settling them in front of the computer, we moved to his conference table as he explained the process.

"I'm not really the one who will work this case for you, but Tamara will update me as needed. Basically, we're trying to prove the church put undue influence on Brian and his decision making for the will's provisions. Even if we can't pull that off, which I think we can, especially given the"—he glanced at the kids as though remembering to monitor his next words—"circumstances with the biology, we still have another angle to pursue, which is to question Elaine's role and whether she agreed willingly with Brian's wishes."

I looked over at the kids, who were deep into the computer game at my dad's desk, and I leaned back in my chair. "This is going to be long and messy, isn't it?"

"Long? Yes, likely. Working with churches in this sort of dispute is kind of a sticky business. Messy? Not for you. That's what Tamara and her assistants are for." His casual confidence and nonchalance were why his firm continued to be successful. I might have been biased and reassured because he was my father, but based upon what I had seen and heard, I could tell he was also the real deal.

"Tamara should finish with her conference call soon, so I thought I'd take the kids down to the pond to feed the ducks while you two talk."

I smiled. "They'd like that a lot."

He patted my hand before presenting his duck-feeding proposition to the kids, who readily accepted it. The computer game forgotten, Lucy led the way, skipping with the bag of bread crumbs bouncing in her hand while my dad and Mikey followed, hand in hand. I snapped a quick photo with my phone before Tamara arrived.

Tamara oozed competence. She had short black hair with flips and curls in all the right places. She wore a deep-blue button-down blouse and dark-gray trousers. I imagined, briefly, having a job where I would have to dress more stylishly, a sign of a job going somewhere instead of nowhere. I suddenly felt wildly out of place. She gave my hand a single solid shake, yanking me back into the moment. I listened intently as she related everything I needed to know in confident tones and simple explanations, and it occurred to me she had been well trained by my dad. She asked me questions to verify I understood everything, paused for my questions, and patiently listened to the odd, extraneous information about my relationship with my brother that I somehow felt compelled to insert.

"I wish I could tell you more," I said. "In spite of something that should have theoretically bonded us, it never did. I could have been an anonymous egg donor for all the contact we've had."

She waved me off. "Don't worry. The crux of the case will really be what we learn about their relationship with the church."

Their relationship with the church. Amid all the mess, I suddenly considered how the kids had a relationship with that same church. They probably did Sunday school or something, had special seats they always sat in at services, and sang in a kids' choir at Christmastime. I had to put effort into separating the life I was creating for them from the life the church seemed to think they should have. The money wasn't for me. It was for them.

I signed a bunch of documents to clear Tamara to continue on the case and went to the window after thanking her and saying goodbye. I watched Lucy fling the last of the bread crumbs and look up at my dad, seemingly to ask him a question, since he responded by dropping to her level and making gestures to explain something.

Watching my dad crouch next to the kids by the pond brought back memories of him sitting next to me at the kitchen table as I worked on my homework. I didn't yet have a desk in my room like Layla did. He didn't join me in the kitchen often since he frequently worked late. I would like to believe that when he did join me, he enjoyed keeping me company. In reality, I think it was a way to hide from an attention-seeking Layla and a younger and wilder Brian. It wasn't that I didn't think he specifically enjoyed being with me. Rather, I provided an excuse for him to have a quiet place to read his newspaper and law journals.

If I had a question, however, he always took the time to put down whichever thing he was reading and give me an answer, work through a math problem with me, or quiz me on my spelling words. But after walking in on him and the receptionist the first time, I'd stopped doing my homework in the kitchen.

It wouldn't be the last time I discovered his affairs, but armed with my new knowledge, I found the homework sessions uncomfortable. If he ever wondered why I stopped, I didn't know since he never asked about the change. He kept up his usual routine in his same spot even while I studied away in my room and hoped I understood enough of my math homework to pass the tests.

He and the kids headed to the building, so I swept through his office to make sure everything was in place and cleaned up after the kids. As I glanced over his desk, I noticed a Post-it note with the words, "Lisa - Tues." *Lisa, as in my mother?* I shook my head. There were any number of other people with the same name that the note could refer to. Besides, my dad and the kids returned, and I didn't have more time to think about it. *Not everything revolves around you, Julie.* With everything going on, it was easy to forget.

Mikey rushed over with a smile and hugged me while Lucy merely skipped about the office.

"Looks like you guys had a good time," I said.

"One empty bag of bread crumbs and many fat and happy ducks," my dad replied. "I trust Tamara has you filled in and everything's ready to go?"

"Yes. I guess the whole thing's in motion now."

"This was the right thing to do, Julie. Trust me."

"I'm trying."

"The earlier version of his will didn't look like this. I don't like what that church did to your brother."

"This can't be at all easy for you to do."

He gave a small shrug. "If it eases things for you down the road, though, that helps."

He followed up his comment by bestowing a kiss to my forehead in the way only fathers could do. "Let's do this again, except with Nora. Come to our house for dinner."

"Do you have ducks at your house?" Lucy asked.

"No, but Nora has fish. Good enough?"

Lucy agreed, bouncing in full approval.

"Thanks, Dad. Shoot me an email or a text." I suddenly hoped more than anything we would follow through with his invitation.

Later in the day, my mom came to my apartment for my first cooking lesson. We'd decided on broiled chicken, rice, corn, and canned biscuits—more of the trusty Pillsbury. My first test had been to remember to put the chicken in a marinade—and not a premade one. Instead, I made it from a spice packet.

"The timer is your best friend, especially when you're new to cooking," Mom said as she pulled out a brand-new one from her purse. "And having more than one is very handy."

None of what we were making for dinner seemed especially challenging, except for the rice. I normally did the microwaveable kind because I could never get the "real" stuff from the bag to work. The tricky part to the whole thing seemed to be the timing, so the gift of the timer was my mother's first stroke of genius.

Since we wanted to broil the chicken breasts, she said we would bake the rolls first then throw them in the oven again to reheat while getting everything else on the table. As we cracked open the can and lined them up on the baking sheet, I told her about visiting Dad at lunch.

"Oh, I'm so glad. Did you take the kids? I know he wanted to meet them."

"Yes. He had doughnuts. He even remembered I liked the jelly-filled ones."

A soft tone filled her voice as she extracted the last roll from the can. "He always was good with young children. It was only when you all got older that he never figured out how to act or what to say."

"Well, I guess we both forgot how." I put the pan in the oven and set the timer—the new one. Mikey came in, holding up a toy container for me. I looked at his expression to determine his question. "Let's set it on the table. Now, take a look all around it. How is this container different from the others?"

He turned it and studied it carefully. When he had turned it full circle, his eyes lit up. He found the tucked-under tabs and popped them open before pulling off the lid. He gave me a thank-you smile and darted off with his new project.

"You should look at cooking like you do everything else," my mom said.

"How is that?"

"Like a problem to be solved. There's a reason I call you to help me with home projects, honey. You handle the situation like you just showed Mikey what to do with his box."

"Isn't following directions on a recipe exactly that?"

She laughed. "If it were, you wouldn't be needing me to teach you anything right now, would you?"

"How do I 'solve the problem,' then?"

"I haven't the foggiest. That's your problem to solve. In the meantime, I'll help you make the rice." She directed me to the pot and measuring cups. "So, was it a casual lunch with your dad or business?"

"Business. I never thanked you, by the way, for asking him to come up and sit with me through handling the paperwork of Brian's estate. I'm sure it wasn't easy."

"Why would it have been hard? Your father and I talk often, actually. I talk to him far more often than I do to you kids combined."

"Reprimand duly noted, Mother, but moving on... You talk to Dad a lot? For work?"

"Once the rice boils, the first thing to figure out is how low to reduce the heat to still keep it at a simmer. The second part is knowing when to remove it from the heat entirely."

She searched the cupboards for dishes, and when she found the right one, she grabbed four plates for setting the table.

"Yes," she said. "We've talked for work—sometimes. It's usually social. We chat on occasion. We've never been enemies, you know."

"Hence all the cheating on each other."

"The cheating only ever bothered you and your brother and sister, which is why we decided we should split up in the first place."

"What? You're not seriously trying to tell me you had some sort of 'open' relationship, are you?"

"No, not exactly. I just mean we both forgave each other, and instead of trying to make it work, we agreed to split up. It seemed best."

Her lackadaisical attitude felt off somehow, and I wondered if I didn't want to accept it or if she wasn't exactly being forthright. I suppose it had been over fifteen years and she was well over it.

"Besides," she added, "we still get together when he's between wives."

I nearly dropped the silverware and cups upon hearing that tidbit. "'Get together?' You mean, like...? Oh God, never mind. I can't believe I almost asked that question. I don't want to know."

"You were always sensitive about sex."

"*Mom*. I'm not sensitive about sex." I suddenly realized where we were having our conversation. Though the kids were pretty well absorbed in their play, with my luck, Lucy would hear "sex" and decide to ask what we were talking about. "Forget it. I don't want to talk about this right now." *Or ever.* Except I secretly wanted her to tell me about the Post-it note. However, if "Tues." meant a social engagement, then I didn't want the information after all. I refused to travel back to that time of my life.

We turned off the heat sources and transferred the food to serving dishes. When it all made it to the table, pride washed over me at what my mother had helped me create—real food. Nothing fancy, but I didn't care about impressive stuff. The chicken and vegetables were easy. I could reproduce them. I was less sure about the rice, but with the timers, maybe I could pull it off.

Mealtimes with Lucy had calmed down considerably, and though her tantrums hadn't gone away, they were less frequent. During our current meal, she was full of pleases and thank-yous, and best of all, it was absent of complaints. Mikey ate a little more than usual, Lucy entertained my mom with stories, and my mom shared stories about Brian. Talking about Brian and Elaine was like roulette—I couldn't guess what memories or emotions the stories would trigger. Sometimes, the trigger for sadness was immediate. Other times, I would see a delayed reaction, such as the search for a recorder or a picture from Mikey with everything blocked out in a torrent of heavy color.

Mikey's middle-of-the-night screams remained consistent. I'd gotten over the shock of the gut-wrenching pain behind them, and while I still took him into my arms, held him tightly, and said soothing words, they came out on autopilot. The entire event usually took less than ten minutes, and falling asleep again became less difficult for me. Occasionally, that made me feel guilty, but I'd discovered quickly how important sleep was for our smoother days.

I had materials from the social worker and the county about counselors and therapists I could call. When I looked into the kids' eyes, everything still seemed so raw and frightening, and my instinct told me to hold off. We were all still new to our situation, so I waited. When my mother left, Lucy dug out their toy motorcycles to make jumps for them while Mikey drew a picture of a kid playing baseball. Meanwhile, I breathed a sigh of relief we'd actually made it through a full day free of flying objects or children curled up in protective shells. I hoped it was a sign we really would make it through everything.

Chapter Ten

Walking into the community center on my first day back at work in two weeks brought relief. Dropping off the kids at Sophie's was difficult though not as dramatic as I imagined it would be. Lucy hadn't wanted to get out of the car. One strike against me was not anticipating the many challenges involved with getting the kids and myself ready early in the morning and on a schedule. Taming Lucy's hair, for example, practically undid us both. She finally let me douse it all in water and use the detangler spray to comb it out and put it into a ponytail. With one trauma behind us, we still had the one ahead.

In the car, she had tears spilling down her cheeks, nearly causing my own to burst free. Unexpectedly, Mikey took Lucy's hand and reassured her, keeping her meltdown at bay. Inside the door, they clung to me, and the tears I held back reflected both the pain of abandoning them and, God help me, the mounting irritation of wanting them to please, please *cooperate*. Once again, Mikey took charge and let go first. As they walked over to the kitchen table for breakfast, I watched in amazement as Mikey put his bunny under the chair Sophie directed him to and promptly sat down.

Sophie smiled at me. "It looks like they've done this before."

Of course. Only a few weeks earlier, they did this same routine with Lynette. They would adapt. It gave me enough peace of mind to give them kisses and I-love-yous and be on my way. Then slowly, on the drive to work, muscles from my neck down to my toes loosened from their tight grip. I treated myself to a latte from Caribou Coffee and imagined all was the same as it used to be.

I savored the lightness of my step as I reentered a world where I knew exactly what I was doing. All the questions about class locations, membership, and how to use the database were ones without any guessing games. They were questions I had answers to.

Gemmi met me for lunch—bringing fast-food burgers and fries, God love her—and she blew cheer and confidence back into me.

"Mai! How is it being back at work? What's it like being a mom? When can I take the kiddos to get their first tattoo?"

I laughed at her last question and showed her the makeshift flower Lucy had colored on my arm the day before. I tried to wash it off, although secretly, I was glad it didn't all go away. "I think they're ready now. I'll have to set up a time when we can visit our favorite henna artist. Mikey's the true artist, though. He'll want to create his own design."

"Perfecto. We'll do tattoos and sundaes. Kids like those, right?"

"I'm pretty sure it's in the instruction manual for them, in fact."

"Ooh, I bet you've been wishing those manuals really existed."

"No joke." I swallowed a french fry and licked the delicious salt and grease off my fingers before grabbing a napkin. "A single reference would be fantastic. Everything out there conflicts with something. Don't give kids a choice. Always give kids a choice. Say no. Always find a way to say yes. It's okay to let them watch some TV. It's never okay to let them watch any. Whatever you do, you're sure to do the wrong thing."

Gemmi unwrapped her scarf, a light, gauzy pink one, and draped it over the back of her chair, probably to avoid contact with ketchup and grease. "Has it been pretty bad?"

The best thing about Gemmi's question was knowing she wouldn't judge me if I said, "Yes, it's horrible." She always understood my views about having kids and remained uncertain about whether she wanted them herself. Her boyfriend, Demitry, wanted kids, an is-sue that seemed to prevent them from stepping into marriage.

"No, I guess not. I mean, it's been hard, and sometimes, it's really bad, but you won't believe this." I paused, less certain about revealing the next part. "I already love these kids."

She smiled so readily and sincerely at my admission that my mood immediately lifted. "Of course you do."

"Really? I feel like a fraud admitting it."

"Why?"

"Because of how I've always viewed the idea of having kids, how vocal I've been about it. I'm a hypocrite."

"First, you'd be a hypocrite only if you were saying you loved them to make yourself look good. Or if you made it seem like every-one else was wrong for having kids. You and I both know neither of those things is true."

I smiled at her. "I've missed you."

"I've missed you too. I've been trying to give you space since everything happened, but it's been *hard*. Sean keeps asking when we can stop by for mojitos and Yahtzee."

Nostalgia and happiness collided inside me. Maybe we couldn't quite return to our three-amigos days, but Gemmi's reassurance boosted my worries about losing our connections altogether. "Soon! Except we might have to skip the mojitos or at least limit ourselves to one round."

Gemmi laughed. "If I promise Sean I'll take him out later, he'll be no problem. How's Zach reacting? He was pretty cool up in Du-luth. He was really excited about everything. He's got plans for you, girl."

"Well, then, he's thinking too far into the future."

"Uh-oh. What's up? I thought you liked this guy."

I picked up a fry and twisted it around in my ketchup. "I did. I do. He's been great, and the kids really like him."

"But?"

"I haven't told him the full story. Gem, I actually broke up with him a few days before I found out about Brian. He showed up at my door after going over arrangements with my mom, and he smiled at me with those kind eyes…"

"And he was the right thing at the right time."

"Yeah."

"And now?"

"He still might be."

"It might be crass to say it, but Demitry is jealous of this whole situation. Obviously, he doesn't want one of my brothers or sisters to die or anything, but he seems to think having kids appear would solve all our problems."

"Do you agree with him?"

She grabbed my hand. "Tell me honestly. If you could undo it all, would you?"

What a question. I considered for a moment then met her gaze head-on. "Probably."

"You see how things are between me and Demitry."

I squeezed her hand. "I'm sorry."

"Me too. And thanks for being honest, even if you'd say no if asked the same question again right now."

When I picked up the kids at the end of the day, Sophie told me, "All things considered, they had a good first day."

I determined "good first day" overshadowed the mysterious "all things considered" and counted it a win. At least Lucy hadn't thrown anything, because for all I knew, during the trial period, it might mean game over. The kids were quiet on the drive home. I figured they were tired since they woke up earlier than usual and it was a new situation. I let them watch TV when we got home while I figured out how to make a homemade dinner on my own.

Things were going fine in the kitchen until I got to the rice. I ruined the pan and still had no edible rice to show for it. Distracted by trying to get the rice right, I forgot about getting the green beans ready. I crossed my fingers and hoped that when the timer beeped, the pork chops would be okay. We could manage with carrots and some bread or crackers instead of the failed rice and green beans.

I smiled when I cut into one of the pork chops and saw clear juice emerge. The most expensive thing came out great. Another win.

The kids were quiet as we ate. I tried to extract information about their day with Sophie. "Did you have fun?"

Lucy shrugged. Mikey's expression was inscrutable.

"Did you play with the other kids?"

"Sometimes."

"What kinds of things did you do?"

"We played with toys. We went outside."

"What did you have for lunch?" I asked.

"Grilled cheese."

"Was it yummy?"

"Not as good as Daddy's."

And not a word more.

At work the next day, others told me the short answers were normal.

"Kids forget the little specifics all the time," said Misha, one of our regulars. "I usually got the food and possibly the very last thing they did before I picked them up. Then the things they remember, like the cool shirt their friend was wearing, is the stuff you don't care about at all."

"Typical, isn't it?" another had chimed in. "Kids will remember you told them months ago how you'd let them have that huge rainbow lollipop when you next go to the amusement park, but what they did that morning? Nada."

The stories bolstered me, even if I'd left out the other part of the equation—Lucy's normal chatter and the kids' busy play had also been absent. They were subdued throughout the evening and went to bed early. To my surprise, I missed their activity. I hoped they wouldn't be as worn out every day.

Of course, when energy returned, so did tantrums. Issues of all kinds colored the rest of the week. If it could bother Lucy, it did. Playing with toys the wrong way, serving her food wrong, itchy clothing, bathwater in her eyes, tangles in her hair—everything caused screams and tears from both of us. Poor Mikey barely made it out of his curled-up ball all week.

By the weekend, we were thankful for the break, the chance to sleep and not have to rush off in the morning. A breakdown on Saturday had Lucy sobbing into my chest about how much she wanted her mom and dad back. Though her admission was not some surprise revelation, the reminder bulldozed me as I registered the events of the past week. While I had juggled my return to work, daycare, and a new schedule at home, I foolishly let everything override the immediate nightmare still haunting them. Mikey, who seemed to know how to cry only in the middle of the night, crawled next me, and we sat for a while under the weight of the current boulder of sadness until we had the strength to shove it away.

"I have an idea," I told them. "Let's brainstorm all the things we like about your mom and dad and put them on colorful shapes to make a mobile."

"What's 'brainstorm'?"

"Brainstorm is when you try to think of as many ideas as you can. It's your brain raining out ideas super fast, like a storm."

Mikey jumped up, ran and got crayons and paper, and brought them to the table. Lucy brightened and joined him. I suggested they draw shapes and cut them out. I would write down all of their ideas and transfer them onto the shapes.

"Mama made yummy cookies."

"Yeah? What kind did you like best?"

"Chocolate with chocolate chips."

"Wow. Those sound amazing. How about you draw a picture of the cookie on the other side of the paper?"

"And make it cookie-shaped!"

The smile filled her face and warmed me. Mikey's expression lost some of its melancholy.

"Tell me more."

Mikey hugged me then looked up expectantly.

"She gave you good hugs?"

He nodded.

"And Daddy did too!" Lucy added.

"Of course he did."

They kept going. Mama smelled nice. She was pretty. Her hands were soft. She took us to the park. She sang to us. Daddy used funny voices. He let us ride on his shoulders. He played games with us. It was such a great list. Lucy surprised me once by telling me I smelled nice too.

"Thank you, Lulu. Anything else?"

"Mama prayed with us, and they both took us to church."

I paused, knowing church was one area I hadn't been giving enough attention. I still hadn't any idea how to handle it. "Do you miss going to church?"

Lucy took a moment as if thinking about her answer. "Some-times."

"Would you like it if we prayed together?"

"I don't know. Maybe."

"What about at night? Before you go to bed?" I turned to Mikey. "Would you like that?"

He nodded and hugged me. I swallowed my nervousness over my personal doubts about God and religion. I didn't know how ingrained some of Brian's beliefs were in them, and though I loathed some of those beliefs, I knew they couldn't be all bad. It hardly seemed fair to undo their entire upbringing solely because I didn't share the same faith. For all I could guess, the kids might have been dealing with their grief and continually new situations with their faith. To shatter it might destroy everything surrounding it.

As we bundled together before bed, the kids showed me yet again how to get what they needed. We said the Lord's Prayer, which miraculously came back to me. Then they taught me some basic rhyme obviously meant for children. Finally, they had me read a prayer from one of their books I hadn't much noticed before.

So with our prayers floating up around the new "memory mobiles," as we called them, we managed the rest of the weekend in a transient peace. A peace we desperately needed since the week to come would wreak havoc on it all.

Chapter Eleven

" Take her to Hair for Littles," Patty suggested. "Their entire store is all bright and colorful, and they let the kids choose a movie or show to watch on TV while they cut their hair, which sounds like something Lucy might need in case she freaks out on you again."

"Oh yeah," Misha chimed in. "They can't do jack with Black kids' hair, so I've never taken Amalia, but I've heard of them. Might be a good place to go for your first experience."

"I hope she doesn't change her mind after the first snip of the scissors. There's no going back after the first cut, you know," said Mrs. Lasky.

Mrs. Carson followed up quickly with, "Don't make her look like a boy." Sean would have loved to take Mrs. Carson down for that one.

Tracy said, "Instead of cutting it, you should get some ideas for how to style it."

Gemmi would have given her bug eyes and asked, "Have you looked at Julie's hair lately?"

Everyone had an opinion. I didn't remember them always having a plethora of advice for me. Maybe I noticed it because it was painfully obvious to them I had zero parenting experience. According to them, whatever happened with Lucy's hair, it would probably be wrong. At least I knew where to take her to help me make the worst mistake ever with her hair.

It had seemed like such an easy decision earlier in the morning when I'd discussed it with Lucy. I put in the daily effort to comb through the tumbling tangles without producing tears. I was rarely successful. Somehow, my mother had dealt with that for Layla and me every day too.

Zach might have affectionately compared my hair to the "beautiful chaos of jazz," and I had long since learned how to tame it—or at least manage it—but it had never been less than a wiry mess when I was young. If I cut it super short, it was a sad excuse for a white-girl afro, and when it was long, it was awful to brush. A ponytail hid the mess a bit more.

I'd figured out some tricks for taking care of it, and Gemmi had been my go-to person regarding the right length—a great in-between one. My hair was my best feature, so I learned to spend time on it. People never said things to me like they did others, such as "Oh, you're so pretty" or "You're so smart, though!" But my hair was a winner. Men always loved it, and Zach was no exception. Some of my coworkers were actually jealous of it, and I'd never had anyone ever be jealous of anything about me in my life.

Lucy, however, did not have the natural curl to work with. Her hair was thick and straight and reminded me of Emma Watson's Hermione in the Harry Potter movies. If Lucy had the patience, we might have held off on the cut because, in spite of Tracy suggesting I should find out how to style it, styling was one of my few solid parenting skills. I had mastered braids, twists, and curls. Most of the time, however, the morning ended in a fight with a final, painful rush into a ponytail. After the most recent fit and tears, I suggested the haircut.

Lucy almost looked shocked. "Really?"

I wondered if the shock was disbelief at the suggestion or merely surprise. "Yeah, really. It's just an idea. We don't have to do it."

She flung her arms around my neck and squeezed harder than I'd ever felt her squeeze before. "Yesyesyesyesyes! When?"

I nearly cried at her unexpected joy. Such wins were rare, yet sometimes, they overshadowed the overwhelming failures. "How about after I pick you guys up from Sophie's today?"

"Yay!" She jumped off the counter and raced around the apartment.

I checked on Mikey, making sure he was dressed and ready to go. I found him sitting primly on the edge of his bed, Bunny and thumb in the usual places. I sat next to him and looked at his hair. His tightly cropped hair recently showed signs of relaxing. I liked it and had no particular desire to cut it and hoped he didn't either.

"Do you want a haircut too?"

He shook his head.

I snuggled him into me and kissed the top of his head. "Good. I like your hair a little longer."

It had been such an auspicious start to the day until I opened my mouth about it all at work.

Mrs. Carson added, "You should give this more thought. If she were your own daughter, you'd probably never dream of cutting off all her beautiful hair." No one else contradicted her, seeming to imply a secret agreement.

That one hurt.

She *was* technically my "own" daughter, although they weren't privy to that information. I supposed the DNA knowledge was also beside the point, yet the sting of the comment was about more than the DNA. People really had no idea how terrible it sounded to act as though we didn't all have the same mad love for our children, no matter their biological background.

I loved my hair. I loved Lucy's hair. Cutting it would make her happy, and I refused to let everyone else tell me otherwise. She was my daughter, not theirs.

The certainty buoyed me. Lucy and Mikey were my kids. Mine. Suddenly, it didn't matter what anyone else said. They didn't know what they were talking about. They didn't know my kids. Not wanting to mess with my new confidence, I texted Zach to cancel our lunch date. I didn't need his judgment about the whole thing to interfere with my good mood.

At day's end, I walked through Sophie's back gate, and Lucy flew into me.

"Hey, Lulu!" I lifted her into a big hug, relieved she still had her bouncy mood. Mikey's little hands tried to reach around my waist and latch on in a similar greeting.

"How did it go today?" I asked Sophie.

"It was kind of hot and cold with Lucy. She had a hard time calming down sometimes, but she's clearly been excited about something. Pretty good overall, I guess I'd say."

Progress. Somehow, though, Sophie's tone sounded off. Our two-week trial period was up the next day, and my brain niggled at me to do some more questioning, but we didn't have time.

"Let's go! Let's go, JuJu!" Lucy bounced in my arms.

"Mikey, why don't you grab your bag and make sure Bunny is ready to go, okay? Lulu, sweetie, you're getting a little heavy. Mind if I set you down and you walk?"

Mikey's path cut wide around almost everyone as he dashed to get their bag. I wouldn't have given it much attention, except his return made it clear he was dodging contact with any of the other kids and even Sophie.

"See you tomorrow," I said. Though Sophie bid us goodbye, too, I noticed Lucy and Mikey didn't give her a second glance. I searched my brain to determine how often kids failed to do that. I tried to picture the kids who might have left Sophie's before we did or the kids at the community center for lessons or camp or whatever. It seemed like such a little thing, but I felt like all the little things were adding up to some big thing, and I didn't know if it was the same big thing we had been dealing with all along or a new big thing.

Cowardice prevented me from exploring further. I wanted to focus on Lucy's excitement. I needed her joy. *She* needed her joy. She sang all the way to Hair for Littles with me joining in every once in a while—I was finally learning some of the words to kid songs—and our singing was enough to loosen up Mikey.

As we approached the salon, however, Lucy's mood shifted instantly. We weren't ten feet away when she let go of my hand and stopped walking.

"Lulu?"

"No."

"No, what?"

"No haircut," she said.

"Why not?"

"I don't want it."

"You were so excited, though. I don't understand. What's wrong?"

Her volume ratcheted up. "I don't want to!"

Right. No reason. Nothing. *What? What is it this time?* I couldn't figure out what was going on for the one-hundred-eighty-degree switch. Mikey shrank in on himself.

"Okay." I mustered what little calm I had and invited the kids to sit on the curb with me.

"No!"

I inhaled deeply and slowly exhaled, willing myself not to cry and working to still my shakiness. I took another deep breath. Better. I squatted in front of Lucy and took Mikey's hand, hoping to reassure him at the same time.

"Lucy. I won't make you go in and get your hair cut if you don't want to. I promise. I just—" I paused to make sure my request stayed in a measured, reasonable tone. "I would really like it if you told me why."

"I just don't want to."

"I need more than that."

"No! No! No!" she cried. "Mama will be mad!"

Oh.

I took her hand. She let me. "Oh, honey. Why would she be mad?"

She cried without answering. I looked at Mikey, who sat down and scrunched into my legs, attempting to disappear. I looked at Lucy for a moment before closing my eyes. I focused on more deep breaths, desperately trying to force my frustration away. I wanted Mikey to *talk* so he could explain what was going on with his sister. I wanted Lucy to tell me what was going on instead of crying or having a tantrum. I just wanted it all to work for once. We were so close to something, but it was all slipping away. I breathed out one more time and opened my eyes.

"It's okay." I released her hand and attempted to pull her into me. "We don't have to do it. It's okay. You don't have to tell me why."

Her shaking subsided, then a little voice came out, still attached to a sob. "Mama says my hair is too pretty to cut. She won't let me do it."

"Your hair is beautiful, Lulu." I stroked her back.

"If we cut it, I'll be ugly, and Mama won't love me anymore."

Never would I have guessed such a reaction. Kids' ideas were wild sometimes. Sure, some of the ideas came from adults, yet I couldn't fathom how the messages got all mangled in their brains.

I let go of Mikey's hand and gently pushed Lucy away enough to hold her shoulders and look her in the eyes. "Your mama will always love you, no matter what. Nothing can change that. Guess what? Your hair is *always* your hair even when it's short, which means it is always pretty. Always."

"Cutting it doesn't kill it?"

Oh God, my heart. "No. Our hair is always growing. Did you know that? Cutting it makes it healthy and happy!"

"Like when I eat my vegebles?"

"Exactly like when you eat your 'vegebles.'"

I let her sit with our conversation and returned to Mikey, who had nearly dissolved into me. I rubbed his back, trying to convey reassurance that the worst of the Julie-Lucy conflict was over. For once, I somewhat understood the issue. I wondered about Elaine's control over Lucy's hairstyle. Either Elaine really did refuse certain styles, or it was simply Lucy jumbling the ideas about it all.

"Mama won't be mad?"

"No, honey. She only wants you to be happy. Will cutting your hair make you happy?"

She nodded.

"Should we go inside?"

Another nod. She was still uncertain, but I took the risk. I mentally crossed my fingers, hoping we would make it through the entire cut without incident.

The transformation was adorable. When Lucy saw herself, the smile on her face gave her a fresh glow. Where her thick tangles had sometimes dwarfed her face, after the cut, her full profile and bright eyes took center stage. The stylist cut her hair to chin length and thinned it. It rested in gentle waves, floating back and away from her cheeks.

"You look just like your mama," the stylist said with a smile.

"Really?" Lucy's eyes raised hopefully.

"You think so?" I asked simultaneously.

"You don't see it?" The stylist turned to me. "You have beautiful hair too. I bet if you pulled it back, you'd see how your eyes and face shape are alike."

I glanced in the mirror and noticed Lucy's confused expression. I realized my mistake with a jolt. Lucy and I were not imagining the same person. For a moment, I unthinkingly felt Lucy really was my daughter. Genealogy had validated a new connection. I saw what the stylist saw and thought, *My daughter looks like me.*

Reality came back quickly. For Lucy and Mikey, DNA meant nothing. Before Lucy questioned her, and before the stylist inadvertently triggered a scene, I smiled at Lucy. "You *do* look like your mama, and she is smiling down at you right now and clapping her hands at how pretty you are."

Lucy's smile returned. "Can I touch it?"

I laughed. "Of course! It's soft, isn't it?"

I could tell she agreed by the way she stroked her head. "Do I still look like a girl?"

Yet another worry. No wonder she'd broken down in front of the salon. It pained me to see how a single haircut had brought about such angst. "Absolutely. Besides, you *are* a girl. However you wear your hair always means you look like a girl."

"Mama wouldn't be mad?"

"Are you happy with it?"

She nodded.

"Then so is your mama, and you know what else? I love it. What do you think, Mikey?" I twisted his chair around so he could focus on his sister.

He smiled.

"See? Full Mercer family seal of approval!" As though to further show our support, I gave Mikey's chair a spin, eliciting a rare giggle. One of the other stylists gave me a disapproving look, probably worried about the chair or something, but I ignored it, giving Mikey yet another spin, yearning to hear more of his beautiful laughter.

Music. The best kind of music.

Lucy skipped to me, joining in with her own giggles, sharing in her brother's happiness. I paid for the haircut, and we left feeling light and free. Jubilant.

I remembered my mother playing a record once—"Ob-La-Di, Ob-La-Da" by the Beatles—and pulling Lay, Brian, and me away from the TV and into a dance. It was an exceptional moment of spontaneous, unfettered joy.

As we left the salon, with Mikey laughing and Lucy joining in, my heart could have flown us out of Hair for Littles and all the way home. Lucy skipped to me, then I picked up her then Mikey and spun them around before I had to set them down again. Giggles followed us into the car, and we danced in our seats the rest of the drive.

The high spirits carried us through dinner. The kids were so enthusiastic that an optimistic Lucy asked, "Can we stay home tomorrow?"

Those hopeful eyes almost worked. I imagined a day of games and make-believe and fun, as though we'd fixed everything with a single haircut.

"Oh, honey, I'm sorry. No." And like a sugar high, we crashed into the ground, their bruised expressions making the impact clear. "It's only one more day, and then we have the weekend together. We'll go somewhere or plan something special."

However, Lucy was done. I stopped her from throwing dishes—we'd progressed on that front—but the angry yelling continued. I might have told Gemmi all the parenting sites made it sound like any parent was doing at least something wrong, but Lucy was an expert at making me feel I did everything wrong.

Mikey's sad face looked at me, my betrayal complete. Layla, I was sure, would have known the exact right thing to say to him. Zach would have suggested they go bang on the drums. I had nothing. I cleared the table and cleaned up the kitchen. When I looked at Mikey's seat, he had disappeared.

Chapter Twelve

Friday morning proved the most challenging of the week. Both kids resisted in every way possible. I had to carry Mikey from the apartment to the car and from the car into Sophie's. I worried he might not make it through the door at Sophie's, but once inside, he moved into autopilot. Lucy scowled at me, and neither of them returned my goodbye. Sophie's look implied that if they had a bad day, it would be my fault. With no time or inclination to explain anything, I simply left. We had been running late, and while I couldn't afford to take the day off like the kids wanted, I also couldn't risk being late for work. Carl wasn't one to put up with tardiness. I'd already crossed him earlier this week when I was late.

I tried to hold on to our brief run at normal happiness from the day before. Not every moment of the week had been terrible, but mornings had deteriorated, and the time between coming home and dinner encompassed the brunt of meltdowns.

Zach had come by one evening, and the change-up kept us all from killing one another. He made dinner for us and played with the kids while I took a hot bath and watched TV on my phone. After putting the kids to bed, he joked about how strict I must be if most of my nights were usually like that one. My expression made him backtrack and apologize.

"You have no idea how hard I'm working at this."

"I do, Jules, I really do. I'm sorry. I overestimated your tolerance for a little teasing." He pulled me down next to him on the couch and massaged my shoulders.

"I have no tolerance for anything. I'm too tired." The massage felt nice—definitely tolerable—until he changed his tune and started kissing my neck and moving his hands to my chest and stomach.

I squirmed away. "What are you doing?"

He chuckled. "Helping you relax."

"Trying to get laid."

"That too."

I stood. "Not tonight."

"Okay." He stood too. "I have to work all weekend. Can I see you between one of my shifts and my gigs?"

"Ask me tomorrow when my tolerance level is higher."

His crooked smile cheered me. "How about I ask you at lunch tomorrow?"

"Yeah, okay."

Of course, I ended up canceling lunch, but since most of the day had gone pretty well, I agreed with the repeat request when he texted me later. Maybe we could try the whole "cooking together" thing again.

I had forgotten I would be especially busy at work because school-age kids in the area had the day off. It was my least favorite scenario and always made me thankful I didn't have to work weekends. Parents complained about our minimum-age requirements for leaving kids in the pool or open-gym area, and others complained they didn't know they would have to pay extra for childcare during their workouts.

Our system crashed for an hour, and I helped process check-ins at the counter instead of fixing the system glitch. I worked through my normal lunch break, and by the time I got the database back online, Livestrong Freak wore a familiar expression—the one forecasting an unbroken string of whiny objections. I wanted to shake my bottle of Coke and open it in his face.

"My insurance company won't give me the discount for this month's dues because they said I only visited eleven times, but I know I came twelve because I keep track. Someone here is going to have to pay for this mistake."

"Do you have your record with you?"

He pulled out a folded sheet of paper from his stupidly expensive armband wallet and slapped it on the counter. "Of course."

"Okay. Give me a second to print out all of our scans for you last month."

"Will this take long? I already waited until after the crowds of screaming children left, and I have to get back to work."

"It will take as long as it takes for a sheet of paper to go through the printer since I've already sent it there." I leaned over to the printer to grab the readout and stood with a pen at the counter, ready to check off the dates he'd read to me from his list. I waited as he opened his meticulously folded record. *Will this take long?* I wanted to ask.

I listened to his clipped recitation of dates, and we found the one in question.

"There. *That's* where you guys messed up."

When I looked up, his finger was pointed menacingly close to my face. I eyed it with my own warning glance, and he dropped it to the counter. "Wasn't the fifth when we had the big snowstorm?"

"What's your point?" he asked.

"You didn't come in that day. Hardly anyone did."

"Of course I came in. I don't let snow stop me. It must be you didn't scan my card correctly."

I resisted telling him how nice it had been with him not showing up. How not showing up at his exact same time and day was nearly impossible to miss. The snowstorm day had been a fun, peaceful one—more so because of his absence. Instead, I went with his lie. It was too exhausting to fight it, and it wasn't like I cared if he did or didn't make his insurance quota. We got paid either way. In fact, granting him his quota meant we would for sure get paid by his insurance company.

"That's possible. Look, I'll print out a correction form for you to send in to your insurance agency."

"Why should I have to do all the work for your mistake? You should give me the discount up front."

"It's a form you sign and mail to them. Then they'll reimburse you. You'll still get your money back."

"*You* should have to pay for the mistake."

I didn't understand his problem. Maybe it was his way of making his big stand against us and getting us to "pay" for all of his insane grievances.

"How about this? I'll print the form, you sign it, and I'll mail it in for you. I'll even cover the stamp."

"You don't seem to understand what I'm saying."

I might have been able to maintain control over the situation if a group of screaming kids and their mothers hadn't passed by. One child yelled, "No, I don't want an apple. I want a fruit snack!"

And I snapped.

"No, Mr. Kline, *you* don't understand. I'm doing all I can to help you here, and for some reason, it isn't good enough for you. We didn't make a mistake, yet I'm jumping through hoops to keep you happy. I worked on the snowstorm day in question, and you did not come when you say you did."

"I most certainly did. I wrote it down."

"Do you realize how ridiculous your remark is?"

"I want to talk to the supervisor."

Fuck Carl's titles. "I *am* the supervisor."

"Then your boss, whoever he is."

"That would be me." Carl suddenly showed up.

Either someone ratted me out, or his timing was oddly impeccable.

He extended a hand to Freak. "Carl Preston. What seems to be the problem?"

As the freak retold his story, Carl nodded sympathetically, and I wanted to shoot him. I could already tell what was going to happen next.

"Julie, please wait for me in my office while I finish helping our esteemed guest." Carl's condescension injected a smug smile onto Freak's face.

It took everything I had to keep from punching them both as I stepped away. I left and paced in Carl's office, hating how he'd effectively sent me to the principal.

When Carl finally showed up, the fake persona he put on for our guests disappeared. "What the fuck was that?"

Ah, so this is how the conversation is going to go. Any frustration I'd siphoned away came blasting back in spades. However, I was on thin ice. "I need this job" played on repeat in my head.

I tried not to gag on the words I forced out. "I'm sorry, Carl. I don't know why I lost my temper with him. It won't happen again."

"Damn straight it won't. You try to handle something in the same manner again, you'll be done here. You are *not* the supervisor. You are a program *liaison*. If guests have issues, you refer them to me."

"I usually handle guest complaints or issues. It was in my job description when you hired me."

"I doubt it. And regardless, you'd better not be performing any more made-up duties in the future."

I swallowed the bile. "No, of course not."

By the end of my shift, I nearly sprinted out the door, eager for a weekend to decompress. However, relaxation wasn't in the cards. When I got to Sophie's, tension ratcheted right up again.

I cringed when the first voice I heard as I approached the backyard of Sophie's house yelled "Move!" It would have been no surprise had Lucy voiced the frustrated "move" demand, and I was relieved that it wasn't her. Plus, I was proud of myself for knowing her voice well enough to make the distinction.

As I reached the fence, a new dread washed over me. Mikey was the target of the demand. He and the speaker, a girl about the same age as Mikey—Malorie, maybe?—were on trikes. Mikey seemed to be blocking the path, and Malorie was unhappy and showed it by banging her trike into his. Mikey was unresponsive. I had an unnatural urge to shake Malorie. *Stop it! He's not hurting you*, I yelled at her in my head instead and quickly opened the gate.

"Hey, Malorie. Can I help?" Though focused on Mikey, I scanned quickly for Lucy, wondering why she wasn't unloading her wrath upon Malorie.

"He won't move." She followed up her frustration with another bang on the back of Mikey's trike. I wanted to cry seeing Mikey give no reaction and tamped down the desire to bang on Malorie's trike.

"Okay, but honey? Can we figure out some different ways to talk to him instead?" I stepped in and moved her trike away from Mikey. She scowled but didn't fight back. I remembered how Mikey had skirted around all the kids the other day and wondered if the Malorie situation wasn't the first time a kid had rammed into him in one way or another.

I crouched next to Mikey. "Let's help your—" I was about to say "friends" before I realized the presumption. "Let's help the others out a little and move over here. Do you want to ride over there or get off and we can push the trike?"

He looked at me, his eyes projecting "help." I held out my arms, and he raised his to me. I lifted him, and he immediately wrapped all of his limbs tightly around me as I reached down and picked up the trike. When I turned, Sophie showed up. I had momentarily forgotten about where she might have been during the whole event. She was carrying one of the babies, who was screaming bloody murder, so I imagined her distraction was related to that.

"Hi, Julie. I tell you, this child does *not* like getting her diaper changed."

I watched her expression shift and realized I must have looked as distressed as I felt.

"Is everything okay?"

"Yes... Well, I don't know. Malorie here seemed to be pretty upset with Mikey, and Mikey froze. Have things been going okay?"

"Oh yeah. I mean, as well as they always have been, I guess. Mikey doesn't say anything, and you know how other young kids can be. They're still learning patience and turn-taking." She bounced with the baby. "Hush, sweetie. We're all done now."

Her response made me uncomfortable, even though I wasn't sure why, and the baby's crying grated on my already-frayed nerves. The grip on my emotions threatened to fail at the prospect of addressing whatever odd situation was at play, so I nodded noncommittally. Sophie wasn't paying any attention to me. I should have said something, anything, but Mikey held on to me tighter and tighter, and my anxiety rose to match his hold on me.

"Where's Lucy?"

Sophie glanced around and released a frustrated sigh.

"She went inside," another girl said.

"She must have come in while I was changing the baby."

"I'll go find her," I quickly told Sophie.

"Don't forget to take off your shoes and let me know where she was!"

My stress level continued to escalate. With Mikey still clinging to me so hard I barely had to hold onto him, we moved past the sliding glass door, and I called out for Lucy.

When no answer came after two tries, I illogically asked my silent, traumatized child to help me. "Mikey, where might she be?"

He leaned back and pointed toward the living room. Ignoring the reminder about the shoes, I charged on through, calling out Lucy's name again, and found her kneeling, hands clasped before her, looking up at a gold cross hanging on the wall. Relief trickled in upon seeing her actions were innocent. I half expected to find her amid a pile of broken dishes or standing in front of permanent marker across the wall.

"Lucy? It's time to go."

She crossed herself before standing and coming over to us.

I reached for her hand with my free one, and we all stumbled outside, where Sophie immediately asked about Lucy's whereabouts.

Lucy's hand tightened in mine as I replied, "She was in the bathroom." I didn't know what compelled me to lie, but my instincts took over.

Sophie's eyes narrowed slightly, and I wasn't sure if it was because she guessed I was lying or because of Lucy's transgression. I didn't give her time to voice anything she might have been suspecting.

"We really have to run. Have a good weekend."

I tried not to run to the car, but my heart was racing anyway when we reached it, and all I could do was lean against it and stroke Mikey's back while trying to tell him it was okay.

I was failing with Brian's kids. I was so wrapped up in the idea of all Mikey's behaviors surrounding his grief over his parents that it didn't occur to me there might be real, unrelated problems going on at his daycare. No one could blame Mikey for continuing to keep his mouth shut when kids were treating him so poorly every day. I wondered if they waited until Lucy wasn't looking or listening because, surely, she would scare them away from him. Then again, maybe Lucy was a different kid there. I'd heard mothers talk about how good their kids always were for childcare but how they were holy terrors at home.

After I buckled the kids inside the car, I took a deep breath in the driver's seat.

"Are you mad, JuJu?" Lucy asked.

"I am a little but not at you guys, okay? I promise. I'm not mad at you at all."

"Okay."

She accepted the response and stayed quiet as we traveled to the grocery store, a stop we unfortunately needed to make on our way home since I didn't know if we had enough supplies for even the most basic of meals.

Probably the one advantage of working an earlier shift than most others was the post-work grocery-store crowd, which wasn't as bad as, say, the five o'clock one. I appreciated the grace of being able to at least move through the aisles with ease, since Lucy determined everything else should be difficult.

"I don't like that kind of macaroni and cheese. Kraft. It has to be Kraft."

"Lulu, they're the same. And Kraft is three times more expensive than the generic. Can we please try it?"

"No! Mommy always gets us Kraft."

I gave a frustrated sigh and considered that Kraft macaroni and cheese was probably not going to break the bank.

"Fine." I grabbed three boxes and threw them into the cart. "The almighty Kraft company and you win."

Lucy glowered at me. I glowered back, hating myself. I knew I should pause and count to ten or something Zen-like, but I was worn down. I was tired of losing all the arguments and so tired of how ridiculously difficult it was to take care of children.

We moved on. Lucy and I battled through several more food choices until I gave up. The week before, we'd made it through the grocery store without problems, yet it was all suddenly impossible. *The daycare.* It was nagging at the back of my brain. Plus, it was Friday, and I was exhausted. I understood the whole working-mother thing so much better, and I was only two weeks in. I tried to imagine it getting easier. My efforts failed with Lucy's complaint in the next aisle.

"That's not the right kind of rice. You're supposed to get it in a bag."

"Lulu, rice is rice. If I get the kind from a bag, I'll screw it up, and you'll throw it all over the place. Do you get what a mess that is? The red box is the best I can do."

"I don't like it."

"It's what we had last time, and you liked it fine."

"I did not."

"You did too." I groaned inwardly at my childish response. I determined we would jump to the cereal aisle then get out of the store. The rest of the groceries could wait.

"*I did not!*" Lucy picked up the box out of the cart and threw it to the floor.

Then I lost it. I yelled at Lucy. She yelled back. Mikey curled into a ball.

"See what you did now?" Lucy screamed at me. "You made Mikey sad. I hate you!"

"Good little girls mind their tone and pick up after themselves," another shopper interceded, her expression one of extreme disapproval.

"I hate you too!"

Oh, Lucy.

"You deserve a time-out, young lady," the shopper scolded, and suddenly, I couldn't take a moment more of that damn store.

"Don't talk to my daughter like that. You don't know what she's been through. Give us all a break, will you? Can you all just give us a fucking break?"

I grabbed Mikey's and Lucy's hands and nearly ran out of the store. Everything around me was a fog. We made it to the car, and the only one crying by then was me.

It took everything I had to pull it together and ask with as much normality as possible if they had their seat belts on, then I told them we would order pizza for dinner. The visual in the rearview mirror told me they were buckled, but no other responses came. I didn't blame them. I wouldn't dare say two words to me yet either.

I turned on the radio, desperate to find music to calm and distract me. The first thing to blast through the speakers was the Wiggles, and it nearly made me let loose all the curse words flying through my head, which were many, including the Spanish ones Gemmi had taught me. My fingers jammed the eject button and rapidly hit a preset button. In my head, I magicked the kids out of my car and imagined cranking up the music and singing whatever the hell I wanted at the top of my lungs. It worked until I started through an intersection and didn't notice that the cross traffic didn't have to stop. A horn blasted, and I looked up in fear as a car slammed on its brakes, stopping a mere few feet away.

My breathing turned ragged. My body shook, and I got us out of the intersection and pulled over to the side of the road, trying to process how I nearly let the kids get taken in the same way their parents did. I flicked off the music and rested my head on the steering wheel, directing my breathing to slow and my mind to focus. I faced the kids. They held hands. Mikey buried his face in his bunny. Lucy's eyes were wide.

"I'm so sorry, you guys. We're almost home. Pizza and a movie safe and snug in our living room, okay?"

Lucy's eyes relaxed, and I took it for acknowledgment, if not acceptance. It was enough for me to concentrate and get my head in the game and drive us home without further incident.

Once inside our apartment, I called to order pizza then fell into the recliner. Moments after I sank into the chair, two small bodies crawled in with me. We held onto one another tightly.

"I've made a mess of things. I'm trying as hard as I can. I love you, and I will do better. I promise."

They didn't let go. I did my best to believe they gave tacit consent. I wasn't sure how I would make good on the promise but hoped we all had the strength to make it until I did.

Chapter Thirteen

Saturday morning. A fresh start. At least, I hoped it would be. Certainly, it had to be better than the day before. The evening had been quiet. We never made it to laughter, but a calm still settled in. We had a smile here and there with the movie we watched together, snuggled on the futon. After Mikey's midnight wake-up call, we all ended up in the same bed for the rest of the night. A sleep of forgiveness.

I'd asked the kids lots of times about how their days were going at Sophie's. I'd asked how they liked it and whether they were making friends. Lucy usually couched her answers in obscure stories about how no one did things the way she was used to. I always assumed that was an issue of learning to adapt to yet another new situation but suddenly realized I had been missing something. Likewise, Mikey's responses were difficult to read. He would pull Bunny closer to him and stick his thumb in his mouth. I could imagine his experience was different from Lucy's.

After I put the kids to bed and before Mikey woke up, Zach called, and I spilled some of the awful details of the day, mostly my worries about the daycare. Zach attempted reassurance, which meant him trying to say all the words he assumed I wanted to hear. I appreciated the effort, but I needed someone to work through the issues with me, not placate me.

Calling Layla seemed the exact right thing to do.

"Hey, Jules, how's it all going? How are my adorable niece and nephew?"

"Things are... I need your advice."

"God, Julie, it's about time."

"Since when have you started holding back?"

"Since Sheila made me promise. It ain't been easy, and for someone who admitted she knows nothing about what she's doing, you have been ridiculously closed off from everyone."

I didn't have a reasonable reply. She was right.

"I know. I just—"

"Don't want everyone to see how you're fucking everything up because then they'll judge you for assuming you can raise two traumatized children. I get it. It's another wonderful female character trait we can thank men for. They can fuck things up, and it's no big deal. Women fuck things up, and it's because they're overemotional, PMSing, or—"

"Yes, right, stupid men," I said. "Got it. Can we move on?"

"On some level, you know I'm right. So, what did you fuck up?"

"Probably everything. Lucy and I had a screaming match with each other and with everyone else in the grocery store last night. I'm betting the employees are hoping we'll never shop there again."

"Actual screaming or just the sass-and-scold thing?" Layla asked.

"I'm pretty sure we were not using our inside voices. Lucy is prone to tantrums."

"She's got fire. I love it. She got fire out of you, and I love that too."

I nearly snorted at her positive characterization. "I'm worried I messed up with the daycare." I told her about the situation from the prior day, Sophie's vague answers, and how I couldn't get solid information from the kids.

"Mikey's still not talking?" Layla asked.

"No, and I'm not getting useful answers out of Lucy. I don't know the right questions to ask."

"Try getting specific. Ask about what happens right after you drop them off. What do they do? What do they eat for lunch? You could work your way into the more sensitive stuff, like what happens if a kid says something mean or takes someone's toy away."

"I don't want Lucy to think I assume she's any part of those problems," I said.

"That's why you build up to it if you have to. You could ask what happens when that Malorie chick is all snotty, because chances are if she was snotty to Mikey, she treats other kids the same way."

Layla had good, solid ideas while clearly showing whose side she was on. It was why I called her. Confidence trickled back in and buoyed me.

"Okay. The thing is, we have a two-week trial agreement which ended on Friday," I said.

"If you make a decision this weekend, you can call before Monday, right?"

"I suppose."

"Look, I agree it's not ideal, but it's not about the daycare person. It's gotta be what's right for the kids. She must think so, too, if the trial is part of the contract," Layla said.

"Right."

"What's your gut telling you?"

"I think I've missed a lot of hints." I told her about what happened on Friday then about all the other little things I presumed were related to the kids having a hard time adapting to everything.

"Babe, cut yourself some slack. You're doing fine. Look, if you decide to pull them, let me know, and Sheila and I can come up for a few days and help, okay?"

A lifesaver of an offer. Though it was true I had some money in savings, it wasn't much, and if I had to keep taking a bunch of unpaid days off, my savings would disappear. Every penny of my paycheck covered the usual expenses, which, with the kids, meant a higher budget for food, clothing, and daycare. I had almost no wiggle room. Pressing down on it all was me resting on the hairy edge of losing my job, given the way Carl was handling my new situation.

I thanked her and promised to call again before the end of the weekend. Courage and determination returned, even if the whole idea of Sophie's being an unhappy place twisted my insides. I didn't talk to the kids about everything right away; emotions were still too raw. Instead, we played together, drew pictures, read stories, and walked to the park.

We ate lunch, and after reading them another story, I took on the challenge.

"Tell me about your days at Sophie's, like your routine. What's the first thing you do after I drop you off?"

"We eat breakfast," Lucy said.

That, of course, I had seen. Some mornings, it was cereal and some fruit. Other days might be toast and yogurt.

"Then what?"

Mikey pointed down.

"You go downstairs?"

He nodded.

"And what do you do once you're down there?"

"Play," Lucy said.

"Do you get to choose what to play, or does Sophie have some activity you all do?"

"We get to play what we want at first, and then we all learn about the letter of the day. But we know all of our letters, so we have to be quiet so we don't ruin it for the kids who don't."

I frowned. The activity sounded nice, but I didn't like Lucy's wording about "ruining" it for others. "What do you do during the letter of the day? Talk about words with the letter or try to write them?"

She told me that Sophie had a basket of things beginning with the letter and might do a craft using it. If they wanted, they could trace the letter on a piece of paper. When I asked what Sophie did with the projects and papers afterward, Lucy told me most went into a drawer.

"Mikey usually draws his own pictures instead."

I turned to him. "Yeah? Maybe they weren't about the letters, though, huh?"

He shook his head and waved his hand at me.

I wasn't sure what he was trying to tell me. "No, they weren't?"

"For the letter *M*, Mikey drew a macaw like we saw on the animal show we watch," Lucy supplied.

"Wow, Mikey. Really?"

He nodded and smiled.

"I'd love to see it. Did your macaw drawing go in the drawer too?"

He tipped his head to the side before shrugging.

I didn't understand why Sophie wasn't sending home the kids' art. The rest of the routine I pulled out of the kids seemed normal enough. Things got a little dicey when I asked the more personal questions.

"Who did you like to play with?"

Mikey pointed at Lucy at the same time that Lucy said, "Mikey. Sometimes, Lucas."

"Does Sophie play with you?"

"She plays a lot with Cassie and baby Jackson. She doesn't talk to Mikey very much. I think she forgets," Lucy said.

I looked at Mikey, wondering how this matter-of-fact comment affected him, because it sure hit me hard. I wondered what Lucy meant by "she forgets." *Forgets to talk to him? Forgets he can still hear but just doesn't talk? Forgets about him altogether?*

"Now, how could she possibly forget our Mikey?" I put my arm around him and hugged him tightly. "You're too busy all over the place to go unnoticed."

He wrapped his hand over mine. I meant it. He was quiet, but evidence of his presence was everywhere in his block creations, his drawings, his touch, and countless other ways.

"Mikey, is Malorie always kind of mean to you, like she was yesterday when I picked you up?"

He looked up at me, and while his mouth didn't move, something changed in his eyes. It wasn't quite sadness, more like... resignation, as though it was to be expected.

"Sometimes, she's okay. Sophie tells people not to bother him 'cause he won't do anything back anyway."

I closed my eyes and told myself to breathe. The lump in my throat expanded; I worried I might choke on it. I was angry that someone who was supposed to be nurturing children saw Mikey as merely an extra body in her home and not as a curious and interactive child.

"What about you, Lucy? Are the other kids nice to you?" I asked.

"I guess so."

"What happens when you don't follow directions?"

"I have to sit on the time-out mat."

Mikey held out his arms as though to reflect a large object.

"It's a big mat?" I asked. He shook his head. "Something else is big?"

He shook his head again. He pointed at Lucy and gestured again.

"She sits there a lot?"

He nodded.

It was Lucy's turn for a tight hug. "What happened the last time you had to take a time-out?"

"I forgot to say thank you for the snack."

Good God, how ridiculously over-the-top. "Was it something you didn't like? Did you get mad at her for what the snack was?"

"I didn't throw anything, JuJu." She started to cry, then I fully recognized how exaggerated Sophie's reports were of Lucy having "a hard time." "I was good, I promise. I didn't mean to forget to say thank you."

I released Mikey for a moment to embrace Lucy fully, my heart cracking at how exhausted Lucy must have been each day, trying to be as cooperative and polite as possible. No wonder she'd fallen apart at home. "Of course you were good, sweetheart. You're very good at pleases and thank-yous, and you did not deserve a time-out for that."

"I did something else bad yesterday, JuJu. I'm sorry."

"What are you talking about? When?"

"At Sophie's. We're not supposed to go in her living room."

"Yeah, I figured. But you weren't doing anything bad in there," I said.

"But then you lied to Sophie. That's *bad.* That's breaking one of God's big rules."

"What if I had told Sophie the truth? What would she have done? Another time-out?"

She nodded into my chest.

"Nothing else?"

She shook her head.

"Do you ever get a punishment different than a time-out? Does she take anything away or spank you?"

"No."

I let out a breath of relief for small favors. I didn't know what I would have done if there had been more. Probably signed them over to Layla and Sheila after all. I wasn't sure I was getting the full story, but if she worried about me breaking one of "God's big rules," then hopefully, she wasn't doing the same.

"Were you praying in Sophie's living room?"

"Yes."

"Did it help?"

She shrugged, and I made a decision I'd been wrestling with for several days.

"Do you want to go to church tomorrow?" I looked from one to the other to make sure they understood I was asking both of them. They didn't answer right away. "It wouldn't be your same church, but my friend Gemmi goes to a church I hope you'll like. Should we try it out?"

Mikey looked at Lucy, and she looked at him. I caught one of those rare moments when they truly seemed to communicate telepathically, answering together. When Lucy met my eyes, I had no doubt that her agreement reflected the feelings of them both. I squeezed them to me and kissed the tops of their heads.

"Okay. I'll let you guys play now, and I'll call Gemmi. I love you two munchkins." They scrambled up, and little arms wrapped around my neck in a wonderful chokehold.

I had been to church with Gemmi only once, for a wedding. I was her plus-one. Though it was a nondenominational Christian church, Gemmi boasted about its strong community. Only a month after I accompanied her to the wedding, she had met Demitry there.

The worship space provided a familiar atmosphere, with a central altar and an area for the musicians. The congregation sat in a semicircle instead of the straight rows I had more often seen. If the wedding I attended was representative of the regular community, the kids and I would be in good hands, regardless of how different it likely was from what Lucy and Mikey had experienced in Duluth.

Gemmi and Demitry greeted us out front. Gemmi matched Demitry in height—she on the tall side and him on the shorter—and they carried themselves with a grace and spirit I'd always admired.

"Hey, Demitry. It's been a while." I smiled at him.

"So long you sauntered off and picked up a couple kids along the way, huh?" With the twins glommed onto me, our hug was mostly one-way. "I'm sorry about your brother," he said softly into my ear.

"Thanks."

He crouched to talk to the twins, and as he did, I shared a moment with Gemmi. Her expression conveyed appreciation for her kind boyfriend and regret for what they might lose. My heart splintered for her.

"C'mon, you guys. Sean's inside, saving us some seats."

Demitry won Lucy over, and she skipped inside with him. I took advantage of my newly freed hand and grabbed Gemmi's as we followed. I looked down at Mikey to see how he was faring. As we entered the church, he relaxed. Different as it might be, there was surely some familiarity, and I was grateful.

Sean greeted us cheerfully as he made room for us in a row about halfway up. Lucy studied him before I finally asked her to share her question.

"Are you a boy or a girl?"

"Yes," Sean answered with a smile. "I might be one of those. Or neither of those. What do you think?"

Lucy scrunched her eyebrows together as she took in Sean's short black knots with a low fade, eyeliner-sculpted lids, earrings, pink T-shirt, black skinny jeans, and tattoos.

"Boy."

"Great! Let's go with that."

"Which one am I?" Lucy asked.

Sean cocked his head and tapped his lips. "Hmm. Neither. You are clearly a butterfly."

Lucy giggled. "Nope! I'm a girl! See?" She twirled around, letting her dress float along with her, which to me surely proved Sean correct.

"Look at you!" he exclaimed. "You flutter like a butterfly, but if you say you're a girl, I believe you. What about your twin? Are they a butterfly too?"

Mikey, glued to my side, slunk behind me.

"No." Lucy transitioned from twirl to bounce. "He's a boy. He doesn't like to talk." She climbed up onto a chair and looked at Sean more closely. "I didn't know boys wore makeup or earrings. You don't have as many earrings as Julie, though."

He grasped her hands and held up her thumbs. "It looks like you found her rings too."

Lucy loved trying out different rings every day. Because of the obvious difference in our sizes, I didn't often let her wear them outside of the apartment; it took too much time to find some yarn to shrink them down. We made an exception for church. She said she wanted to look her best for God.

Mikey sneaked from behind me and held up his right hand to show his pointer finger to Sean, who praised it appropriately. Mikey only ever wanted to wear the silver one I had let him try back when Layla and Sheila first visited, and it pretty much came off only when he took a bath. I was secretly happy knowing something of mine had earned some form of attachment from him.

Throughout the service, I glanced at the kids to see how it met their expectations. Frankly, the fact they paid any attention at all impressed me. Lucy openly bounced to the music while Mikey swung my hand occasionally.

I was glad we came. I couldn't promise them regular attendance, but I had to figure out a balance between what I believed—or didn't—and what they needed. I was also grateful to my friends for creating a situation in which I didn't feel awkward and ignorant. By telling the kids what would happen next in the service, they told me too.

Afterward, we picked up lunch and ate at a park, allowing the kids—and Demitry—to run and play. Sean, Gemmi, and I sat along one side of a picnic table, watching them.

"Look how happy he is with them," Gemmi said. "I could do it, couldn't I? Have kids?"

"You can't just do it for him, and you know it," I said.

Sean agreed. "And don't go doing anything stupid either."

"Like what?"

"Like 'accidentally' getting pregnant, that's what."

I nearly laughed at Sean's comment until I sensed Gemmi stiffen next to me and caught her expression. *Oh God.* Her silence lasted too long.

"Gemmi?"

She turned to me sharply. "No. I'm not pregnant, and I'm still on the pill."

I held onto her gaze, willing her to understand I was on her side, no matter what.

Her eyes softened. "I know. Sean's right. It would be stupid."

Sean pulled Gemmi into him, and I took her hand.

"Babe," Sean said, "I am *always* right about stupidity."

We laughed. "Thanks for taking one for the team, Sean," I told him, "because obviously, we won't ever let you forget that comment."

Thanks to Sean, we'd put a smile on Gemmi's face again, and when the kids dragged Demitry back to the table, Gemmi smiled at him and kissed him as though our conversation had never happened. It was an imperfect resolution but one I could relate to. No sense fixing something that wasn't broken.

Back home, the kids tucked themselves away in their room for some quiet time, and I tried for the same. I had barely closed my eyes when I awoke to two little faces next to me. I glanced at the clock to find out I had, in fact, slept for almost half an hour. Considering how TV shows always seemed to depict kids jumping on their parents to wake them up, I appreciated the gentle prods from my two.

"Hi, munchkins. You have very serious expressions right now."

Lucy's eyes suddenly filled, and Mikey pulled Bunny closer.

My stomach contracted. "Hey, it's okay. Tell me what's wrong."

"Do we have to go back to Sophie's?" The tears spilled down her cheeks, and I imagined the courage it took for them to ask me what was obviously a painful and scary question. In a defining moment, I knew that I couldn't send them back. I had called Sophie a day earlier but only got her machine, and I left a vague message. I'd aimed for getting a more complete story of what was going on since I'd gained more concrete answers from the kids. However, everything was clear. I couldn't possibly send them back.

"No, sweetie. You don't. We'll figure something else out." They snuggled under the covers with me, and I ignored the swell of anxiety that insistently returned despite all my efforts.

Chapter Fourteen

Then Grant showed up at my door.

The kids and I were playing car bowling, a new game Lucy and I had invented. We set up a pyramid of blocks then raced the cars into them, hoping to knock them all down. It was wonderfully loud, not only from the cars hitting the blocks and sending them all tumbling but also from Lucy's shrieks of glee each time it happened. While I restacked the blocks, she scurried over to get the cars and set them up again in giggly anticipation. Sometimes, the crashes elicited a smile from Mikey too. I wondered if we could play car bowling forever.

With the knock at the door, I cheerfully told them, "Aunties Layla and Sheila are here!"

That earned another joyful shriek, except it wasn't them. Instead, it was a tallish, well-built, not quite as well-dressed man. He wore faded jeans and a more-faded-still Washington Cougars T-shirt revealing heavily tattooed arms. His dark hair curled at the ends. His five-o'clock shadow gave him a rugged outdoorsman look, like the sort of man seen on pickup truck commercials or in beer ads, which fit, because he was also a little soft in the middle. I was pretty sure I'd dated a guy like him a few years back, and he kept calling me Mint Julep, which I hated, which made him say it more, and that wasn't even the least of the problems in our short-but-not-short-enough relationship. My greeting to the stranger was crabbier than it should have been because I was irritated that a conjured memory might destroy the fragile and temporary joy I'd experienced with the kids.

"Hey. Are you Julie Mercer?"

"Who are you?"

"Sorry. Right. Grant Masinksy. Elaine's brother. Also known as 'the sperm.'"

"The sperm whale is the hugest animal ever," Lucy's voice chimed out. "We learned about it on *Wild Kratts*."

Perfectly timed. Clearly, "The Sperm" did not realize the results of his contribution were on the other side of the door. His face registered the appropriate embarrassment.

I held out my hand. "Yes, I'm Julie Mercer. The Eggs."

I stepped away and gestured him inside, and he started in on a rambling introduction.

"God, I'm sorry. I didn't know, but I should have guessed. That was stupid, which is pretty typical of me. You might as well know that right away, but I guess that's already pretty obvious. I should have called first, but my phone is out of minutes. It's just one of those buy-it-off-the-rack phones—you know, a burner phone—but I'm not a criminal, I swear. I know I should have come earlier, but I didn't even find out about..."

My irritation fell away. I didn't know what he didn't find out about—the kids, his sister, or maybe me.

The room had gone suddenly quiet. The kids had fled. *Shit.* Another stranger. If I had thought for one second before inviting The Sperm in, I would have remembered their potential reaction.

"Hold on. I'll be right back."

I found them in their bedroom, sitting in the corner, holding hands. I sat before them, cross-legged. "Hey. I'm sorry I didn't warn you. He surprised me too." They crawled into my lap, and I squeezed them. "He's family, though, okay? He's your uncle. I bet he's here to see you. You don't have to come out, but you can skip right on over to me if you do."

Upon seeing them calm, I left them to their own devices while I headed into the new upheaval awaiting me.

In the living room, I found The Sperm pacing. Before I could say anything more, my sister and sister-in-law walked in.

"We come to save the day with junk food for dinner! Where are my rascals?" Layla called out before she saw the wrinkle in our evening. "Oh. My rascals have turned into a strange, slovenly, Y-chromosomed creature."

"Layla, Sheila, meet The Sperm."

"Ah! Well, you're kind of late to the party, Sperm-boy," Sheila said.

"Also known as Grant," I said.

"I think I like Sperm-boy better."

"Layla." Sheila's tone carried a light warning.

"Yes, okay," Layla said. "Grant." She narrowed her eyes at him. "Why are you suddenly here? Unannounced?"

It was a valid question, yet Layla seemed a little on edge at his presence. It occurred to me she might have been playing the protective older sister.

"To see the kids, Lay," I said. "Just like you."

My comment brought her back to the moment and her purpose, which was to see Lucy and Mikey.

"Where are the kids?" she asked.

I tipped my head toward their bedroom. "They got a little spooked at a new face."

Layla's entire demeanor changed.

"Here." She unloaded onion rings and a cheeseburger for me. "Sheila and I will go picnic with the twins in their room while you, you know, figure some stuff out. We'll work out a way to convince them to come out later and meet Sper—their uncle Grant."

Sheila gave my arm a supportive squeeze as they slipped away. I looked at my food and recalled The Sperm—Grant—saying he'd been driving for three days.

"Here." I held out the cheeseburger. "I'm not very hungry. I'll have the onion rings, and you can have the rest."

I could see him contemplating turning down my offer, but he took the proffered burger. I grabbed a couple of beers and some ketchup from the fridge and took them to the table. "I'm sorry about my sister. She's kind of rough around the edges and a little more so lately."

"Yeah, I imagine rough edges might be true of all of us."

He had no argument from me. I wondered whether my edges would ever be smooth. "Three days in the car. Washington?"

"Home? No. I haven't been home in years. California."

"Were you close to your sister?"

He paused—a familiar reaction. It was the pause in which one considered what the answer should be and not what it was. "Not really. We were kind of close when we were kids. Then we both left home after high school, and we talked and emailed sometimes, but that's about it. Of course, there was the whole donating-sperm thing. I guess if you wanted to call donating sperm to your sister 'close,' then there's that."

"Oh, you mean donating reproductive stuff makes you beloved by someone? Then Brian and I were super tight too."

He gave me a half smile, which I returned.

"So, you gonna tell me what made you decide to come out here?"

"I heard you talked to my mom, and I can imagine how pleasant *that* was, since she usually saves all of her charm for me. Anyway, she called me as an afterthought one day, and by one day, I mean two weeks after you and my parents had Elaine cremated. I pulled a few more teeth in asking about Brian and the kids because for all I knew, it was only Elaine who had died in the accident. Mom told me about you having custody of the kids, and I thought maybe I had some responsibility in this whole thing. So I got in the car, and here I am."

"Responsibility? They didn't name you their guardian. Your name wasn't on the documents at all."

"Considering Elaine didn't have any more information about me than my address, it was probably a solid decision on their part. And I don't know, with them gone, I figured my biological role meant I should do something. Helping, getting to know them, or... something."

"You're their uncle. Wasn't the family relationship enough before this turn of events?" Never mind how little of a role *I* had been playing in their lives before the accident.

"No. I was a shitty uncle, but now it's like you're the girlfriend who just told me she was pregnant, and instead of assuming it has nothing to do with me, I'm trying to show I'm ready to man up."

"Except we're not girlfriend and boyfriend. I'm really not sure how the analogy applies."

"You're not going to give me anything here, are you?"

He stared at me, and I stared back. He won. I looked away. I didn't know why I was being so hard on him and so self-righteous. As if after a month, I was suddenly the hero instead of the only one who happened to be at the right place and at the right time. I was drowning, and another weed had tangled around me and threatened to pull me down farther. Hearing how awful his mother had been to her own son about the whole thing threw me too. We were all a train wreck.

"I gave you the cheeseburger," I finally replied.

Then he laughed, which made me smile, because it was the best thing I'd seen since he walked through the door, besides the fact he'd actually traveled cross-country to "man up," whatever that meant. I laughed too. The entire situation was ridiculous.

"I'm sorry," I said after catching my breath. "I don't know why I'm being difficult."

"If I just dropped in on me unannounced in this situation, I wouldn't have even given me the cheeseburger."

I chuckled and saw Mikey peek around the doorway to the kitchen and encouraged him to come out by extending my arms. He raced over and climbed into my lap, with Lucy close behind. Both avoided looking at Grant. After settling them in my lap, which was hard because they weren't exactly little toddlers, I looked at Grant. He stared at them with what I suspected was the same expression I wore when I first saw them at Lynette's—awe at how two such beautiful children were mine. To Grant's credit, his expression lacked fear, which mine definitely held when I initially took them into custody. I supposed the reaction was different when one was free of the responsibility of being the primary provider, and I had a moment of jealousy over his unappreciated freedom.

It was brief, though, as they nestled into me. I would never have guessed how powerful the sensation of a child's snuggle could be.

Grant pulled out a sheet of paper from a nearby notebook, and with a pen, he drew a big smiley face on it. He handed it to me.

"Look, you guys. This is from Uncle Sperm Whale Grant."

The nickname brought a snort from Layla, who had been waiting in the hallway with Sheila. It was odd that I hadn't noticed her right away. She always made her presence known.

I spoke to the kids again, still showing them the picture. "Do you think he has this same expression on his face right now?"

They shrugged.

"Hmm," I said. "You should probably check. Take a peek."

They slowly turned their heads, but Grant wasn't smiling. Instead, he'd plastered on a goofy expression—eyes wide, cheeks puffed out— and succeeded in making Lucy giggle and turn to me. They looked at him again. That time, he had on a different goofy look.

More giggles came from Lucy, but Mikey was still unsure. No smiles yet. Grant stood and moved to the living room, where he started arranging the blocks into roadways for the cars. As he took a car and maneuvered it through the roadways, making car noises along the way, Lucy slipped off my lap and joined him.

"I was using that one," she told him.

"Of course you were. It's one of the coolest ones here. Which car should I use?"

She studied the small collection, picked out the hot-pink one, and handed it to him.

"Perfect." He smiled, taking it without reservation.

Lucy turned to me with a grin of joyful surprise. I smiled back. Zach had always liked to amuse Lucy with a juge show about how he needed the biggest, toughest-looking car then tried to look and act tough once he picked it out. On the living room floor was a man who looked far tougher than Zach ever would, and he accepted the girly car without question. I wondered what the comparison said about them. Maybe nothing.

"Do you want to play cars with them?" I asked Mikey.

He shook his head.

"I can play right next to you."

He shook his head again, holding onto me tighter. A moment later, he gripped me tighter still because apparently, Grant's hot-pink car had no muffler. A loud roar came from him, startling all of us and eliciting an excited scream from Lucy.

"Don't let the color fool you. Pink doesn't have to mean soft, right?" Grant told Lucy.

His eyes glossed over Layla then rested on me. I gave him a reassuring smile. He was doing good with Lucy.

"See, Lay?" Sheila said. "Pink isn't evil."

"He obviously hasn't walked into a toy store recently."

"Do you want to color?" I asked Mikey, hoping to move on from the diatribe against all things feminine that Layla might have unleashed in a wrong moment. Mikey nodded at the suggestion, which Layla caught, and she left and returned with crayons and blank paper from the twins' bedroom. She scooped up Mikey from my lap before moving him to her own lap at the table, where she drew pictures and he colored them.

Sheila and I moved to the couch in the living room, and for a few minutes, we simply watched the kids interact with their aunt and uncle.

"I like how he jumped right into playing with them," Sheila started quietly.

"Yeah. Me too."

"What's his story?"

I shrugged. "I don't know. I'd guess he doesn't really know either. Sounds like he's trying to figure out what he should do and what his role should be."

"You don't think he has thoughts of fighting for custody?"

"Um. Look at him. What do you think?"

She laughed. "I guess I can't imagine it, but seriously, you never know, right? I mean, you should probably be careful."

Great. Because it wasn't still stressful enough, Sheila—and presumably Layla, earlier—had to bring up a concern I never would have considered. I might have had official guardianship, but he also had biology. I had signed paperwork during the egg-donation stage, as I assumed Grant had also done, but maybe everything changed with Brian and Elaine's deaths. Grant could easily contest my sole guardianship, unless he had some awful strikes against him.

I decided not to worry about the possibility. My brain was overloaded enough. The evening was supposed to have been a break. Layla, Sheila, the kids, and I would have dinner, and I would go out for a little while on my own, possibly meeting up with Gemmi. I was going to forget about the mountainous list of new daycares I had to vis-it the next day. Layla had taken a couple of days off to help me out with the kids so I wouldn't lose more of my paycheck—or my job.

We'd had a better time of it than the day before but not by much. But it wasn't because of any of Lucy's tantrums—it was me. With all of my mental and physical energy tapped out, I'd lost count of how many times I'd said "I'm sorry" to the kids. At one point, I let them watch a movie while I tried to nap. I managed twenty minutes, which became the new "enough" to get me through the last of the after-noon.

Layla came in with Mikey in tow, and he huddled next to me on the couch.

"Lucy's hair is adorable, and she positively beamed at me when I told her so."

"Thank you," I said, appreciating the validation more than she might guess.

"I can better see the resemblance between you two."

"Now you're buttering me up for something."

Sheila laughed. "Layla, babe, I *love* that we are hanging with your sister now. I need someone else who's got your number."

"Hey, I was being sincere," Layla scoffed. "Anyway, there's still time to get out of here for a little while, Jules. We can babysit the man too."

Grant's head shot up. "What? Nope. No babysitting necessary. I'll get myself gone."

I waved him away. "I'm too tired to go anywhere now. It's all fine."

"We'll help put the kids to bed at least," Layla said, standing and ready to gather them for the nighttime routine.

I looked at Mikey. "Do you want to go with Layla and Sheila?"

He nodded before sliding off the couch and wrapping his arms around my neck.

"Sweet dreams, honey," I whispered into his ear as though the message might actually settle into him and work magic.

Lucy skipped over and flung herself into me. "Night-night, JuJu."

"Sleep tight, Lulu."

They scampered off, leaving me with a warm glow. Happy kids—or at least not unhappy ones—restored some of my energy.

"Which came first? Lulu or JuJu?"

Turning to Grant, I smiled. "Lulu. She modified my name almost right away after I started using it. She's pretty quick."

"I like it."

He stood with his hands in his pockets. I didn't move from the couch. The next move was probably mine.

"So," I said.

"I'm sorry for ruining your night."

Leaning forward and rubbing my face with my hands, I sighed. "It's fine. My sister will be in town for a couple more days. I'll have another opportunity."

"I would have called if... Well, I should have called, I suppose, but I thought I'd lose my nerve to come and actually meet you and the kids. Of course, it obviously didn't cross my mind that no warning would not really set a good first impression for me, and I don't really have a plan in general—"

"It's no big deal," I interrupted. "I mean, I guess I'm not sure what I would have told you to do if you'd called first, especially from California. How about we figure things out tomorrow? Stop on by in the morning."

The relief seemed to roll off him, and it occurred to me I'd forgotten something important.

"I'm sorry about your sister."

Sadness seeped into his expression as he gave me a gentle nod. "I'm sorry about your brother."

After Layla, Sheila, and Grant walked out together, I flopped down on the couch and didn't move for an hour and a half. I caught most of an old *Prime Crime* episode starring one of our homegrown Minnesota actors, Rick Calloran, then flipped to more TV reruns starting with *Everybody Loves Raymond*. The episode featured Raymond and Deborah's kids, and it stressed me out. I flipped again and found *Scrubs*, which was better. By then, I'd recovered some energy and got up to grab a snack.

I stared into the cupboard, battling a wave of nostalgia over Twinkies. Fruit snacks didn't come close to filling a Hostess void. I grabbed a package of the gummies nonetheless and headed to the living room, arguing with myself to go to bed. Instead of returning to the couch, I turned off the TV and stared out the window, reflecting on how things had shifted yet again. A California license plate caught my eye in the faint glow of one of the parking lot lights. It belonged to a banged-up-looking Ford Explorer. Seemed like it could have been Grant's car. Possibly he'd returned, or my better guess was that he'd never left. I contemplated going to investigate as I worried about his potential lack of lodging. Something told me he didn't have much money.

It was ten o'clock, and if patterns held, the kids would stay sound asleep while I went down to see if, in fact, the Explorer was Grant's and if he was in it. I locked the door behind me and headed to the lot. Sure enough, I found Grant sleeping in the driver's side, seat reclined as far as it could go. I decided to trust my instincts, which I usually didn't, but Gemmi always said it was because I second-guessed them until I ultimately forgot what my original instinct was. I held onto the current instinct. Grant had come a long way, and I didn't think it was for money. He might want the kids, but I honestly didn't think he was going to kidnap them or anything. I could do a little more detective work once we got inside.

I tapped on the window. Obviously, my second-guessing side won because the tap was ridiculously soft, and it was no surprise he didn't wake up. I took a deep breath and rapped on the window. He startled slightly as he opened his eyes then raised his seat up. He tried to lower his window, and I laughed as he apparently realized power windows meant a need for power. He dug for his keys, but I cut the motions short by opening his unlocked door.

"Hey," I said.

"Right. So, I have no money because I completely ditched everything in California. I quit my job, cut out of my apartment lease early, which also forfeited my deposit money and probably ruined my already terrible credit, slept in my car mostly at rest stops on the way out here unless a state trooper caught me, and took my first shower in three days this morning at a truck stop. I'm down to my last one hundred dollars and just saw my sister's kids for the first time and am stupidly thinking I'll be able to do anything at all about any of it."

He was a nervous talker—a painfully honest one. I thanked my instincts and shrugged. "Okay. Wow. Whatever. I'll process all of that later. For now, how about you grab whatever you need and come on back up. You can sleep on the couch. I'll meet you there, because Lucy and Mikey are asleep, but I don't want them to wake up and find out I'm not there."

I didn't wait for a response. I took in the state of his car's interior before I headed back to the apartment, and I didn't doubt a word he'd said. It wasn't as trashed as I might have expected for a car driven by a single man traveling cross-country, although his stuff was definitely all over it. He had few belongings—a couple of bags, and the front passenger seat held empty or half-empty snack bags, Red Bull cans, a water bottle, a razor, and a toothbrush sticking out from underneath a towel.

When he got up to the apartment, I had a blanket and pillow ready for him on the futon, currently converted to a bed. "Look, I'm super tired and don't have the energy to go into everything we'll need to work out, but you're welcome to stay here for a few days until we do figure stuff out. Okay?"

"Yeah. Of course. And... thanks."

I nodded and headed to my room. I closed the door and fell onto my bed, reflecting on all the "stuff" ahead of us the next day. Despite my "few days" offer, I knew a man who had only one hundred dollars to his name and no job would not be moving out soon. My brain was already wrapping itself around a new idea. It would give Grant a purpose and solve a couple of my more immediate problems. Maybe, just maybe, I could keep things from falling apart for a little while longer.

Chapter Fifteen

Later, when Mikey's screams rang out, I ran into Grant in the hall, as though he was planning to go in and comfort the boy.

"What are you doing? He doesn't know you yet." I didn't wait for an answer as I rushed past him and into the kids' room. Bunny had fallen to the floor, so I retrieved him and put him into Mikey's hands before picking him up. Mikey and I fell into our customary position of his legs and arms wrapped around me as I held him securely, rocking and spilling out my usual soothing words. He quieted, and I continued to hold him, gathering my own peace from his return to a deep sleep. The day had called into question for the millionth time my ability to handle anything, and I also doubted my plans to deal with Grant. I closed my eyes and rocked with Mikey until my breathing matched his, and only then did I kiss his head and tuck him into his bed.

I leaned over to Lucy and kissed her head as well before noticing Grant was still waiting in the hall.

"You okay?" he asked.

I had been, but with the simple question—from a stranger, no less—my walls crumbled. I couldn't risk answering because there was no way I was going to fall apart in front of him. So I didn't. I bolted for my room and quickly shut the door before falling into bed and sobbing into my pillow.

I awoke to Lucy but not from her elbow or foot digging into me. Rather, it was the tone I had become too familiar with.

"No! You did it all wrong."

I wanted to creep into a shell and never come out. My taut nerves were ready to snap at any moment. I raised my arms and tightened them over my head as I fought the rush of tears. I was so tired of being stressed-out. I was so tired of walking on eggshells. I was so tired of everything.

I gasped for air until I could breathe in and out normally then propelled myself to the kitchen to find Grant picking pieces of toast up from the floor.

"You said you wanted butter and jelly."

Lucy's voice clung to the high-decibel level. "I don't like it cut. Mama never cuts it!"

"Lucy," I interrupted firmly, "he didn't know. Throwing your food on the floor and yelling at him is not the way to tell him."

I expected her to fling something else, but she merely folded her little arms and scowled.

"I'm sorry," Grant told me. "I was trying to help. They came out while I was making coffee, and I thought they would freak out on seeing me, but it seemed to be okay, then I thought I could get them some breakfast. I figured you might get a little extra sleep, and it started out okay, but then—"

"Oh God, Sperm Whale. I got it. It's okay. Chill."

"Right. Okay. I'm sorry. "

I turned to Lucy. "If you want another shot at breakfast, you need to figure out how to make it happen." At least coffee was ready and waiting. I poured myself a cup and shifted to Grant, feeling bad about the name I'd used with him again. He looked like he was going to apologize once more. "It's fine," I said before he could.

"You want some toast?" he asked. "My talent for making toast inspires passionate responses."

I laughed, loosening the knot in my stomach.

"I'm hungry!" Lucy wailed, threatening to tighten it up again.

I refused to let the threat take over. I sat next to her. "Honey, I know, but I'm kind of tired of this tantrum stuff. Aren't you? You need to say you're sorry to Grant then ask us nicely to find something else for you." I turned to Mikey, who'd already finished his toast and banana. "Hey, Mikey. You and Bunny doing okay this morning?"

He smiled and gave me a hug. Based upon his reluctant reception of Grant the night before, I was impressed Mikey had allowed him to make his breakfast. It was like the two had planned their switched roles. I glanced over Mikey's shoulder and saw one possible explanation for the warm-up—the two plates at Mikey's spot. One of them might have been for Bunny. I didn't know if I was happy about Grant's ability to have figured out a way to Mikey's heart so quickly or if I was jealous. Instead, I was comforted that Lucy had unleashed her wrath upon Grant, even if I was being unfair.

I wandered to the fridge to grab a yogurt when Lucy's quiet voice came through.

"I'm sorry, Sperm Whale."

I turned away quickly to hide my laughter. Lucy might have originally come up with the name, but I had reinforced it. That wasn't a bad way to warm us all up to Grant's presence. He gave me a nudge, which made me want to laugh harder, but Lucy's small voice brought me back in.

"May I have more toast, please?"

"After such a nice apology and polite request?" Grant replied. "I'm totally on it. Maybe you could tell me *exactly* how you want it this time."

I smiled as Lucy slipped out of her chair in order to help. She got out two pieces of bread and handed them to Grant, who put them in the toaster.

"You have to butter the whole thing. Then jelly. Then put the bread together to be a sandwich."

"A sandwich?" Grant squatted to meet her at eye level. "That sounds like the best way ever to eat toast. A toast sandwich!" He held up a hand for her to high-five, which she did with zeal.

She looked at me for approval.

"See how much better your politeness worked? Thank you, Lucy."

She smiled and bounced in place as she waited for the toast to pop up. I grabbed a spoon and sat at the table. Mikey moved to the living room, constructing something with blocks—mostly one-handed, as he wasn't far enough into the morning to release Bunny completely. Grant set Lucy up with her toast and joined us with coffee.

"Please tell me you're not skipping breakfast out of some sort of guilt right now."

He glanced at me before looking away. Definitely guilty.

"I told you we'd figure something out, which means I will feed you and house you and let you use stuff. Okay?" I got up and grabbed another yogurt, along with some Pop-Tarts and a banana. I deposited it all in front of him and sat down. "Eat freely, Sir Whale."

"The new name's never going away now, is it?"

"Nope. Lucy rubber-stamped it. Sperm Whale it is."

Lucy giggled. Grant chuckled. I smiled. A crash of blocks came, and I saw Mikey give a rare grin. I didn't know if it was from the terrific crash of his structure or our conversation, but I glimpsed teeth and a sparkle in his eyes again. I felt hope.

"So," Grant said, "what's going on today? Do you have to work or something? Do the kids go to a daycare?"

"Yes, I normally would work today. We had a snafu with daycare. I took some more time off to figure out the next option."

"What's a snafu?" Lucy asked.

"Everything wrong with Sophie's house."

"Oh. Like her broken dishwasher?"

"Yeah. Something like that."

Grant opened his Pop-Tarts. "Me showing up right now could be good timing. Will you let me help?"

"What were you thinking?" I asked carefully. I definitely had my own ideas, but his opening sounded promising.

"I don't know. We could try tag-teaming. I could stay with the kids while you go to work. You know, until you find something else for them."

In fact, his suggestion had already occurred to me. I'd looked him up online to find out more about him. No TikTok. An Instagram and Facebook, although he didn't post much. I even found his old, barely used MySpace account. I didn't see any red flags, though, and his location checked out. I found a Grant Masinsky listed on staff at a youth rec center in North Hollywood, and that information was probably the most compelling in helping me feel more solid about my decision.

"You're really willing to take care of the kids all day?" I asked.

"Yeah. I mean, I may not have had the save-the-day scenario in mind, but I meant it about doing my part."

"Have you ever spent all day with young kids before?"

"Had you?"

I narrowed my eyes at him. It was a fair question. "I had no choice. Now I do."

"I guess I can be rude too. I've helped a lot with babies and kids older than ten. So, I suppose I don't have the experience with younger kids, but I can do it. I want to do this."

"Okay."

"Yeah?"

"Yep." I watched as Lucy cleared her dishes and joined her brother in the living room. "I have zero days of vacation or sick leave left at work and am in the hole several days of paid work already. I hate having this as my big concern instead of being able to focus entirely on the kids. Except, if I can't pay for food, let alone daycare, we're all screwed. My mom helped for a little while earlier in the week, and Layla came up to help me out the rest of this week. Only for part of the day today, though, because she has a meeting, and Sheila had to head back. So..." I took a deep, steadying breath. "Maybe in the next couple of days, we can figure out some time to give you and the kids a trial run together on your own, and if everything works out okay, I can go back to earning some money for a few days before resuming the new daycare search."

"I think it's a great plan. I can do this, you know."

"Am I already expressing doubt in your ability, or are you trying to reassure yourself?"

He shrugged. "A little of both, but I want you to know you can count on me. I don't really know what all you've gone through in the past few weeks. What I saw last night and this morning gave me some idea."

I scraped the inside of my yogurt container, turning the cup as I went along. "They're really good kids. They're just going through a tough time, you know?"

"Yeah, definitely. I didn't mean they weren't. Of course, it's all tough, for everyone, really—"

Oh God. He was about to go off the rails again. "Sperm Whale."

"What?"

"It's okay."

He huffed.

I continued, "I also want to reassure you about Lucy. Her tantrums don't happen all the time. I mean, it can freak you out at first."

He nodded. "What else do I need to know?"

"Mikey doesn't talk. His one a.m. screams are a regular occurrence, and it's pretty much the only thing proving his vocal cords do, indeed, work. I let him take Bunny with him everywhere. He is slower to warm up to new people, and he curls up into a ball when he feels anxious about things around him, most often when Lucy is having one of her fits. He's quite affectionate and has his own ways of expressing himself nonverbally. Lucy will likely help you interpret if you get stumped."

"Got it. Lucy?"

No, Grant. You don't have it all. Mikey also has the most tender touch when he wants to soothe Lucy or me. His face is wonderfully expressive, and if he doesn't use actions, you can still often guess what he's feeling. When he lets go of Bunny, you get a jolt of hope and joy he has reached a certain amount of security to let go of the pain and live in the moment. His smile, rare though it may be, is adorable.

I wasn't sure why I didn't share the rest of my thoughts. Maybe it was because I wanted to test him. I continued with Lucy.

"She has a ton of energy, most of it positive and inventive. Lynette, the daycare provider Brian and Elaine used, says the tantrums are new. I don't know if they'll go away again as she adjusts to her new situation or if they are new in general. They really are less frequent than at the start, so I'm hoping they're only related to the whole awfulness of her new life, which is terrible to say, but there it is. She likes things a certain way. Mostly only food, though. I find it easiest to ask her for specifics. When she gets high-tempered, she'll sometimes throw stuff, but the tantrums are short-lived. She apologizes and, in a snap, continues into active and happy mode."

He accepted everything without hesitation. I supposed it helped he'd already seen some of it earlier. What he hadn't seen was her dancing and singing around the apartment or how she helped with everything without being asked. She took care of her brother and easily shared affection. She was inquisitive and smart, and her smile and laughter melted my heart.

"Look, about last night," Grant started.

"I'm sorry about how I reacted. I get it. You were only trying to help. I was tired. I'm not at my best in the middle of the night, obviously. I don't have any idea how mothers of newborns do it."

"Does Mikey have any memory of it?"

I shrugged. "I haven't been able to figure that out yet."

"And he's been doing it every night?"

"Yes."

"God, you must be exhausted."

He had no idea. "The past few days have been harder. Much more change and upheaval."

"I'm not helping by providing more change, am I?"

He wasn't wrong, but if things worked out with him, it might get better than it had been. "I don't know yet."

"Fair enough. Let me attempt to earn my keep. You go take a long, hot shower and take your time getting ready. I'll entertain the kids."

"An offer I cannot possibly refuse." I stood to take care of my breakfast dishes. "I'm not sure when Layla is going to stop by. Consider this fair warning you might be on your own with her while I give myself the spa treatment."

He chuckled. "Thanks for the heads-up."

When I finally emerged from my imaginary spa, feeling closer to my old self than I had in days, I discovered my sister had arrived, and she and Grant were playing nicely together. In fact, they all were as they attempted to create the tallest tower they could with any object they could find.

"What about these?" Lucy held up two wooden train-track pieces.

"Perfect!" Layla said. "Try them out."

Lucy clapped excitedly after successfully stacking them. The kids, Layla, and Grant had started with a foundation of blocks, but also stuck in there were books, a couple of stuffed animals, and miscellaneous toys flat and stable enough for building. It was a remarkable feat. The stuffed animals looked like they surely would have brought about a collapse.

Mikey saw me first and raced over with a hug. I lowered myself to return the hug properly, and he put his small hands on my cheeks and smiled. God, he had a special talent for giving me all the gooey feelings. "Are you saying I clean up good?"

"You definitely do," Layla said. "Feeling human again?"

"I really am."

"Good. You look better. Now, the next step in the plan is to get all of us out of here. I'm taking the kids to the hotel for swimming and whatever else. The whale over here is leaving too."

"To where?"

"Who cares?"

I glared at her.

She continued, ignoring me. "The point is even though we couldn't get you back to work today, at least you can actually take some time for you."

I looked at Grant, who was helping Lucy add another railroad track to the tower, which started leaning precariously.

He looked up at me. "What? Don't worry about me. I've got plans."

"See?" Layla added. "Okay, you rascals. Let's grab your swim gear and go have an amazing morning with Auntie Layla!"

"Can I knock down the tower?" Lucy asked.

"Of course. It's the best part!" Grant agreed as he let Lucy take the first blow, and he helped scatter the rest before they all picked up the debris and returned it to its rightful place.

Before Grant left, I made sure he had my phone number, and as Layla and the kids hovered at the door, I asked her, "You really don't know or care where he's going?"

"Not much, no. But if it will set your heart at ease, he said something about getting familiar with the area and finding the library. I sent him a screenshot of a map on my phone since his phone is shit." She put her hand on my arm. "Try to relax while we're all gone, okay? Everyone is fine, and you can let go of the anxiety for a bit. We're going to solve all the problems later. Right now, do whatever you need to do to take care of yourself."

I pulled her into a hug then followed up with goodbye hugs to Lucy and Mikey. With the close of the door, I turned around to face the rest of the apartment, taking in the quiet emptiness. Really, it was just quiet. Everywhere I looked, I saw the kids. There was the stool in the kitchen for them to reach the sink. The place mats that Mikey made on a daily basis. The pictures on the wall. Gemmi would be happy.

I considered keeping the daycare visits I'd planned, but the kids needed to be a part of those visits. I relied on their reactions and instincts, since mine had already failed them before. I called to cancel, knowing it probably meant losing the spots by the time I was ready to start again. The whole thing set me on edge anyway after dealing with Sophie. On Sunday, I'd called again, leaving her a message to say we'd decided the arrangement wouldn't work after all.

On Monday, I'd called again in case she hadn't received the messages. The exchange had quickly gotten nasty. Her tone lost all traces of kindness or courtesy. She'd demanded I send her a check for the next two weeks for the contractual notice for termination. I argued we had only used the two-week trial. She'd countered, saying the trial ended at the close of business Friday.

"I left you messages about the situation over the weekend," I said.

"I don't deal with work on the weekend. It's my family time. I'm sure you're the same."

"Which is why I called you first thing today."

"If you don't pay me the two weeks, I will take you to court. I've done this before, and I have won."

"You go ahead and do that." As I'd hung up, I was shaking. I couldn't believe I'd ever thought she was the right person to take care of my kids. I didn't know what I'd do if she did take it to court. I couldn't lose another day of work to go there. Paying her was more than a day's earnings, but if I lost my job, I was out a whole lot more money than simply paying Sophie for two weeks. She'd continued to call daily, leaving messages since I refused to talk to her.

Instead of dealing with any daycare stress while I had the apartment to myself, I chose the TV. And later, sleep.

Layla and the kids returned before Grant did, giving me time to work out the new plans with her, since she no longer needed to stay the rest of the week.

"I can, you know."

"I do, and I appreciate the offer more than I've actually told you. Instead, I'm giving Grant a chance these next couple of days, and you can save your offer for next week if things don't work out."

She gave me a hug. "Okay. But call me if he doesn't work out after only a day, all right? Don't wait until you've fallen apart again." She pulled back and smiled as if reassuring me she wasn't entirely scolding.

"Yeah, yeah."

Grant returned as Layla was leaving. "Don't fuck this up, Sperm," she told him without preamble.

"Right."

Lucy skipped up to Grant and grabbed his hand. "Come play cars, Sperm Whale."

He joined her, and I returned to my game of Candyland with Mikey. A few minutes later, my phone rang. I almost let it go, assuming it would be Sophie harassing me again, but when I looked, I saw Zach's number.

Oh. Right.

I got up and answered as I walked to the dining room. "Hey."

"Hey, Jules. How's the chaos going?"

"It's something new every day."

Cars crashed in the background, and Lucy and Grant's voices cheered together.

"Is someone else there?" Zach asked.

"Well, that's the new thing of the day. Grant."

"Who's Grant?"

"Lucy and Mikey's uncle. On their mom's side. Look, why don't I meet you somewhere so we can talk? I can leave the kids with him." I looked over at Grant to see if he was listening, and he nodded. "Twenty minutes?"

Getting the okay from the kids, I took off and hoped the new thing of the day passed the first test of the caretaking experiment, not yet knowing who needed to pass it.

Chapter Sixteen

I met Zach at the Taco Bell around the corner.

"I don't get it. He quit his job and totally left everything in California? He's their uncle. He couldn't use some vacation and plan a visit?"

This is why people should tell stuff to friends and family a lot earlier. It was like I was on some TV show. I imagined the audience yelling at me, saying, "You idiot. You should have told him *ages* ago." I would probably agree with that audience.

"He is their uncle, and yet he isn't. It's complicated."

"I'm listening."

Of course he was. Except it seemed like he had gone into pharmacist-listening mode instead of boyfriend mode. Maybe detached-listener mode was better.

Direct. Getting right to the point seemed the best way to do it.

"Lucy and Mikey are biologically mine and Grant's."

"What?" The pharmacist expression was gone. Zach was back.

"Brian and Elaine ran into all kinds of problems while trying to have kids on their own. They tried in vitro fertilization using my eggs and Grant's sperm."

Zach didn't say anything at first, presumably taking time to process, I guessed—and hoped. Or he was working out the biology.

"Okay. Um, wow. This is all really unexpected. Why you? I mean, I gathered from our drive up to Duluth you and your brother weren't exactly close."

I told him the story, including the part about how I had never wanted kids, which might have surprised him more than anything else. If he had foreseen a future for us before we originally broke up, I wondered whether or not having that information would have made it easier for him to let me go.

"Why in the world didn't you tell me all this before?" he asked.

"I honestly didn't know how you'd react."

"About which part?"

"Any of it. Not wanting kids. Donating my eggs. Lucy and Mikey in some ways really being mine."

We sat in silence. I waited for Zach to respond.

"Well, I'm glad you made the right choice, anyway," he said.

"Which choice?"

"Taking responsibility for your kids. You might not have wanted kids, but obviously, they're meant to be with you."

"So, what, God intended for Brian and Elaine to die to rectify some mistake?"

"Jeez, Julie, that's not what I meant at all. I'm not your brother, okay?"

"It sure sounded like you were making a judgment."

"I'm saying I'm especially glad you didn't agree with Layla's proposition. If something had to happen to Lucy and Mikey's parents, I'm glad they came back to you."

"I almost said yes to Layla."

I wasn't sure what crossed his expression—sadness, disappointment, or maybe surprise. Whatever it was, he recovered quickly.

"What changed your mind?" he asked.

"I don't know. It felt right."

"What's Grant's deal, then? Does he want custody of the kids instead? Or shared custody?"

"No, I don't think so. He says he wants to do the right thing and help, be a part of their lives."

"Do you believe him?"

I didn't like Zach's tone. I didn't like how he was the second person to doubt me. I didn't like how I was doubting myself. "I don't have any reason to think otherwise."

"You have every reason to question his motives. You don't actually know this guy, do you? He randomly shows up on your doorstep—three weeks late—and conveniently has no money and no address? Everything about this situation is suspect, and you don't see the problem?"

"Yeah, when you arrange all the facts just so and forget everything else, then sure, there are some things to be aware of. I'm not as naïve as you sometimes assume I am."

"This is probably the first time I've ever worried you were."

"Brian told me Elaine had no contact with her parents. A while back, Lucy confirmed this. Grant said he only heard about his sister's death last week. I'd say, if anything, he's the clueless one for dropping everything and moving to the other side of the country to a family he's never met."

"So he gets a free ride with you now."

"He's helping with the kids. I'd say it's working out for both of us."

Zach leaned back and sipped his drink. "Are you saying you trust him already?"

"I neither trust nor mistrust him. He's family. Sometimes, we decide things differently with family. We take them at face value."

He raised an eyebrow.

I shrugged. "Family in general. My own immediate family is different. I have too much experience with them."

The slurping noise from Zach's straw indicated an empty drink. He leaned back on the table again. "How can you be sure he won't be as bad as Sophie's?"

Nothing like having your boyfriend throw you a sucker punch. Like I hadn't beaten myself up enough for the situation with Sophie. "Ah, I fucked up with her. Therefore, my judgment can no longer be trusted at all?"

He didn't answer.

"What's this really about?" I asked. "I'm guessing it's not about custody or whatever anymore."

"Fifteen minutes ago, I found out you've been holding onto a secret about how these kids really belong to you and not your sister or even your brother, and the 'father' waltzed into town, and this strange guy is now closer to my girlfriend than I am. Or possibly I'm a little disappointed some random guy gets to live with you, but I can't even spend the night anymore."

"He's not some random guy, and it's not like he's sharing my bed or anything."

"For the love of... Give me something here, will you? Could I get a little reassurance I actually have some importance in your life?"

I wrapped my hand around his. "You do." Understanding the real problem, I lowered my prickly defenses. "I'm sorry. It's a lot to take in. Trust me. I get it. I'm still trying to figure everything out, and right after I do, something new comes my way. Grant's arrival is going to be a good thing, though. I need the help right now."

"You'll find a new daycare as soon as you can, right?"

"I honestly can't say. Come back with me and hang out for a while. Get to know him to set your mind at ease."

"I can't. I've got a gig tonight."

"Then trust me. Trust I know what I'm doing."

He slid into the chair next to me and stroked my face. As his hand embraced the back of my neck and head, he moved in and gave me a gentle kiss. I loved how soft his lips were.

"I do trust you. I'm sorry too."

I leaned into him, and he put his arms around me. "I'm beat, Zach, and I don't want the kids to be scared or sad anymore."

"At least having Grant around let you take a break for dinner with me tonight, right?"

I merely nodded, since I hadn't found our dinner to be much of a break. Having to defend my life and decisions the entire time didn't relax me. I was doing a poor job of navigating my life.

"Maybe you can slip out later, too, and come see me at the Crosswalk. We can hang out between sets."

"We'll see. Let me see how Grant did while I was gone. I don't want to overwhelm him as he goes into tomorrow on his own." What I really hoped for was to go to bed early so I might make it through a full day of work without falling asleep on the job. Or losing my cool with a guest.

We walked out and stopped at his car. He offered to drive me back, but I wanted the walk to loosen up and clear my head. He took me into his arms and kissed me long and deep, and it felt good, easing the tension between us.

"I miss you," he whispered into my ear afterward.

"I miss you too."

He gave me another quick kiss, and I went on my way.

As the warm breeze floated across my face, I wondered how I missed the changeover from the cool April temperatures to those of mid-May, signaling summer's upcoming arrival. I wasn't even sure if I had summer clothes for the kids. I wondered whether they played sports or something I didn't know about and if I was supposed to be signing them up for stuff. *Fabulous. A whole new set of things to worry about.* It was no surprise my mother always ended up stepping back from us. She couldn't keep up with everything without getting overwhelmed.

When I walked into the apartment, I found things well under control with Grant. He was working on a farm puzzle with Mikey while Lucy built with Legos nearby. The kitchen was already cleaned up from dinner, and the kids appeared calm and content. That should have made me happy. Instead, a wave of jealousy and anger hit me. I was gone an hour and a half, and Grant had everything under control. I couldn't remember the last time things were that calm and easy for me.

"Hey, that was a short evening," Grant called out.

"Zach's got a gig tonight, and I thought I'd get the kids to bed so I can turn in early."

"I can put them to bed."

"No, that's—"

"Yes! Uncle Whale can read to us, JuJu! Please?"

"Oh. Fine." *Great. All under control.* I tossed my bag onto the table and tried to deal with the unexpected edge creeping into me. I saw clean dishes in the sink and put them away—a little too loudly. Grant came into the kitchen.

"You all right?"

"I'm fine." I slammed a cupboard door.

"Then maybe you could tone it down. You're scaring the kids."

Of course I am. He's got it all down after only ninety minutes. I glared at him.

"I'm guessing things didn't go well with Zach."

"He's not happy with our living arrangement."

"I don't blame him. I'd be jealous too."

"You've got it all figured out, don't you? I'm not sleeping with you."

"Jesus, I didn't say you should. It's just where guys' brains always go. And what do you mean? What have I got all figured out?"

"Nothing. Go read to the kids like they want."

He gave an exasperated sigh, and we headed to the living room to find it empty. The kids had fled. I darted to their room and found them sitting side by side on Lucy's bed, holding hands. I sat on the edge of the bed. I needed to stop fucking up.

"I'm sorry for scaring you."

Grant was right behind me. "Could I speak with you in the kitchen for a moment?" His tone was icy.

I considered saying no, but we'd already spooked the kids enough. I agreed and told the kids I would be right back. I joined Grant in the kitchen, and before I asked in irritated tones what his problem was, he turned on me in a fierce whisper.

"What have you been doing to these kids?"

"What?"

"I mean, when you get frustrated or impatient, what do you *do* to them?"

"What the *hell* kind of question is that?" I asked. "You drop in out of nowhere only two days ago with no money and no job, weeks after I've been doing all I can to help these kids adjust to a world where their parents no longer exist, and you have the nerve to accuse me of *hurting* them?"

"What else am I supposed to think when I see them acting that way?"

"Oh, I don't know. Maybe it's because they've had to leave everything they knew and have had to meet new people on a daily basis for the past three weeks?"

"There's something more to their behavior."

He stared at me as I worked through what he'd said. No. I couldn't possibly have been missing something that big. I analyzed the kids' behavior to determine if there really was something more going on. I didn't know. With me, the Sperm was way off base, but I could see why he might jump to the wrong conclusion.

"Look, I get why you might think it's me, but I swear to God it's not. My brother was a jerk, but I don't know if he was horrible, and if he was hurting these kids—" I sat down heavily into a chair and put my head in my hands. "I am in way over my head right now. I have no idea what I'm doing."

Grant joined me at the opposite end of the table. I looked up as he ran a hand through his hair. "Fuck."

I listened to the hum of the refrigerator and wondered if it was loud enough to mask our voices. "I need to go check on the kids."

I slipped into their room again, chagrined to find them in their same positions. "I'm sorry, you guys. Look, everything is okay. Do you want to watch TV for a while before we get you ready for bed? You could watch one of your *VeggieTales* DVDs."

Lucy nodded and scooted off the bed, pulling Mikey with her. "Let's watch Lyle!"

Sometimes, I could almost hear the switch. Her excitement about the video overrode everything. Poor Mikey did his best to hop on the wagon. I picked him up, reassured by the arms wrapped around me.

I got them set up and gave each a kiss on the head before I rejoined Grant at the table.

"I'm sorry for being a douchebag," Grant said quietly. "I was totally out of line. You're right. I came waltzing in as though biology gives me the right to anything when instead I should appreciate you letting me walk through the door at all. Thank you for allowing me to stay here and to do the right thing for once in my life."

"What makes you think there might be more going on with them?"

He was quiet for a moment, which gave me another bad feeling. Grant smoothed his hand back and forth on the table, his stare following the motion.

"My dad was good with a belt. He drank a lot but usually preferred to ignore us in his drunken state. Sometimes, he'd see us instead. My mom preferred things less likely to leave permanent marks. Her hand, of course. A fork. You know, because the tines could be sharp but not quite sharp enough to break the skin, even if she pressed really hard." He quickly pulled his gaze away from his hand, which he flexed and released. "I was a little more partial to hiding in the closet. An extra door was always nice to have."

His open confession both surprised me and hurt my heart. We barely knew each other, and he'd shared something deeply personal.

"I'm so sorry." The phrase sounded ridiculously trite. "I think you're wrong, though. Brian and Elaine argued a lot, and I think the kids have learned to hide from adult conflict."

Zach's doubt in me, followed by Grant's accusations and subsequent confession, had me in a tailspin. Grabbing the controls and voicing my opinion leveled me out. I'd been in my brother's home and met Elaine. I'd gotten to know those kids, and while I might have been wrong about their history, I didn't believe I was. Their parents were unhappy, but they didn't take it out on the kids—at least not directly.

"Projecting," he said, resting his head in his hands. "I used to work at a runaway-teen shelter, although some of them weren't necessarily teens. They weren't this young, but they were young enough to share a common expression on their faces, you know? I'm probably projecting. One of the counselors there helped me a lot with how to avoid that when working with the runaways, but obviously, I've forgotten how. I mean, you said there were problems with the daycare." He looked at me and quickly backtracked. "That's not your fault, though. I don't mean... shit. I can't believe I made another accusation. I'm sorry."

I wondered if Grant had started out as one of those runaway teens. Zach was right. I knew almost nothing about Grant, but what I did know was important. He'd kept in contact with Elaine enough to help her and my brother. He'd driven almost nonstop to meet the kids and me. And he'd had a shitty childhood. I didn't know whether it was enough information to trust him. I hoped it was.

"It's okay," I said. "I guess this means we need to get to know each other a little better."

He agreed, and hearing the kids' video approach its end, I asked if he still wanted to put them to bed.

"Yeah, but not if it's going to make you upset. I swear I'm not trying to take over. I came to help."

"I know. I'm fine." I waved him off. I was being stupid. I knew it wasn't a competition, yet I couldn't help feeling like everyone else was better suited to be around the children than I was. My mom had the cookies and bikes. Layla made Lucy laugh within minutes. And next was Grant, who acted completely at ease with them. I wondered why people assumed women held the corner on caretaking.

I gave Grant the rundown on our bedtime routine then gave the kids kisses and hugs good night. The last thing that drifted through my mind before falling asleep was how before the kids, I didn't doubt myself as fully as I suddenly did on a daily basis.

Chapter Seventeen

Zach dropped in at my place the next day between his class and his gig at Crosswalk. We'd had lunch together earlier, and I encouraged him again to stop by and meet Grant to help him feel better about things. He seemed off when he arrived, and after a few minutes, I realized he might be jealous. He looked defensive and kept slipping in "Julie and I did this" or "Julie and I like that" statements. I'd dated a guy several years ago who was the jealous sort, but he had been jealous about everything. It felt different with Zach.

Zach riddled Grant with the standard who-are-you-and-where-do-you-come-from questions. I kept waiting for Grant to babble, but he held his own. Maybe it was because he'd already done the intro routine with me earlier. Or maybe it was because he had readied his own jackpot question for Zach.

"Julie says you do some jazz with a group?"

"Yeah. It's a side thing. We do mostly smaller venues."

"Do you guys do more of a blues or swing kind of traditional jazz? Or are you more fusion?"

Zach's whole demeanor settled down into his customary loose attitude. First with the kids, next with my current partner. The Sperm had magic powers.

"We're more traditional, but I like the fusion stuff. You listen to any fusion?"

Grant shrugged. "You mean like Chick Corea or the Brecker Brothers? Yeah, I've heard a little."

"Cool." Zach nodded. "You should stop by Crosswalk sometime when my band's playing. Sometimes in our second set, we get into fusion or some funk."

I wanted to agree wholeheartedly. If Grant started going, then I wouldn't be expected to go all the time. While his jazz wasn't really my style of music, Zach was a lot of fun to watch—super upbeat, and he clearly loved playing. I usually went to see him and not necessarily his whole band. With my new lifestyle, however, I had a hard time imagining staying up until his usual late start time, which was sad, really.

"Speaking of," Zach said, "I gotta get going." He gave me a kiss and asked about the weekend.

"I've got a thing with my dad on Saturday evening. Afterward?"

"You got it."

I shut the door behind him and turned to Grant. "You know about jazz?"

"Fuck no. I looked a bunch of stuff up earlier today so I'd know a little bit and have something to talk about with him."

I wagged a playful finger. "You gotta stop with the R-rated language with the kids around."

"Oh man, you're right. I'm sorry. I'm working on it, I swear, although I guess it sounds stupid to say 'I swear' in that situation since that's what I'm not supposed to do, but I haven't really been in this family kind of situation in a—"

"So," I interrupted before he took the conversation way off the rails. "You did some research to talk to my boyfriend."

He took a deep breath. "Yeah."

"Why?"

He fell into a chair and ran a hand through his hair. "I just, you know, get really nervous, and when I get nervous, I talk continuously."

I smiled and tried not to laugh. "Um, I already know *that*. I mean, why the research?"

"It gives me something solid to focus on. Keeps me from launching into some stupid babble making me sound like an idiot. I know about four things in tons of different subjects. It's usually enough to get me over the hump." His hand imitated a ride up and over an imaginary hill.

"Makes sense."

"You think so? Because it feels like all kinds of fu—messed-up crazy to me."

"You're prepared. But seriously, you've listened to some Chick Corea?"

"I might have," he said.

"Yeah, right."

He gave me a sheepish smile. "I didn't mean to make that up, but we can look him up and listen to him on YouTube or something, right? Then I'll have some real stuff to bring up next time."

"Oh, now I have to be a part of this?" I gave a mocking shake of my head. "Tut-tut." Of course, I didn't know the difference between fusion jazz and any other brand of jazz either. I'd seen Zach play, but we didn't talk about his music much.

"Either that or listen to me ramble on about every single drugstore I've ever been in as an attempt to sound like I know anything about pharmacy stuff."

"Your two-minute conversation with Zach about music was the more intelligent route, for sure."

"You haven't heard my drugstore stories yet." He grinned. "The PayLess brand of Advil makes me puke. It was a great way to get my mom to think I was sick so I could stay home from school. I used to live by a drugstore so small, it had an honest-to-God soda fountain in back. They still have part of the counter there as a tourist attraction."

"Hmm, about thirty seconds so far but not too bad for stories."

"I've got more. The Rite Aid by the shelter I volunteered at had the cold medicine in aisle ten, while the Walgreens had it in aisle seven. The best deal on candy—"

"Buzz! You lost him at 'candy.'"

"You mean it wasn't my intricate knowledge of product locations?"

Eyeing him with skepticism, I challenged him. "Band-Aids."

"Aisle nine, CVS."

"You are so full of shit."

"Hey, watch your language."

Laughing, I gave him a playful shove as I reached over to the coffee table to grab my laptop. "Okay, Mr. Smarty-Pants. I'll help you make good on your lie about Chick Corea, but this means you owe me."

"I don't know if I like where this is going. What does it mean to owe you?"

"Eh. I'm sure I'll come up with something."

We started with Chick Corea and Branford Marsalis for a few minutes then rapidly spun down into the YouTube vortex while eating Swiss Cake Rolls and drinking Fanta Orange pop. It made me miss Gemmi, because while she liked to go out more often and hit the bars and clubs, she would sometimes humor me and stay in to watch TV and spend way too much time on things like TikTok and other ridiculous videos and photo memes. Zach liked to stay in with me, but there was definitely no gorging on Little Debbies.

For the first time in almost a month, I felt less alone.

"I should head to bed and catch a couple of hours before Mikey wakes up."

"Let me get him tonight. You should get some sleep."

The idea sounded way too appealing. "I don't know if he'll calm down for you." As soon as I said the words, I realized how foolish they sounded. Grant had some magic charm. Obviously, Mikey would be fine for him. *Shouldn't I be happy?*

I agreed to let him try, and I set off to bed.

Right on schedule, Mikey's wails jolted me awake. I'd told Grant he could give it a go, but I got up anyway. I found Grant frozen in the hallway outside the kids' door, looking terrified. I slipped past him and scooped up Mikey like I always had. I hugged him tightly, whispered the soothing words, and stroked the back of his head. When I glanced up at the doorway, Grant was gone.

After I calmed Mikey and tucked him in, I stopped in the living room. Grant was lying on the couch, back to me. Based upon his stiff-looking shoulders, I suspected he was still awake.

"It's okay," I called out softly. "You'll be ready tomorrow."

He didn't respond, and I didn't press. As I got into bed, I considered how a couple of hours earlier, I'd been jealous of Grant's confidence and the idea he would be able to take over my job of comforting Mikey. Not anymore. I empathized far too well with his fear.

The next morning, I woke to both munchkins snuggled up next to me. I reveled in the cozy warmth, laughter slipping out after I considered how far I'd come in finding contentment through sharing a bed with kids. Or maybe the new giddiness of a treasured weekend influenced my mood. Weekends meant no rushing and pushing to get the kids ready to go. With Grant around, though, we'd avoided a lot of chaos during the past couple of days. I warned myself not to get too used to it.

On the other hand, "no use borrowing tomorrow's troubles," as Ms. Lasky at the community center would say. I decided to enjoy the peace while I had it.

I glanced at the clock and saw Mikey's eyes already open, though still a little sleepy. I smiled. He smiled back—a fresh and new one I knew to treasure, since the rest of the day was wildly unpredictable.

"Ready for some breakfast?"

He rubbed his eyes and nodded.

"Let's be quiet in case Sperm Whale is still sleeping, okay?"

Another nod, our expressions indicating a shared conspiracy.

We tiptoed into the kitchen, where I started the coffee while Mikey found a cup and pulled out the milk.

"Do you want to go peek and see if he's awake?"

He set his cup on the table and disappeared into the living room. When he returned, he shook his head.

"Was that a recon mission that just went down?" Grant's tired voice floated our way.

Mikey's eyes grew big, and he covered his mouth as though to quiet himself and his surprise. It seemed like a reassurance of a "before" habit of needing to actually make himself quiet. I grinned at him.

"I guess Mikey still has to work on stealth," I called back.

"Pretty sure you're the one who broke protocol with the coffee aroma and the noisy brewing."

"Are you complaining?"

"Not a chance." He shuffled into view in sweats and a T-shirt, mirroring my sleeping attire. It was amazing how quickly one could get comfortable with appearances when they had to. I worried only briefly about how wild my hair looked after seeing the mess on his head. I was pretty sure he looked better.

He ruffled Mikey's hair. "Hey, Mikeadoodle. Got your own cup of joe going?"

Mikey showed off his cup and took a gulp.

"Good man. We gotta have our morning beverages to brace us for the day ahead, don't we?"

I handed Grant a mug, smiling at the little routine they'd developed. Grant paused the coffeemaker and filled our mugs. I took my first sip and reached into a cabinet for a box.

"I was thinking pancakes this morning, Mikey. What do you think?"

"I want pancakes!" Lucy showed up with an enthusiastic vote.

"Me too," agreed Grant, "but no boxed stuff." He returned the offending package to the cabinet. "I'm going to make you guys the real thing."

"Yay!"

"You can cook too." I didn't muster the same enthusiasm as Lucy.

"Not really. I can make about five things. Pancakes happen to be one of them."

Since the kids were excited, I extinguished my argument. "Is cooking like your conversation starters? Know a little bit about the whole thing?"

He snapped his fingers and pointed at me as though I'd hit the jackpot. "Exactly. Unfortunately, the other four things aren't as impressive." He searched through the cupboards for dishes and pancake ingredients.

"So, what are those four other things?"

"Scrambled eggs, grilled cheese, spaghetti, and ramen noodles."

My jealousy and irritation fell away, and he caught my smile. "I told you the other things were far less impressive."

Secretly, I thanked him for the small gift of shared incompetence. "You've still got me beat by having pancakes on the list. What about mashed potatoes? That's my newest accomplishment."

"Sounds like an addition to the list of many new things to learn. Measuring spoons?"

I pointed at the drawer behind him. "You're welcome to join me in my next cooking lesson with my mom. Actually, I think we're going to try some baking next."

"Count me in."

The kids scampered off to play, apparently not interested in helping cook like they usually were. Maybe they were still getting used to Grant.

As I watched him mix the flour and other dry ingredients, his expression turned serious. "I'm sorry about last night."

"Don't be. Mikey's screams used to scare the crap out of me at first."

"Yeah, but I bet it didn't stop you from going right to him the first time you heard him."

"Only because there was no one else to do it. I had to."

He shifted his weight uncomfortably on each leg and focused on stirring the milk, eggs, and oil. I waited for the onslaught of anxious chatter. None came. His face wore tight lines of worry or frustration. I couldn't quite determine which one.

"Hey," I said, "don't worry about it. I'm used to it by now."

His silence was unnerving. I didn't know what he was battling, but I concentrated on distracting him. I started a new conversation.

"I'm taking the kids to my dad's tonight for dinner. He's invited you to come, too, if you want."

It probably wasn't the best topic switch, as he started to ramble. "Really? I mean, why would he invite me? Wait, I didn't mean it to sound like—I mean—he doesn't know me at all, and I don't know him. Is he worried about me staying here too? I can understand—"

"No, he's not worried. He's being polite, I guess." Chatter was better than silence, except I turned him into a chaotic ball of anxious energy. I tried yet another tack. I got up to find a frying pan big enough for cooking pancakes. "Can you help me figure out when to flip them? I always seem to do it too soon or way too late. I can't get the stove temperature right either."

Success. Everything about him smoothed out again. "It's all in the bubbles. Right before they're ready to pop is the best time to flip."

"Yeah, but how do you *know* when they're in the right-before-they-pop stage?"

His smile returned as he explained the best temperature and how pancakes in the first batch were often practice ones. I couldn't blame him for being nervous about having dinner with my dad. I would feel weird, too, if I were him. Dad had wondered whether I was going to bring Zach. I was glad Zach had to work because I wasn't ready for a true "meet the parents" thing with him at my side. I'd met Zach's parents, a friendly couple and much like Zach himself. The whole thing of getting to know my parents again, however, was strange enough to navigate on my own, let alone with anyone else.

Things with my mom were going okay. We had short check-in conversations every once in a while, and although they weren't anything special, they were still more than we'd ever had. She'd helped with the kids on my first Monday morning after deciding not to return to Sophie's. It was only until I could find someone to come finish my shift at work. What I remembered about her and her ability to handle kids hadn't changed—she wasn't willing to do more than occasional babysitting.

She loved the kids, and they loved spending time with her, yet she maintained a certain distance with them. I recognized it all too well. Where my mother and I *were* improving was in normal, adult conversation. We discovered sharing stories about community-center guests and real-estate clients brought us together in a different way. It was nice.

She was the first person I'd talked to who was unreservedly happy about Grant's arrival. She made it sound like everything was working out according to some secret plan of hers. If he had been part of some master plan, I wished she had clued me in on it.

Chapter Eighteen

Grant gracefully bowed out of coming along with the kids and me to my dad and Nora's house. The kids expressed some trepidation about meeting Nora, yet another new family member, and it took them a little longer to warm up to her. I talked with her awhile as the kids glommed onto the fish tank. I found her fairly down-to-earth, and it didn't take long for her to connect with them through their shared interest in fish. She taught the kids about the variety of fish and creatures in her expansive tank in the living room. I discovered any kid would befriend an adult who took the time to talk to and sincerely listen to them. Later, my dad and I sat on the deck, lemonades in hand, leaving the kids with Nora in the kitchen, happily helping with dinner. My dad asked me about the latest update from Tamara.

"Not much news yet. She's working on finding out if Elaine had any other draft of a will before the one that mirrored Brian's. And now with Grant here, we're kind of wondering if he would have been in some earlier version. But it's likely she didn't have one, so Tamara's continuing to prepare depositions with some of the church officials."

"You probably don't have a will either. Do you?"

I shook my head.

"Something else for Tamara to help you with. Sooner rather than later, okay?"

"Yeah, you're right. Until then, if something happens to me... Layla and Sheila."

He nodded, but the conversation brought us up short.

My dad finally broke the painful silence. "How are you enjoying being a mom?"

"It's exhausting. Hard. Stressful. Then there are those moments when it surprises me how much I actually like it."

He chuckled. "Yep, your mom used to say the same thing. She might have appreciated having the daycare option, though. I don't know why we didn't look into care for you kids. A couple of days a week probably would have helped a lot."

I felt contradictory emotions. It was like he was saying Mom would have been happier if she hadn't had to be around us. Yet I knew I was happier when I went to work. It probably wasn't fair of me to hold such a double standard. My mother deserved to have her own career like anyone else.

"Daycare's a crapshoot, let me tell you."

He raised his eyebrows. I told him the story.

"You'll win easily in small claims court."

"Possibly at the cost of my job, though. My boss, Carl, has been giving me a lot of grief. I can't miss any more work."

His silence left me wondering whether he had no more to add to the conversation or was simply thinking about it all. I knew I should talk to Sophie. Possibly, I could get her to worry about how she'd left the kids outside and unsupervised on the last day. However, I was barely functioning in normal conversations with people I liked, let alone with someone who angered me. If I came across as unstable or threatening, that would definitely not work in my favor.

Lucy fluttered through the screen door and fetched us for dinner. If my dad had anything to add, he didn't share it with me.

Dinner was spaghetti with homemade sauce, salad—but only the carrots and celery for Lucy—and garlic cheese bread.

"We made the garlic, JuJu," Lucy told me proudly. "Nora put it in the pressy thing, and we had to squeeze really hard, and it made garlic for the bread!"

"More perfect garlic I have never seen made." Nora smiled.

"I can't wait to try it," I told the kids, patting my stomach in anticipation.

"They sure are pros in the kitchen. You've been teaching them well."

I nearly choked on my food with laughter. Lucy giggled, and Mikey grinned, making me laugh harder.

Nora looked at my dad. "I'm not sure what I said."

He merely shrugged.

"I'm sorry," I mustered after taking a deep breath. "It's... Well, I'm *terrible* in the kitchen. Them learning anything from me is highly unlikely."

"You're getting better, JuJu!" Lucy's unexpected compliment touched me.

"Only because of your help."

She beamed.

After dinner, we all agreed upon ice-cream cones from Dad and Nora's freezer to enjoy on our walk to a nearby park. Watching the kids travel the sidewalk on the way to the park provided entertaining insight into their personalities. Mikey alternated between holding my hand and walking slightly ahead of me yet at a steady rate so he could eat his cone. Lucy would skip ahead then stop to get a decent bite of her cone.

The walk gave me insight into my dad too. Once, when I looked behind me to make sure we hadn't lost them, I noticed the affection between him and Nora. They held hands and walked the casual stroll of two people comfortable with each other, and I wondered if I had ever seen the same easiness between him and my mother. I also wondered whether what my mother said was true about them splitting up because they'd agreed it was best for us. Maybe she'd wished they could have simply stopped cheating on one another.

Or maybe I was reading more into it than I should. Nora was my dad's fourth wife. For all I knew, he'd strolled like that with every single one of them.

At the playground, I chased the kids around then left them to dig tunnels and make castles in the sandpit. I joined my dad and Nora on a nearby bench. We watched the kids work seamlessly to make whatever creation they had in mind. They communicated effortlessly; even Lucy spoke very little.

"Twin telepathy?" Nora asked.

"They definitely have a connection, especially now while Mikey's not talking."

"Clearly, you've picked up on ways to communicate with him too," she added, giving me a smile. "It's been pretty impressive how much conversation passes between you two despite his silence."

I sat with that observation and analyzed it. Mikey was quiet, but I had never really considered him silent. Increasingly, I discovered he had more and more to say, and I learned how to read his moods and feelings. More than anything, I didn't want him ever to feel forgotten again.

"I bet Lucy talks for him a lot," my father suggested, correctly. "She's a lot like you, Jujubee. You used to do a lot of talking for Brian."

"Obviously not enough to stifle him, since he sure found ways to speak for himself later."

He shook his head. "No, I don't mean like that. More like you spoke on his behalf—in defense of him. Mostly when you were both younger. I remember one weekend, taking you two to the park. Your mom was taking a client round to some houses, and Layla had something going on with a friend. Some kid who probably wasn't much older than Brian, maybe two or three years old, threw some of those little playground rocks at him. You marched right on over and gave the kid a piece of your mind." He chuckled. "I thought we were going to have to make a quick getaway, but you eased up, and then you crouched down to your brother and said, all grown-up-like in spite of your seven-year-old self, 'Brian, you have to stand up for yourself. You tell kids to stop if they're being mean to you. And if they don't, then you come get me, okay?' You were a spitfire, all right."

I didn't remember the incident, but I did sense a familiarity in the lecture to my brother. "Mom taught me to stand up for myself."

He nodded appreciatively. "Sounds about right. Your mom can be a real spitfire too."

I snuck a glance at Nora to see her reaction to my dad's compliment about his ex-wife. If she felt any discomfort, her face didn't show it. Layla, unfortunately, was probably the only one of us forced into taking my mom's words to heart. I was proud of how strong she stood against others, defending her right to be who she was to a world wasting its time attacking her. Worse still was that one of the "mean kids" was her own brother. More appalling was how I seemed not to be there through much of it. I hoped she'd been able to get help when she needed it.

When the kids' energy finally waned, we trekked back to my dad's house and wrapped up the evening.

"I'm glad you invited us, Dad."

"You're always welcome."

I let the comment go, because even if it was true, he'd never called or tried hard to keep in contact before. I realized I was glad he'd made good on the offer that time. There were parts of his life I wished I had never known, but I missed many other things about him, things I thought I'd forgotten. I recalled my kitchen homework sessions and my subsequent move to my bedroom. Sure, I had moved there because of my distress over his affair with his secretary, but not more than a couple of weeks later, my dad bought me a new desk. I felt both happy and guilty at the same time. I had already started to miss working in the kitchen. His presence reassured me, and his thoughtfulness in buying a desk without me asking for one felt nice. Back then, I didn't know how to differentiate his behavior regarding his marriage from his actions with his family.

It occurred to me I still wasn't sure how to separate it all. I had been taking all of his affairs personally, but surely, I could let them go. And if my mother really was okay with it all, I should have been okay too. My father loved me. Maybe his love for me should be enough.

I shooed the kids into his house to pack up anything they'd brought from home. As we waited, my phone rang, and I took it out, only to growl in frustration. I held the phone up to my dad. "It's Sophie again."

He held out his hand. "Pass it on over."

"What for?"

Palm still outstretched, he hooked his fingers inward. I handed him the phone.

He pressed the talk button. "Trevor Mercer. No, she's not available to talk to you. I'm her legal counsel. You can speak to me instead."

I couldn't quite hear Sophie's response.

"Yes, she is aware you intend to challenge her end of the contract, except I don't advise you to do so."

All I heard was the tone of her voice, high and challenging.

"Most judges will recognize that since 'close of business' is not specifically stipulated in the contract, the spirit of the clause indicates the provider's interest in finding new clients to fill the spot, which could only happen over the weekend, which you then communicated you do not do, although clearly, you've negated this claim again by calling Ms. Mercer today, a Saturday, signaling a troubling inconsistency. Further, evidence supports extenuating circumstances apply regarding the level of care the children received. Finally, it is my understanding when Ms. Mercer arrived on the last day within the trial period, her child was under attack by another, all while you were absent from an area requiring supervision. Should this altercation have escalated before Ms. Mercer arrived, I believe it would be she who would be taking you to court. Now, if you have any other questions, you may direct them to my office, Mercer and Associates. Additional calls to Ms. Mercer will be considered harassment with appropriate charges to follow."

More angry tones from Sophie.

"Yes, I understand. Good day." He hung up the phone and passed it back to me. "There. You don't have to worry about her anymore. She won't be pursuing her complaint against you."

Holy shit. My jaw might have actually dropped open during the interchange. "Dad. What? Oh my God, that was awesome."

"You have enough on your plate right now. It's the least I could do."

My awe slowly converted to gratitude, followed by my own raised eyebrows that time. "Under attack? Altercation? You do realize you were talking about four-year-olds, don't you?"

His matter-of-fact expression softened into a smirk. "Ten-dollar words for a fifty-cent claim can be very effective."

I flung my arms around him, startling him. "Thanks, Dad."

"Get some rest, Jujubee. I want to see your fire come back again."

I gathered the kids and thanked Nora for a delicious dinner and for letting the kids help. As Lucy and Mikey sped to the car, I suddenly considered my dad's use of the word "altercation."

"Dad? What if Brian was hurting Elaine? Would it make any difference with the will?"

A cloud filled my dad's expression and unsettled me. Then the cloud passed, and his voice slipped back into its normal, even tones.

"What makes you suspect this was happening?"

"Something Grant said. He thought maybe—" I paused, deciding it might not be a good idea to reveal the accusations against me.

"Well, based on some of the kids' behaviors, he thought it was possible Brian and Elaine were hurting them, except I don't think the theory fits. His observation isn't all wrong, though. Maybe they saw something else. Brian and Elaine didn't seem quite happy together."

Dad put his hands in his pockets and didn't say anything. I wished I knew what he was thinking.

"I'll let Tamara know. A relationship under duress could certainly be an angle to pursue. I'm not sure if it's one that benefits you directly."

"What about Grant? Could it help him?"

"Perhaps. We're still in a long haul of information gathering, so there's time enough to zero in on the endgame."

I thanked him again and left him to ponder the situation. I hadn't told Grant about contesting the will, and since he hadn't asked about it, I assumed he didn't necessarily know anything. With my concern over Brian and Elaine's relationship, I worried about telling him anything at all. If Brian had been worse than I thought, and if he was hurting Elaine, I couldn't imagine how Grant would feel about me, the monster's sister, having Elaine's kids.

Chapter Nineteen

Four days straight at work with no kid interruptions or drama. I had gone home each day at the beginning of the week filled with relief. Grant was getting on great with the kids. If he struggled or secretly hated it, he did a good job of fooling me. The kids were settling in too. The past couple of days had even been tantrum-free.

I came home to a quiet apartment. I reveled in the silence and memories of the days when I plopped down on my couch—back when it was mostly a couch and not a bed—and napped or watched whatever TV show I wanted. Back then, I snacked on chips and salsa, later having it for dinner too. And yet, it was only a memory. As well as things had been going the past few days, I was okay with living in the past. My present didn't threaten me as much anymore.

I looked around for a note but didn't see one. They were probably at the park. I glanced out the window to see if Grant's car was still in the lot but didn't see it. I called Grant to find out when they would be back for dinner.

No answer. I left a message but saw their absence as a sign of them having a good time. Or Grant had silenced his phone so as not to distract from flirting with some single mom at the park. I smiled at the idea and nearly laughed as I imagined the rush of information pouring out of his mouth as his nervousness kicked in. Or maybe he didn't get nervous when flirting. He had the looks to boost him, and some women might see charm in his nervous chatter. I supposed I could have seen the same charm had our meeting happened under different circumstances. I kicked off my shoes, grabbed a box of crackers, and crash-landed onto the couch, hoping the remote lay within arm's reach.

Thirty minutes and one rerun of *Friends* later, I still hadn't heard back from Grant. No texts. I called him again. It occurred to me the calls were jumping straight to voicemail. If I hadn't thought to feel nervous, my body helped bring me to it as my heart pounded and a jittery restlessness took over. I stood and paced. *Why isn't he answering my call or returning my messages?*

An accident? If there really was a God, it couldn't possibly be so cruel. Brian's God, maybe, but not Lulu's or Mikey's. I stared through the window, pointlessly bouncing my eyes on every single car in the lot, imagining the Explorer simply sat, parked, waiting for Grant and the kids to bound out of it. I called Gemmi.

"Mai, it's only been a half hour, right?"

"Forty minutes now."

"A little over a half hour. Not long at all. Probably his phone died, and they're stuck in traffic."

"Where would they have gone involving a traffic jam? And wouldn't he have a car charger? What if they got in an accident? What if..." I didn't want to voice the other fear I'd been stuffing down for the past week.

"What if what?"

"What if he took them?" I whispered.

"Loca mamacita. You've become a crazy little mama. Forty minutes, mai. It's nothing. Okay?"

I hung up, my fears somewhat tamped down. I was sure she was right. Plus, I probably overestimated Grant and his likelihood of owning a car charger. He'd been using buy-by-the-minute phones until recently, and his cash flow likely prohibited the purchase of accessories.

I suddenly understood our workout maniacs at the community center. I could have used a treadmill or a rowing machine to distract me from my increasing anxiety. I cleaned the kitchen instead, scrubbing away an unaccustomed agitation.

Four forty-five. Still no answer on Grant's phone. I called Gemmi again.

"An hour and fifteen minutes, Gem. I don't know when they left. He didn't leave a note, which means either he intended for them to be home before I got back, or he doesn't want me to know where they are."

"Okay. Let's think this through for a minute. I listened to the traffic news on all the different stations for you, and there haven't been any major accidents. A couple of fender benders. One on 35E and another on Highway 10. If we go with the accident route, those locations don't make sense."

"What if it wasn't on the highway? They don't talk about those."

"Yeah, okay. I guess we could call hospitals. This isn't a TV show, though. I mean, is anyone in an ER actually going to give us information?" Gemmi asked.

"I don't know. Fine. What about if he took them? Is it too early to call the police?"

"That's major stuff you're talking about. Don't be ringing that bell too soon."

"What is too soon?" I heard my voice rise to a horribly loud and high pitch. "What if he left with them at lunchtime? Or earlier? I haven't talked to him since this morning, and it would be an almost seven-hour start. They could be anywhere!"

"Or they're still in town because it never crossed his mind to take them away. What is up with you? Think rationally."

"Fine. Help me with rational ideas. One, he arrives at my doorstep out of nowhere and at the exact convenient time I need his help. Two, he tries to act all victim and hero at the same time with being broke, supposedly wanting to do the right thing. Three, the kids trust him and love him. Four, he is biologically their father and therefore has every legal right to custody."

"Five," Gemmi said forcefully, "he concedes to all of your decisions and loves those kids. People who love their children don't go taking them away from their families."

"They do if they think the family is wrong for them."

"Qué locura. Okay. Fine. We play your game. Go see if any of the kids' stuff is missing. Like clothes and stuff. He wouldn't leave without packing some things for them, right?"

It was a place to start.

I went into the kids' room. It wasn't like they had a ton of stuff, so I had a hard time determining whether anything was missing. Bunny was nowhere to be found, but Mikey took Bunny with him everywhere. Pillows were still on the beds, and Lucy's doll remained nestled in the comforter. Clothing was missing. I raced out to the living room. Grant's big duffel bag was gone as well as his clothes. I looked for other traces of him. His book still lay on the coffee table. I couldn't find much else. My heart pounded harder. My hands shook, and breathing suddenly became unmanageable.

My phone rang. I didn't recognize the number.

"Hello?" I barely recognized my voice.

"J?"

"Where are you?"

"We're fine. Everyone's fine. We're at JP's. The car died, and I had to get it towed. We were at a park near the laundromat and on the way home when my car completely kicked the bucket. I tried to call you, but my phone died, too, which meant I couldn't call anyone for a tow truck, so the kids and I had to walk a couple of blocks to a store and borrow a phone there, and then after I got off the phone with the gas station, Lulu had a meltdown, which meant we had to get out of the store, and she finally calmed down when the tow truck arrived and she got to watch the whole process, but then when she found out we'd have to get in the truck to go to the gas station, she flipped out again, and Mikey was nearly in a ball at that point…"

I allowed him to rattle on while I closed my eyes and waited for the initial relief to replace the panic that had suffused my body for the past ninety minutes. I grabbed my wallet and keys.

"Okay," I interrupted. "I'm on my way."

"Okay."

I thought he said something else—probably another apology, as there had been a couple of others within his ramble—but I'd already hung up. I didn't want to hear any more.

JP's was my usual gas stop, located not far away. One of Gemmi's brothers used to work there and gave me free pop when I visited. When he left, I kept going there. It was one of the places I told Grant about to help him get acclimated to the area. At least he'd had the sense to take the car where I recommended. At least he finally called. At least he apologized.

As unfair as all the calming statements were in my head, I used them as an attempt to keep the rising anger away. It wasn't working because one more "at least" expression kept intruding and brought an overpowering anger.

At least he didn't take the kids and skip town.

Only moments after I got out of the car, the kids came running through the door of JP's and into my arms. I held them as close as possible, yet it wasn't close enough.

"I'm so happy and relieved to see you two. I was worried."

"Why were you worried, JuJu?" Lucy asked in a cheerful voice.

"It's a little later than I expected. I thought I'd see you sooner. I bet you're hungry for dinner. Should we go home and eat?"

They readily agreed, showing off baggies with crumbs remaining from eaten-up Goldfish crackers. I stood and finally looked at Grant, anger bubbling up. "No note. No messages. No call. No nothing. *An hour and a half.*"

"Here, Lulu, Mikey." He handed them their booster seats. "Why don't you take these and go wait for us in JuJu's car, okay?" He looked at me after they ran off to fulfill his request. "I'm sorry. Everything fell apart, and I obviously didn't make phone calls in the right order."

"Some of the kids' clothing was missing. Your bag was gone. All of your clothes were gone."

He stared blankly at me. "I don't get your point. We went to do laundry."

"The apartment building has a laundry room."

"Yeah. I didn't know about it until Lucy told me after we'd stuffed all of our clothes into the washers at the laundromat." I heard a touch of impatience in his voice.

"I thought you took the kids." I turned and started back to the car. Grant grabbed my arm.

"What?"

"Let go of me," I snarled, pulling my arm out of his hand.

He released his grip immediately. "You need to tell me exactly what you mean by your accusation." His expression was as fierce as I had ever seen it. "'Took the kids.' As in kidnapped them?"

"Yes."

"Jesus, why the fuck would you jump to that conclusion?"

"Because I don't know you! I don't know anything. And everything was missing," I said.

"My clothes were gone. *That's* what's got you going? So, what, this entire week was an act on my part? I should have stayed in California and checked out Hollywood if I'm such an amazing actor."

The only thing that kept me from slapping him right then was the kids.

"Do you have money for the bus? I don't want you in my car right now."

His expression tightened. "Yeah. I'm good."

I didn't wait any longer. I strode to my car, but before I got in, I leaned with my back against it and took a deep breath, head in my hands. After regaining control, I got inside and checked that the kids' seat belts were buckled. As I pulled away, I avoided looking at Grant. He stood where I left him, and I wondered about what I'd done and whether I had destroyed the one week when things had finally taken a turn for the better.

The kids stayed inordinately quiet on the short drive home. I glanced in the rearview mirror to see Mikey hiding behind Bunny and Lucy staring straight ahead with her hands clasped in her lap. I'd made another big mistake, yet I didn't want to admit I'd overreacted.

As we walked up the steps to the apartment, I tried to overcome it all. "Sounds like you had a little adventure this afternoon, huh? I bet watching the tow truck in action was fun."

No response. When I opened the door, both kids shot past me and went straight to their room. *Shit. Okay, J. Hold it together for a little while longer.* I debated following them and opted for getting dinner ready instead. Not taking any chances, I focused on peanut butter and jelly, spreading the exact right amount on the bread, edge to edge. I leaned into the calming effect of the methodical concentration on the task. I pulled out the new Doc McStuffins character plates we'd bought at Target last weekend. I counted out eight baby carrots. Poured the milk.

I was ready to approach the kids again. I knocked gently on their door before entering. They sat on Lucy's bed, holding each other's hands and clinging to Bunny and Dolly respectively with their other arms. I knelt by the side of the bed.

"Hey. It's okay. I'm sorry. I'm not exactly sure what's going on, but I'm sorry. Tell me what's happening."

"You and Sperm Whale got mad. We're supposed to go to our room when Mama and Daddy are mad. We're not allowed to talk or come out until they remember us."

Don't cry. Don't cry. Don't cry. I took a deep breath. I imagined them sequestered for far too long. I should have followed them into their room immediately. I should have known that by then. Wordlessly, I held my arms out, and they fell into them. Again, I tried to hold them as tightly as possible, trying to make them a part of me, to make them know I would never forget them.

We ate dinner, and about halfway through, the kids finally opened up about their afternoon at the laundromat, the park, and the tow truck. As I listened to Lucy's animated chatter and Mikey's giggles—one of his newer, more regular and beautiful sounds—my chest tightened as the guilt pressed down on it. To hear Lucy tell the story, Grant handled the situation well by making everything manageable for them. Lucy admitted getting mad after the car broke down, which Mikey emphasized by kicking his legs really hard, making his whole body shake. She scowled briefly at her brother, then she skipped right into a detailed description of the tow truck man and riding high up in the truck to the gas station, which must have been a bumpy ride, based upon Mikey's bounce in his chair.

It was after 7:30 p.m. by the time we finished dinner and played a quick game of I-Spy Bingo. It took little to convince the worn-out kids to get ready for bed. As they brushed their teeth in the bathroom, I noticed, with still more guilt, Grant's toothbrush and razor resting on the counter. I hadn't thought to look in there. *What is wrong with me?* Gemmi had it right. Locacita mamá.

The kids went to bed without a fuss, and I sank into the couch, leaning back with my eyes closed in exhaustion and shame. After everything Grant had done and tried to do since he arrived, the kidnapping idea hit me as the most ridiculous conclusion. I opened my eyes and stared at the stark-white ceiling, wanting to blend into the nothingness it seemed to represent.

I wondered at Grant's long absence and reached for the book he'd left on the coffee table, *The World According to Garp* by John Irving. I considered how I yelled at him about not knowing him, and while it was mostly true, we had learned something about each other. I knew he liked to read, and he sometimes got frustrated with how slow he was. He liked to challenge himself with his reading choices. He said he enjoyed reading action-type books occasionally, but they didn't really pull him in. It had been one of those moments when he surprised me—again.

In the past several days, he hadn't complained at all about watching the kids all day. Not once. I was jealous of how well they spent time together. Grant stumbled with cooking, but so did I. He was surprisingly open about his life. There were many things I hadn't learned about him yet, but he could say the same of me. I didn't have the impression he hid anything, which made my wild assumptions from earlier all the more unfair.

I opened up his book and started reading. BuzzFeed was more my speed. I'd never really had much cause to read anything else. That day seemed reason enough to change.

The knock on the door came around 10:30 p.m., waking me up from one of the many times I'd dropped off to sleep while trying to read Grant's book. I glanced out the peephole to find Grant leaning against the opposite wall, arms crossed. He had his head down, and I couldn't see his expression. I opened the door, and he looked up. No help. I had no read on him.

"Hey," I said.

"Hey."

"No key?"

"This seemed best right now."

I stepped aside as a sign for him to come in. He picked up his duffel—the one carrying only clean clothes and nothing else—and entered.

"I'm sorry," I said as I shut the door. "I'm sorry I was so... I shouldn't have jumped to such a stupid conclusion. I was wrong and really overreacted."

"Yeah, but you know, you weren't all wrong."

We stood, watching each other, neither of us sure about who should go next. I suspected it should be me. I'd considered the words all night, but nothing surfaced. I was wrong, plain and simple.

"I would never, ever take the kids away," he said.

"I know."

"No, you don't know, but I want to say it anyway. I mean, the words are kind of worthless because you're right—you don't know me. I've never had any intention of taking them or fighting for custody. If nothing else, you at least have the words for now. I'm not exactly sure how I'll show you to prove it, but one way is I got a job. I'd been looking online and keeping an eye out since I got here. I figured it was more urgent now. I'm staying. And don't worry because it's a night shift, so it doesn't interfere with helping out with the kids during the day. I couldn't call tonight because my phone's still dead, but I'm calling my parents tomorrow, and I'll get them to lend me money enough to find my own place as soon as possible. I'm sorry. I'm really sorry."

Suddenly, I saw the boy who would come home each day, terrifyingly uncertain of what his fate might be with his parents. He'd probably given them a ridiculous number of unnecessary apologies. I'd spoken to his mother on the phone; I knew what she was like. No way would I let him crawl to them for help.

"No. Don't do that."

"I should have done it in the first place."

"No, not with your parents, you shouldn't. Not before, not now. You told me you're trying to prove you make good on your commitments. Let me do the same. I said we'd work it out and you could stay here, and I meant it." I waited for him to agree. When he finally nodded, I took a deep breath and sat on the edge of the couch. "Look, the thing is, I don't know why I automatically jumped to this idea of you taking the kids. On my own, it never occurred to me you would. A couple of other people brought up the idea, and when you were so late today, the stupid seed weeded its way through."

"I probably should have made sure my phone was charged."

"Yeah, or left a note, or called me before the tow truck. I would have come and helped with everything."

He leaned forward with his arms on his knees. "This is all pretty new to me. I didn't think anything through."

"Oh God, I can't believe I just made you say that." I laughed in embarrassment. "I have no idea what I'm doing. Ever. I guess it's obvious given how I handled this whole thing." I told him about the kids' reactions when we got home. Their fear and doubt and, later, my discovering how they saw everything as an adventure with him. Suddenly, the pinpricks of tears threatened to spill. I looked away, hoping to toss them back where they came from.

Grant's hand on my arm only made me want to cry harder. "Hey, I'm sorry I scared you and made you worry. I promise I'm not here with some other plan than to be who I'm supposed to be to these kids. My promise doesn't mean much yet, but it's all I've got."

"It's enough. I know you won't take them away. I really do. I'm such a mess, and I swear I'm not always such a bitch. I don't understand what's happened to me."

"Major life change. I'm pretty sure you get a few free passes right now."

"I'm pretty sure I've used them all up." I went to the bathroom to blow my nose and to get a grip. When I came out of the bathroom, Grant stood in the kitchen, holding up a beer and a Fanta Orange.

"Which one?"

"What a stupid question."

He laughed, opened the beer, and handed it to me. I headed to the living room and pointed at the book on the coffee table.

"I tried reading your book, but I kept falling asleep."

He picked it up to see how far I had gotten. Page four. "You should skip the first few chapters. Here, let me give you a summary, then you can start in where it gets to be more about Garp and not his mom. It isn't really about his mom, although she's kinda important. See, she's this super-independent woman who becomes a nurse when everyone is waiting for her to get married and have kids. Only, she doesn't want the traditional thing. She ends up getting pregnant in a... well, in a weird way—"

I raised my eyebrow at him.

"Okay, in the standard way, except it's a weird situation, and how it happens doesn't really matter. Trust me. She raises her son at a boarding school, and he decides he wants to be a writer. They go to Europe so he can learn more about the world to help with his writing. And that's where you should start."

"Everyone says she has to get married and have kids? 'Cause it's what women do."

"In the thirties and forties, yeah."

"And she basically got a kid in a weird way," I said.

"Yep. I suppose you can't relate to any of this at all?"

"Nope. Not at all like my life right now."

He grinned and held out his beer bottle. "Cheers."

I clinked his bottle with my own. "Cheers." We sat quietly for a moment before I spoke again. "Are we good?"

"I think so. I'm good. You?"

"Yeah."

"Child abuse and kidnapping. We're on a pretty good roll, huh?"

I laughed. "Let's try not to outdo ourselves, okay?"

He held out his fist. I gave him the bump.

Chapter Twenty

Grant and I moved past our high-strung behaviors. We started the next morning fresh. Grant joked that since he didn't currently have a car anyway, I was stuck with him. To prove I'd been serious about trusting him with the twins, I gave him my car to use when he started at his new job bartending at a hole-in-the-wall called Lucky's.

He had a short first shift, scheduled only to prove he had experience and to train him on their specials. I was still up when he came home; I hadn't gathered the energy to roll myself into bed.

"Sorry," Grant said, coming out of the bathroom bare-chested after showering. "My shirt got wet."

"It's not like you came out here without your underwear." He might not have been Mr. Rock-Hard Abs, but he still had a pretty good frame on him. I certainly wasn't complaining, especially seeing more of his art exposed.

He had far more tattoos than had been visible. A smoke-and-flame pattern stretched along his side, and an expansive geometric design wrapped with a snake spanned his back. There was one tattoo, though, that wasn't like any of the others. I probably shouldn't have, but I burst out laughing. "Oh. My. God. You are *that* guy."

"What?"

I pointed at the tattoo. He looked down. *Christy*, it said in swirly script over his left pec.

"I don't know what you mean," he said evenly. "You can laugh all you want, but she was the love of my life."

Oh, shit. He was serious. I searched my brain for what to say to make up for my callousness. "I'm sorry. I shouldn't have—"

He grinned. "I'm just messing with you."

I rolled my eyes. "Put on a shirt, jackass."

He laughed as he dug in his bag for a clean shirt.

My smile returned. "Who was she, really?"

He pulled the hem down around his waist and relaxed onto his bed. "Well, I probably believed she was the love of my life at the time, and we were kinda serious for a few months. Then she started the whole drug scene, which was never my thing, so that was the end of that."

"C'mon. 'Kinda' serious? I mean, you got her name tattooed on you. Sounds like more than 'kinda.'"

"She wanted me to prove I loved her. It seemed like the thing to do. I was young."

"I bet it's gotten in the way since then, huh?"

"I like to tell them it's the name of a daughter I never get to see."

I groaned. "Oh God, you are awful. I bet they fawn all over you in sympathy, right?"

He smiled at first, then his expression grew serious. "You're right, though. That's pretty bad," he said. "If it makes you feel any better, I haven't used such a line in a long time. I used it in my younger partying days."

"What about that one?" I pointed at what looked like Greek letters on the inside of his left forearm.

"Ah, the beginning of my partying days. Sigma Alpha Epsilon. One of the biggest social frats at UCLA."

"Wait, I thought you didn't go to college?"

He snorted. "I wasn't going to school there. I found a way in with the frat crowd. By getting the tattoo, I got in easier. Way cheaper drinks than at the bars."

"And the girls were easier prey?"

His expression clouded. "Yes." He looked away and got a little fidgety. I sensed a babble coming on, but he only said, "It's a pretty scary environment for women. I never did more than flirt."

I wondered about his body language, reminding me of what he'd told me earlier about his parents. "What did you see?"

He looked at me, his eyes darker. "Too much. Too much I should have said or done something about. One time, I got in a fight trying to stop something because it didn't look right. I never went back to one of those parties."

I leaned forward, putting my elbows on my knees and resting my chin in my hands. He was so interesting and clearly had a lot of stories. I wanted to hear them all, but I was creeping close to getting too personal. I shifted back to the tattoos. Around his biceps, he had some of the Celtic-type stuff I'd seen before. I moved to his right forearm.

"And the dragon?"

His eyes scrunched as if in confusion before he realized the topic shift and held out his arm to show off the art. "Oh, the dragon's more recent. Got it a couple of years ago after reading some Anne McCaffrey."

I shook my head.

"She's one of the definitive authors on dragon lore. Not a fantasy reader?"

"No. I don't read much." More like not at all, but he was already upstaging me enough on the interesting scale. Not that it took much. I tried to make it sound like I didn't have a total write-off of a personality. "I've been reading a lot of *Curious George* and kids' Bible stories lately."

That response got me a smile and a nod. "Are you all pretty religious?"

"Oh God, no," I put in quickly, cringing briefly at my ironic language. "But the kids are. I've been trying to figure out what to do for

them. My friend Gemmi invited us to her church a couple of weekends ago, and it was kinda cool. Brian, Layla, and I grew up Luther-
an, sort of. I don't have any idea where Brian got his religion."

"Elaine. From what I got, she convinced Brian to go to that one
church up north with her—"

"And Brian fell in hook, line, and sinker. Wow. That place was—"

"Nuts. Scary."

"Right?" Even though I'd guessed it before then, I was glad to
get confirmation we were on the same page with Brian and Elaine's
church thing. "The kids don't seem overly affected by it all. Lulu
will sometimes say something like 'maybe she still hasn't been saved'
when she sees someone do something mean. I'm never sure how to
reply."

"You don't just say they're going to hell?"

I laughed. "I usually say they need to be saved from *something*,
for sure. To be honest, I'm pretty much agnostic. I haven't decided
how to deal with the whole religion thing for them. I don't want to
confuse them."

"Because they aren't confused enough already? Their situation
should swing you to atheism instead."

"Is that you?"

He paused only a moment. "It's an option I like better than others. What the fuck kind of god puts kids in situations like mine and
Elaine's when we were growing up? Or Lucy and Mikey's now?"

"Brian might say it was God's will they ended up back with their
biological parents."

"Are you serious?"

"I didn't say *I* would say that. It feels like a Brian pronouncement,
though. I was always kind of surprised they went this route for the
kids. Wouldn't it be God's will they couldn't conceive on their own?"

"Huh," he said, appearing to process the idea. "You're right. It's
weird, isn't it? Then again, I didn't know my sister well." He slid over

to the end of the couch that met my chair and put a finger on the stem of my tattoo, the part of it on my triceps. "I've been dying to find out where this vine leads."

"How do you know it leads to anything? It could just be a vine."

"Nope." He lifted my arm up. "It winds differently from here..." He traced from below my elbow, finishing where my shirt sleeve ended, mid-triceps. "To here. Plus, there are the stray petals."

There were only two, but almost no one noticed them. Each one caught between the leaf and the stem, kind of hiding them. Even Zach had never commented on the ones on my arm. If he'd ever noticed them, he certainly hadn't said anything. They were bluish with a tinge of red. I reached over to pull up my sleeve to reveal the bright-blue flowering clematis covering most of my shoulder.

"I knew it." He grinned appreciatively, his eyes bright and cheerful again. "Awesome." His hands circled my upper arm, and his thumbs traced the pattern as a sculptor might gauge texture and shape. It felt... intimate, though not in a sexual way. Zach usually avoided my tattoo altogether. For a musician, he acted awfully strait-laced. I wasn't some wild child, but to have someone actually understand some of my choices gave me a sense of freedom.

"You've got brilliant color," Grant continued. "Look at the red edges. Did you pick it out?"

"Gemmi helped." Except for the stray petals, which I didn't tell him about. Those were my idea. I had more of them, and though he wouldn't see a couple of them, I wondered if he would notice the others more likely to be visible with the warmer weather. "She has a great artist she goes to. You should see the sea dragon around her neck. It's amazing."

Embarrassment crossed his expression as he apparently realized where his hands rested and released my arm. "Sorry. I wasn't thinking. It's just really cool, and I couldn't believe how bright the color was and—"

"You're fine." I straightened my sleeve. "Relax." I smiled, and he leaned back on the futon.

"I'll have to check out Gemmi's artist for some more ink," he said.

"More?"

"Gotta cover up the 'Christy' tat now, don't I?"

I laughed. "Not on my account! Probably a good idea for your future love life, though. No more using kids for sex."

His face fell into mock disappointment. "Wait, what? I can't use Lucy and Mikey while I'm at the park scoping single parents? You haven't seen the attention I've been getting there the past couple of days."

"What is it about single dads?"

He gave me an inscrutable look.

"What?"

"Did you just call me a dad?" he asked with a little smile.

I shrugged. "Yeah, I guess so. You are, aren't you?"

"Yeah. Technically, I am, huh? I guess in my head, I was sort of thinking maybe. When you said it out loud, it sounded... *real*. I liked it."

And there it was. After less than a couple of weeks, he already acted and felt the part, yet after almost a month, I still struggled with mine. At the grocery store, when I'd yelled at the nosy woman who scolded Lucy, I had a rush of something, but I wasn't sure what the something was.

"Well, those parents at the park see you as Lucy and Mikey's dad too. Any potential?"

He laughed. "Nah, not really. A couple of them are married. One mom is single, I think, but she's kind of strange. There's another dad who might be single, and he's a good guy."

"Do Lucy and Mikey play with the other kids?"

"Not really. Mikey swings most of the time, and Lucy is branching out a little more. She's all over the playground equipment. She doesn't join in with the other kids yet."

"I don't suppose the most recent daycare experience helped at all," I said.

"Or suddenly losing her parents in a car crash. Neither thing is your fault. She'll be okay. Kids have a way of adapting."

I folded up my legs in the chair and looked down at my Coke, thinking of Mikey and whether he was adapting or if he was still simply reacting. Though he smiled and laughed more, he still wasn't talking, and the awful night horrors remained.

Grant cleared his throat, pulling me out of my thoughts, and I looked up to see him nervously wiping his hands on his sweatpants. "The other night, you know, when I didn't go to Mikey... it wasn't only because it was jarring. I mean, it was, but it was more than something startling. It... I recognized it."

My breathing shallowed at his nervousness.

"I don't remember ever waking up screaming like he does, but I know the scream. The feeling. I still..."

"You still feel that way sometimes," I offered.

He looked up at me and held my eyes as though waiting for judgment or teasing. I hoped he found none.

"Yeah," he said.

He'd been incredibly forthcoming ever since knocking on my door. I owed him something, so I shared my story. "Two years after I graduated from high school, my roommate and I were walking home from a bar. We lived close by and didn't want to waste money on a cab. It was February and frigid cold, so we took a route we wouldn't have normally taken because it cut through an area where drug traffic was high. But it was shorter, and we figured we had each other for safety. Two guys approached us, one with a gun. Fortunately, all they did was take our purses and run."

That wasn't exactly true. They had forced us against the wall, palms and cheeks scraping the brick. I caught myself bringing my hand to my face and quickly brought it down to my lap. The man without the gun had done some groping, too, but the other yelled at him for wasting time. I had thought about the self-defense course I hadn't yet taken while also doubting it would matter with a gun pointed in our faces.

I refocused on the point of telling Grant my story. "I had nightmares for over a month from the single incident. I imagine yours might never go away." When I looked up again to tell him that last part, I discovered him leaning forward, arms along his knees, hands clasped. His eyes were still on me, and his gaze softened.

"Thanks," he said, his voice muted. "And thanks for helping me get some perspective."

"I didn't mean to minimize anything. My point is your history is bigger than my one brief moment, especially a moment so many years ago."

"I know, but your not-so-little moment could still be in your present and future. Mikey's present is currently bigger than my history. And both those things help me renegotiate my own present."

Whatever the renegotiation meant for him, it worked. At two a.m., I found Grant at Mikey's side before I got there. It took a little longer than usual for Mikey to calm down, and I almost charged in to take over. But then the sobs subsided. Watching the two of them, I saw a mutual solace. When Grant looked at me, I gave him a reassuring nod and let them be.

Chapter Twenty-One

Grant's work schedule started in full swing the next day, and after a couple of weeks, we all fell into an easy routine. I paid for his car repair, much to his discomfort, and after every shift, he left his tips out on the counter for me and later signed over his first paycheck. I assumed he was being smart enough to hold on to some of the tips for cash on hand, but he didn't like talking about the money situation most of the time.

On Saturday morning, I made my way quietly into the kitchen. I'd prepared everything before bed the night before so that all I would have to do was press Start on the coffeemaker. I peeked into the living room to make sure I hadn't woken Grant, and my heart squeezed upon seeing Mikey curled up next to him, thumb in his mouth. He'd obviously woken a second time, since I was with him for the first. I wondered if Grant encouraged Mikey or if Mikey wandered out and into Grant's bed on his own. Looking at Grant, I guessed the latter, as he appeared to have dropped straight into bed upon coming home. His shoes lay tumbled upon each other at the foot of the futon, and he wore jeans and an untucked polo shirt. I smiled, recalling his scorn over the idea he had to dress at all nicely for such a dive.

Almost a month had passed since he showed up at my door, and him filling in was only meant to be temporary. As much as I didn't want to, I had to start the search for a more permanent childcare situation. The kids would turn five in July, technically in time for them to start kindergarten. Naturally, all kinds of mixed advice came my way about enrolling them right away or waiting another year. Zach said I should enroll them because it would be good routine and socialization. I wasn't sure. I felt like it was too much pressure with all the changes they were going through. I had so many doubts about Mikey and whether he would start talking before September. I worried his teacher wouldn't understand, just like Sophie didn't, and whether the school would allow him to be there if his not talking wasn't a physical issue.

I supposed they couldn't actually disallow his enrollment. I also knew, though, that not all teachers were created equal, and Mikey could get passed over a lot if he didn't talk.

"They won't ignore him. They'll want to help him out," Zach had told me.

"Yeah, says the guy who was a good student all his life. I'm sure teachers loved you. Teachers liked me well enough at first, too, until I started shutting down in eighth grade, and from there on out, it didn't take long for them to stop trying and give up on me."

"You have to want to keep trying, too, right?"

"But Mikey will be five, not fourteen. Five's too soon to expect someone to 'prove' himself."

He'd shrugged. "I bet once he starts school and sees all the normal behavior around him, he'll talk. At some point, he would have to, right? I mean, he's got it easy with you when you don't make him say out loud what he wants."

I flinched inside at Zach's use of "normal behavior." Mikey's muteness seemed 100 percent normal. Same with Lucy's meltdowns. I didn't see how anyone could expect differently in their circumstances.

"Look," Zach continued, "all I'm saying is when my nephew went through a stage of being snotty and demanding things without talking nicely to my sister, she ignored him. She wouldn't give him what he wanted until he changed his tone. Maybe it's the same with Mikey. If you stop giving in to him for a while, he'll figure it out."

The next day, though, had been when the first warning bell about the daycare had occurred, and I hadn't had the heart to enact any sort of sanction on Mikey's wordlessness. Besides, it went against all my instincts to force words out of him. He simply wasn't ready.

His silence came in handy as I peeked in on him and Grant on the futon. Mikey opened his eyes, and when he saw me, he tumbled off the futon with Bunny and scurried over. I scooped him up into a hug.

"Ready for our weekend breakfast?" I whispered in his ear.

He nodded and squirmed for me to put him down. Dragging his bunny behind him by one ear, he grabbed the syrup from the cabinet then pattered off to the hall closet and got our picnic blanket. I pulled out a box of frozen waffles from the freezer, snagged my coffee, and picked up the toaster as I followed him into his and Lucy's room. We found Lucy groggily rubbing her eyes as she woke up. It didn't take long for her to perk up, though, when she saw the toaster.

"Yay! Waffle picnic day!"

We'd started the tradition the week before, when I determined we had to find a way to let Grant sleep on the weekends. He'd asked for limited shifts during the week so he could get up before I left for work and still be able to function all day with the kids. However, he made up for it by working longer shifts on Fridays and Saturdays. He went in at four and stayed until close. He wouldn't get home until after three in the morning. With the kids usually waking at six, it hardly seemed fair to invade his space and wake him prematurely.

So in a spur-of-the-moment idea after one of those late shifts, we had a picnic breakfast in the kids' room, and it officially became a fun ritual. We toasted waffles, tore them into strips, then dipped them into a bowl of syrup. Next, we played a game or two of Candyland or Mr. Potato Head. We talked about where we would go after our lazy start, leaving a quiet apartment for Grant. We would go to a park, and sometimes, we ran errands.

Currently, however, it was pouring rain, so we took more time with the games. We tried to stick around at home a little longer, but the kids got antsy and rambunctious, and we still had a few hours to kill until Zach expected us at his place for lunch. *Target.* Target would be open, and the kids needed sandals.

Cheered by the new option, we cleaned up, got dressed, and slipped out the door without disturbing Grant.

We returned home at two in the afternoon, wet, sloppy, and giggly.

"Looks like you got caught in the rain, huh, kiddos?" Grant greeted us, smiling.

"We splashed in puddles!" Lucy told him gleefully.

"Sounds like the perfect thing to do today. You, too, Mikeadoodle? Did you splash too?"

I watched Mikey give Grant his best smile as he slapped Grant's hand for a resounding "five."

"He didn't want to at first, but JuJu said Bunny could watch us from inside Uncle Zach's house, and then he did it!" Lucy burst with pride for her brother. I hadn't been sure we would convince a cautious Mikey to try it. Once he did, he loved it.

"Did Uncle Zach splash with you too?"

"It was his idea," I said. "We should get Lucy and Mikey some raincoats and rain boots too. Then we might be able to stay out longer. We had to turn on the heat in the car on the way home."

"Sounds awesome. What do you think, kiddos? Time for some warm baths to clean you up?" At their nods, he looked at me. "Unless you wanted to shower first, J?"

I shook my head. "I'm fine. Kids first."

He roared and scooped up the kids, causing happy shrieks. He then carted them off to the bathroom. As I peeled off my clothes in my bedroom, I appreciated Grant's easy, warm reception of everything. Zach might have suggested the splashing, but he hadn't realized I would let the kids do it with bare feet. The kids had the new sandals from our Target trip, but I hadn't thought to get the waterproof kind. I didn't want them ruined already. Zach also made me worried the play area at the mall we stopped at was a bad idea and that I was neglecting the kids' safety by letting them jump into unknown curb gutters. There could be hidden broken glass or other things, but we had already lost the joy of the morning. Next, Zach assumed he'd made a kid-friendly meal of macaroni and cheese, except he had gotten all fancy with the frozen stuff instead of the Kraft box. Mikey had poked at it, and Lucy had a fit. Zach tried to tell them it was all the same, and later he tried to wheedle a verbal thank-you from Mikey, an effort that I crabbily dismissed. I sympathized with Zach trying to deal with Lucy's tantrum, but it was like he hadn't been listening to any of my stories.

He tried. He kept calm. He let me scavenge his kitchen to find things they liked. I apologized a billion times. He said it was okay, but he acted as if it were my fault they wouldn't eat his food. Like I should have force-fed the meal to them.

"I'm doing the best I can," I told him, trying to hold it together.

"It's okay. They'll learn."

"They'll learn what?"

"How to behave more appropriately when they don't get what they want. How to eat different stuff. I don't know... all of it."

He must have seen how defeated and tired I felt, because he pulled me in for a tight, reassuring hug. "I'm sorry. You're doing great, and this is all new to me too."

I sank into his embrace, appreciating the admission. I often assumed he knew more than I did. He had several nieces and nephews and spent more time with kids. Just when I started trusting my instincts, he showed me how wrong they all were. I didn't want to tell him we had been using the toaster in their bedroom, because surely I was creating a fire hazard.

After the lunch fiasco, Zach wanted to make up for the meal by suggesting the puddle splashing. We argued about going without shoes, and I told him he could go buy new sandals for them afterward. He sighed then gave in. We enjoyed ourselves once we got outside. At first, both kids took small, hesitant steps into the puddles. After Zach and I jumped in full force, they caught on and took little leaps before moving to all-out kicking and splashing. I couldn't help thinking about Grant and how playing in puddles would be right up his alley. He wouldn't have thought twice about it.

I was making some hot chocolate for the kids when Grant came into the kitchen, telling me they were getting dressed.

"Thanks for cleaning them up."

"No problem. Least I can do. I'm kind of jealous I missed out on the rain party, though."

"It seemed like your kind of activity, for sure."

He eyed me suspiciously. "I'm not sure if that's a compliment or something else."

I smiled. "I was part of it, so if it's something else, I'm saying the same thing about myself. But given the other activity today, maybe it really is the something else."

"What do you mean?"

"Well, we've usually been going to a park. The rain ruled out the park, and the kids were getting antsy. I remembered the mall has an indoor play area. We got a snack from the food court, then I let them loose."

His eyes lit up. "Brilliant. I'm so totally stealing the idea for the next rainy day when we're going bonkers."

"Really? You think it's okay? Zach kind of implied I was welcoming a germ fest. He had all kinds of stories about gross things in those kinds of play areas."

He waved me off. "They sanitize those areas all the time now. How about I throw them in the bath right afterward? They love baths. It's an entire half a day full of win, if you ask me."

"They did love the superlong tunnel slide there," I conceded, feeling better about the day the longer I was home.

The kids came bounding out of their rooms in fresh, dry clothes, ready for the rest of the day.

"Yummy hot chocolate," Lucy exclaimed when I showed them their mugs. "And cookies! Can we have some, please?"

"Sorry," Grant said, looking at me. "I didn't mean to leave it out where they could see it. It's a cookie-decorating kit. I thought it might be something fun to do tonight."

"It does sound fun. You didn't want it to be for this afternoon? Should we have come home sooner?"

"Nope. I got it purposely for you guys."

"Can we decorate cookies?" Lucy asked again.

"Of course," I agreed, enjoying their happy bounces, then turned to Grant again. "And all I got you was a new bottle of shampoo." I smiled. "Doesn't seem like a fair trade."

"A trade? No way. The cookie kit was a fun treat for you guys. I'll pay you back for the shampoo."

"Don't be ridiculous. It was only a couple of dollars."

"I don't think we should do that," he said.

"Do what?"

"Start covering expenses for each other."

"Expenses? Seriously, it was like two forty-nine or something. I'm not worried about it."

He glanced at the kids, who bobbed their marshmallows in the milky brown liquid, and put a light hand behind my arm and guided me into the hall.

"Look, I know I let you take me in out of sympathy, even if it helped you out with the kids. I really appreciate you letting me into their lives like this. We both know I didn't need to be living here in order to help, though. It's not like we've been friends forever. It may only be two and a half bucks, but what if we hate each other after a couple more weeks and we suddenly resent that tiny thing? I don't want to get to the point where we're nitpicking about those dumb kinds of things."

I stared at him, trying to determine whether he was being for real. He seemed pretty anxious. "All right. Can we at least round to the nearest dollar? Because really, literally counting change will make me hate you faster than buying fun activities for me and the kids."

"The cookies are even prebaked in the kit. They're Julie-proof," he said.

I gave him a light shove. "You think you are sooo funny."

He laughed. "Thanks for noticing I needed shampoo."

"Give the ladies crappy service tonight so you'll be able to pay me back in small bills. I don't give change."

"Even my crappy service gets me the big bucks." He grinned.

"Oh, look." I tapped my watchless wrist. "It's time for you to get going. Don't want you to be late." I brushed past him to check on the kids while he chuckled, making his way back to the living room to pocket his wallet and keys. He returned to the dining room and planted kisses on the kids' heads.

"Enjoy the decorating, kiddos."

"Bye, Sperm Whale," Lucy called as Grant waved on his way out the door.

I felt a strange pang as the door closed behind him. For all the ups and downs of the day, it had been a relief to come home to him. It surprised me how quickly I had gotten used to him sharing my space. It wasn't always convenient, like the weekend mornings, but we made a good team. I kind of liked his schedule, allowing me evenings alone after the kids went to bed. I really liked him around on his days off too. He made me laugh.

Sometimes, he tried to send me out to meet Zach, Gemmi, or Sean. To help give him a break, I never wanted to go until after the kids were in bed, and when post-bedtime routine ended, I was often too tired to go anywhere. He'd befriended a couple of his coworkers, so I made him go out, too, thinking of how much he had left behind in California. At one point, though, we argued about the whole idea of "making" the other go out and finally agreed to accept each other's answer, yes or no, to the "wanna get out of here?" question.

With Zach's classes nearing the end of the term, his and Grant's paths rarely crossed, which was probably a good thing. Zach acted pretty cool about everything, yet he had his jealous moments. He questioned Grant's presence while nagging me about how he surely had enough saved up to be moving to his own place. He hadn't, I knew, since I saw his paychecks, though I got him to hold on to the latest one instead of signing it over to me. I never told Zach about paying for the car repair, which had been pricey, because I figured he would get upset with me about it.

There was a lot I didn't tell Zach, and that was a problem. I wanted to believe he would understand all of my decisions and support them. Increasingly, I felt judged. What I hadn't quite been able to name when I broke up with him the first time came into focus as my life became so much... more. Sometimes, it was like he made me a project. *Let's show Julie how she can eat better. Let's show Julie how she can be interested in more than TV.* And then there was the latest development, *Let's show Julie how she can be a mom.*

I also didn't tell him about the missteps Grant and I had made with each other at first. I shared little about Grant's past, as that was

Grant's story to tell, not mine, and I shared even less about what I was learning and remembering about my past with my parents. I didn't reveal my worries about Brian and Elaine's relationship.

And yet I knew how Zach *could* be. He could be accepting and supportive. He could absorb my anxieties and frustrations. He could take me in with those kind eyes and keep me there with his smile. He could be patient and gentle with the kids.

Maybe all I needed was to work harder at remembering that.

Chapter Twenty-Two

I knew something was wrong when Lucy hardly ate anything at dinner and didn't have a tantrum about it.

"I don't feel good," she said, her voice smaller than ever.

I pressed a light hand to her cheeks and asked if it was her stomach. She shook her head. She felt a little warm but not too bad. I was glad *Moana* was the only thing on the docket for the rest of the day. We'd been busy, and a quiet evening was a good way to end the day. Mikey offered to help clean up, and I let Lucy lounge on the couch. Afterward, he ran to his room, only to return with Lucy's dolly. My chest filled with gooey happiness at his sensitivity.

Lucy declined popcorn and fell asleep before the movie was over. Mikey and I finished the movie, and I got them both to bed. I figured Lucy would sleep through the rest of the night, but an hour later, she woke, crying with skin hotter than I thought was safe for such a small child. She shivered uncontrollably, and I wrapped my arms around her, trying to calm her. She drifted back to sleep, and I tucked her into her bed, covers snug.

Searching my bathroom cabinet, I discovered I'd never prepared for childhood illness. I had Advil, but the package clearly indicated a single tablet would be too much for a four-year-old. I had nothing else except bandages and antibiotic ointment I'd bought after our first visit to the park. I didn't know at what point I should be alarmed and whether I should take Lucy to the ER.

Less than twenty minutes later, Lucy was awake and crying again. Her cheeks flamed red. I scooped her up, blankets and all, and took her into the living room, hoping not to wake Mikey. Panic rose and wound itself around my chest. With a deep breath, I grabbed my phone and called Grant.

"Hey, what's up?" Voices, laughter, and cheers overpowered the music in the background. It was a busy Saturday night. I wasn't sure why I thought he would have time to talk or help.

"It's Lucy," I blurted out. "She's sick."

"Okay. Hold on a sec and let me call you back."

I hung up and touched Lucy's forehead again. She whimpered, and I leaned down to give her a kiss followed by empty words of re-assurance. My phone buzzed.

"I'm sorry." Grant's voice came through right away when I an-swered, his apology sounding sincere and ridiculously unnecessary. "I needed to get someplace quieter. What's happening with Luce?"

"She feels super hot and is really upset. I don't have anything to give her, and I don't know what to do."

"How hot? What's her temperature?"

"I don't know. I don't even have a thermometer. What kind of mother doesn't have this stuff for her children?"

"Like, a million of them, J. It's okay. What did Zach have to say?"

Zach. The pharmacy intern. And my boyfriend. Also, the guy I had just spent the day with.

"I didn't call him... yet. You're right. He'll know what to do." Probably my mother and every other person I knew would too. *What is wrong with me?*

"Call me back if he's not around, okay? I can take a longer break and pick up some medicine or something."

I closed my eyes and inhaled slowly then exhaled.

"Hey." Grant's voice dropped into gentle tones. "I'm sorry I'm not there. She's gonna be okay, though. Kids get sick all the time. You're doing fine. Do you want me to see if I can leave early?"

Remembering the noise I'd heard at the beginning of the call, I knew it was surely too busy for him to leave. I also realized I was overreacting. And in spite of not thinking things through, I was glad Grant had been my first call.

"No. I'm sorry for freaking out. You're right. I'll see if Zach can come by, and if not, I'll call my mom. Thanks for answering. I know it's hard to do at your job."

"Don't be dumb. I'll always answer or call you back as soon as I can."

I smiled and would have cried, a sure sign I was overtired, except Lucy beat me to it. I thanked him again and hung up. I pulled Lucy into my lap and rocked her gently in my arms, trying to settle the trembles rolling through her. When she calmed once more, I dialed Zach and let his earlier admonishments sink in. *The play area, the rain.* I'd gotten her sick.

With no answer from him, I left both a message and a text then moved on to my mom.

"Should I take her to the ER?"

"No, of course not. I'll be there in a few minutes, okay? She's got a bug like all kids get. Hang in there."

I nearly cried at her response, too, which was when I realized Lucy wasn't the only one who had come down with some virus. My body aches weren't just from holding Lucy. I could do something about myself, however. I slipped away from Lucy long enough to grab some Advil and some juice.

Juice. Yes, of course. *Well done, Julie. You've finally let your brain kick into gear.* Liquids. Lucy needed liquids. Hydration. I poured an extra glass for her and hoped I would be able to get her to drink.

By the time my mother arrived with supplies, I had regained some of my composure.

"How's she doing?"

"Sleeping fitfully on the couch. We've been alternating between sleep and watching pieces of a *PAW Patrol* episode."

Together, we took her temperature—102.3—got her to chew some Tylenol, and urged some more water into her.

"Do you think she got sick from the mall play area I took her to? Or from the rain? We splashed in puddles with bare feet. The kids got cold."

"No, honey. It's a random virus she picked up a day or two ago. It could have been anything."

Zach's criticisms kept flooding my brain.

When I tried to put Lucy back into her bed, she balked and asked to sleep in mine. Bed sounded good, so I tucked her in with me while my mother cleaned up all the mess I hadn't gotten to before—dishes, toys, and whatever else I had left in our wake since coming home. I texted Grant to assure him things were all right. His return text was almost immediate, expressing relief and asking if I was okay.

I was. I wasn't proud of how I'd panicked, but I felt calmer and much more confident things would be fine. I felt stupid for not knowing how to handle a simple fever, like I had never been sick before. Like I hadn't helped take care of my brother when he used to get sick.

My mother came in and sat on the bed and passed gentle fingertips along Lucy's temple to clear her hair away then pressed her palm on my forehead.

"Hmm," she said. "I thought your eyes looked a bit glassy, but you feel okay."

"I took some drugs earlier. You know, after I realized what an idiot I was."

"Welcome to motherhood." She smiled. "It turns us all into basket cases. It's hard when the kids get sick. I hated seeing you guys feeling miserable."

"Is that why Dad always took care of us when we were sick?"

She laughed then choked some of it back, clearly mindful of a sleeping Lucy. "Maybe. Especially during the times you had stomach bugs. He was pretty good at it, wasn't he? You wouldn't guess it, but he enjoyed caretaking."

I knew what she meant. My dad was clearly not one to emote or talk things out. I remembered him bringing us soup and reading us stories, though. Considering recent events, I realized he hadn't changed much.

"Thanks for coming tonight to take care of me, Mom." I paused before asking my next question, considering whether I wanted to open up the conversation. "Did Dad take good care of you? Is his caretaking part of why you still get together with him between wives?"

She cocked her head and tucked her hair behind her ear. "Your dad always supported my decisions. He's the one who got me started with real estate. He paid for the classes toward my licensure and used his professional contacts to get my first clients." She leaned back against the head of the bed and stretched her legs out on the mattress. "I guess that kind of support is part of what I miss about him. Things are very easy with him."

"Do you ever think your... interludes will lead to you getting back together? Because he looks pretty happy and content with Nora."

"Oh, honey, he always looks content with his wives. He was happy with me, even when we were cheating on each other."

My skepticism obviously showed because she continued, "I told you, things are easy with him. He's a man who loves but doesn't seem to fall *in* love, and it's easy for us all to make him look fulfilled. I don't have any delusions, trust me. He's comfortable. Plus"—she gave me a sideways glance—"he's very good in bed."

Her smirk broke free, and I rolled to my back and groaned. "You really loved mentioning the sex bit, didn't you? God, Mom, would you have actually wanted to hear your mom and dad talk about their sex life?"

"Oh, I suppose not." She chuckled. "I just couldn't resist this time."

"Yes, hit me while I'm down."

"Of course. It's a parent's job to embarrass her children whenever she can."

Lucy moaned next to me, though she didn't wake. Her cheeks were a more normal color, and I loosened the covers around her, hoping the excess heat would escape.

"Do you remember the weekend I went away and left you in charge?" my mom asked.

A wariness overtook me as I looked up at her. "Yes."

I'd come home from school to find a note on the table, short and vague. She would be away until sometime on Sunday. No phone number. No information on where she'd gone. My parents had split up a year before, right before Layla graduated from high school, and by then, it was only Brian and me. I was angry because it was a weekend I took off from work, and I actually had plans with friends, a rare occurrence.

Brian wasn't yet thirteen, and while he didn't need direct supervision, my comfort level wasn't high enough to leave him for a long time at night. I tried calling my dad, but he was out of town on "business," as I was sure my mother was too.

"I spent the weekend with a woman. I wanted to... try it out."

Ah. Turned out I was right, just not at all in the way I was expecting.

"Try what out?"

"You know. Sex."

"Oh, Mom. Really?" I wondered why she was telling me and not Layla. I didn't want to have that conversation with her. I'd determined to try harder for things to work between us, so I kept at it. "What did you find out?"

"Nothing surprising, I guess. I'm not actually attracted to other women. My friend caught on pretty quickly, and she was very kind about it all. She'd already suspected, and if nothing else, I learned a lot."

I caught a blush. "Why? Why did you do it?"

"I really admired your sister for putting herself out there, and she seemed so happy, and I thought, oh, I don't know, I guess I'd try it too."

"You know it doesn't work that way, right?"

"Yes. Well, I guess I do. To be honest, I don't fully understand it. I mean, it seems like as happy as Layla has been, she's had to go through some hard stuff too. It would have been easier if she'd stuck to boys."

"But *why*, Mom? If Layla really was your inspiration, and you admitted it was hard for her, why would you want to go through the same thing?"

She looked away then returned her gaze to the bed, where her fingers worried at a stray thread. "I was sad, Jules, and was searching for something. I thought if I did something completely new and different, it would wake me up and make me happy."

I let my head drop to the pillow, taking in her melancholic tone. It was the first time I'd heard actual regret about her past. All the times I'd thought about her affairs and how she seemed distant from us, it never occurred to me she might have been unhappy.

"Back then," she said, "I had friends who talked about starting with this 'new' drug, Prozac, to help with depression, but I didn't have depression. Sometimes, you can just be sad. I missed your father. I missed Layla, and I wished I hadn't destroyed the years of growing up where we could have become friends. I wasn't any good with you as small children. Sometimes, I imagine I could have been good with you in your teen years if I hadn't been so careless. And even though the woman I spent the weekend with wasn't someone who was sexually attractive to me, she reminded me to get myself out there and embrace all of the change. She helped me find myself again."

Embrace all the change. It was all I'd been struggling with, and I couldn't fault her for experiencing the same thing. I reached over Lucy to rest a hand on my mom's arm and gave it a gentle squeeze.

"For what it's worth, I'm pretty sure Layla would say good for you and be proud of you."

"And you? What do you say?"

"I say I'm just glad you didn't 'try it out' in the kitchen."

She laughed loudly and freely, obviously forgetting about waking the kids. Lucy's eyes fluttered open for a second before quickly closing again. I laughed too.

Mom put a hand on top of mine. "Sweetie, you look absolutely beat. You need rest. Will you be all right if I go?"

"Yeah, I've got my head back on again."

"I'm glad you called me."

"Me too."

Over the past several days, Mikey's middle-of-the-night screams had morphed into full wake-up cries. The change twisted my insides. Before, the pain seemed to exist outside of him, since I wasn't able to discern if he remembered the nightmares. With the change, however, the sadness threatened to overwhelm me as I discovered he had become aware of them. He only clung to me tighter instead of giving me yes-or-no responses to my questions about the dreams. If he remembered his dreams, he wasn't ready to share.

That night was no less difficult, as my emotional state was rubbed raw from worrying about Lucy and not feeling well myself. I breathed a grateful sigh for small favors as his cries subsided; Grant was obviously home. A couple of minutes later, they showed up in my doorway, Grant whispering and pointing at Lucy. I imagined the fear running through Mikey upon seeing his sister's empty bed.

Mikey squirmed down and, before Grant could catch him, scrambled into bed with me and flung his arms around my neck. I tried to move us all over to make room, but it was slow going. My body felt achy and sluggish. I guessed the drugs had worn off.

I glanced over at the other side of the bed, missing the soothing presence of my mother, regardless of the awkward conversation. It was something I hadn't had with her in a long time. I barely remembered her leaving. I must have conked out quickly.

I turned back to see Grant squatting next to my side of the bed. "How are you guys doing?" he asked quietly. "Lucy been sleeping? Are you getting any sleep?"

"Yeah, mostly. The drugs have surely worn off by now. We'll see if her fever spikes again." I looked at the clock. It was only midnight. "Why are you home early?"

"Paul let me off. I feel bad for not getting away sooner."

The black curls he kept pushing back fell along his temple, and I resisted the temptation to brush them away. He smelled of beer and sweat, but his unique musky scent still pushed through, especially at close proximity. Of their own will, my eyes traveled from his sympathetic brown eyes then down along his shoulders and forearms resting along the edge of the bed.

"Don't feel bad. It's only a virus, and I overreacted, something I've become very good at in recent weeks. You answered when I needed you. That made all the difference."

He put his hand around mine and gave it a squeeze. I squeezed back.

"You should sleep in Mikey's bed tonight," I said. "I bet it would be a nice change from the lumpy futon."

"Yeah, maybe I will." His other hand came up to my forehead, a cool and soothing touch. "Ah, I thought your cheeks looked a little too red. You have a fever too. Go back to sleep."

"Mm-kay," I agreed, my eyes already closing. I held Mikey and Lucy closer to make up for the absence I felt with Grant leaving the room, and when I imagined him on the bed where my mother was earlier, I dropped right into sleep.

Chapter Twenty-Three

The next several days flattened both the kids and me. Somehow, Grant escaped the clutches of the virus. I couldn't remember the last time I felt so miserable, and as hard as I tried to avoid it, I had to call in sick on Monday.

Zach had shown up on Sunday morning, carrying a whole pharmacy and a string of concerned apologies. In his arsenal were a regular thermometer and an ear thermometer in case the kids wouldn't sit for the regular one. Chewable and liquid Tylenol. Throat lozenges. Cough medicine. Pedialyte. It was all overwhelmingly sweet and Zach, through and through. It was the Zach I wished I could keep.

Amid the standard apologies for not having his phone on in between his work shift and his weekend gig, he made a promise.

"When you're feeling better..." He lay on the bed next to me and whispered, "I'm going to take you out for a night on the town. No gigs. Just you and me."

Maybe I could keep this Zach.

I was late to work on Tuesday, burning the bridges of goodwill I'd tried to rebuild over the past few weeks. Still recovering from illness, I overslept. Carl made it clear he was adding my late arrival to my "file." Great.

"Since you still have not earned any more leave," he told me, "you can choose to take the dock in pay, or you can work next Sunday's day shift, since Nicole told me she needs the day off."

Oh, joy—a weekend shift. It wasn't an early one, though, so I crossed my fingers and hoped Grant would understand. As additional punishment, Carl had me doing everything in addition to my regular tasks. I helped in the childcare several times, cleaned up messes in the locker rooms, and filed. Maybe it was a test. I didn't understand what had gotten into him, especially since he never used to micromanage me, but failing the test was not an option. I didn't have time to find a new job to fit the schedule I needed.

Of course, if I found a new daycare, maybe the schedule wouldn't be an issue. The idea of starting a daycare search again created a band of pressure and unease. I knew the next place I found wouldn't necessarily be like Sophie's. Surely there were still some great places out there. Some of the more promising ones might currently have openings when previously they hadn't. It could work out totally fine.

Or I could hope Grant would take the job permanently.

However, Grant had said he would help out, not take over. When he drove across the country to help, becoming the nanny probably wasn't what he'd had in mind. I needed to find the courage to talk to him about it.

"Have you ever thought about going back to school?" Grant asked while we vegged out in front of the TV, both of us wiped out from our respective days. Mikey was still recuperating from the virus but had some comfort with Lucy snuggling him as they slept in my bed.

"Not really."

He didn't follow up. After a while, I picked up the thread again. "What about you?"

"Yeah. I guess." He turned to me. "You really don't think about it?"

Great. Someone else who sees me as a loser for not going to college. I liked my life the way it was. The key words were "the way it was."

The idea of school had crossed my mind recently. I liked my job, its precarious position in recent weeks notwithstanding. I knew it wouldn't lead anywhere, though, and raises didn't come often. I wasn't likely to earn enough to feel comfortable down the line, and with my lack of education, my options were limited.

He must have caught the scowl on my face, because he started chattering.

"Not that you should or have to. I mean, people always expect college is what you're supposed to do, right? But it's not for everyone, not that you couldn't do it or handle it. That's not what I mean. I just mean not everyone likes or wants it. It just seemed like you're really smart, and I didn't really know why you never went to college. Maybe you wanted to and couldn't, or maybe you think it's snobby or something. I hate when people ask me about college like I'm an idiot for not going or something, and then here I go doing the same thing to you, and God, aren't you going to interrupt and stop me? I'm dying over here."

"I wanted to see if you ever actually stop on your own." I grinned. It had a been a little too enjoyable to wait him out, wondering about the deep holes he dug for himself.

"You're evil."

"And you're a pain," I quipped, still smiling.

"Christ, I know." He dug his fingers into his hair.

I pushed down an unexpected urge to put my own hands in his hair by elbowing him good-naturedly instead. "I do hate when people ask me about college as though I'm a fool or must not have been smart enough," I started. "I never used to think much about college because people might be right about me not being smart enough for it. Lately, though... I feel like I need to have some better future for these kids. What's got you bringing it up right now?"

"Kind of the same thing. Don't get me wrong. The money's not too bad in bartending, but it's not like there's this exciting future in it. I don't have any *Cocktail* dreams, you know? I just... I want my life to mean something."

"Like working in a shelter for runaway teens."

His eyes met mine, and I watched them move from warm to taking on an excited flash. "Yeah. Or counseling teens or kids. I think I could be good at working with kids."

Light shone from his eyes, and I breathed through the twinge of jealousy I felt for his focus, his confidence in what he wanted to do with his life. It mixed with happiness for him, because what he wanted to do fit him.

"You would be great," I told him sincerely.

"You think?"

"Of course I do."

"What would you want to do if you got a degree in something?"

"I haven't the slightest idea. My dad says I should start with taking the basic classes everyone has to take in order to get my feet wet."

"He's right. We could take one of those classes together," he said.

"How in the world would we manage a class together? Who would watch the kids?"

"We do it online. I was looking into the community colleges Paul told me about, and they all offer online options for most of their courses."

Holy crap. He's all set to go. Sweat formed on my palms. We'd spent only two seconds talking about going to school, and suddenly, he was signing me up for a course.

"I'm not... I wasn't thinking..." My incoherent response tumbled to the floor.

"No, no. That's cool. I mean, you're right. We wouldn't have to enroll in anything right away. I can't afford it right now, anyway."

I tried to let out my breath of relief quietly as I redirected my attention to the TV screen. The disappointment in his voice stayed with me. Or maybe it was embarrassment. I'd wrecked his enthusiasm. Just because I didn't have my shit together didn't mean the same for him.

Besides, I didn't know what my problem was with his plan. It wouldn't kill me to take one course. He probably wanted to take some book course or something. I was having a hard time even getting through his *Garp* book. *Math. I would enjoy a math course.* Or science. Zach could help me with stuff in those courses. I used to quiz him on things like how different drugs affected various parts of the body. I supposed the class wouldn't be that advanced, though.

"Student loans," I said.

He turned to me. "What?"

"You can get a loan to help pay for your classes."

He muted the TV. "Does this mean you think it might be a good idea after all?"

"I'm not saying *I'm* committing to anything, but that doesn't mean you shouldn't do it."

"C'mon, J. It'll be fun. We can choose a class together. We can help each other out. Look over each other's papers. Quiz each other as we study for tests."

Clearly, he'd clicked into full excitement. "Why is this such a big deal for me to do with you? I can still help you study for quizzes and read over your papers. Well, I'm not sure about helping with the essays, but I can help with other stuff."

He twirled the remote and drummed the fingers of his other hand on his leg. "I guess I'd be more likely to trust what I was doing if you were doing it with me. You attack everything with such confidence, and I figured on sharing a shot of your determination."

"Except I'm terrified to go back to school. I was never very good at the whole school thing. Your reliance on my supposed confidence is slightly misplaced."

His hands stilled as he looked at me again. "No, it's not."

I expected him to say more, but he held my gaze. "I'll think about it, okay?"

He broke into a grin. "I can live with that."

I laughed and shook my head as I reached over to steal the remote. "You're a pain." He had won me over, and he knew it.

"I know."

"Look, since we're talking about the future, sort of, we should also talk about the kids."

His grin faded. "What do you mean?"

"Nothing bad," I reassured him. "I was thinking about daycare. I should probably start looking for something more permanent for them."

"Oh."

"You were doing this to help me, and I really appreciate it, and it's been fantastic for the kids and all. I'm sure you've been wondering when I'd finally get around to starting the search."

"Yeah. Well, no. I guess I wondered if you'd be wanting to find a new daycare for them, but I haven't felt it's taken you awhile to bring it up. It's just... Do you think it's a good idea? Should we really put them through yet another change?"

"I don't know. Maybe not. I don't want to impose on you, though, either."

His hands gripped his legs, and I tried to figure out what I'd said or done to upset him.

"Am I messing things up?" he asked. "Do you want me to do something different with the kids? I know I don't always know what I'm doing, but—"

"What? No! No, you're *great* with the kids. I didn't mean that at all."

He closed his eyes and breathed a sigh of relief.

"Look," I said, "to be honest, I would like nothing more than for us to keep this thing going indefinitely. In fact, drop the rest of the car-payment thing as me paying you to do this."

"Well, that's stupid. I'm not taking money for being with basically my own kids. Ever."

The adamance of his statement nearly took my breath away. It wasn't at all *what* he said but the conviction behind it. He was all in with Lucy and Mikey. "So, we're good with our arrangement?"

"Yeah. I suppose I gotta get my own place one of these days and get outta your hair, but I love being with the kids all day. Even after days when they drive me crazy, I get up the next morning, and they'll be smiling and brand-new again. So yeah, I'm more than good with our arrangement."

Mark his answer in the column of "ways to decrease stress."

"To express my gratitude," I said, "I'll let you have the remote back."

"Truly big-bucks payment coming from you, for sure."

Chapter Twenty-Four

"Now he's making you take a class?" Zach asked.

"He's not *making* me do anything," I said.

"I suggested a long time ago that you go back to school."

Another pissing contest. Great. Before I got upset about it, I reminded myself Zach had been supportive—mostly—about my situation. It had to be hard for him, seeing another man as my roommate. Plus, it didn't help that the man also had an immediate connection with me that Zach didn't share. That night, Grant was out on a date, something I hoped would ease Zach's mind. It did, and I enjoyed cooking dinner with Zach. It helped that we were doing it at home, and everything was comfortable and all it should be until I brought up the conversation about going back to school.

"Yes, you did suggest it. A few months ago, there was no compelling reason to go back. I only had myself to worry about. I need a better job now to help take care of these kids."

"So, you can't afford to come to my gigs, but you can suddenly afford a college course?"

I put my fork down onto my empty plate after our post-bedtime dessert and looked at him in disbelief. "What? Why are you making this about you?"

"I'm not. Tuition's expensive. Where's the money coming from?"

"It's a community-college course, so it's a lot cheaper, and I don't suddenly have the money for it. I haven't exactly figured it all out yet. I might get a loan."

"When were you thinking you'd have time to do all the work for it? Seems like your days and nights are already pretty filled up."

"You mean will I choose to study instead of going to see you play at one of your gigs?"

"That's not what I meant," he said.

"It sure sounds like it. You said you were the one who originally thought I should go back to school, and now you're making it hard for me to even talk about it. I assumed you'd be happy about this." It had been a topic of past conversations, especially when I helped him review for exams. I hadn't considered he would be upset about it not being his idea.

He slipped his hand underneath mine and held it. "I'm trying to get used to all of these changes."

I wanted to be fair. I wanted to admit he was right. He was going through changes too. I looked at his hand around mine then up at his face and its worried expression. "I know. I get it. These things affect you, too, but you have to understand this decision is about *me*, and it's about the kids. I can't just focus on only today any-more. I have to look at tomorrow, next month, next year. I've never had to worry about more than myself before. I never *cared* to think about more than myself. I was never planning to have kids. Brian and Elaine named me guardian without my knowledge. Shouldn't they have *asked* me about taking their kids?"

I stood and paced. "I offered my eggs because *I* didn't need them or want them. How dare Brian assume DNA act as the sole factor for the kids to go to me? Why didn't he make the same assumption with Grant? Because I'm the girl? Compare him and me, and it's obvious who is more suited to the whole parenting role. The thing is—"

The thing is, I want these kids. I loved Lucy's energy and spirit. I loved how she knew her own mind and expressed it at normal vol-umes or at the top of her lungs. I loved Mikey's creativity. I loved his charm and empathy. I loved them both, and I loved that they were mine.

"The thing is what?"

"I love these kids. They have come so far. It amazes me how they've adapted. How can they expect me to do any less? They need everything I can give them, and if how I go about doing it doesn't sit right with you, then you are with the wrong person."

Zach stood, too, and gave me his crooked smile. *Why is he looking at me this way?*

He made his way over to me and, before I could think, pulled me into a kiss, his arms around me securely, his lips warm and sure. Oh God, what a kiss it was too. It reminded me of when we first started seeing each other, when I felt my attraction for him reach all the way down to my toes. Except it was more.

"God, I just fell so hard in love with you right now," he whispered, lips still on mine.

I got lost in another tingling kiss, and for a moment, it felt completely right.

"I knew you had some passion in you. I knew it."

I melted into him, deepening the intensity of each kiss. His hands moved up my skin and under my shirt. When his thumbs reached the sides of my breasts, reality jerked me back. With labored breathing and my heart racing, I backed away.

"We have to stop," I said.

"Why?" He inched closer, pulling me in by my hips. His mouth made it to my earlobe, and he tugged at it gently with his teeth. "If I'm not mistaken, we are on the verge of fantastic sex."

I gasped as his tongue made its way down my neck. I closed my eyes in bittersweet pleasure. I pushed him away again.

"No. We can't. The kids—"

"Are sound asleep." His arms wound around me, and one of his warm, sure hands moved up my back and under my shirt while the other caressed the back of my neck. He kissed me again, but it wasn't the same. First Mikey flooded my brain, then came memories of walking in on my parents, breaking the magical spell between Zach and me.

"They're asleep *now*, but what about later? Mikey has been waking from a nightmare almost every night. Most mornings, I discover Lucy has crawled into my bed, and I don't know when she got there. I can't do this with you now, here, like this. You know I can't."

He sighed heavily and dropped his head, his expression hidden. I secretly thanked him for the small favor. He could keep his disappointment and frustration to himself.

"I'm—" I realized I was about to apologize and stopped myself. I was through taking the blame for his lack of understanding. It wasn't my fault he didn't like my new situation. It wasn't my fault the kids—my kids—lost their parents in a car accident and had their whole lives turn into a crazy, upside-down land. It wasn't my fault that I had a larger responsibility placed upon me.

"I'm sorry too," Zach said, angering me. I was angry he'd correctly guessed what I was going to say and angry for the presumption.

"I didn't say I was sorry."

He looked at me, confused. As I pushed away, Grant walked in the door, cheerful and whistling.

He stopped mid-whistle. He took in my stance, and he tensed. "Hey, guys. Everything going okay?" He gave me a questioning look.

"Weren't you on a date?" I asked.

"I was." He shrugged. "It wasn't really working out. You two wanna bust out of here instead? I can stay with the kids tonight."

"Perfect," Zach said while I said, "No."

Grant looked from me to Zach to me again. "Okay. Well. I'm gonna go change. Let me know if you decide on something."

I nodded to reassure him everything was okay, and he walked out. My eyes met the floor tile. I wasn't ready to look at Zach.

He spoke first. "You're mad."

"I guess."

"You gotta get over this thing."

"Why? Because the movies say sex in the kitchen is hot?" I asked.

"No. This guilt and anxiety you've started carrying around. I want you to be *you* again."

"What if this is the new me?"

"It's not. Some of that spark I saw earlier proves it. But you're right. It's a lot of change. We can work through it."

I let my forehead fall onto his chest. "Okay. Not tonight, though."

He nodded, and I walked him to the door. Zach's hand snaked through my hair. "I meant what I said earlier. I love you."

I was sure he was hoping, waiting, for me to say it back. The words weren't there, so I tried to convey something in my kiss. It couldn't possibly have been enough.

"Meet you for lunch tomorrow?"

And because he looked at me with such kindness and patience, I gave his funny ears an affectionate tug and agreed.

As I closed the door, Grant was suddenly at my side, holding out a beer. I guessed he had heard almost everything Zach and I had said. Instead of embarrassment or irritation, relief swept through me. He walked me over to the couch, and we sank into it, side by side.

"What happened with your date?"

A long, low, rumbling chuckle poured out of him. "You're not going to believe this, but my date turned out to be kind of a double date. Dana brought her twin sister."

"Twins? You mean every man's dream?"

"Next to the whole girl-on-girl thing, yep. Except for your sister, of course. Layla's too much. Sheila, though, with someone else."

I smiled. "It didn't work out? How in the world did you sabotage it?"

"Why do you assume it was *my* fault?" he asked in mock outrage.

I raised an eyebrow.

"Okay, okay. Except it wasn't *all* my fault. The sister's name was *Dolly*. No joke. After Dana introduced her to me, they stood together and said, 'See? Double D's.'"

"Oh God."

He busted out laughing, and he had such a fantastic laugh, it invited me to join in. "It sounds like the perfect night for you. An easy lay, right? And doubled, no less."

"Is that really what you think of me? That I sleep around with women, just for kicks?"

"No, I..." I paused. "No. I don't."

He stared at me, probably trying to decide whether he believed me. I hoped he did but also wasn't sure why it was so important he did.

"All jokes aside, I don't know. Every time Dana said her sister's name, or I tried to, all I could hear in my head was Lulu asking 'Where's my dolly?' or you... your voice reassuring her that her dolly was safe. Weird, huh?"

I shrugged, recalling what had stopped Zach and me earlier. "Nah. Not at all."

"Anyway. It wasn't going to work out."

We sat quietly a while longer. I was thinking about bed until Grant decided I wasn't to be let off the hook.

"Love, huh?"

"That's what he says."

"You don't believe him?"

"I don't know. I got all wound up earlier about him, my family, the kids... mostly the kids, and he said he fell in love with my passion. It was a single moment, so I'm not so sure it means anything. How will he feel tomorrow when he sees I'm still the same me from before?"

"I don't know what you were like before, but anyone can see you've got passion. Shit, it's been there for a long time. I'm surprised Zach only noticed it tonight." He tipped his bottle to his lips and swigged down the last of his beer.

I was a little thrown by the idea I'd been showing passion without actually knowing it. I desperately wanted to ask more about it but felt inexplicably tongue-tied.

"What about you? Do you love Zach?"

It should have been a simple question to answer. I wasn't lying when I expressed doubt about Zach's proclamation. Suddenly, I was making changes he had always wanted, and yet I didn't think they measured up to his vision of my journey. I wasn't sure if he understood the implications of my choices. I wondered if he had fallen in love with the idea of my new situation rather than with me.

"Do you want my opinion?" he asked.

"No."

He nodded and reached for the remote. "All right."

I put my hand on his arm to stop him. "Yes."

He leaned back into the couch again as I reluctantly released his arm. "You won't like all of it."

"Warning noted."

"First, I'm glad you didn't give Zach a knee-jerk 'I love you too' in return. It put him in his place. That guy is far too presumptuous about you. Plus, people respond with 'I love you too' too often. You should only say it if you mean it. Second, you deserve to be with someone who doesn't make you have to work so hard."

"Strong relationships take work."

"By both people."

"Zach does his part. He's had to give up a lot lately."

"Like sex with you tonight? Yeah, I imagine that probably is tough. Poor guy has to go home and jack off on his own instead. Then he'll sleep for eight to ten hours without interruption. He'll go to work without a second thought about what he's leaving behind. Then he'll show up at the community center with lunch, looking like a hero, go to a class—already paid for—like always, and play on his drums later just for kicks. Maybe his girlfriend who only got a couple hours' sleep the night before will stop by at midnight, and if she's lucky, she won't have had to pay the twenty-five-dollar cover charge—the twenty-five dollars that could have gone toward the new shoes she needs—for the fifteen minutes to assure him she hasn't forgotten about him. Then she'll go back home, trip over the crap the guy she never invited left on the floor while he takes over the living room, try to comfort a kid whose parents died when he was too fucking young, and forget once upon a time her life was unencumbered and didn't involve taking care of everyone around her."

I remained silent. I had no desire to defend Zach, nor did I really have anything coherent to say in response to the other stuff. It felt good to hear everything he said since he was partly right about Zach. I learned that with Zach's eyes on me, I did a lot of self-judgment, and I didn't like it. Zach rarely said anything about what he didn't like about me, yet he clearly wanted me to change, and frequently, I fell short of what he wanted. With Grant, I could always be myself. He never judged me and, more often than not, supported my decisions about me personally and about the kids.

Except it wasn't really fair to say I was the one making decisions about the kids. Grant and I figured things out together. We had become a good team, and the idea he was probably going to move out soon made me sadder than I cared to admit. It was more than losing the live-in caretaker for the kids. He had also become a good friend—one of my best friends.

"I said you might not like all of it." Grant broke the silence and my thoughts.

"Well, I'm not exactly arguing with you right now, am I?"

"Yep. I suppose that is a sign of something. Just don't know what yet."

I laid my head on his shoulder in weariness and suggested TV. It might have been a sign of something else, though, that the movie *When Harry Met Sally* was on, and before it got to the part where Harry and Sally finally slept together, I suddenly felt uncomfortable and went to bed.

Chapter Twenty-Five

The following weekend, the kids and I headed down to Rochester to visit Layla and Sheila. We were staying over on Friday night, then I was going to drive back up on Saturday for my date with Zach while the kids stayed in Rochester for the night. I would stay with Zach at his place like he'd wanted for so long. I was nervous about leaving the kids, but I knew they were in good hands with Layla and Sheila and my mom. My mom planned on driving down Saturday, staying overnight, and bringing the kids back up on Sunday.

It had all sounded like a great plan before work happened.

At work, Carl handed me an unexpected ultimatum. "We made a schedule change, Julie."

That didn't sound good at all. "What kind of change?"

"Melissa's doing the kickboxing class in the morning instead of the evening. She'll cover the desk in the morning until the class, and because she doesn't want to split her hours, we'll be shifting your schedule by two hours."

My shift would end at five o'clock. Grant had to work at four. Obviously, that presented a major problem.

"Since when do you make fitness-programming changes?"

"I always reserve the right to step in when necessary."

"What made it 'necessary'?" I couldn't help my insolent tone. He had already imposed his own snobbery on me.

"Melissa says she didn't have a chance to run it by you because you're never here. I guess you're always sliding in 'just on time'"—he used the air quotes to show his doubt that I was on time at all—"and rushing out at the end of the day."

"That's bullshit, Carl, and you know it."

Carl's expression turned stony, and I was pretty sure I'd crossed the line.

I kept going, anyway. "She can't talk to me during any other part of the day? Leave a note? Email me? What's really going on here?"

"You know what's going on, Mercer? Melissa's not calling in sick or coming in late because of her kids. She's not having to take off all the time to figure out daycare or whatever."

"I never took a single day of sick leave before Lucy and Mikey came to me. I volunteered to work on holidays. I covered shifts on weekends."

"That was then. I get it. You have kids now, and they take up a lot of time and get sick. I'll give you a week to figure it out. I can probably get someone to cover the last couple of hours of your shift next week, but beyond that, you need to have it all worked out or take the reduced hours until I can find someone else to fill your position."

"So you're firing me."

"If you can't manage the new schedule, then yeah, I'll need to find someone else who can."

I had a great many more things I wanted to say, but few of them would help me. What he was doing obviously wasn't fair, but I had to figure out if any of it might also be illegal.

Once upon a time, losing a job wouldn't have ruffled me. I'd had a lot of different jobs over the years, and rarely had I missed leaving them. Carl's ultimatum sent me into a minor panic. Having to support two small human beings changed everything.

I decided not to worry about it until Sunday.

Layla and Sheila lived in one of those housing-development neighborhoods where all the houses looked alike with minor differences in the landscape. Their yard was picture-perfect, with multicolored ground cover and decorative rocks bordering the sidewalk from the street to their front door. My mother would approve.

The kids tumbled into Layla's arms. "Here are my munchkins! Sheila and I are super excited to have you here. We've got all kinds of things planned!"

Layla told them about fort building, Play-Doh, cookie making, and numerous other things as she took the kids and their gear upstairs to their room. Sheila hugged me, expressing equal enthusiasm.

"We may have bought a few things in a bit of overzealousness." She smiled, her eyes shining. "Come out back with me for right now. While Layla wows them with everything, you can help me shuck the corn for dinner. It called to me in the produce section, even though it's obviously not Minnesota corn."

We passed through the kitchen, where a pot of water was presumably working its way to a boil, and out onto their deck, where brats were already cooking on the grill. We each picked up an ear of corn and peeled away the husks.

"So," Sheila started, "it sounds like things are working out with the Sperm Whale, huh?"

I smiled at her use of the nickname. "You know, it really is. In fact, we worked it out so I won't have to find new daycare for the kids."

"He's going to stay indefinitely?"

"With the kids, yes. Not necessarily living with us. He doesn't have enough money saved to move out yet. It doesn't matter, though, because the living arrangement has been working out okay."

Sheila snapped off the end of a husk and tossed it into the paper bag between us. "It's not crowded with the living room doubling as a bedroom?"

"Sometimes on the weekends, which is why coming down here this weekend works out nicely."

"An excellent excuse for sure, and for our sake, I'm especially glad. Layla's quite impressed with how you've handled the situation with Grant."

"Well, we both had our not-so-great moments with each other at the beginning," I said.

"Can you imagine if it had been Layla in your place, though?"

I thought about the accusations Grant and I had made about each other then considered Layla's likely reactions. No, things between those two would not have gone well. I chuckled. "Maybe he could have pitched a tent in the backyard?"

She laughed. "And then dug his own latrine."

"He might lure her back out, though, for some campfire stories. He's led an interesting life."

"She does like a good story. Anyway, I'm glad it's working out. How are you feeling about everything these days? Do you... like being a mom?"

Her hesitation unsettled me. With Gemmi, admitting my fears and shortcomings felt safe. I liked Sheila, and she was family, yet I struggled with how much to share. I still didn't know her well. I was nervous about revealing my mixed feelings. Some days, I wanted to run away and pretend I'd never accepted the kids into my life, but most days, I couldn't imagine what life was like before the kids came. I hadn't realized how much my life lacked focus. I wondered if she would believe me or if she would judge me for the "run away" part.

"It's the 'mom' word that throws me. I love these kids, and I know technically and biologically, I am their mother. I know now, circumstantially, I am their mother. Yet sometimes—well, a lot of the time—I don't really *feel* like their mother. I am simply their aunt who might love them beyond measure but can only guess at how to raise them."

My fingers worked away at clearing the last of the silky strings on the final ear of corn from the pile. So much of the silk clung to the ear, and just as I decided to leave the stray bits to hopefully boil away in the pot, Sheila's hands came around mine, holding everything in place.

"Loves them beyond measure? Guessing at how to raise them? Both those things sound exactly like a true mother to me."

I looked up to see her warm smile.

"I don't know how to help you feel like a mother instead of an aunt. I can tell you, however, I already know it's true, regardless of how you see yourself."

Layla surprised me by being a wine drinker. It seemed a soft beverage for her, and I kind of liked it. We sipped away while kicking back on the deck into the night. The kids had taken some time to settle, and Mikey seemed a little nervous about the new setting, so we read extra stories and had some extra snuggles with Bunny. The kids were in sleeping bags on the floor next to the bed I would use. I was under no illusion they would actually stay there. No doubt they'd end up in bed with me before the night was out.

"I'm still not sure about how tomorrow night will go. Maybe I should come on back down after the date."

"You said Grant was able to calm Mikey down, right?"

"It took a little extra effort, but yeah, he did it."

"We will too."

Most of me knew she was right. Another small part of me doubted. In some ways, a month ago would have been better, because at least Mikey hadn't been fully waking up from his nightmares back then. With his current fear and sadness, I hoped Layla's attempts wouldn't throw him off. They seemed to have a connection, those two; I did my best to rely on my faith in their bond.

"This will be good for both you and them, you know," she said. "You've calmed down some since the first weekend we came up to visit and meet the kids, but you're still wound pretty tight."

"I know. I feel like everything got broken, and I've been caught in a continuous fix-it cycle. Figuring out the childcare situation with Grant takes care of one thing. Now it's on to the next."

"What's the next thing?"

"The kids in general. Work. Zach. Me."

"Sounds like the wrong order."

I looked at her dubiously. "The kids have to keep the first-place ranking for now, you know?"

She shook her head. "No, you're mostly right, except I didn't mean them. I meant you. You should come before the other things. Before Zach and work."

"Work just fell apart, so no dice there."

"What happened?"

I gave her the rundown of the conversation with Carl. "I'm not under contract, which means he pretty much can do what he wants with my hours."

"Maybe. He still has to abide by the FMLA. The law says you can take time for childcare and not lose your job. Sounds like he's discriminating, too, for you having kids. He can't do that."

I had considered the discrimination piece but hadn't thought about the family-leave part. It was definitely more ammunition. I knew I had a decent argument to take to Carl. One problem, though, was that I didn't think it would prevent him from cutting my hours. The next problem? Potential for more payback, like he'd already been doing.

"You should talk to Dad," Layla suggested.

"No."

"Why not?"

"I can't keep going to Dad with all my problems. He's been fixing too many things as it is. Everyone's been bailing me out of everything lately."

Layla grunted and drained the last of the wine in her glass. "It's okay to accept help, you know. I'd forgotten how ridiculously independent you always were."

"I've been really good about accepting help lately. Too good. I can figure this one out on my own." I poured some more of the wine. "I do like talking things over with you, though. Why did we stop being friends so long ago?"

"Are you asking a real question, or are you just being nostalgic?"

"It's a real question. I missed you when you started having this new life. It didn't include me. Or Brian, either, I suppose."

"The 'new life' being the one after I came out to you."

"I guess." I thought about it and realized it made sense, except I knew she was closer than friends with one girl the year before, and her coming out to me hadn't been some big surprise. They hadn't always been exactly quiet in her room, but at least they were in her room and not on the living room couch or the kitchen table.

"You guess? Jules, you would cringe when I talked about another girl being attractive. Your mind would jump straight to sex and deciding you thought it was gross. How could I not believe you thought I was gross for wanting another girl instead of a boy? I never thought my sister would think or believe the same thing everyone else around me did. You were my best friend. Until then."

Shit. I couldn't believe that was what had started her pulling away from the family and me. She was right. I was grossed out but not for the reason she thought.

"Lay, I never thought sex between two women was specifically gross. I was grossed out by sex entirely. Man-woman. Man-man, woman-woman, whatever. I thought the whole damn act was the most disgusting thing ever. I had seen too much with Mom and Dad, too many times. The whole thing totally turned me off. I was young and inexperienced and couldn't imagine any good coming from sex. It was never from thinking *you* were gross." I rested my hand on her arm. "You are the opposite of gross. You and Sheila are beautiful. You have everything I didn't even know I wanted."

I had always thought age had influenced Layla to move away from me, and while newfound adulthood was probably part of it, I felt horribly sad knowing it was more, and the "more" had hurt her. All of those years, I thought of myself as being the forgotten child, the afterthought. Instead, she was the one ostracized by her siblings. "I'm sorry I made you feel that way. I didn't know."

"I suppose I shouldn't continue to be mad anymore, hearing you say that. I really wish I'd understood all of those feelings back then. You were great when I told you. Then it seemed like the reality of it had sunk in and you didn't like it. I never considered how our parents' ridiculous sexcapades could have shadowed everything."

The thing we all saw but never talked about. The thing we still saw and still didn't talk about.

"Mom told me she hooks up with Dad when he's between wives."

Layla snorted. "Mom hooks up with Dad when he's *with* those wives."

I leaned back and closed my eyes. I should have figured Mom wasn't telling me the total story. She knew I wouldn't want to know it all. She was right. I remembered the Post-it note on my dad's desk with her name and a day written on it. It might have been a rendezvous, after all. Then I saw the happiness I originally thought I observed as being unique to Dad and Nora. I felt the new roads I'd been creating with my parents start to crumble.

After pulling my legs up to me on the chair, I wrapped my arms around them and asked, without really expecting an answer, "Why do they do that? Why can't they just be loyal to each other?"

"I think Mom cheated on Dad first."

"Why do you say that?"

She looked at her empty glass, and her finger circled the rim. "I don't know. It feels like she never fully wanted to be with us, so she did things to keep herself happy and... too bad for the rest of us."

I understood that interpretation. Remembering my mother's confession of unhappiness, I also learned it was no longer as clear for either of us to assign blame. "I can't say you're wrong, because I have no idea who cheated first. Suppose it was Dad, which caused her to find someone else to make her happy. Or maybe he cheated first because, like you said, Mom didn't really want to be with us and he figured, 'Fuck it, I'll be with someone who does.'"

"I don't figure Dad for a 'fuck it' kind of guy."

"That's all bullshit, Lay, and you know it. It takes two to cheat. Cheating on his wives with Mom is still cheating. I don't understand why, if you're willing to assign blame or give free passes, Dad is getting the pass instead of Mom."

She pursed her lips and tilted her head. The moon gave enough light to provide a striking silhouette of her strong jawline and straight-lined nose. But something in her manner warned me of some unknown secret, some untold story. I unfolded my legs to return my feet to the wood and leaned forward.

"Lay?"

Her glance revealed pain-filled eyes, a sadness I would never normally associate with my sister. She had always been fiercely confident with no time for self-pity or sadness. Her eyes usually held challenge, anger, or plain old self-assurance.

"What happened?" I asked gently.

"A few years ago, Sheila and I decided we wanted kids. We wanted to have a baby. The idea of using a random sperm donation didn't appeal to us, and Sheila and I had a good friend who served as the donor. He had no interest in raising the child but wanted to be involved. We had contracts. Sheila got pregnant then miscarried about fourteen weeks in. Our 'friend' sued on the grounds that Sheila was somehow responsible. She didn't eat right or exercised too vigorously or whatever other bullshit he could come up with. Dad stopped the charade from even getting off the ground. He never questioned Sheila or me about anything. He went straight in and blew the whole lawsuit out of the water before it could gain traction, and I have never been so grateful for something in all my life."

Multiple emotions coursed through me as I listened to the obviously abridged story. They'd lost a child. Two women who were clearly built to be amazing parents had a chance and lost it. That anyone whom they trusted could betray them so thoroughly with those accusations gutted me. It crushed me to know their "friend" thought Sheila would have done something to jeopardize the pregnancy. Then I remembered the unidentified emotion Sheila'd had when she helped me figure out daycares. It was pain. Or maybe regret.

What my father did to help sounded exactly like him. Helping us was his way of loving and taking care of us. I'd never doubted he loved me—us—but much like my mother, he'd never been very expressive about it or exhibited much desire to be involved with us.

Yet he had shown up in Duluth to help with the will. He took care of Sophie, the daycare provider, for me. He would probably be happy to fix the situation with my job too. Maybe that kind of love was the most either of my parents could offer. For my sister's sake, it was certainly more than enough from our father, and I finally understood, as an adult, that maybe it was enough for me too.

"I'm so sorry," I said. "I can't imagine what you went through. The joy and hope, and then to lose it all, followed by such awful accusations? I'm sorry."

She nodded but didn't look at me. "Our baby would have been about Lucy's and Mikey's age right now had she lived. I always thought she might be a girl."

I imagined our children playing together during our visit. I imagined having never drifted away from Layla in the first place and having known the little girl of her dreams, or of having been able to simply hold my sister, as I reached over to do. For the first time I could remember, she let me hold her and comfort her. She let me pretend to be the big sister. But only for a moment.

She pushed me away, tears still building in her eyes. "No, stop. Don't comfort me because you won't like what I have to confess next." She wiped at her eyes. "The night we found out about Brian and what was to happen with the kids, before Sheila and I went up to Mom's house, we talked and planned far more seriously about taking on the guardianship of Lucy and Mikey than you might think." She stood and walked over to the deck rail before resting her fists on top of it. "I was so angry Brian left those kids to you. I knew there was no reason to believe he'd leave them to me, but still, *you?*"

Her disbelief in me didn't upset me; it would have been ridiculous to dispute it. Obviously, I had, once upon a time, agreed with her assessment.

"It wasn't fair how at the same time we had lost our future family, Brian was getting *two* children and at the hand of my own sister. It felt like a betrayal. When Brian died, it all came back to me, and I called Dad to see about legal means of getting you to give up your guardianship rights."

Then silence pushed its way between us, the way air in a revolving door pressed against someone moving within the door. I let it press me into my chair as I stared into Layla's back. Up in Duluth, my dad had suggested Layla as a guardian made more sense financially. He didn't mention Layla herself had tried to take the kids from me. Maybe all that time, he would rather have been helping Layla.

But no. I stopped those thoughts. I understood my dad better, and he was right about the financial logic, but he'd also never questioned or doubted me in my role with the twins. He'd sat at the kitchen table to support me while I did my homework. All those years later, he was still sitting at the kitchen table for me.

Unlike my sister.

Layla turned toward me and looked as though she expected me to say something. Utter disbelief, shock, and anger ate up all my words.

She broke the silence. "He said no, Jules." She said it as though it were an obvious conclusion. "He said it would involve discrediting you and proving you were unfit and how I couldn't see why you were the natural choice, and he would have no part of it."

Anger was the winning emotion, propelling me to my feet and giving me words. "You didn't even *know* me, and you thought I'd be a crappy parent? Enough to take legal action? Against your own sister? It's not my fault Brian was an asshole to you. Helping him and Elaine is *not* the same thing as betraying you. If I had sperm, I'd have gladly given it to you and never have *thought* of staking a claim on your child." I didn't know if any words coming out of my mouth made sense or were true. Maybe the wine had gotten to me, or maybe the whole thing rang a little too close to the truth of how I had always felt. I'd always thought it would have made sense for Layla and Sheila to have the kids. And after seeing Grant in action, he would have made sense too. It was crystal clear the kids should have gone to Layla and Sheila. Or Grant. Maybe I wasn't the logical pick, but I couldn't believe she thought I would have been the *worst* choice. I had been figuring it all out. Lucy, Mikey, and I had been doing okay. I was doing everything I knew how to start a new life for the kids.

"I know you would have helped us," she said.

"He didn't even *call* me when the kids were born. He never invited me to come up and see them. I gave him my eggs, no questions asked, and never got the courtesy of being their aunt. I might never have wanted kids of my own, but it didn't mean I didn't want to be part of the family or know my niece and nephew. The only reason I'm the guardian is because there weren't other options, or I don't know, maybe it was obligation. In Brian's fucked-up life view, he couldn't possibly have left the kids with their biological father or his lesbian sister even if they were the most logical and natural choices ever to be parents."

"Jules."

"It's still me they're stuck with. Am I that ridiculous of a choice for raising children?"

"No, of course not."

"And yet you'd seek the law to say I am."

"No, I wouldn't," Layla said. "At least, not anymore. I'd like to think if Dad had agreed, I would have realized my mistake by the next day. As soon as you said no to me, I knew I was wrong. You refused me with such conviction, and I realized it wasn't just to spite me. You wanted to take on the responsibility. I don't know what Dad knew that I didn't—and should have—but I do know he was right, and I'm sorry for ever doubting you."

My self-righteous anger fizzled, leaving me tired and confused. I walked over to the rail and rested my elbows on it in order to support my face in my hands. "I've made a lot of mistakes."

Layla walked over and looped an arm around me. "Babe, that's the definition of parenting. Let me tell you what I know now about you. I know you think the kids warm up to everyone else more easily than to you, but you're wrong. What you haven't seen is how they rely on you to determine what's safe. You haven't noticed they look to you first, before going to someone else. They have security with you. Do you think they would have warmed up to me, Sheila, or Grant as quickly if they didn't know it was because you showed they could trust us? They trust *you* and know you'll still be there for them, even after we leave. Who do they go to when they're sad or scared? When they race off to their room, who is the one they wait for to tell them it's okay?"

I shifted my head enough to look at her. "They would have felt the same with you, though, if you'd taken them in."

"God, Jules, you're missing my point. Yes, you're probably right. Except Brian didn't entrust them to me. He entrusted them to you, and you've proven him right. You understand those kids. It shows in everything you do with them."

Exhaustion gave way to tears. "Thank you. I really needed to hear that."

Layla put her arms around me and held me close. "We're family. I've got your back."

Chapter Twenty-Six

The twists in my back and the cricks in my arms and legs woke me the next morning. Instead of the kids ending up in bed with me, I'd joined them on the floor. I looked with concern at the top of Mikey's head, which rested on my stomach. After my conversation with Layla, I'd barely crawled into bed before Mikey awoke, his cries full of fear and sadness, filling me with my own fear.

"Was your dream a sad one?"

To my surprise, Mikey had an answer. He shook his head.

"A scary one?"

A nod.

"About your parents?"

He buried his face in me and gripped me tighter. He shook his head again.

I held him close. "Your sister?" No. I frequently wondered what his nightmares entailed. Lucy never talked about any dreams and rarely woke from nightmares. "Whatever it was, you're okay now. I've got you. It's okay. I love you, honey." I rubbed his back and repeated the words over and over until I could feel him relax. By then, I'd been too tired to move and simply curled up on the floor with him and Lucy.

I gently looped one of his curls around my finger. His hair was finally growing out, and it made me smile to see how it mimicked Grant's. I analyzed Mikey's dream process. He was finally moving toward something, and part of me recognized it as good progress while another realized it could mean his grief might surface more fully. I didn't know what his grief would do to him or how it might affect Lucy and me.

A different tangle of hair bobbed by my side as Lucy unfurled and sat up with a smile. "You camped out with us!"

"Yes." I smiled back. "I guess I did. How about you start a spy mission to figure out breakfast?"

She readily agreed and scrambled out the door.

Though Mikey hadn't moved from his position on the floor and on my stomach, I knew he was awake. "Hey, sweetie."

He twisted around to face my head instead of my feet.

"Are you about ready for breakfast too?"

He hid his face into Bunny.

"Okay, we'll wait." I sat up against the wall, and Mikey crawled into my lap and rested against my chest.

"Last night's dream was different, wasn't it?"

He nodded.

"Sometimes, our dreams are our mind's way of figuring things out, of helping us with our feelings. The nice thing, though, is the dreams themselves aren't real." I tilted his head to face me then placed my hands on either side of his face, as he had done for me in the past. "If you ever need to be sad or mad without saying why, you can, okay? It's okay to be sad."

I brought my hands back, and he put his arms around my neck and squeezed. When he let go, he placed his hand on his stomach, letting me know he was ready for breakfast. I smiled and told him to head on down. I would follow in a minute. As he traipsed out of the room, with Bunny trailing him, I tried to take in Layla's words from the night before. I hoped with all my heart Mikey really did feel safe with me.

My mother arrived later in the morning, and after lunch, we set out for a quick shopping trip to find a new dress for me to wear for my date with Zach. I'd already set the parameters of two stores and done. The kids wouldn't last longer, and it wasn't like I couldn't wear something I already had. After thirty minutes, the score stood at my closet, one, and the mall, zero, as store number one stalled out, and we progressed quickly to store number two.

My mother wandered off with the kids to look at clearance racks of raincoats while Layla, Sheila, and I perused the dresses.

Sheila picked out a dress that made me think of Grant. It was a deep-red cottony thing meant to hug every part of my formless body. I worried about the spaghetti straps and no jacket to hide my tattoo. Zach was taking me to some surprise place, and I didn't know how fancy it was. Regardless, he wouldn't want my crass side on display. Not that he ever used that word to describe my tattoo, but his attitude had been clear in other ways.

"Grant would like the red one," I said.

"He has excellent taste, then. What makes you think so?"

"I think it was some actress on TV once. She wore something similar and had all the right curves."

"So we're getting this dress for you, right? You've got the hips for it, which is enough to make this work on you." Sheila took the dress off the rack and held it up next to me. "Grant would definitely approve."

"Except I'm supposed to be impressing Zach."

"Isn't it a given if one man will salivate, the other will too?"

The idea of Grant salivating over my appearance appealed to me far too much. I decided not to dwell on it. "I'll need a wrap or something to go with those thin straps."

"Why? It's supposed to stay warm all through tonight and into tomorrow."

"Zach thinks my tattoo is too flashy."

Layla, who had been only half listening while checking email and texts, caught the radar ping. "Why are you still with this guy, anyway?"

I'd thought about the question a lot lately. "I don't know. I already broke up with him once before."

"Wait. What?"

They turned to me in surprise. Funny how I had always failed to mention the key bit of my and Zach's history. For a while, even I had forgotten.

"When?" Layla asked.

"Before Brian and Elaine died."

"Comfort?"

"I guess. I mean, I didn't call him. He showed up at my door the day after I found out. He didn't know about Brian until I invited him in. And then yeah, I suppose it was comfort. He was there for me and simply stayed—no questions. Well, until he found out about the kids, but everyone questioned the kid situation." I looked at Sheila, who remained mute, which I supposed meant I was to keep talking. "He's a good guy. He really is. It just wasn't going anywhere."

"Is it going anywhere now?"

I shrugged. "He says he loves me, except I don't think he loves *me* but the me he wishes I were."

"You don't love him?" Layla asked.

"No."

"Yet we're shopping for a fancy dress for a date with him."

I shifted, resting my weight on my right hip. "I like him. I keep thinking the spark will ignite one of these days. Maybe it will on this date."

The expressions on their faces clearly suggested I was being ridiculous. My mom rejoined us with the kids and noticed the awkward moment. "Well, that didn't take long. I've already missed something juicy, haven't I?"

"Apparently, we are buying a dress for a fake date," Layla answered.

"Any date is as good of an excuse as any to buy something," my mom answered. "Especially this dress. Is it the one we've decided on?"

"Yes," Layla said. "We're not sure if Zach will like it, but Grant will love it, so naturally, this is the one we must get."

"Layla," Sheila murmured.

"I'm sorry I don't have my life all figured out perfectly like you do, Lay. Don't you think I want what you and Sheila have? I'm trying to get it with Zach. Maybe he *is* that person. I haven't given him much chance."

"Uncle Zach's teaching me how to play the drums!" Lucy suddenly chimed in, then Mikey's hand was in mine.

I didn't know how he always knew. He was too young to be so empathetic. I gave his hand a light squeeze and smiled at him to reassure him I was all right.

"Babe, I'm sorry," Layla cut in quietly. "I guess I don't know Zach, but what if you're trying too hard with the wrong person? I just want you to be happy."

"We all do, honey," my mom added.

What scared me was that Layla was probably right. I let things get too far. "I can't cancel on him today. This is the first time he's done something like this, and I've messed up things with him enough."

Layla threaded an arm through mine. "Then let's check out the jewelry next. We have to get something to match this dress."

I blinked and swallowed the surge of emotion and managed another grateful smile. "A necklace. I've already got earrings to match, but I need a necklace."

"Jewelry!" Sheila cheered. "My favorite thing."

After a successful shopping trip, we rewarded the children and ourselves with ice cream. Mikey ate little of it, and by the time we got to the house, he'd started his isolation techniques—coloring with his back to us and hiding away on his own in the indoor tent Layla had set up. It wasn't until I was about to leave to head up to the Cities that I understood more fully why.

Lucy danced my way and gave me an easy hug and kiss goodbye. Mikey, however, nearly had me canceling all my plans for the rest of the day. In an unexpected display of more outward emotion, he latched onto me much like he did at night. Curling into himself, shrinking away, and ignoring—these had been his normal reactions to pain or difficult situations. He didn't cry—he rarely did, outside of his nightmares—but it wasn't for lack of desire. He fought the tears, making me do the same.

"I'll see you tomorrow morning, sweetie. I promise." He almost pushed me away then raced out of the room.

My mother read the indecision on my face. "He'll be okay. He needs some time to adjust and get used to the idea." She put her hands on my shoulders. "Go. Have a good time and enjoy the time for *you* tonight."

I didn't have a full smile to reassure her but gave her what I could. "Don't wait too long in the morning to bring them back, okay? Call me before you leave, however early it is."

Though the agreement came through in an obviously placating tone, it nonetheless yielded an agreement, so I took it and started home. I found my seventies-music radio station and blasted it, taking myself all the way home and pushing away most of the tension. I stuffed down my anxieties about Mikey, my job, college, and wills and concentrated on trying to guess where Zach would take me for our date.

It had been a long time since we had truly gone out on a date. Before I found out about Brian and broke up with Zach the first time, we had fizzled into homebodies, partly because of the frigid Minnesota winters that caused hibernation and partly because of Zach's heavy course load. We would order takeout, and I helped him study for exams or format his reports and case studies. Then we vegged out in front of the TV. He worked several evenings a week, and other nights, I went to see him play.

He'd said he wanted to surprise me, but I would have been thrilled with any old place if it meant I didn't have to cook or clean. I looked forward to food that provided no guessing game for those at the table and that would also stay there and not get tossed to the floor. I anticipated time to simply eat and enjoy a meal from start to finish with no rush. Maybe we'd take in a movie afterward or go straight to his place and recreate what I had ruined a few days earlier.

Apprehension swam through me. I'd let myself believe our entire relationship was riding on one special date, which was ridiculous. Maybe my nervousness stemmed from the solitude I was unaccustomed to in my apartment. I didn't know what to do with myself. Once upon a time, it took me ages to get ready. Jitters and new experiences had me speeding right through my preparations. I slowed down when I got to my hair and makeup. I wanted to impress Zach.

I pulled my hair away from my face, considering the comment that the Hair for Littles stylist had made about how Lucy and I shared the same eyes and cheekbones. I studied myself, searching for the resemblance. Maybe with the right makeup techniques, I could work some magic. I knew what Zach wanted, though, so I let my hair fall around my face. I successfully coaxed the wisps, curls, and waves into all the right places and smiled at the result, imagining his expression when he saw me.

Everyone had talked me out of the wrap to go with the dress, saying the color of the fabric contrasted well with both the color and design of my tattoo. The choker we'd picked out had green flecks to match the color of the stem, and I wore some of my less ornate rings to avoid looking too wild.

When the knock came on the door, I found Gemmi on the other side instead of Zach—a welcome surprise. I'd taken the kids to church again recently, but she hadn't joined us, and we met up with only Sean there. In fact, I hadn't talked to her in quite some time. I missed her.

"Hey! What are you doing here?"

Her panic-stricken expression didn't match my happy greeting. I pulled her across the threshold and quickly tried to process whether our lack of contact might not have been entirely my fault after all. I seemed to remember an unreturned phone message or two. "C'mon in. Tell me what's wrong."

She walked a few paces from me and pressed her fingers to her forehead. "Oh God, Jules. I made a mistake. A really, really big mistake."

Her breath came out in muted gasps, and her body trembled. I went to her and wrapped my arms around her. "It's all right. Whatever it is, we'll figure it out, okay?"

The sobs spilled out of her, stored-up emotions cascading around me. We stood there, letting the initial flood pass through before she choked out, "I don't see any way to figure this one out."

I moved us to the couch, and as we sat, I took her hands. "We will."

"I'm pregnant."

Oh. *Oh.* "Fuck."

She started to cry again. "I know. God, mai, I'm so stupid. Sean was right, and you can't tell him. Promise me you won't."

"Of course I won't. I promise. I take it this means you haven't told Demitry either?"

She shook her head. "You're the only one. I knew you'd understand. What do I do?"

"What do you want to do?" My heart hurt at the pain in her expression. "I know it's a crap way to answer you, but what I'm trying to ask is if you didn't have to worry about what anyone else thought—*anyone*—what would you want to do?"

Three months ago, if I had been in the same situation, I might easily have experienced the same panic. But three months ago, I would have been ending a short-run relationship with Zach instead of a long-term, committed one like Gemmi had with Demitry. As I thought it over, I wondered how I would react within the context of our current status. I loved Lucy and Mikey, but I didn't think I had changed my opinion about having any other children of my own. The thought of suddenly finding myself pregnant while I was with Zach terrified me.

And what a message that was.

"I don't know," Gemmi answered. "Being pregnant, giving birth, raising a child—it'll change my whole life. I love my life right now. I don't want to give it up." She regarded me as though realizing her implications about my own life.

"I get it," I told her. "And you're right. It changes everything."

"You didn't have a choice."

"And you do."

She hesitated, her eyes welling up. At the same moment came the knock on the door from the expected visitor. Gemmi scanned me, suddenly noticing my attire. "Shit, Jules, you have plans—"

"Don't worry. Hold on a sec."

I opened the door to see Zach dressed to the nines in a navy suit with a deep-green tie. He stepped forward to come in, but I guided him back into the hall, following him and shutting the door behind me.

"What's going—wow, Jules, you look fantastic."

"Thank you."

"You'll probably want some sort of jacket or sweater or something, since the club will probably blast the air with this heat we've been having."

There it was. Once again, though not direct, the message still came through. "I'll be fine. Can we shift everything a little later?"

"What's wrong?"

"Gemmi showed up, and she needs my help. I can't leave her yet."

"Anything I can do?"

I kissed his cheek. "No. We need a little more time. That's all."

"Yeah, okay. We have a reservation at the Blues Lounge, which I can try to change, but the Lux Trio is playing, so I bet they'll be full up."

"Wait, I thought you said no gigs tonight?"

He cocked his head and drew his eyebrows together. "Right. I'm not playing, but I thought it would be fun to see these guys play. They're top-notch."

Somehow, when he'd said "just me and you," I'd thought he really meant it. While it was true that the Trio wasn't his group, it was still all his thing. It felt like an intrusion. I couldn't explain why and tried to rearrange my attitude, which caught me in the gut. It had always been my "attitude" that was the problem.

Whatever. Gemmi first then Zach. "Okay. I'm sorry about the reservation, but Gemmi needs me right now."

"It's okay. I'll see what I can work out. Call me when you're ready."

As Zach walked down the hall, I took a deep breath to help shift gears and stepped into my apartment. Gemmi was curled up along the side of the couch, clutching a tissue box.

"I'm sorry about screwing up your date."

"You're not screwing it up. To be honest, I take full credit for it." She looked at me with questions in her eyes, but I waved her off. "It's nothing. Really."

She looked calmer, which told me she'd gotten closer to some decision.

"So, we were talking about how you have a choice."

She shook her head. "I don't really have a choice, do I? Not in my case. I'm not pregnant from some random guy I'll never see again."

"You *always* have a choice, but you're right about how maybe you shouldn't make this decision all on your own. Especially knowing how Demitry would feel about it. Especially knowing how you feel about Demitry."

"I can't get an abortion without telling Dem. No way can I do that to him. He wants kids, but he didn't mean he wanted them *now*. And I don't even know if I want this baby at all. I'm so stupid. I can't believe I did this."

"What happened?"

"Dem brought up marriage again, and he looked so happy and excited. His enthusiasm pulled me in, and the next day, I was holding my birth-control-pill packet and staring at it. I thought, if I get pregnant, then I won't be able to lose this happiness we have together. I won't be able to use it as an excuse to break up, and then... I threw the whole thing into the trash."

With Zach, it sometimes seemed like he was more attracted to me because of the kids, of some idea that we were becoming a family. It was after I ranted about them that he determined he fell in love with me. He loved giving me advice about how to raise them. *When was the last time he really listened to what I want or what I care about?*

Gemmi didn't have the same issue with Demitry. Anyone could see Demitry loved Gemmi. When she moved out of my place to go live with him, I let her go far more easily because I knew how Demitry felt about her. As much as he wanted kids, though, Gem was right. He might have had suspicions about her motivations.

"You need to talk to Demitry," I said. I didn't know how he would react in the short run, but something told me he'd hang in there. "You need to tell him everything. What you did, why you did it, and how you feel."

"What if he hates me for thinking I can't have this baby?"

"Then I guess you know, right?"

"*Ay Diós.* Is this you saying he might?" Gemmi asked.

"No. Well, I don't think so. But we tell it like it is, right? No sugarcoating?"

"A little sugar might be nice about now." She gave the smallest of smiles.

"Okay, then. Give me a sec." I went to the kitchen and rummaged around for my secret stash of Little Debbie snacks and found some Swiss Cake Rolls. I came out again and tossed one to her. "Hostess called these Ho-Hos. Here's a Ho-Ho for the ho who got herself pregnant with a man she'll probably marry. How's that for a 'little' sugar?"

She couldn't help it. The giggles took over. "I am a total ho. You're right."

"You know I am. You left *me* for him. It's the only explanation."

She laughed, then I got serious.

"Look, do you trust him?"

She leaned her head against her knuckles and took in my question. "Yes, I think I do."

"Then I guess you know what to do, right?"

"Yeah."

I smiled and reached over for a hug. "You don't have to do it tonight. Stay here. You can sleep in the kids' room."

"Thanks, but I think it's best if I went home to Dem tonight. Do you mind if I hang out here for a while by myself, though?"

"Take all the time you need. Grant doesn't usually get home until around three."

She hugged me again and thanked me for listening. I wished her luck, but I knew she wouldn't need it, at least not yet. She had nine more months of needing luck and maybe many more years, depending on what happened.

I, on the other hand, sure needed luck for what I was going to do next.

Chapter Twenty-Seven

I sat at the bar, off to the side, wanting to be unnoticeable to anyone except Sean.

"Julie. You're looking way overdressed for this joint. Got a hot date coming for you?"

"More like escaping the hot date early."

Sean gave me a sympathetic look.

"Gemmi's not working tonight, but I can trash ex-boyfriends with the best of them, you know."

"I do know. Why do you think I came here?"

"Problems with Zach?"

"Not anymore."

"Ah, well, good riddance, I say. I didn't like him, anyhow."

"Really?" I asked. "Or are you only saying that because I'm here to get drunk about the situation, and you think it will make me feel better?"

He shrugged. "First, second, and third drink's on me, my love. What'll it be?"

"How about a mojito? Wait, no. Vodka tonic. Or vodka anything."

As he poured me the drink, he asked about Gemmi. "She's avoiding me, which is hard to do when you're business partners. It's been all 'shoptalk only' lately. Is she talking to you?"

"Yes."

His scrutiny was intense enough for me to expand the tiniest bit. "I can't tell you, so don't ask, but she'll come to you. She will." I discarded a thought about warning him to be compassionate; I didn't have to. Based upon Sean's "don't do anything stupid" comment a few weeks back, I understood why Gemmi would be worried. But when it came down to it, he would be there for her.

"I gotta go take care of these other customers. You okay here?"

I waved him away. "Yeah, yeah. I'm good. Just send someone over to top me off every once in a while, huh?"

He smiled and slid over a basket of pretzels as he moved away to help a couple at the end of the bar. I would have gone home to Gemmi if I hadn't known she already had problems enough to deal with. Sean could trash-talk like nobody's business and also keep it all light.

I grabbed a pretzel and looked down the bar to see one man sitting on a stool with the other standing close, his arm slung affectionately around his partner, a thumb gently stroking his arm. The gentle scene of companionship suddenly hit me with what I'd just lost and made me doubt I'd ever had it.

It hadn't been an easy breakup.

I pulled out my phone and dialed Grant, letting it ring three times before I panicked at what I was doing and ended the call. He was working, and that wasn't the relationship we had. We didn't get drunk and pathetic and expect the other to pick us up off the floor. Besides, I didn't need him seeing my stupid wallowing.

I downed the last of my drink, and Mason, another bartender, got me going on my next and then my next. I averted my eyes from the romantic couple and took in the rest of the club. It was a country-and-western theme night—so far out of both Sean and Gemmi's wheelhouse, I wondered how they'd landed on it—and I admired the hats and boots galore. I thought I still had a decent pair of boots somewhere in the back of my closet, perfect for line dancing.

My phone buzzed. It was Grant. *Shit.* I let it go to voicemail. A minute later, though, a text from him came through. He was worried about the kids. *Double shit.* I was selfishly sitting in a bar, thinking

I didn't want him to hear my sauced-up sadness, forgetting I would never be the first thing to come to his mind. It was a good thing. He was a good dad. Actually, he was a fantastic dad. Looking at him, people jumped to the conclusion he was some sort of immature loser, but they were wrong. He took responsibility for everything he did. He probably wouldn't be caught sitting on the corner stool of a bar, downing alcohol simply because he broke up with someone.

I texted back. *Kids are fine. They're still at Layla's. Don't worry.*

He volleyed back. *Call me now.*

Then came *Please.* I remembered him telling me he would always answer when he could. I owed him the same thing.

"Where are you?" he asked upon pickup.

"At the Grey Shade."

"How messed up are you?"

"Well on the way to fantastically messed up. Sean's got a Lyft for me later."

"What happened?" he asked.

"Broke up with Zach. It's no big deal. I didn't want the night to go to waste, you know? It's country-Western night here. I can't pass that up."

"Right. I'm sure you blend right in there."

"I really do. Turns out a spaghetti-strap red dress matches plaid flannel. I'm missing the finishing touches of a cowboy hat, but—"

"Okay, I got it. I just wanted to make sure you were okay."

"I'm at the top of my game, baby."

I was pretty sure if he hadn't been mad before, he was when we hung up.

Sean brought me another drink. "Top of your game?"

"Yep, and you ain't seen nothin' yet. I'm going to show you guys how I'm going to be even higher. I'm gonna *top* the top of my game."

"Maybe this should be your last drink."

"Yeah, okay. You're the best, Sean. Keep 'em coming." Maybe I should have eaten a few more pretzels before slamming down the vodka.

Loud cheers rang out, and I looked over to see a line dance starting with Tim McGraw's "I Like It, I Love It." The monitors filled with shots of a shirtless McGraw, and everyone on the dance floor looked wildly happy. A photo on one monitor showed off McGraw's tattoos, which made me think of other tattoos. I pulled my eyes away and stared into my glass.

At one point, Zach had asked me if breaking up with him had anything to do with Grant. In so many ways, it didn't, but I couldn't deny he was probably mixed up within it all too.

It would have been better if I'd lied about it, though. Zach lost sight of everything else and blamed it all on Grant, as though I'd been cheating. Hearing—directly, for once—about all the things wrong with me had been far more difficult to take. I let him go on for a bit before I finally had the wherewithal to walk away.

It was a relief, really.

"Still at the top of your game?"

I know that voice. Grant. I forced my gaze away from my glass to him. *What the hell is he doing here?* Somehow, him showing up made him look freaking hot. Or maybe it was the environment. I hadn't been on anyone's radar since entering the place, and suddenly, there was a new possibility when there shouldn't be one.

"Did you lose your job too?" I scowled but not before his gaze traced a path up and down my body then snapped back up to my eyes.

"What? Lose my job 'too'? What are you talking about?"

"Oh yeah. I didn't get a chance to tell you about that. Carl's fucking with my hours." I held up my empty glass. "Cheers." *Welcome to uncontrolled conversation starters.*

Sean appeared as Grant slid into a seat next to me. "Beer?"

Grant shook his head. "Nah. I'd better stick with a Coke."

I leaned into him. *Mmm.* He still smelled good. "The guy a few seats away is already checking you out. You should, you know, spill something on your shirt so you won't look as appealing."

He chanced a glance over at where I nodded. "He's not really my type."

"You have a type?" I wondered about the other father he knew from the park.

He shrugged.

Something crossed his expression—a memory, maybe, and it wasn't a bad one. I rested my head against my palm. "Tell me about him."

He smiled lightly. "There was this one guy about three or four years after I left home. It wasn't long after I stopped doing the frat-party crashing. I met him at a bar. We talked. Went to breakfast. Went out again the next night, and things progressed from there."

"How long did it last?"

"Only about a month or so. He grounded me. It was probably the beginning of when I focused more on things with a purpose."

"That's pretty hot."

He laughed that free, happy laugh of his, and I no longer needed another drink. "See? That's how men feel, but you all just roll your eyes at us."

I grinned.

He rested his forearms along the edge of the bar and cocked his head. "However, you are the rare creature who admits to the possibility. I think *that's* pretty hot."

I felt the flush move from head to toe. *Did he just call me hot?*

"Did Elaine know?" I asked.

"Know what?"

"About the guy. Or guys."

He looked down into his glass, tipped it away, then took a swallow from it. "It's possible. Might explain the 'God can save you' emails."

The weariness of it all weighed me down.

"What happened with Zach?" he asked, changing the subject to an equally exhausting topic.

I shrugged. "It was really bound to end again sometime."

"Again?"

"Yeah. Weird, huh? I didn't think this was going to last, then he had to go and say he was in love with me. It was hard enough to break up with him the first time. He's a good guy, you know?" Mostly. Until that night, anyway. Then again, couples weren't usually nice to each other during a breakup. At least not in my experience.

Grant didn't answer and drank his Coke.

"He seemed like a better guy before, and he isn't a *bad* guy. I might have stayed with him for the sex. He really was good in bed. Not that we've had any sex since before the kids. Wait, no. There was one time. Wow. Maybe that's why he thought he loved me. He let his brain take over and fool himself." Gotta love alcohol. I was sounding like The Sperm.

"First of all…" He looked at me. "You did not just tell me Zach, that stringy, self-centered know-it-all, gave you good sex."

"I know, right?" I lifted my glass and tried to find any remaining drops of vodka. "He knew what to do with his hands."

"If he did, you would have gone home with him last week when I offered to let you get away for the night. Or at the very least, half your clothes would have been off you when I walked in."

"That moment was not about sex," I said.

"Sure looked like it to me."

Sean had disappeared, and I needed another drink. Raising my hand, I caught his eye and waved him over. I pushed my glass toward him. "Fill 'er up, oh, Danny Boy."

Grant's hand shot out and covered my glass. "She's just mad at me, Sean. As soon as I apologize, she won't need the refill."

Sean waited. I met his eyes and shrugged. He nodded back and went to help the guy who had been eying Grant earlier.

"I'm not entirely sure what I'm apologizing for, but I obviously said something wrong. I'm sorry," Grant said.

"Besides, half my clothes being off when you walked in would *never* have happened."

"Okay."

"I'm not one of those women who has sex in public restrooms."

"I don't really understand that comment, but I'd like to point out that the kitchen in your own home is not a public restroom."

God. Why am I talking about this with him? "When you've seen your parents fucking around everywhere they please and with anyone they please, then come talk to me about how the kitchen may as well be the Mall of America. Lucy and Mikey don't need to see that."

I rested my forehead on the bar as I thought about how my home experience was nothing compared to the hell he'd lived through with his own. I didn't know why he wasted his time coming to the bar. "Fuck."

A string of celebratory whoops passed through our silence. Another line dance was in progress.

"Second of all"—Grant cut into my drunken self-hatred at my stupid, unimportant pity party—"in spite of his ego, he definitely is, or was, in love with you."

My head spun as I bolted upright. "What? Are you trying to tell me I made a mistake? I shouldn't have broken up with him?"

"Fuck no. I'm glad you dumped his sorry ass."

"Okay, then. So, what *are* you doing?"

"You made it sound as though you couldn't believe he might actually be in love with you. Zach might have been stupid about a lot of things, but how he felt about you was not one of them."

"I'm so confused," I said.

"Drunk can do that to you."

"I can't believe not a single guy has hit on me since I've been here."

He laughed.

God, I love his laugh. "You think I'm too drunk to remember where I am, but damn it, I look *hot* tonight. It would be common courtesy to at least pretend to be straight, don't you think?"

"Fools, all of them." He stood and came behind me then guided me off the stool. I leaned into him for a moment. "C'mon, hot babe. Let's get you home. I've got some aspirin waiting to hit on you."

Grant's hands on me, even platonically, aroused me and caused me to rethink the whole "Zach was good in bed" conversation. Maybe I'd missed another cue. Except I wasn't too drunk to know that it wasn't the time to start anything.

I'm not too drunk.

Then we exited the cool, air-conditioned bar, and the comparative heat and humidity buffeted my head, making me feel thick, which then signaled my stomach.

"Oh God, I'm going to hurl."

He shoved me over to a garbage can, and if I'd thought I could hold it in, the smell from the trash changed the thought as I swiftly emptied the contents of my stomach. It all left me feeling weak and shaky, and I was about to sink to the ground, but Grant caught me instead.

"Oh. No, you don't. A sidewalk full of dirt, gum, food, and who knows what else is no place for that dress of yours. Let's move over to those bricks." He led me to the side of the building with a brick border. After he asked if I was okay there while he went to grab some water, I nodded. I closed my eyes and concentrated on staying upright—a metaphor for the past two months.

A cold bottle against my cheek made me jump, and Grant's subsequent laugh had me smiling in spite of myself.

"Thanks." I took the bottle and sipped, letting the water cleanse my throat. The next day was not going to be a picnic. I hadn't gotten drunk like that in a long time. I swayed and leaned into Grant's shoulder. "Sean would have gotten me safely into a Lyft. You didn't have to come."

"I know."

"Do you have to get back? I'll be fine once I pass out in my bed."

"We'll see." He stood and pulled me to my feet, making me dizzy. He wrapped an arm around me to keep me mostly steady as we walked. I couldn't believe I'd made him leave his job early a second time. All for another pathetic meltdown as though I were the first person to have sick children. The first person to break up with someone. I was a self-centered, selfish bitch.

"Don't be ridiculous. You are not."

I guess I said the last part out loud. Or did I say it all out loud? Fuck it. I hope I did say it all out loud. First step is admitting you have a problem, right? Hello, my name is Julie, and I think I'm the center of the universe.

"S'okay. You don't have to be nice. I'll still let you have the money from the will if we win. That's less selfish, isn't it?" I asked, apparently starting more random conversations.

"What are you talking about? What money?"

We got to his car. *God, how is this pile of metal still running?* He helped me inside and shut the door. I focused on latching my seat belt, and it occurred to me I hadn't ever told Grant about contesting the will or about my suspicions about Brian and how he might have been treating Elaine.

Grant slid in behind the wheel and, as he started the car, asked again, "What money are you talking about?"

"Brian and Elaine's. Besides the trust funds for the kids, every single other stupid penny they had they gave to their stupid church. As if the *church* were going to raise them. Never mind how we gave them the means to have their children. Let's let the homophobic, sexist cult spend all the money on indoctrinating more weak-willed people to be the same way too."

"Okay, but—" He paused, maybe to think about what he should say, or maybe it was to concentrate on driving. "Why would you give any money to me?"

I wondered whether I'd never shared my reasons with him for his sake or for mine. Probably for mine. I didn't want him to blame me for my brother's actions. I didn't want him to change his mind about helping me with the kids. I didn't want him to think less of me, period.

"Because it turns out my brother was probably more of an ass than I thought. He might not have been hurting the kids, but my lawyer—ha, listen to how pretentious that sounds, 'I have a lawyer'—says there might be reason to believe he made your sister's life miserable. Emotional and verbal abuse. If we can pry the money away from the church, then it sure as hell ought to go to Elaine's blood rather than Brian's."

"How long have you been thinking about this?"

"Since not long after you showed up at my door."

"Why wouldn't you talk about it with me?"

"Because admitting to you my brother might have been mistreating your sister makes me feel horrible. Like I should have known or done something."

Grant honked at someone who cut in front of us. I imagined it felt good. Probably not as good as yelling at me might feel, though.

"Are you trying to tell me you somehow feel responsible for him? That's stupid. He was a grown man. He's responsible for himself and his own actions."

"I was at their house last year for dinner and heard them argue."

"Elaine too? Or just your brother?"

I thought about sticking my head all the way out the window like a dog. I no longer wanted to talk about it. "Both of them."

"Sounds like mutual arguing, not necessarily single-sided verbal abuse."

"Do you really believe that, or do you just want to believe it?"

We reached our apartment-building parking lot, and Grant sped into a space, slamming on the brakes once we were fully in the spot.

"I don't know," he growled. "Does it matter? She's dead, and I can't do anything about it. Whatever she went through is over and done with. What about you? Do you believe Brian was a fucking tool, or do you just want to believe it? Does it feel better to be glad he's dead because of that?"

His anger smashed into me, pinning me to my seat. Starting in my throat, which constricted my breathing and moving outward throughout my body, every muscle seemed to contract in tension. Oh God. *Is that it?* Maybe I'd thought it easier to feel nothing about his death under the guise of hating him rather than simply not having known him well enough. My stomach rolled again, and I relaxed enough of my body to pull the seat belt free and get out of the car. I took the few steps over to the bushes and heaved into them.

A moment later, Grant's hand rested gently on my lower back as I remained bent, and he offered the water bottle again. I took it, swished and spit, and rested my palms on my knees, not ready to face him.

"I'm sorry." His hand moved to my shoulder. "I didn't mean what I said."

I straightened and drank the last of the water. "It's okay. You might be right."

"I don't know how things were between Elaine and your brother. Her email messages certainly didn't give me any reason to believe she was in some abusive relationship, but it doesn't mean shit when all I ever really got from her were daily quotes from the Bible. Either way, though, it's not your fault and is certainly no reason to suddenly think I deserve anything because of it."

I pivoted to face him, standing close enough to rest on his car for support. I felt like I might fall over. "I'm sorry about the whole will thing. I should have told you about it."

"I don't really know why, but I don't care. Look, let's get you upstairs and into bed. You look like hell."

Agreeing, I latched onto his arm. He walked me up the stairs, through the apartment door, and set me down on my bed.

"You gonna be all right?"

"Yeah. I don't remember the last time I ate, so I'm pretty sure I don't actually have anything left in my stomach right now."

"You know where I'll be."

I gave him a weak smile as I sent him out so I could change and fall into what I hoped would be a dead, dreamless sleep.

Chapter Twenty-Eight

"J..." Grant's voice pierced my dense fog of sleep. "J, wake up. It's your sister on the phone."

I tried to orient myself to where I was and when it was. Grant sat on my bed, holding out a phone, looking worried. "It's Mikey."

Suddenly, I was on full alert. I stopped breathing for a moment and grabbed the phone. "Lay? What's wrong?"

The cries and screams in the background, I would know anywhere. Mikey. *And do I also hear Lucy? Shit.* It was foolish to have thought it was okay to leave them so soon. I looked at the clock—one a.m.

"I'm sorry to call, Jules. He won't calm down or let either Sheila or me near him. He keeps pushing us away and asking for you. I figured if he could hear your voice, it might help."

Asking for me? What is she talking about?

"No!" I heard over the line. "Mama JuJu!"

Wait, that isn't Lucy's voice.

"Put him on, Lay." My heart pounded so hard in my chest I thought it might leave a bruise.

"No."

"Mikey, honey," I started in right away as the scream came through louder.

"Mama JuJu!"

"Yes, it's me. Mama JuJu. I'm here. It's okay."

"No," the little voice sobbed. "Not here."

I swallowed my tears and felt I might choke on them. I twisted the phone away for a second to heave out a breath and struggled to take another. Grant's hand wrapped around one of mine, and I pulled together another moment of control. "I will be. I'm coming down now. Let Auntie Layla hold you until I get there, okay?"

Mikey didn't answer, and Layla came back on the line. "He's still crying, but he's calmed down. I think it'll be okay."

"I told him I was coming. We'll be on the road as soon as I hang up."

"Jules, I don't think—" She stopped, probably because by then, I didn't have the control anymore. I was crying too. "Okay. Yes, of course. We'll leave the door unlocked for you."

I hung up and vaulted from the bed to pull on some shorts and a T-shirt to cover my thin tank top, all while trying to spill out what was happening and what we needed to do.

"He's so scared. I shouldn't have left him. I knew it was wrong when I did. He didn't act like other times, and his nightmares—" I couldn't finish because Grant had pulled me into him, and I buried my face in his chest, soaking his shirt with my tears. He held me tighter, since I couldn't stop shaking either.

"Hey, it's okay. You didn't do anything wrong. It's not your fault." He spoke quietly yet firmly. "I know it feels like it is, but it's not."

His tight grip helped with the shaking, and I forced myself to concentrate on deep breaths to stifle the tears. "Okay. I think I can function again."

Grant slowly released me but held me in place with his hands framing the back of my head, thumbs along my jawline. He met my eyes. "He's going to be okay."

"How do you know?"

"Because he has you."

I thought of how Grant had told me he understood some of Mikey's pain, and taking in his eyes, I grasped the message.

"Because he has *us*," I said.

He briefly nodded before letting go, and we rapidly pulled on shoes before heading out. Grant grabbed a box of crackers and a Coke from the fridge and handed them to me. "I have a feeling you could use this about now."

"I don't know about the crackers yet, but I'll definitely take the Coke. Are you awake enough to drive for an hour and a half?"

He shrugged. "Oh yeah, I'm good. I haven't even slept yet. Normally, I'd still have a couple hours left of my shift, you know?"

"I'm sorry."

"About what?"

We got into his car, and I wondered vaguely what was going to happen with my car downtown. "About making you cut out of work early to bail me out."

"Don't worry about it. Paul's cool with it, so you should be too. Besides, it's a good thing I did, since I don't think you're in any condition to drive yet."

I leaned my head back and opened the window, thinking it was unfortunate that I didn't have my car. His didn't have any working air-conditioning. On the other hand, I could use the fresh air. Keeping my emotions in check was my immediate battle. I sipped the Coke, and despite still reeling from my earlier binge, I thought a beer sounded better.

We didn't talk any more for a while, letting me replay the events of the past forty-eight hours.

The first time Zach and I had broken up had been quiet, if not a little sad. The second time, not so much. An angry Zach turned out to be someone I hadn't seen before, and I was glad. Cruel, cutting statements razored into me, leading me to leave a blood trail all the way to the Grey Shade, where I nursed my wounds as best I could.

"After everything I've done for you?" Zach had asked in the parking lot of the Blues Lounge, where I'd met him after leaving Gemmi in my apartment.

"What are you saying?" I'd asked. "I'm supposed to stay with you out of obligation?"

"No, but I didn't have to stick it out with you, you know."

"And I didn't have to take you back when you just showed up outside my door."

"But you'll take in anyone, won't you? I thought having the new responsibility of children would help you finally grow up. Instead, it was all about 'playing house' with an equally immature guy off the street."

Wow. "Help me 'grow up'? What does that mean?"

"C'mon, Julie." Zach had held out his hand and made a sweeping gesture from my head to my feet. "Look at you. Piercings, tattoos you insist on calling 'art,' no education, and no ambition. At least the kids were starting to point you in the right direction."

"That's right. I was a *project* for you. And let me add that Grant is the twins' father in every way. He and I have been doing everything to raise them since losing their parents, and all you've been doing is playing 'Uncle Zach.'"

"It's all you've been allowing me to do. And at least I've been trying to give them real meals. All you can do is boxed stuff and McDonald's. All I wanted was to help you do right by those kids. But go ahead and fuck it all up without me. You're doing a fine job on your own."

"Fuck you," I said, no other words at my disposal to fend off the razor slashes. Then I'd walked away.

I was grateful for the "guy off the street" in the driver's seat. If giving him a chance had been a risk, then it turned out I was doing something right. We hadn't been "playing house." We'd been giving Lucy and Mikey a home.

"So, he's talking." Grant's voice broke through my thoughts. "That's something, huh?"

Amid the stress of knowing what Mikey was going through, that fact hadn't been lost on me either. I didn't know if Layla understood the significance of what had happened. I wasn't sure either.

"Yeah. I just wish... I guess I'd always thought when—or if—he started talking again, it would have been in happiness." *Or I would have been there.*

"Me too. He called you 'Mama JuJu.' That's pretty big, right?"

Oh God, more tears. I really could have used another beer.

"Of course," Grant continued, "before that was the word 'no.' Sounds about right for first words, don't you think?"

I tried to smile. I tried to rein in my emotions and focused on Grant's effort. "And he said it first to Layla. That must count for something too."

He laughed. I laughed. Mine came out as more of a snort, since I was still half crying, which made him laugh harder.

"Hey, stop laughing at me."

"Stop snorting, then."

I covered my mouth as I attempted to settle my laughter. My worries lessened.

"I wish my boss were as 'cool' with things as yours," I told him without segue.

"You gonna tell me what's up with your job?"

I sighed and slowly at first, then quickly picking up speed, spilled everything from the past couple of days. The issue with Carl at work, the conversation with Layla, Gemmi finding out she was pregnant, and an abbreviated version of breaking up with Zach.

"I think it took me imagining myself pregnant with Zach's baby to realize we were wrong for each other. Kids bind you together in uncontrollable ways. I thought I wanted things to work out between us. Then I saw it from a different perspective…" I didn't want to talk about him anymore and especially not with Grant.

The Sperm Whale had nothing to say about Zach, however, and had been a good listener. It felt good to dump everything out to him, to someone who really listened to me and asked how I felt about it all.

"I guess I'm not surprised by the need to get drunk after all you went through. Look, about your job. I can talk to Paul and see if I can't jostle my hours around more. I can talk to a couple of the other guys and see what flexibility they have to trade some shifts or something so I can start later."

"You don't really think you'd be able to start as late as six, do you?"

He shrugged. "I've been getting on well with Paul. He might work with me on it."

"I appreciate you wanting to help, but I'll get it figured out. Hey, take this next exit." I directed him the rest of the way to Layla and Sheila's house, and when he shut off the engine and turned off the headlights, I took a deep breath before getting out and gearing up to face Mikey.

When we walked in, all was quiet. I crossed my fingers, trusting it was a good sign. As we headed up the stairs, however, a fresh round of cries rang through, and I hurdled the remaining stairs two at a time. From the entrance of the guest room, I could see only Lucy, sleeping soundly with her dolly and in her sleeping bag. Sheila met me in the hall and beckoned me to their room, where Layla sat with Mikey, slowly rocking and singing.

"Mikey, honey." I called out and met him halfway as he pushed away from Layla and buried himself in my arms, sobbing hoarsely. I held him tightly and let him wrap his legs around my waist as I knelt and swayed with him on the floor. Layla, Sheila, and Grant spoke to one another, but I didn't hear what they said over Mikey's grief.

Without further thought, I stood with Mikey in my arms, saying the soothing words I always did and trying my best to add more. I walked past everyone and felt his body quiet, along with his cries. Back in the guest room, I kicked off my shoes and, without letting go of him, curled us into the bed. I ran my fingers through his hair, gently rubbed his back, then went through the pattern again and again until finally, he dropped into sleep, his breaths changing from choking wheezes to a calm, regular rhythm.

Layla tiptoed in, and I almost shooed her out again, not wanting to disrupt the precious calm. I changed my mind when I saw how worn-out she appeared. I recognized Mikey's sleep and knew he probably wouldn't wake again as long as I was there. Layla knelt by the edge of the bed and gave me a tired, gentle smile.

"Thank God for Mama JuJu," she whispered.

"I'm sorry. I should have known he wouldn't be ready yet."

"It's okay. After we called you, he slept in brief spurts and didn't cry the entire time. He let me hold him in my lap, at least. We probably could have made it through the rest of the night, but I admit it would have been painful." She nodded toward the hall. "His was not the male voice I expected to answer your phone tonight."

"Long story."

"Tomorrow, then."

I nodded and asked about Mom. "Has she been any help?"

"Good God, no. She left shortly after dinner because she couldn't handle Lucy's minor tantrum."

"Lucy doesn't have 'minor' tantrums."

"This one was nothing, honest. One of the toys wasn't working like she wanted, and she threw it down and yelled about it for a tiny bit. Normal stuff. Everything else went great, really."

I felt annoyance with my mother for running away. I understood her better, yet she still was who she was.

"Go flop into bed and dream of rainbows and unicorns, Lay. You've earned them."

"Deal. Give this whippersnapper some extra kisses from me throughout the night. He's earned them too."

The sun woke me the next morning. As I opened my eyes, the intensity of it surprised me. I reached over to my phone and saw it was past ten. I felt lost for a moment about where I was, what day it was, and what I was doing. Suddenly, I heard a cheerful shriek, certainly belonging to Lucy, and when I turned over onto my back, Mikey was next to me, lying on his belly and drawing as though it were the most natural thing in the world.

"Hey, Mikeadoodle." I borrowed Grant's nickname for him, earning a return smile, one I wasn't sure would come back.

He dropped his colored pencils and flung his arms across me for a hug, followed by a kiss on my cheek.

"How're you doing, kiddo?"

Admittedly, part of me assumed he would tell me in words. Instead, he held up his picture, which had a house with four windows. A face peered out of each one. Him, Lucy, Grant, and me.

"Are we all together again, safe and sound?"

He nodded before setting it aside and curling up next to me. I let the calm settle into me until my stomach growled, making Mikey giggle. "I'm finally hungry, which is a great sign. Do you suppose the kitchen is still open?"

He rolled off the bed and came around to pull me out too. We drifted into the kitchen, where I got my next surprise.

"Dad? What are you doing here?"

"JuJu!" Lucy slid down from Grant's lap, pushing aside my question, and leaped into me with such exuberance, I nearly fell down.

"Hey, Lulu. How's my fireball doing?"

"You slept *forever*. I wanted to wake you up, but Sperm Whale said no. Grandpa's here! We had doughnuts. Sperm Whale and I went to the park. We started writing a story. I can tell it to you. Want to hear it?"

Grant laughed, probably at my expression, as I was sure I looked shell-shocked. Maybe I should have stayed in bed a teeny while longer.

"We can tell it to her later, Luce," Grant said. "Maybe we should let her eat something and wake up some more, first. Okay?"

I half expected Lucy to get upset with further delay, but she simply said, "Okay," and skipped off to find something else to add to her already full and busy morning.

Sheila offered me a cup of coffee, which I readily accepted, while I grabbed a banana and leaned against the center island, ready to re-ask my question. "I'm awake enough to want to know why you're here, Dad."

"We are doing exactly what you don't want us to do, which is solving all of your problems," Layla answered. "You can yell at me now and thank me later. Or thank me now and later, which would also be fine."

Seeing everyone gathered around the table and possibly talking about me both made me extremely uncomfortable and slightly touched.

Grant came around with the box from the table and opened it. "I hear you're a sucker for jelly doughnuts. We saved one for you."

I eyed it only briefly before grabbing it. "Fine. Bribery wins. I don't see what problems there are to solve to require all of this work, though."

"Dad's making sure we've got the legalese down so you'll be able to keep your job and hopefully your hours."

"At minimum," my dad finally said, "we'll buy you time to find something else in case you still have to put in your notice."

Mikey, who hadn't yet left my side, followed me to the table and pulled his chair right up next to mine. I held out my doughnut. "Want a bite?"

He shook his head. I sought Grant's eyes and questioned with a quick mimic of my hand to illustrate a talking sign. He shook his head and surreptitiously flashed a "zero" with his fingers. Mikey hadn't spoken a word since his cries on the phone the night before. I frowned, worried the wrong emotion had gotten him to say any words at all, and my leaving him too soon was what caused the damage and might prohibit him from saying anything more.

Sheila leaned in behind me and whispered in my ear, "Mikey hasn't left your side for more than just going to the bathroom."

A fresh wave of guilt washed over me for having thought he was ready for the overnight trip away from a home he'd barely gotten used to. I put my arm around him and squeezed him to me, kissing the top of his head.

"Okay, problem solvers, let's figure this out."

Both my dad and Sheila explained that the change in my family status gave me the right to access the Family and Medical Leave Act, which allowed me up to twelve weeks off, six of them guaranteed with no loss of my current position. It also didn't have to be consecutive days or weeks as long as it was within a year following the change. Using up my vacation and sick leave was within the purview of a company, but whether to grant the time was not an option. The tricky part came in proving that my hours and benefits were being cut because of my option to access that leave.

"Carl made his first mistake in bringing it up in conversation. It's enough to give you some leverage," my dad said. "A lot of prevarication exists in his dialogue regarding the changes. Technically, he isn't laying you off or firing you, since he is simply changing the parameters of the position under the guise of company need. To be honest, I think you'd have a tough case in proving he was directly discriminating or failing to abide by FMLA laws, regardless of what he seemed to imply. However, you might have reason to report him to his supervisor for an ethics violation."

I leaned into the table, resting my chin in my hand and tapping my lips. I thought about something Carl had said. He'd mentioned the change in structure due to "company needs." If I focused on the "company needs" and not the legal stuff, maybe there was a way to keep what I had and make it work for everyone. Sure, I would throw the legal crap in Carl's face to help defend my cause, but if I could present a logical plan, it would strengthen my position. I needed access to the database and to make a spreadsheet.

"See?" Grant interrupted my thoughts. "Attack with confidence. You've got a plan, don't you?"

My dad smiled at me. "She definitely does. I remember that expression well."

Ignoring them both, I asked Grant if he was ready to go sooner rather than later. "I need to stop at work today, while Carl's gone and not breathing over my shoulder. Maybe you want to let the kids swim?"

"What do you think, Mikeadoodle? Should we do some swimming today?" Grant asked.

Mikey shrugged and wrapped an arm around mine, pulling himself close.

"I guess we'll figure out other stuff later," I said. Then I glanced at my family around me. "Thanks, you guys, for all of this and all you've been doing. I really appreciate it."

"Well," Layla said, "it's what families are supposed to do. Our family is just a little late to the party."

"Speaking of late," I said, "it's time to wrap up this party and let all of you get some rest. I think I have a car to pull out of the impound lot too."

"Nah," Grant said. "Sean took care of it. It's probably parked back in the apartment lot already."

"God love him. Okay, I'm going to go pack up the kids' stuff, and we'll be all set."

Mikey grabbed my hand and tagged along, as did Sheila.

"Do you remember how we teased yesterday about who the dress was for?" Sheila asked as she rolled up one of the sleeping bags in the guest room.

I flicked my eyes over to her briefly before throwing Lucy's clothes into our bag. I didn't answer.

That didn't stop her. "I think you bought it for the right person after all."

My heart gave an uncontrollable leap, and though I didn't give voice to it, I hoped she was right.

Chapter Twenty-Nine

Mikey spent the remainder of Sunday glued to my side, back in silent mode. While I worked at the computer at the community center, gathering what I needed to study the schedule at home, he sat on the floor at my feet, drawing or simply sitting with his bunny. Without Mikey, Lucy opted against swimming, and I wondered if I shouldn't have plotted with Grant about possibly extracting information from her about her brother. Maybe she would be more open to a conversation without Mikey being there.

Mikey's silence had me almost convinced I was only imagining I'd heard him say anything the night before. I didn't know how to trigger any more words, save leaving him again, which I obviously had no plans to do. Every time I replayed Layla's phone call in my head, my heart sped up and my chest tightened, making breathing difficult. No, I had no intention of recreating that scenario. Regardless, he was the Mikey I had always known—thoughtful, creative, communicative in his own way, and still giving out smiles.

Besides, maybe I could set aside my disappointment about his not talking and focus on a recent development. Monday morning, I discovered he'd slept through the night without nightmares. Both children had slept in my bed Sunday night because Mikey still wasn't amenable to leaving my side, and Lucy, not to be left out, chose my bed first too.

I couldn't remember the last time I had slept more than four hours at a stretch. It felt great. I hoped Carl was ready for me, because

I was well rested, had the law on my side, and carried a restructuring plan bound to impress him.

In fact, I'd reexamined the full schedule and history of staffing and found some odd anomalies. I didn't know whether questioning them would help or hurt me, but at least it gave me more to work with.

On Monday, Carl didn't give me a chance. I asked for a meeting, but the only time he said he was available was at the end of the day, when he knew I couldn't stay longer. I pulled out the FMLA argument and reminded him of his insinuations in our conversation last week. That got his attention, and he agreed to a meeting the next morning. What he also didn't know was that I had been made privy to interesting gossip about his relationship with Melissa and of a relationship before her with another fitness instructor. It explained the anomalies I'd found, and even if I couldn't prove anything, I had time to consider how or whether to bring in the information.

To siphon off some of my nervous energy after work on Monday, the kids and I planned a "fancy" dinner. Mikey made new place mats, and Lucy folded our napkins into interesting shapes and made place cards. Together, we roasted potatoes, which sounded much more complicated than plain white rice, but I discovered with joy how much easier it was. We boiled corn on the cob and pretended the frozen chicken nuggets were really fancy chicken strips from a restaurant. I let them have Fanta Orange for our "champagne."

I didn't think mojitos and Yahtzee with Gemmi and Sean could have topped our evening.

At the end of the day on Tuesday, I left work feeling invincible. I'd been walking a tightrope with Carl for several weeks, carefully avoiding falling off, knowing I had no safety net. Finally, though, I realized I had not only the safety net of my family but also a trampoline in the form of my ability to bounce back. No matter what happened, I would be okay.

And everything turned out better than I'd hoped. I had drafted a schedule—which had always been a part of my job description, as I'd reminded Carl—and I had the law to back me up. I'd successfully pressed Carl in between the proverbial rock and hard place. It probably would have been enough to bring up the FMLA issue, but when he wavered about the "necessary" changes, I only had to allude to his affair with Melissa to find him dropping his protests faster than Lucy could fling herself into a tantrum.

I walked into the apartment to find Grant working the air guitar while Lucy stood on the coffee table, singing "More Than a Feeling" into her spoon, and Mikey swayed, rattling his prescription-bottle popcorn shaker. The performance matched my mood perfectly.

"Hey, look who's home!" Grant called out, pausing to turn down the volume of the Boston song to a more manageable level.

"Guess who still has her same job and her same hours?" I asked.

"Yes!" Grant cheered and high-fived me. "Hurray for Mama Ju-Ju!" he told the kids.

"Yay, Mama JuJu!" Lucy joined in, and I wanted to gobble her up for using her beautiful name for me.

"Yay, Mama JuJu!" came Mikey's voice, which silenced both Grant and me but not Lucy.

"Mikey talked! Mikey talked!" She jumped and clapped then flung herself at her brother, wrapping her arms around him like a sausage, while he merely smiled at Lucy's happiness. "I knew you could still do it!"

Grant and I grinned foolishly at each other. Lucy didn't know about Mikey's words at Layla's, and after a while, I almost doubted I'd ever heard them. To hear him in that important moment flooded my heart with hope. Grant held out his fist for a bump then held out his hands for the kids. "High fives all around."

"High fives for Daddy Whale!" Lucy bubbled, and I thought I might cry to see the joy not only on the kids' faces but on Grant's too. All the times his face had shown joy when I called him a dad were like nothing compared to Lucy bestowing the name on him. And when Mikey added his "Yay, Daddy Whale" cheer, Grant couldn't contain himself any longer. He pulled them into a hug, giggles pouring out of all of them as they tackled him to the floor. I picked up the remote and increased the volume of the current song, which was the Doobie Brothers' infinitely appropriate "Listen to the Music."

By the time the weekend rolled around, we had much to celebrate. Mikey, though using words again, used them sparely, as if still trying it all out. We didn't question it or push—not even headstrong Lucy—and felt every instance of speech as a gift instead of an expectation.

We decided on a visit to the beach, since many were opening for the summer. The early onset of hot summer temperatures had us optimistic about swimming at a lake for the unofficial start of summer on Memorial Day weekend. Others definitely held the same hopefulness at the beach as Lake Nokomis filled up. Plenty of people were splashing in the water, and if it was icy cold, no one complained.

We set up blankets and towels on the sand and got ready to hit the water. The kids helped slather sunscreen on each other, and I stripped down to my bikini, trying not to think about why I felt self-conscious about it in front of Grant.

Fortunately, his back was turned to me, and when he removed his shirt, I was taken in by the huge ink design on his back. The "Christy" tattoo had taken up my full attention last time I had seen him shirtless, but there was a lot more story to explore on his skin.

"Wait, I never got a good look at this mural on your back. How long did this take?"

"Four different sessions, each one about four to four and a half hours."

I put my hands on his shoulders to stop him from turning.

"It's nothing special, really. I mean, it's not like I designed it myself or spent a lot of time figuring out some masterpiece. You saw how I did the frat one just for drink discounts. The dragon one is probably the only one I more consciously thought about for the design itself, and it's not like yours at all—"

As he drifted into more nervous chatter, I wondered what was making him uptight.

Until I saw the scars.

I sucked in my breath and realized I had tightened my grip on his shoulders. Grant stopped talking, and I slowly released the air I held and relaxed my hands. I knew I didn't have long, and I scanned his back as quickly as possible, an unknown force compelling me to count. If I hadn't considered how it felt to get lashed with a belt, I got a sickening perception of it after that scan. I got to five, but his head was still bowed, and I suddenly felt cruel and invasive, bringing to light what he had obviously tried so hard to keep dark. It was wrong of me to expose him like that. I gently thumbed over a scar close to my hand.

"Well," I said, trying to keep my voice light. "Specially designed or not, your artist did an amazing job. It's like a painter's brushstrokes and fantastically symmetric. I was thinking lately of doing something on my left shoulder. I haven't decided what yet." I let go of him and pointed. "Another flower? Or should it be something more abstract?"

He turned around, and I met his gaze, which proved difficult to interpret, although at least it didn't seem angry.

"I kind of want to keep it all thematic somehow. Or not. Too corny?" I gave a half smile.

His face relaxed. "No flowers but nature, and no, not too corny. A bird, maybe. Like a hummingbird."

"Those are small. I was thinking something bigger."

"How about a big butterfly!" Lucy jumped into the conversation then fluttered around our place in the sand. "Can we go in the water now?"

"Last one in gets dive-bombed by the Sperm Whale!" Grant yelled with a grin.

Mikey tore away so quickly I almost panicked that Grant had truly frightened him. Mikey looked behind him, though, with a huge smile. Lucy shrieked as she followed her brother, and Grant looked at me, mischief in his eyes. "You think I was only talking to the kids?"

We took off at the same time, with me edging him out at the last second. I supposed he let me win, but I didn't care. We'd moved past the awkwardness and had an afternoon of sun and cheer ahead. Maybe we would talk about what happened later—or not. For as open and startlingly honest as Grant could be, he still kept some stories to himself. Much of his past had not been easy.

Surely Brian had known of Elaine's history, although Elaine's perspective had also been different from Grant's. From the stories Grant did share, I respected the choices he made once he moved forward. I wasn't ashamed of my decisions about my life, but it didn't stop me from admiring the goals he had set for himself, not to mention the unknown detour he took when choosing to leave California.

From all I could see, it was a positive detour. Acknowledging the kind of aunt I had always been, I didn't think I would have thought less of him had he not shown up when he did. I hadn't ever expected to meet him. As I watched him splash with the kids, I realized it would have been quite the loss for all of us if I hadn't.

We enjoyed the water, built—well, not quite sand*castles* but sand structures—then split up for the changing rooms.

"How about we do a quick rinse here and worry about a full shower at home?"

Lucy agreed, and afterward, as I helped comb her hair, she hit me with an unexpected question.

"How come Daddy Whale doesn't sleep in your bedroom?"

I paused my combing, suddenly acutely aware of the people around us listening in.

If she had known the full biological truth, the question might have been far more complicated than she imagined. However, on the surface, regardless of my changing feelings toward Grant, the answer remained fairly straightforward.

"Grant and I aren't like your mom and dad. We're friends but not friends who sleep in the same bed."

"You should get bunk beds. Connor and Sam at Lynette's had bunk beds."

I smiled. I loved kid solutions to things. It sort of amazed me Grant had survived as long as he did on the futon. Those things weren't terrible, but I was sure the futon hadn't been great long-term.

"JuJu?"

"Yes?"

"Sometimes, I don't miss Mommy and Daddy as much as I used to. Is that bad?"

Something in her voice tugged at me—a need for validation along with a fear of the same validation. I could only try to strike a balance in my answer and hope it would be enough.

"No, honey, it's not bad. I think they are happier when you aren't so sad about them. Sometimes, some days, you might miss them so much it will hurt, and that's okay too. Remember, I'm here for you on those days, okay?"

"Okay. Can I put on my sandals now?"

"You bet. Let's go see what your brother and Daddy Whale are up to."

The kids crashed quickly at bedtime, and not long afterward, I did too. Neither Grant nor I had Memorial Day off, so the next day would be back to our normal routine.

At some point, a loud *thud* and subsequent crash woke me. Worried one of the kids had fallen out of bed, I jumped up and hurried to find them safe and sound under their covers. When I went into the living room, Grant sat on the futon, head in his hands, shaking.

"I'm sorry. That was me." His voice cracked.

I went to him straightaway and was about to put my arm around him, but something about the way his hands were gripping his hair stopped me, so I simply sat next to him.

"What happened?"

"I didn't wake the kids up, did I?" His voice sounded strained.

"No, they're fine."

He said nothing more, and I wasn't sure what to do. I still didn't know what the noise was, and he appeared to be trying to regain control of himself.

"Hey," I said. "I'm going to put my arm around yours, okay?"

His fingers relaxed in his hair. I waited. Without looking at me, he nodded. His left elbow rested on his knee, and I laced my arm through that space and around his bicep then leaned along his shoulder.

"Talk to me," I said.

"It's stupid."

"No. Whatever it is, it's not."

"It was the book. I threw it at the wall."

I looked across from us and scanned until I saw where it lay, splayed haphazardly among the toys it had taken down.

"Why?"

"There's a scene... or there's going to be a scene with a car accident... and kids, and I just know that—"

"Something's going to happen to the kids in it."

"Yeah." He lowered his hands and turned to me, his expression raw. "I don't know why I got so mad. It's like I felt as though the author was doing it to me personally." He shook his head and looked down. "I told you it was stupid."

"With everything going on? Hardly. You're always telling me to cut myself a break. I'm pretty sure the sentiment applies to you too."

"Yeah, I guess. It's just…"

I tightened my arm around his, trying to reassure him. Obviously, there was more going on than the scene in the book. I just didn't know what. He broke away abruptly then stood up and paced.

"It's just what?"

"Everything. The kids. Elaine." He stopped and stared at me. "Just everything."

I leaned back into the couch and took in his expression. I guessed there was more or at least something more specific than simply "everything." Maybe it was me and my invasion of his privacy earlier in the afternoon. Maybe it was what my invasion had dredged up from his memories. Or maybe it was him thinking like me every day, trying to figure it all out and freaking out when he couldn't.

"I should have been better about keeping in touch with Elaine. She left, and I was mad, you know? Like, how was it she could escape and leave me trapped with Mom and Dad? But I could have left then, too, right? I didn't have to stay."

"What, and become a runaway teen? Where would you have gone? Would you have known there were places you could go to get help?"

"I don't know. For a long time, I used to be mad she didn't take me with her, even after all the times I—well, just after everything."

"You protected her, didn't you?"

His eyes gave me my answer. He went on. "Then I realized I was only mad at myself because I let her go. She'd email me and text me, but all I ever promised was to tell her where I was. My new phone numbers and addresses. She was getting her life figured out, and I was fucking around and feeling sorry for myself. Maybe if I'd kept in better contact with her, things would have been different."

"Different how? Like you might have magically become closer?"

He'd stopped pacing and leaned an arm along the wall. "I don't know. I guess. Or maybe I would have gone to college for real, or maybe I would have been here when she asked me to donate my stuff for the kids. I could have been here and been the better uncle, the one who isn't scared every day he's going to mess them up somehow."

"Mess them up? How? You are great with them. I mean really great. I'm insanely jealous of how good you are with them."

"All I do is wing it every single day. I can't imagine what you're jealous of. I accused you of hurting them after only two seconds of meeting everyone. Look how long it took me to manage getting Mikey in the middle of the night. What if something happens to them on my watch?"

"You're not your parents."

"How do you know?"

"I know what you've told me and not told me about them. I know the conversation I had with your mom when I called about Elaine. I know what I see when you're with the kids, and I know how much they love you. Do you remember when I made *my* awful accusation about you?"

He gave a brief, painful nod.

"And do you remember when I started crying? I wasn't crying because I was scared or upset about the whole situation. I was crying because I didn't have the connection with the kids you had formed with them immediately. They had been with me for almost a month, and I didn't feel like a mother, whereas you came in, and the word 'dad' oozed out of your pores."

I loved his face every time I used the word "dad" with him. It was always how I knew I'd made the right decision about having him stay with us. The parenting thing had clicked for him right from the start. And while I was confessing how I'd felt when he first arrived, I didn't feel the intense jealousy anymore. I'd gotten to a point where I truly *knew* Grant, and it wasn't as if he ever rubbed my face in his relationship with the kids. It was just right.

He sat down next to me. "In other words, I'm being stupid."

"Sperm Whale, that's not what I'm saying. I'm saying you're not alone. We're in this together. 'Winging it' together."

"Then I'm stupid for not telling you back then what I'm going to tell you now. Those first days? Lucy spent most of the time telling me all about you. 'Julie makes our lunch this way.' 'Julie says we can't do such and such.' 'We like it when Julie reads.' 'Julie's nice.' And then of course there was, 'When's Julie coming home?' You were a tough act to follow."

My throat, my chest, my stomach—they all tightened. It might have been awe or disbelief. His words meant more to me than he could have possibly known. I gradually came around to the idea I was doing okay by the kids. Layla's and Sheila's words helped, but it was sinking in through the kids' words and actions too. To know what they were saying long before I came to my own realizations touched something deep inside me.

"Thank you for telling me."

He gave me a little smile and a gentle lift of one shoulder.

I walked over to pick up the book he'd flung. "So. Want me to put it in the freezer?"

His smile widened, and he chuckled. "Nah. I think I'm done reading it altogether."

"So I'm off the hook for it too?"

That earned a full laugh. "Yes. You can go back to your BuzzFeed articles."

"Oh, thank God." I gave him an exaggerated sigh. "You have no idea the suspense I've been in not knowing what animated GIFs to use when describing the latest season of *Survivor*."

He laughed harder.

I loved it and said, "You have a great laugh."

A blush bloomed across his face as he turned away.

"What?" I tossed the tainted book onto the table and flopped into the armchair. "Surely others have told you so before."

"I don't think so. I also think you're being far too nice to me tonight. You should go back to bed before I do or say something dumb again to change your opinion of me."

"Yeah, okay. Tomorrow's work and all. Not a bad idea." I stood and rested my hand on his shoulder before heading to my bedroom. "You're okay?"

He brought a hand up to mine and squeezed it. "Yeah. No more throwing things tonight. Promise."

Chapter Thirty

I didn't fully know why Grant would give up sleep for the St. Paul Family Festival but opted not to question it when he said he wanted to go there with us one Saturday morning. The kids weren't the only ones excited; my stomach was doing more and more flip-flops around Grant. There had always been something appealing about him. I had never really let myself wander into that territory while I was with Zach, nor had it been high on my radar when my relationship with Grant focused on co-parenting.

With Zach happily in my rearview mirror, I felt my emotions were heading into a new adventure.

The kids kept themselves occupied first thing in the morning with building something or other, while Grant and I packed a back-pack with food, drinks, and sunscreen.

I stood at the counter, bagging up snacks, when Grant approached behind me to open the cupboard above my head.

"Excuse me a sec while I grab the juice boxes..." He drifted off, and I understood why. His hand on the cupboard didn't move when I realized his other hand rested on my hip, presumably for balance. He said nothing as I leaned back into him, ever so slightly. My breathing shifted. I turned around and into him tightly, feeling his hand trace my back. As I moved my hands up his chest, across his broad shoulders, and let them rest at the top of his arms, Grant clearly forgot about the juice, dropping his hand to frame my other hip.

My whole body flushed with a fantastic heat. My heart raced. We stared at each other, and the way his eyes changed as he looked at me was *hot*. Those hands on my hips tightened, and my fingers curled into him. If I weren't nearly trembling in his arms, I might have laughed at myself for involuntarily licking my lips when his eyes dropped to look at them. He was going to kiss me, and I was going to kiss him back. Hard.

"Mama JuJu! Daddy Whale! Lookit lookit lookit! We made a huge castle!"

Grant's expulsion of air matched the force of mine. We turned to see Mikey bouncing, his hands in the air to show how huge the castle was. I grinned at his excitement and all the new words continuing to spill from his mouth. I knew Grant felt the same way even as our separation came reluctantly. My fingertips tingled as they dropped away from him, and the tingle jumped to my feet, giving me a spring in my step as I followed Mikey into the living room.

Lucy jumped up from the floor to give us the "tour" of their masterpiece. "This is the front door. This is where the princess sleeps. This is where the king and queen's knights march to make sure the castle is safe."

"And this is where the secret back door is," Mikey added.

We gave our full, appreciative responses then sat with them at their invitation to add more. I chanced a glance at Grant, admiring the black curls I hoped to soon enjoy with my fingers, provided our moment hadn't changed his mind about what was happening between us. He looked up at me and smiled, very much assuring me he hadn't. The heat rushed through me again as I smiled back then tried to focus on the castle.

"Okay, guys, it's time to get ready to go. I need you to go to the bathroom then put on your sandals."

Grant ushered them into the bathroom, and I finished packing snacks and water before making my way to the bathroom too. We traded places, but when I came out into the hall, I ran into Grant, who tossed a comment over his shoulder to the kids.

"Hang on a second, kiddos. I gotta ask JuJu something. We'll be right back."

He pulled me into my bedroom, closed the door, and leaned me up against it. He took my face into his hands and kissed me. All of my senses lit up as his lips touched mine. It was gentle and wonderful and far too short. He pulled away and stroked my cheek with his thumb.

"I didn't want to act like a hormonal teenage boy all day. If I didn't kiss you now, I would have acted the total fool until I could."

"Do you not know how women get when all they've gotten was a short kiss of temptation? I need one more before we go." Our lips came together again, with more intensity. My tongue pushed through and circled his, eliciting the smallest of moans from the back of his throat. Oh God, he was delicious.

Lucy's impatient reminders on the other side of the door helped us regain control and brought us back to earth. We grinned at each other, both knowing it wasn't enough. But it would do.

We rejoined the kids, slathered them with sunscreen, and headed out. As we walked down the hall and to the car, Grant took my hand. I squeezed it back, feeling giddy over the direction of our relationship.

The day bloomed perfectly. With Grant's shift beginning at four, we got an early start, catching the cooler temperatures before the ninety-degree heat forecast for later on. Gemmi had told me once that Rice Park was probably as close to an actual plaza as we could get in Minnesota. It took up a block in the heart of downtown St. Paul and was flanked by the city library, the Ordway Center for the Performing Arts, and the upscale St. Paul Hotel. In the winter, Christmas lights twinkled on the trees framing the lawn. Walking paths crisscrossed, with benches lining them. The park housed ice sculptures during the Winter Carnival, but under the cloudless sky of summer, brightly colored tents filled the grounds, and the sprightly popping rhythm of bongos reverberated through the air. I could already distinguish the distinct aromas of Greek gyros and Mexican chilis coming from the food trucks, and we watched the young Circus Juventus acrobats flipping and rolling by as they warmed up for their acts.

We stood at the edge, taking it all in. Grant put an arm around my shoulders, and everything felt exactly right. I looked at Mikey, who clung tightly to me, and at Lucy, who stood in front of Grant, backed up into him as much as possible. It was a bit overwhelming, but Lucy's eyes were bright with excitement, and I knew it wouldn't take long for her to jump right in. I lightly stroked the back of Mikey's head.

"You all right there, Mikey? It's kind of a lot, huh?"

He nodded.

"How about we go over and watch the musicians first? Then we can look around and see what else there is to do and make a plan."

Lucy agreed for the both of them and pulled us along to find a spot to sit, although "sit" didn't really match her plan. We sat, and Lucy immediately danced. She twirled, allowing the air to lift her hair and fly with her into her bouncy steps. I looked at Grant, wanting to share the moment with him. There was something in his smile I couldn't quite read.

"What?"

He gave a slight shake of his head. "Nothing." But the expression remained. It wasn't the smile so much as his eyes. I waited for him to change his mind and tell me more, to tell me what he was thinking, to give me the stark honesty that always fell from his lips. Oddly, he added nothing. I wanted to ask, yet the moment felt too precious, as though it might break instead of blending into whatever came next.

"Let's make hats." Mikey's voice slipped into our bubble, expanding it instead of popping it. We looked down to see his finger tapping the map.

"Where do we find the hats, buddy?" Grant asked.

We examined the map and found our route, beginning our immersion in craft upon craft with pauses for acrobatic displays and Lakota dance demonstrations. We created buttons. Lucy's design was an angel who wore striped socks and a bright-orange dress while Mikey drew a rainbow. We helped pin them onto their shirts, readjusted their elf hats, and handed their pinwheels back to them. The backpack soon bulged from other crafts and games—beaded bracelets, stones and diagrams for the Somali game fàh, and paper airplanes.

By noon, I was relieved we couldn't stay much longer because I was imagining lying down flat on the ground right then and not moving for the rest of the day. Grant took Lucy with him to figure out lunch while I hung back with Mikey. Despite the fantastic smells, I knew our lunch would simply be hot dogs. Lucy had increased her tolerance for foods that weren't exactly what she was used to, but we had yet to try anything too far outside her norms. Her tantrums were fewer and further between but could still intrude at unexpected moments. Grant would definitely not risk it.

I didn't know if she'd always been rigid in her food choices. I'd considered asking Mikey, since he was talking again, but that path still seemed muddy and full of land mines. Besides, maybe it didn't matter. If I'd learned anything in the past couple of months, it was that experience shaped everything. Lucy might once have been an even-tempered child, but I couldn't take away her experience of losing her parents and the world she once knew.

She bounced happily alongside Grant, holding bags of chips while he balanced a tray of hot dogs. I loved the image for its simplicity—father and daughter at the park, coming to join mother and son. As they sat next to us on the grass, it was Grant's turn to look at me and ask, "What?" and mine to simply smile and say, "Nothing."

He leaned in and gave me a soft, quick kiss on the lips. I blushed and thanked the heat of the day for hiding it on my face.

We nearly inhaled our food, and before we cleaned up, I heard an enthusiastic voice call out the kids' names followed by excited replies from them—or at least Lucy. Mikey hung back, uncertain. I looked over to see Lynette with her two kids. She was with some other woman who looked familiar somehow, though I didn't know why.

"Who's that?" Grant asked.

"Lucy and Mikey's daycare provider in Duluth." I stood and brushed away extra dirt from my shorts as Lynette, the unknown woman, and their kids approached.

"Julie! Wow, how amazing is this to run into you and the kids here!"

She seemed sincerely surprised, but I wondered. Tamara had told me several members of the One True Path Christ Community Church council were arriving next week. I didn't know if Lynette was on the council.

"Hi, Lynette. It's good to see you." I turned slightly and gestured toward Grant. "This is Grant Masinsky, Elaine's brother."

He held out his hand. Lynette shook it and expressed sympathy for his loss. She then turned to the other woman, who looked rather tense—almost hostile, even. Lynette told her my name and introduced her as Shannon. A light bulb went on in my head. Shannon, the friend I saw in several of Elaine's Facebook photos.

"You and Elaine were close, weren't you?" I asked.

She nodded tightly. "Quite. Closer than her family, I'd say."

Instinctively, I took Grant's hand. He didn't need more guilt. In the meantime, I could feel Mikey slinking behind me, pulling my other hand with him.

"I'm really glad to meet you, then," Grant replied, holding his free hand out to her. "I'm happy my sister found a home with you and everyone else out here that she couldn't find back in Washington."

"Is that how you feel too?" Shannon turned her icy gaze on me.

"Not exactly." I rose to the challenge. "I never thought Brian had to turn his back on us, but I guess I'm glad he was happy."

"Is that where the greed for his money is coming from? His apparent happiness?"

"Shannon, now's not the time," Lynette murmured, eyeing Mikey.

Lucy and the other children were experimenting with juggling toys and Hula-Hoops nearby.

Shannon's demeanor relaxed somewhat upon noticing Mikey, one of her best friend's children. "Yes, you're right."

I tried to remember that the loss of my brother and Elaine had affected other people too. Shannon reached over and ruffled Mikey's hair, but he skirted away, and her hand floated down through the air and eventually found a spot on her purse strap instead.

"How are you doing, Mikey, honey?" she asked in the way people did when they thought they understood everything all at once but really understood nothing at all.

I looked down at Mikey then caught Grant's eye. "Can you—"

"Yep. C'mon, Mikeadoodle. Let's go check out what your sister and friends are up to."

Mikey hesitated, and I might not have pressed, except I had a bad feeling about the whole situation. For once, I trusted my instincts. "Only for a few minutes, sweetie. I'll be right here."

"We can do a shoulder ride instead, buddy. Then you'll have a bird's-eye view of Mama JuJu no matter what."

It was enough to get him to agree, though I knew it would buy me only a few minutes. Once Grant settled Mikey on top of his shoulders, I pivoted to the two women, and Lynette gave me a huge smile.

"You've come a long way, Julie, since I saw you at my house. I could see you had some sort of connection with those kids then, but you were so scared. I worried about you all so much."

"That makes two of us," I admitted. "And I know I need to take them back up north sometime. I think they're still too raw right now."

She waved me off. "No, I know. I'm glad to see they're doing okay. Lucy's doing great. Isn't she something? So much energy and whip-smart. Mikey too. Is he talking yet?"

"Only recently and not very much." I wanted to share everything that had happened with the kids with another woman who already knew so much about them. It suddenly hit me how valuable that would have been. I wished I had thought to call her much earlier. "I'd love to chat with you more sometime about them, learn more about what they were like and what they're like now."

"I'd like that," she said.

"We always called them the miracle children," Shannon added. "They tried for so long to have children and almost went to more extreme measures, but we convinced Elaine our prayer chain would come through, and it did."

Extreme measures. Almost. Prayer chain. Miracle children. I didn't know how I thought rewinding those phrases in my head would actually clarify anything. Evidently, my brain needed help processing them.

"What do you mean by 'almost went to more extreme measures'?" I asked.

"Well, you know, of course"—Shannon gave me a funny look—"they went so far as to get your and her brother's donations, but they didn't actually go through with the IVF process."

It was as though we had suddenly dropped into a vacuum. I could only see and hear Shannon's words, forgetting the cheerful crowds of children and parents swarming around the periphery of the new information.

"They didn't use my eggs? Or Grant's sperm? I don't understand."

Lynette perceived the impact of Shannon's news. "You didn't know?"

My eyes hadn't left Shannon's face, but I heard Lynette's tone. *Shock? Sympathy?* A combination.

Before I responded to her, Shannon replied, "No. Elaine never really wanted to do the IVF anyway, and she was right. If God intends for us to be blessed with children, then we best not interfere with his plan. Only he knows what is in store for us and how we can best fulfill our role here on earth, serving him."

"But..."

"I went with Elaine to one of the appointments, hoping to persuade her from going through with everything, and they made her take a pregnancy test, like they do with all women, to make sure she wasn't already pregnant before she started with the hormone shots. I'll never forget the look of joy and surprise on her face when she found out she was already pregnant. The Lord works miracles in the best way."

"Julie?" Lynette's voice wove its way into my consciousness again. "Are you all right?"

I didn't know how to answer her. So many emotions ran through me. Shock at the new facts. Confusion about why Brian didn't tell me. Irritation at the way I was finding out. Anxiety as I suddenly considered Grant, and when that emotion hit, my brain went into action. My eyes looked for him, and they didn't have to go far.

Grant stood a couple of feet away, frozen, and I knew he had heard everything Shannon had said.

Chapter Thirty-One

Lucy filled the silence during the car ride home. *Connor and Sam hadn't made the pinwheels yet, but they went to the booth for making boats. I wish we had time to make boats. Is the festival here tomorrow? Maybe we can make boats then? Rachel says they're all going to a concert. Can we come back and go with them too?*

I managed a distracted response here and there. Fortunately, Lucy required little interaction and clearly didn't notice the silence from the rest of us. After Shannon's news, Grant launched into a babble so off topic and almost nonsensical, I knew the festival was over for us. I interrupted and mentioned having to get home in time for Grant to get ready for work, and we said our awkward goodbyes. Lynette had caught my arm as we started walking away.

"For what it's worth, I think it's really great you and Grant volunteered to help Elaine and Brian. I like to think God considered it a prayerful sacrifice, blessing them to conceive later on their own."

I might have thanked her, and on some level, I understood her sincerity, however oddly interpreted. Lynette gave Mikey a wave, and torn, he finally waved goodbye and alternated between holding my hand and Grant's, since holding them both seemed out of the question when Grant stayed two paces ahead of us.

He had gone completely quiet after I'd cut off his babble. I couldn't determine what was going on in his head, so I focused on what was in mine. I didn't know quite what it meant to me upon discovering I still really was "just" an aunt and had been all along. I examined whether the revelation would change me or how I did things.

A secret part of me felt relief. Somehow, taking away the direct DNA link eased the pressure of feeling like I was supposed to have an automatic "in" with understanding the children and how to raise them. That it should spontaneously activate the maternal instinct.

I was Mama JuJu, not *Mama*.

I felt... free.

I turned to smile at Lucy's chatter, which she continued with excited gestures and her happy singsong voice. I twisted farther to give the same smile to Mikey, who rewarded me with one back, a smile to transform his troubled expression. Grant's expression remained agitated, and I wished I knew what to say. Everything I wanted to talk about, I couldn't say in the car with the kids. Everything else I could have talked about eluded me.

I stared out my window, and my thoughts drifted again. The mystery remained of why Brian had never told me about what really happened, and what made less sense than it did before was why I became his choice of guardian. When I thought the kids were mine, the decision had seemed logical. Not anymore.

Maybe with his religious views, he and Elaine assumed family outranked all, even the ones they weren't close to. As close as they seemed to be to Shannon and her husband, they would have made much more sense. Instead, my brother and his wife chose the aimless single woman.

When we got home and inside the apartment, Grant mumbled something about taking a shower and disappeared. I noticed Mikey shortly afterward with his hand on the bathroom door. He looked up at me, and I answered his question.

"I don't know for sure, honey. He'll be okay. I'll take care of him."

It appeared to be enough for him, and he agreed to join Lucy and me for stories. I summoned the energy to give them the voices and enthusiasm until Grant appeared at their bedroom door.

"I'm taking off now."

I passed the book to Lucy and followed Grant to the living room. "Just like that? Those are the first proper words to come out of your mouth since we left the festival. Talk to me." I reached for his hand, but he quickly put it in his pocket.

"I don't have time. I gotta go." He turned and left.

I slept on the futon, planning to wake up when Grant came home, followed by forcing a conversation. When Lucy and Mikey woke me for breakfast, my heart sank.

"Is Sperm Whale in your room, JuJu?"

Grabbing my phone, I shook my head at them as I noticed Grant's text saying he'd stayed at a coworker's place. "Nope. He stayed overnight with a friend, so we can have breakfast at the table if you want."

Their faces fell, and I gave them a weak smile. "Oh, don't worry. We can still picnic in your room. Except today we don't have to be super quiet."

They cheered and scrambled to do their thing, getting our breakfast ready. I slogged into the kitchen to grab the toaster, trying to call up the energy to match the kids' mood. However, all I could think about was how Grant hadn't come home. He always came home. Once upon a time, I might have thought he'd hooked up with someone from the bar, but he'd already proved to be a different man. My stomach clenched at the thought of him doing something out of character and, in panic, sleeping with some random person.

I tried to tell myself it didn't matter if he had. It wasn't like he and I had slept together or anything. We weren't even in a relationship. Just because we'd kissed each other—three times—it didn't mean we'd made a commitment. The day before was only like a first date, which meant nothing at all. Living with each other since he'd arrived from California was a mere technicality. We'd been roommates. Stupid, foolish roommates who ruined everything by trying to take it to another level.

And yet, the idea of him having a one-night stand filled me with dread. I wanted more with him.

Get a grip. Grant wasn't a liar. He didn't sleep around. While those facts marginally calmed me down, I still couldn't help fearing I was about to lose him.

I looked at my phone and reread his text. *Crashed at Chaz's place.* Nothing else.

I forced my focus onto the kids to fully engage as a distraction. It worked in spurts, when we were actually within an activity. Building, cars, a walk to the park, stories. The in-between moments had me looking at my phone to see time not inching forward fast enough.

It wasn't until four o'clock that he showed up.

The kids ran to him happily, and he knelt and returned the hugs as though it had been days since he'd last seen them.

Grant asked about their day, and Lucy filled him in on every detail. All I wanted was for her to stop so I could finally talk to him. When Lucy ended by asking him if he could play, I jumped in before Grant could agree.

"Lulu, I need to talk to Daddy Whale for a minute. Can you and Mikey find something to do? Do you want to play games on the laptop?"

I set them up in their room and joined Grant at the dining room table. I had hoped for the couch to be nearer to him. I sat in the chair closest to him, denying him the distance I felt he was trying to create.

"I think I'm going to go stay with Chaz," he said.

"For how long?"

"I don't know. I think it's probably time for me to move out, anyway. Impose on someone else for a while."

"You're not imposing here."

God, I already hated the conversation we were having. I didn't want to talk about his moving out, especially when I thought we were starting something great. Especially when the thought of "us" wasn't even the issue at all.

I grabbed his hand and ignored the tension in it and his refusal to relax into my grip. "For the record, I don't want you to do it. But stay with Chaz or don't, whatever. I'd rather talk about yesterday."

The silence tried to take over, to push us away from each other, but I kept holding his hand, refusing to let it happen.

"Why do I feel like we just lost something?" He asked it quietly with the barest trace of a crack in his voice.

I didn't know if he meant us or if he meant what we thought we had with the kids. "I kind of felt the same way at first, too, I guess, but really, nothing's changed. The kids are still ours."

"Ours?"

I looked at him and suddenly understood his reaction a lot better. We had thought the kids were biologically ours. But maybe everything had changed. They were mine because Brian and Elaine had appointed them to be mine, but I didn't think that suddenly meant they were no longer Grant's. He had become a father to them, in spite of everything, in spite of how completely inexperienced and unprepared he had been. Where I had felt a release upon learning of the new relationship I had with the kids, he must have felt something altogether different. He was released from any ties.

"Yes, ours."

He cleared his throat and ignored my answer. "Well, it was a good practice run for me, right? I mean, I guess I'm still the uncle, right? I'll be a cool uncle. Do all the fun stuff like take them to baseball games and amusement parks."

"No, you're their dad. You'll do more than that."

"How do you figure? I've got no direct hold on them anymore."

"So, what, everything up until now was an act? You'll only be a father to them if they're biologically yours? Now you'll just go back to being a deadbeat uncle?"

"An act? God, no. I love those kids like they're mine."

"They *are* yours," I said.

"No, they're not. Don't you get it? *You* have official guardianship. It's all good right now, while you need me, but you'll meet some guy and get married, and *he'll* become the father, and I'll become nothing."

The pain in his eyes matched the pain I felt at him saying I would meet "some guy." We really had lost something. "I've already met the guy."

Whatever answer he hoped for, I obviously didn't give it to him. He pulled his hand away from mine, stood, and began packing his duffel. He disappeared into the bathroom before returning with his razor, toothbrush, and shampoo. I couldn't move from my chair.

I heard him tell the kids he had to go, and they gave him an unsuspecting goodbye.

Then he walked out the door. Suddenly, the apartment felt too large, too empty. I didn't want to feel the emptiness, so I grabbed the kids and my car keys, and we abandoned ship too.

When my mom opened the door, I second-guessed myself for not texting or calling ahead. I hadn't wanted to because I didn't want her to say no to us coming. I didn't want to hear her hesitation at the last-minute forced invitation. Suddenly, however, I worried about seeing her expression in case she wasn't in the mood for the kids.

"Julie! What... Oh, honey, c'mon in, and tell me what happened."

I breathed out in relief and mentioned maybe we would wait outside the garage, since the kids liked the idea of riding their bikes.

Soon the door rolled up, and Lucy raced to her bike. Mikey, however, got sidetracked by the sidewalk chalk. I loved seeing his face light up at the possibilities.

My mom and I pulled open some chairs, and she asked me again about what happened.

"Grant left."

"What do you mean, 'left'?"

"I mean, he packed up his bag and walked out the door. I don't even know if he's coming back tomorrow morning to watch the kids."

"Jules, that can't be right. Why wouldn't he?"

"Because, as it turns out, Lucy and Mikey are not his kids." I filled her in on what happened at the festival the day before, how he didn't come home later that night, and what he told me an hour earlier.

"Oh no. That's not at all how you should have found out."

With the kids, randomly at a park. Too true. However, something about the way she said "should have found out" struck a chord.

"Wait. Did you *know* they didn't do the IVF?"

Her hesitation stunned me.

"You knew? What the hell, Mom? Why would you not say something? Why would you let me keep believing the twins and I had a connection that didn't exist? Why would you let Grant?"

She fidgeted with her bracelet, finding intricate details to study. "I wasn't really thinking about him. Who knew he would even show up? And then when he did, things started to go much better. You had this genuine partnership and common goal. You had the help you needed so much even when you didn't know you needed it."

Increased frustration streamed through me, and I couldn't sit still anymore. I paced down a few feet of driveway and watched as Lucy got off her bike to crouch near Mikey and offer her ideas on what to add to his chalk creation on the sidewalk. I strode back up to my mother.

"Well, I no longer have that help, and Grant doubts his role with the kids. He's fantastic with them. And now biology—genetics, whatever—is screwing him over. It's like he imagines they won't need and love him as much anymore."

"Do you think he would have developed his same relationship with them had he always known he was 'just' their uncle? Would he have left California at all if he knew?"

I slumped down into my chair, considering her questions. Based upon how he introduced himself when he arrived, Elaine hadn't told him anything either. I couldn't imagine any way he would have known outside of Elaine informing him. And it wasn't like my mother ever would have thought to contact him. Once here, though, maybe he wouldn't have still offered to take care of the kids.

"I don't know. Maybe not in quite the same way, but at least he would have gone into everything with his eyes open. When he showed up, I should have been able to tell him the news. I could have told him his feelings of responsibility were unnecessary. He could have had the opportunity and choice to go back to his old life if he wanted."

"Does he not still have the same opportunity?"

"God, Mom. It's different now. You know it is."

"Is it different for you? Knowing about the kids?"

Lucy had gotten on her bike again and sang as she rode along the sidewalk and occasionally up and down the driveway. My parents had told me Lucy and I shared several personality characteristics, including a temper, at least the one I had when I was a child. The comparisons used to plague me, but after some time, I saw them as coincidence or simply general family traits. Last night, I had enjoyed a different kind of freedom of responsibility. It *was* different.

Yet I knew what my mother was really asking. "No," I told her. "It isn't different at all. I still love them as much as ever. It still doesn't make it right what you did. And it still doesn't tell me why you kept it from me."

"I almost told you when you and Layla argued over guardianship. I know I should have said something then. I saw you wavering, and I figured if you knew the truth, you might have given in to Layla."

"Would it have been so bad?"

"No, of course not. Layla and Sheila would be wonderful parents, but they already had so much going for them. Then you said no to Layla with such resolve, I didn't have the heart to tell you, in case you backed down again."

Layla and Sheila had so much going for them, and I apparently had nothing. I would have been angrier with my mother if it wasn't simply the way she was. Not to say I *wasn't* angry with her, just not enough to press the issue further. At least not at that moment.

"Stay for dinner, honey. I'll make it up to you starting tonight."

"No, I don't think so. Not tonight."

"Julie."

My phone buzzed, allowing me to disregard my mother's plea while I checked to see if Grant had texted. Maybe he'd changed his mind.

But it was Gemmi. "*Big argument with D. Can I come by?*"

I texted her back to tell her yes and that she should order pizza.

"Look, Mom, I'm not going to, like, disown you or anything. But I'm not really in a forgiving mood right now, okay? Besides, something's come up, and I gotta go."

She stood with me. "I'm sorry."

"I know."

Chapter Thirty-Two

"Can we help take care of the baby, Auntie Gemmi?"

"Lucia, nena, you definitely can. I will need all the help I can get."

"What about soup? I have chicken noodle, tomato, and vegetable," I said from the kitchen. The pizza, while it had sounded good when I suggested it, later sounded awful, she told me. She tried a salad, but the smell of the ranch dressing wreaked equal havoc.

"I'm so sick of soup, but it doesn't sound awful, and I'm so fu—freaking hungry. Tomato, I guess."

"If the way Lulu tosses her dolly around is any sign of how she would take care of babies, then I'm not sure of her offer."

"Dolly's not *real*." Lucy pouted. "I will be super nice to a *real* baby."

I covered the bowl and set the timer on the microwave before walking over to Lucy, sitting at the table. Caressing the side of her face and kissing the top of her head, I added, "Of course you would. I'm teasing. You will be great with the baby. You'll be able to cheer him right up when he's sad. Or her."

"Or them," Lucy added. "Sean says some people aren't girls or boys, so we should use 'them.'"

"One hundred percent correct, nena," Gemmi assured her. "You'll help me be ready for whatever this little peanut will need."

Mikey slipped a picture over to Gemmi, one containing his latest artistic subject, birds. I might already have been super biased, but they were pretty damn good birds too. The kid had talent.

"For the baby's room!" Lucy explained for him.

When Mikey smiled, I knew Lucy had gotten it right. He had yet to use any words with anyone other than Grant, Lucy, or me. He didn't talk much with Lucy either. Watching them play together, I could see why. They had a seamless connection.

I set the soup in front of Gemmi, along with some Club crackers. "Have a few bites and tell me what happened with Demitry."

"He wants to get married."

"And you don't?"

"I did. I do. But he's saying it now because I'm pregnant. I wanted him to ask me for real, with a romantic dinner, get down on one knee, or at least have a ring or something. Now it's this rush thing, and it's all a 'you're knocked up, so let's get hitched' deal, and everything feels all wrong." She swirled a cracker in her soup and took a bite. "And then he reminded me he has always wanted to marry me and I'm the one to change the order all around. You can imagine how things went next."

Kids change everything.

Although really, I conceded, maybe they only highlighted parts of our lives we didn't have figured out, exposing all of our insecurities and faults. Gemmi and Demitry loved each other, but the idea of kids had always been a source of conflict for them. But when kids were forced into their relationship and out of the order Demitry expected, they had to face each other head-on. They had to be truly honest with one another.

My mother said she and my dad split up to protect us from their affairs. Zach and I weren't meant to be together; Lucy and Mikey's arrival put a spotlight on all our differences. I had forgotten about all of our problems, and trying to make us work while becoming a parent had only magnified the issues between us.

Maybe Gemmi's pregnancy was only bringing to the surface their own issues about marriage. Or something might have come up later and been even more difficult to fix. I didn't know if they could re-solve whatever the current problem was, but maybe it was better to face it before the baby came and not after.

Gemmi's phone chimed. "He's apologizing and wondering when I'll be home."

She seemed undecided about something.

"Do you want to crash here tonight?" I offered.

"You won't mind?"

"Are you kidding? It'll be like old times."

She smiled for the first time since walking through the door.

In the morning, I suddenly worried Grant wouldn't show up, that his leaving was more than just... well, whatever it was. Hearing the knock on the door filled me with relief and then irrational irritation, since he wasn't in a position anymore to feel like he could walk right in.

"I wasn't sure you were going to show up."

He didn't say anything for a moment, and I wondered at his si-lence, waiting for the string of nervous words to tell me he realized it was all a big mistake. To say he shouldn't have left and he had his stuff in his car, ready to move back in.

"We have an agreement. I wouldn't leave you high and dry. I wouldn't do that to the kids."

So, no nervous chatter. Well, one question was answered, then. "I see. An agreement. So that's what this has all been to you. An agree-ment."

"No, that's not... You know that's not what I meant."

"I have to get to work. By the way, Gemmi's here and still sleep-ing in my room. She's feeling pretty shitty with morning sickness and with everything in general, so I'd probably give her a lot of space if I were you." I walked past him to the kids' room and told them Grant was there.

"Yay! He can help us with our fort!"

Mikey smiled and rushed to me and beckoned me down to him.

"I'll take care of him while you're gone," he whispered, and I hugged him tightly.

When I straightened up again to leave, I found Grant in the doorway with an expression of deep sadness, and he looked so vulnerable I almost went to take him into my arms. Instead, I brushed past him and, at the last second, squeezed his hand, imagining he'd squeezed it back as I continued out the apartment and to my car.

The handoff after work was the same as ever, minus the casual and comfortable way we used to interact with one another and with the additional new knowledge he wouldn't actually be coming back until the next morning. I already missed him, and it had been only two days. The kids accepted the idea Grant was simply spending time with his friends. I hadn't had the heart to tell them he might not—and probably wouldn't—come back to live with us. I didn't know why I hadn't prepared for that conversation since, at one point, I had fully expected him to move out.

I stared into the refrigerator, debating between a Fanta Orange and a beer, then settled on being smart with a Fanta. I stood in the cool air a little longer, contemplating dinner, then registered the fridge was fairly well stocked. Apparently, Grant and the kids had gone shopping. *Should he be buying stuff for us when he isn't living here anymore? How are we supposed to deal with cost sharing now?*

The next morning in my shower, I discovered he'd also bought me shampoo, and I thought of when I first bought shampoo for him. I didn't know what it meant that he'd changed his thoughts about it, only that it made me rest my head against the shower wall and feel too much following an action that probably meant nothing at all. *"It's not like we've been friends forever. It may only be two and a half bucks, but what if we hate each other after a couple more weeks and we suddenly resent that tiny thing?"*

When Grant arrived in the morning, he looked tired. I didn't know where Chaz lived, but I couldn't imagine it helping to lose more sleep with adding the travel time in the morning. I'd lost my irritation with him, and things were less awkward, but conversation still felt formal.

I paused at the threshold of the door on my way out. "Thank you for noticing I needed shampoo."

I didn't wait to see his expression.

I skipped the awkwardness with Grant in the afternoon because of a meeting with Tamara about the will. My mother had agreed to watch the kids so I could go directly to my dad's office after work.

Dad's receptionist greeted me and asked after the kids. I pulled out my phone and showed her a photo I had taken of them at the festival.

"Aren't they the cutest? Look at those curls on Mikey!" she said. "Your dad talks about them all the time. Even with all of his wives, he's never had grandchildren around until now."

My dad wasn't on Facebook, but Nora was, and we'd friended each other. Listening to his receptionist, I considered it was up to me to foster the relationship. Unless Mom had told him, he probably didn't know why I had pulled away. He was doing the best he could.

"Is he here?"

"No. We tried very hard to reschedule the meeting he had this afternoon, but there was just no doing it. He might stop by later if it's not too late."

I nodded and, at her direction, headed to Tamara's office with some apprehension. Tamara told me there was a lot of new information for them to work with; she didn't mention the nature of it. Additionally, Pastor Carl from the church wanted to sit down with me informally and talk. He was coming to the office after my meeting with Tamara.

"Is the new information good or bad?" I asked after exchanging hellos and settling in at her conference table.

"Tough to say, really. It's more like we've been uncovering more facts. Either side could benefit."

"Such as?"

"Such as Brian and Elaine were meeting with Pastor Carl regularly for counseling. We could argue this put undue emotional pressure for them to keep the church as beneficiaries. Conversely, the church could argue this was an invaluable service for your brother and why he left the church his estate and stock portfolio."

A stock portfolio. I must have missed something in the "everything else goes to the church" part of the conversation a couple of months back. "I didn't know he had a stock portfolio. Isn't it part of the trust funds?"

"Partly, yes."

Brian's financials turned out to be a broad and complicated situation. She walked me through it all, and Brian's decisions and money management impressed me. However, we could also see an interesting pattern of how much money had snaked its way into the church's hands. Brian's financial planner was a church-council member, which seemed like a huge thing in our favor. Tamara said it was more complicated.

"We are absolutely building it into our mounting arguments, but there are a lot of holes in the argument against the financial planner. Based upon the many depositions we've already had and the paper trail, Brian made many of those decisions independently."

"Meaning his financial planner is smart, and they all did a good job of brainwashing him."

"Meaning your brother was smart. They might have brainwashed him into giving too much to them, but his financial planner hasn't even made the same shrewd decisions Brian did."

I was beginning to understand what she meant about the ambiguity surrounding their fact-finding mission.

"Julie, about this meeting with the pastor." Tamara turned her chair slightly away from the table and looked at me directly. "He's going to want to meet with you by yourself."

"And you don't want me to."

"No. You absolutely should not meet with him on your own. And though I couldn't promise him, your father tried very hard to get me to say that I wouldn't let it happen."

I raised my eyebrows, questioning.

"The pastor is a smooth talker. Very smooth. We met yesterday with several of the church-council members, all of whom were quite upset over the whole situation. The tension escalated, and Pastor Carl calmed them all down in a way that made him seem quite rational and compassionate. It wasn't hard to see how members got drawn in."

"And you think I'll fall for his persuasion techniques."

She studied me for a moment, and I wondered what she learned. At first, I wondered if my dad's conversation with her was to express doubt in me, but I stopped myself. He was almost certainly trying to protect me.

"Maybe not. I don't know. Think of it as moral support. In any case, I can't emphasize enough how valuable legal protection is."

I didn't really need the pep talk. I agreed without further question. I tackled the next worry. I knew Shannon was on the council, and she'd discovered I hadn't known about not being the kids' biological mother. "Did Shannon give you the news about the kids?"

"Yes. She seemed to enjoy dropping that information. I think she thought it was some big bombshell."

"It's not?"

She looked at me in sympathy. "I'm sorry. I didn't mean it like that. To clarify, I'm sure it was for you, but it really has no bearing on the case."

"Oh. That's good, I guess."

"Look, this is going to sound kind of crass, but had they been from your eggs, the argument would have always been clear that you had already received compensation for the transaction. Assistive-reproduction clinics are pretty thorough in their contracts. The IVF angle wasn't a worthwhile one to pursue. Knowing the kids are biologically Brian and Elaine's means the case is like any other."

A case like any other, which to me meant probably impossible to win. Tamara assured me everything we'd encountered was standard process. Contesting a will was almost never a slam dunk, and they were far from done.

She spent the next fifteen minutes preparing me for our meeting with the pastor. I felt like I was about to take the witness stand in a trial. When Pastor Carl arrived, I understood why. I had expected a bigger man, an intimidating one. Pastor Carl was average in height and girth. He wore a pale-blue polo shirt tucked into khaki pants. His hair was thinning, cut in the standard, conservative suburban style of many white men.

"Hello, Ms. Mercer." He spoke gently, holding out his hand. "I'm very glad to meet you, and let me tell you right away how very sorry I am about your loss. Your brother was a very good man. He spoke quite highly of you."

Ah. Soothing and warm. I returned the handshake and thanked him but offered nothing more.

"Death of a loved one can really affect our behaviors, so much so we are often too close to see it," the pastor continued. "I think if you and I have coffee together and talk about Brian and remember what he meant to us, we can get past some of these other superficial issues."

"Sounds good. I believe there's coffee in the conference room, isn't there, Tamara?" I looked at her, and she smiled.

"Yes, of course. Right this way."

If Carl was unhappy with the turn of events, he didn't show it.

We arrived in the conference room, and Tamara's assistant helped with the Keurig.

"Brian was a devoted member of our community, and God's presence flowed through him freely," Carl said. "We've all been grieving his loss, even if we understand it was God's will."

"And Elaine? Have you been grieving her loss too?"

"Of course." He took a sip of his coffee. "Elaine gave her time endlessly and tirelessly in our women's circle. God always has a plan."

"To take away a child's parents? Tell me more about this terrible plan."

"We can't always know these things for certain, but I believe he gave you children, didn't he? Children you might have given away before now? Or maybe never allowed to come into this world in other ways?"

"Pastor Carl," Tamara started, but I spoke up too.

"That is the most ridiculous 'plan' I have ever heard. Helping others have children seems like a behavior to view as a *positive* thing, not some perverted way of saying I'm denying a child's life."

"I apologize. I didn't mean to imply your gift was not appreciated. God rewarded it by blessing Brian and Elaine with children of their own. And Brian rewarded it by entrusting you with them, did he not?"

"I'm not sure the kids would see their situation as a 'reward.'"

The pastor moved his cup aside and leaned forward, hand outstretched, presumably to take mine. I moved back accordingly. With only a flicker of acknowledgment, he clasped his hands together.

"Brian told me of your visit last year and how skillful you were with Lucy and Michael. He saw a connection. I believe you already know I was helping Brian and Elaine work through some troubles they were having, but I counseled them individually too."

Right. Because *that* wasn't a mess of a situation. Based upon his reaction concerning Elaine, I could guess the advice she was getting. Coming from her home situation, she might have gone along with letting Brian run things, which made me sad. I couldn't imagine Grant wanting his sister to be led along blindly either.

"Brian shared stories with me of how you used to watch out for him when you were children. You took care of him. You helped him with his homework, bandaged his cuts and scrapes, and read with him. All things a mother should do. It didn't surprise me that you were to be the children's guardian."

I looked away from him and bit back the swell of emotion. I had always wanted to know why Brian and Elaine thought of me for Lucy and Mikey. To think Brian actually remembered all of those things from our childhood and that they meant something to him made me overwhelmingly sad for the Brian I had loved. Maybe it wasn't up to me to question what he wanted now that he was dead.

Except I hated hearing it all from *that* guy. I hated everything about the situation and the mess that church continued to make worse for Grant, the kids, and me.

"If Brian remembered everything so well, then he would want the same for his children. If they get sick, I won't be able to bandage them up because I don't have the money to do so. If he wants me to help them with their homework, he'll want me home to do it and not working a second job."

I could tell he thought he had "reached" me somehow, but he recovered quickly. "Ms. Mercer, we have an excellent outreach program, and many of our members have ties to friends and family here in the Cities. We can help you."

"I don't want your help. I don't want any part of your organization at all."

Tamara stepped in. "I think we're done here, Pastor Carl. We agreed to the meeting, and I think it would be best to let our team and yours figure out the rest. As you've said, emotions can run high during this time."

Kudos to the good pastor for the continuously placating and sympathetic smiles. "Of course. I'm sorry to have upset you, Ms. Mercer. May God watch over you during this difficult time."

Tamara walked him out while I stayed right where I was. Maybe Grant was right. It was easier for me to be mad at adult Brian than it was to feel the loss of my kid brother.

A few minutes later, my dad walked in and sat next to me.

"Tamara filled me in. I'm sorry I couldn't be here. How are you doing, Jujubee?"

"Not so good, Dad." I let him pull me into a hug, and I cried on his shoulder.

Chapter Thirty-Three

"Mama JuJu!" Lucy ran to me as I walked through the door. I picked her up and hugged her tightly. She returned the hug briefly, squirming away to return to whatever activity she'd been doing. Mikey tagged in with the next hug, and I took him to the couch to snuggle.

My mom came in, wiping her hands on a dish towel. "Hi, honey. How did... oh no. You look beat. What happened? Are you all right?"

"Yeah, I'm okay. Tired. It was kind of a tough meeting."

"Have you eaten? I saved some dinner for you. You could tell me about it while you eat."

"Thanks, Mom. I'm not up for anything right now. I'll warm it up later. Did things go okay with the kids?"

"Of course. Look, I know you're still upset with me, but I'm here for you when you're ready to talk."

I gave Mikey a kiss on the head and suggested he go join his sister with whatever she was doing. I stood and walked my mom to the door.

"Thank you for watching the kids. The switch went okay with Grant? He got out of here on time?"

"Yes, only... you didn't tell Grant about me, did you?"

"No."

She sighed. "Well, that explains a lot. I assumed you did, and when I apologized to him, he got a little nervous, I think. Does he always prattle on nonsensically?"

I wanted to smile, but my heart sank at her comment. I missed that prattle. "Not lately. I haven't been able to get him to spend more than five minutes with me. I told you he left."

"Julie, I don't want to meddle—"

"Then don't."

She looked me in the eye then reached for her purse. "All right. I love you."

"I love you, too, Mom.

"Just... remember there's more to everything than the kids, okay?"

I wasn't entirely sure what she meant but nodded, accepting the coded message, anyway.

I thought time would thaw things out between Grant and me, and they did somewhat, except with him being absent outside of times with the kids, not much changed. We all felt his absence most on Sunday, one of Grant's two evenings off. The kids asked when he was coming back from his friend's, and I had to give them the only honest answer I had. I didn't know, and maybe not at all.

"He won't stop taking care of us, will he?"

"No, he won't. He loves you way too much."

The following Tuesday, I came home to an empty apartment. Grant had already sent me a text telling me they went to the arboretum in Chanhassen and traffic was slowing them down. There was a note in the kitchen too. Ever since the day I was stupidly awful to him, he'd left nothing to chance.

When they finally tumbled through the door about twenty minutes later, Grant spilled forth apologies galore.

"I'm sorry. I didn't think traffic would be so bad at this time of the afternoon, and I didn't think about how far away the place was either. I hope you don't mind I took them there, but the library had a free pass, and they have cool exhibits for kids to check stuff off on a card, and they were really excited—"

I smiled at seeing a spark of the old Grant. Except, not really. It felt like a big step backward if he was nervous around me again. "Sperm Whale." I paused at the nickname that seemed natural after the run-on explanations from him. But maybe it was the wrong play. I changed course. "Grant, don't worry about it. Why should I mind you took them to the arboretum?"

He shrugged and looked away. "I don't know. Something new. A 'first,' maybe. Or maybe I shouldn't have gone somewhere so far with them. I don't want you to worry about them with me."

"I don't. I *never* worry about them with you. I didn't before Saturday, and I don't now. Nothing's changed."

"Of course it has."

"Not really. I get Shannon's news was a shock, and I think I might understand how you feel, but it doesn't mean you are any less important to them or that they are any less important to you."

"I gotta go."

"No." I reached out and held his arm. "Stay for dinner."

"I can't."

He went out the door, and I followed before closing it behind me so the kids wouldn't hear what I said next. "They don't know and have never known about any of the IVF stuff."

He stopped but didn't turn.

"Nothing's changed for them, and nothing will except for how you treat them. You don't need my permission to love them like you always have."

When he walked away again, I went back into the apartment and grabbed my laptop. "What do you think, munchkins? What should we make for dinner tonight? Should we experiment with something new?"

"Let's make something with noodles!" Lucy jumped up and down.

We searched through doable recipes on the internet and determined we didn't quite have all the ingredients for any of them except spaghetti and meat sauce. They were too tired to walk to the store to get anything extra, so we landed on regular spaghetti. I let them watch TV, and I browsed my computer a while longer before finally gathering energy to cook dinner. Before I got up, I stared at the wall separating the living room from the kitchen and admired the many works of children's art adorning it.

Gemmi had said I lived sparsely, and she'd been right but not any longer. As my roommate, she gave color to my surroundings, and as my new roommates, my kids did the same. Independent did not have to mean alone.

After all, the kids and I just did the most natural thing in the world by sitting together and scoping out our plans for dinner. It was my life, and I didn't need Grant to keep that life.

But I wanted him as a part of that life, and I needed him for the other part of my life. The one separate from the kids. The one including only me. He didn't color my walls, but he kaleidoscoped everything else.

I loved him.

And with that realization, I remembered my mother's cryptic message. *What if it isn't the kids making him run? What if it's me?* All of my reassurances had been about his relationship with the kids, not about his relationship with *me*. I assumed he had changed his mind about us and what had been forming, but maybe I was wrong, like I had been about so many things before.

My hands shook as I grabbed my phone and texted Grant.

Can you come back after the kids go to bed tonight? For a little bit? I knew he had the night off, so he couldn't use work as an excuse. *Please.*

I stared at the screen for a full minute before deciding to pocket it and start dinner. I needed the distraction. He'd said he would always answer, but that was... well, that was before.

I started the pot of water to boil pasta when my phone buzzed. My heart pounded.

OK.

I spent the rest of the evening feeling giddy and terrified. After I got the kids to bed, I flipped through the TV channels too fast to determine if anything was worth watching. I almost wished I liked reading after all to help me focus and relax.

When I heard the knock on the door, I forced myself to take a deep breath before opening it. His hair was still slightly damp from a shower, and he wore a new T-shirt, maybe something from his shopping trip the day before with the kids. He hadn't bothered to shave away the day's beard growth, and it gave him an extra-sexy edge. *Oh God, I'm so far gone on him.*

"Hey," I said.

"Hey."

"C'mon in." He followed me into the kitchen. "Want something to drink?"

He shook his head and leaned against the counter, jiggling his keys. "What's this all about, J? What do you need?"

I should have known he wouldn't be up for small talk, which was fine. It would keep me from chickening out.

"You. I need you."

He sighed. "I told you I wouldn't stop watching the kids. When I talked about our 'agreement' the other day, I was referring to when we thought it was best not to find a new daycare situation right away—"

"No." I took a step closer. "That's not what I mean at all. The kids are fine. I don't care about that. I'm saying *I* need you."

I watched his face. *Oh God. What is he thinking?* I couldn't tell. *Passion*, I told myself. Be confident. Be bold. I moved closer and laid my cards on the table. Win or go home. I placed my hands on his chest, and though I meant it to come out strong and clear, it came out closer to a whisper as I felt his body respond to my touch. "You have been the one I have come home to, and you are the one I've always wanted to come home to. I miss *you*. I miss *us*. I want the Grant who knows where to find Band-Aids in every drugstore. I want the Grant who watches reruns of TV shows with me at night and laughs at the same stupid YouTube and TikTok videos with me. I want the Grant who likes me for who I am. I want the Grant who can make me feel like I'm starting a whole new day after the kids go to bed, one where it's just him and me. With you, I am me. I mean, really me. Please stay. With me."

I heard the keys give a tuneful jingle after they fell from his hand, and I felt both of his hands come around my waist before continuing along my back as his arms pulled me close. His lips met mine, and there was no softness in the kiss, no hesitation. He gave me everything. I could feel it, and I gave him everything back. With his kiss, I was lost within him, and it felt amazing and right. We paused for air for only a moment before he kissed me again. And again. And again. My hands were in his hair. His were warm and sure under my shirt, and God help me, he could have taken me right there in the kitchen, and I wouldn't have seen any problem with it.

"Not here," he whispered, and I melted deeper into him.

Without releasing his hold on me or his lips on mine, he helped us stumble to the bedroom. He locked the door behind him before turning to me as we connected once more. I wound myself around him, and his mouth never stopped eliciting pleasure from every spot it found behind my ears, along my jawline, and down my collarbone.

We stripped each other of clothing. His body met mine on the bed, his hands hot everywhere on me, my own trying to touch any part of him I could.

"Oh God, I'm so glad there were more." He breathed out.

"More what?" Although, based upon where I felt his breath, I knew what and smiled.

"Petals. They are exactly where I'd hoped."

"How long have you been hoping?"

"Since I discovered I had to change one of my own tattoos."

"How presumptuous."

"Is it presumptuous to want a drawer in here now?" He smiled then put his lips on places that made it difficult for me to respond coherently because my ex might have known what to do with his hands, but oh God, Grant definitely knew what to do with his mouth.

"Maybe. I might give you a hanger in the closet. But you should know I sleep in the middle of the bed."

"Since that's where I'll be, too, I think the setup will work out perfectly."

I brought his lips back to mine and released the words. "I love you."

His eyes bored into mine, dark with passion. "I love you too."

"Was that a knee-jerk response?"

He gave a gentle nip on my ear and whispered, "Totally."

I smiled and had sex for the first time with the father of my children.

Epilogue

The mid-July day was hot in a good, occasional-puffy-white-clouds-in-the-sky, sunny, just-enough-of-a-breeze-every-once-in-awhile kind of way. Balloons marked our picnic tables, as well as mostly empty bowls and platters from our lunch, along with a half-eaten sheet cake. Few people remained actually occupying those tables.

My dad stood with Sean, discussing something about the club. I wished I were a fly on the wall for their conversation. The juxtaposition of Sean's almost punk-like appearance next to my dad's expensive dress-casual was beautiful. My mother and Nora sat in lawn chairs under the shade of a tree, discussing the possibility of a goldfish pond in Dad and Nora's backyard.

One of the birthday twins shrieked with joy on a tire swing shared with her friend Connor, while Layla, Sheila, and Lynette all helped spin them around. The other birthday twin giggled while going up and down a curly slide with his friend Sam.

My eyes finally rested on Gemmi and Demitry, who were the only picnic-table occupants, and frowned at their hesitant actions with one another. Some of my worry slipped away as Grant's arms suddenly wrapped around me from behind, and he rested his face against mine.

"They're going to be okay," he said.

"You think so?"

"Yeah. I mean, look at how Demitry is with her. They're being careful with one another now, but you can tell he is *into* her."

"What about Gemmi? Is she 'into' Demitry?"

"What do you think?"

Demitry was trying to get Gemmi to eat something. With each item he presented, she covered her mouth, looking miserable, and shoved his hand away. Yet she wasn't actually pushing him away. Her eyes still met his and smiled behind the temporary distance.

"Yes, she is," I answered then twisted around to face him. "What about you? Are you 'into' me?"

"There's not a single part of me that isn't."

I tiptoed up and pulled myself up to his ear. "God, I fucking love you."

He laughed so hard, and it only made me love him more. "*Language*, J!"

I smiled and kissed him.

The great thing about living with someone before falling in love with him was that when you asked him to move in with you, you already knew it would work. Sharing a bedroom made it perfect. Waking up in the middle of the night to Grant coming home became an excellent trade for Mikey's former nightmare screams.

Of course, the kids hadn't stopped scrambling into bed with us yet. It wasn't both of them all the time, and it was still a good kind of crowded. At some point, I would get annoyed with not being able to wake up with only Grant by my side. My mother suggested I would probably miss it when they stopped doing it. I believed her.

I forgave my mother the moment Grant moved back in. I let her make it up to me by having her watch the kids at our place while Grant and I went out to dinner. A date. All we did was dinner, since leaving Mikey for too long was still out of the question. I didn't think my mother would have made it past the two hours, anyway. It was enough, since the time together reminded us we were an entity of our own—a really good one—standing apart from our identity with the kids.

"Hey, you two lovebirds." Lynette's voice ended our moment and my memory. "The kids and I need to hop on the road. I want to get back before it gets too late, or I'll be a zombie tomorrow morning for work."

"Thank you so much for the memory book for the kids," I told her. "It's perfect and beautiful."

For her birthday present to Lucy and Mikey, she'd put together a scrapbook of photos she found in online photo accounts, her own files, and the collective files of friends and church-community members. The kids giggled at pictures showing them doing silly things as babies and toddlers, and in parts, they fell silent and sad. At one point, Mikey looked up at me, and I simply nodded, arms extended. He ran into me and sobbed uncontrollably, followed by Lucy, and soon not a single one of us had a dry eye.

Lynette felt horrible, apologizing for ruining what was supposed to be a happy day for the kids. I figured after releasing the current round of sadness, they were ready to set it aside again. It wouldn't be their last round of tears, or tantrums, or escapes into silence, but as I'd felt Grant's arms around us, too, I felt thankful for the love and support we all had.

"We're looking forward to seeing you next weekend," Lynette said. "We're still happy to have you stay with us if you change your mind."

"I think the kids are looking forward to the adventure of staying in a hotel, but I really appreciate the offer. I appreciate everything you've been doing, actually."

"I know you don't necessarily believe in him." She smiled. "But I'd say God meant for us to meet each other again at the festival."

I returned the smile and gave a noncommittal shrug. "Maybe."

She gathered her two boys to leave. We weren't completely sure if the kids were ready for the trip down memory lane. If their reaction to Lynette's scrapbook was any sign, it seemed like it might be a good next step after all. Seeing their old house might be the hardest part, and I was a little relieved it had been sold—with the sale proceeds still sitting in escrow—since touring inside of it might have been a little too much. For all of us, really.

Where the estate money would end up remained a source of contention. The entire process upset me. Pastor Carl had gotten to me, and while his motivations might have been suspect, it still reminded me there were actual people involved. My dad, however, kept telling me it was all business and not a personal attack on Brian or his kids. He wasn't the only one who told me that, and I tried to keep the focus on the kids. The money was to help take care of them, not for personal gain.

I had briefly thought about the money helping Grant and me with school but quickly discarded that notion. We couldn't easily get student loans unless we registered as at least half-time students, but taking the one class already intimidated me, let alone two or three. Instead, my dad signed for loans to get us started, until we could get more on top of our finances. I still didn't know what I wanted to do with my life, but the psychology class Grant and I signed up for was a good start.

Grant took my hand and led us closer to the playground, and when we reached the wood-chip boundary, Lucy and Mikey bounded over to us.

"Lookit my tattoo when I run! It's fluttering with me!"

Part of our present to the kids was to get them henna tattoos. They had been over-the-moon excited. Lucy, of course, chose a butterfly. Mikey wondered if he might design his own. The artist we went to was one I'd used before, and I knew she would be able to do a pretty good approximation of whatever he created. He drew a small bird carrying a ring that looked a lot like the one he still wore on his thumb.

"Lulu, are you sure when you were born you didn't emerge from a cocoon?"

She wrapped her little arms around my waist and giggled. "You're silly, JuJu, but I still love you."

My heart had already been so full, I didn't see how it could contain any more happiness, and yet it expanded even more at those words, given to me for the very first time. I crouched to give her a proper hug, though brief, since she pivoted to Grant next, clearly hoping he would twirl her. He obliged but not before exchanging a glance with me, telling me how much he understood what I was feeling at her words.

Mikey enveloped me with his own hug and whispered into my ear, "I love you too."

Somewhere, from someone, I'd been told the death of a child—a sibling—could either tear a family apart or bring them closer together.

But what if the family was already torn apart? Did those options still exist?

I discovered there was another option—the creation of a new family, cobbling together what once was and transforming it into something more durable, more secure. A family that had your back and helped prepare your apartment for new residents, traveled the distance to take care of you, fought the battles you couldn't face alone, and supported you and your decisions.

I'd lived a lot of my life doing everything on my own, but I discovered I no longer had to, and more importantly, I no longer wanted to.

Especially cooking rice. Everyone else could do the fancy stuff. I would stick with instant.

Acknowledgments

I am one of the luckiest authors I know because I have always had nothing but love and support for my writing journey. No one has ever laughed at me or doubted that I could do this. I won't ramble on like Grant, but I can't simply leave my thanks to simply be "thank you, everyone!" because that would be skipping over some key people who helped make this story the very best it could be.

First, my alpha reader, critique partner, beta reader, cheerleader, and keeper of all my complaints about the writing and publishing process, Jen Escue. Thank you for always celebrating my joys with me too.

For my early readers on all or parts of this novel—Carolyn Morain, Phyllis Book, Kathleen Basi, Christine Adler, Cerrissa Kim, and Nancy Ostrom—thank you for all your feedback.

While things didn't go as originally planned, thank you to Jill Marsal, who pushed me in the right direction to strengthen Julie's character, and I know she is all the better for it.

Thank you to Rashida Breen, who loved this story in the same way I do, who gave Julie the proper developmental journey, and who *almost* convinced me I needed to go to the drugstore right away to buy a thermometer.

Thank you to Angela McRae. I truly appreciate her dedication to detail. She tightened this story in a way I couldn't have on my own. Maybe one day she'll get to meet the "real" Rick Calloran.

Thank you to Lynn for giving this story a home. Red Adept is truly a lovely community, and both my novel and I have been in very good hands.

A big shout out for my WFWA colleagues, for Ann's Basement Babes, and the lovely Inksters.

Ever always, all my love to my husband, Andy, who reads my words with a critical eye but also actually likes my stuff. You can't go wrong with support like that. Thank you, love, for supporting my goals and dreams.

To my kiddos, I'm sorry this is still not the Cloud book. One day it will be. I have faith!

And to you, all of my readers, both new and old. All I've ever wanted was for someone to read my words. Thank you for fulfilling that dream.

About the Author

J. Marie Rundquist believes a day isn't complete without time spent reading. Stories she loves best–to read and to write–feature characters from all walks of life who learn from one another. When she isn't writing, you'll find J. Marie exploring all the K-12 public education world has to offer through teaching, learning, and supporting others in their educational roles.

In spite of trying to live in other parts of the US, J. Marie accepted her fate and now embraces six-month winters in Minnesota, showing off photos of hiking in sub-zero temperatures. She lives in the Twin Cities with her family, two cats, and a never-ending supply of Dr. Pepper.

Read more at https://jmarierundquist.com.

About the Publisher

Dear Reader,

We hope you enjoyed this book. Please consider leaving a review on your favorite book site.

Visit https://RedAdeptPublishing.com to see our entire catalogue.

Check out our app for short stories, articles, and interviews. You'll also be notified of future releases and special sales.